SCORPIO RISING

A CELESTIAL SOCIETY NOVEL

BOOK ONE

FIBI MARIE

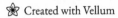

For the dreamers, and the girls on fire.

PREFACE

*LOS ANGELES, THE CITY OF ANGELS. CAPITAL OF THE
CELESTIAL SOCIETY.*

Magic is dying.

Celestials—we're the last of it. 'Children of the Divine'
they call us, for we are the descendants of the old gods. Our
kind exists all around the world, but LA is our homeland. All the highborn bloodlines dwell here because, well, this city was made for us.

Two thousand years ago, magic was the societal norm. Mortals and
gods walked the earth together, along with a plethora of great and terrifying mythical creatures. The skies were alive with the flight of dragons,
the forest crawling with mischievous fae, and the oceans full of monsters
and mysteries. Elemental magic was as normal as fruit stands in the
summer. No one had to hide. It was a glorious, golden age on Earth. But
then the war happened, and shit went sideways. Nothing gold can stay,
and all that.

The story of what *really* happened is muddied since during the
wars, there was book burning, and the destruction of the oldest library
with all the mystical history records.

1

The gist is, the world split in two—the mundane and the magic cleaved apart.

The mortals wanted nothing to do with mysticism or divinity. They turned against the gods and everything to do with magic. Because of this, the gods and their kin began to regress. They need to be believed in and worshiped to thrive. Each generation grew weaker until they became nearly indecipherable from humans.

Once, my ancestors walked the earth as giants, or winged beings, with horns or halos. All of our divine characteristics lessened with each generation until they were no more.

For eons, my people were hunted, persecuted, and demonized by the very mortals they lived to protect and guide, as were all the mythical creatures. Dragons were hunted and slaughtered like cattle until finally, they had no choice but to leave this dimension altogether. Once the dragons left, so did the faeries, the griffons, the phoenixes, and so on.

Four hundred years ago, during a period now known as The Burning Times, to put an end to the bloodshed and scheming, Celestials made a treaty with the elite mortal families. Our kind vowed to step down and blend in with their kind and keep our magic a secret. Form our own Society and leave the mortals to their mortal business.

Humans wanted independence. We gave it to them. And they were running themselves into the fucking ground for it.

An Amnesia spell was cast over the mortal population to make them forget about magic.

Only those elite mortal bloodlines possess this secret knowledge. Humanity's true history was erased and replaced with fabricated half-truths devoid of any magic.

Hiding in plain sight became the Celestial way.

Each of us is born with an element to wield, but it lies dormant within us. A quiet, sleeping power that doesn't awaken until our Emergence, which is the Initiation into the world of divinity and magic. Before we Emerge, though, we're raised amongst the humans. We attend their schools, play their sports, watch their news and movies, and attend their birthday parties.

We need to understand their world to successfully hide within it.

As children, we often inherently know we're different, without knowing why. We are purposely kept in the dark to protect the secret.

Once a Celestial's magic Emerges at the age of eighteen, every mortal we grew up with will fall into Amnesia and forget us.

Upon entering the Celestial Society, we spend five years in a magical academy to hone our abilities. Males and females attend separate academies to learn magic according to their natural divine feminine and divine masculine gifts. The most elite academies are right here, hidden under the glitz and glamour of the LA scene.

We younglings, we're called starseeds. We may be adults in the mortal realm, but in this world, we're babies.

After you graduate, you earn the ranking of Embodied, becoming a full-fledged member of magical society. And if you excel even further, to the mastery of Priestess or High Magician level, you are Exalted.

In the last century, for reasons unknown, Celestial fertility plummeted. Perhaps it has to do with our immortality, or our regression as a species, but today, it's uncommon for Celestials to bear children. Which makes me and all my friends a rarity. We are youngbloods amongst a society of ancient immortals.

You could say we have a lot to live up to.

Social status is everything. Friends are not just friends but allies. We are ruled by our own rank of power. And I am top tier.

CHAPTER I
FIRE BLOODED
NYX

This lipstick was the color of murder, so I named it Wrath. I'd been bending even the smallest details of the world to my will for some time now.

It was originally called Rosebud... I mean, really? Rosebud red? How ground-breaking. The deep, threatening red matched the color of blood spilled in a fit of blind rage more than it did a flower. Mortals rarely managed to grasp the true severity of colors, so I took it upon myself to rename *all* my lipsticks, giving them the thoughtful edge they deserved. I charmed the little sticker on the bottom of the tube to display my name instead, marked with my dragon sigil as well. My inspiration came from things like the seven deadly sins, eighties slasher films, and famous actresses notorious for topless scenes. I had a thing for reds and nudes.

The last spills of sunlight danced through the window, casting golden rays through the center of our room, really spotlighting the fucking mess. I scoffed darkly, flicking my wrist so the drapes shut themselves. With half a thought, I cast all the candles on the mantle alight. Much better.

Clothes and makeup and grimoires scattered around the room, not a free inch of floor in sight. Just the way I liked it. Chaos felt like home.

I rose from my fluffy vanity stool and meandered through the maze of feminine destruction over to the walk-in closet to decide what outfit I wanted to slaughter everyone's confidence with tonight.

My roommate, Natalia, sat amongst the colorful carnage, applying her eyeliner in the reflection of the full-length mirror next to the window.

"You're going to choose your new red dress," she voiced without looking away from her own dark, wide-set eyes in the mirror. She recently got her septum pierced, rocking a gold hoop through the middle of her nose. I liked it. It honored her sun sign, Taurus. She ran her fingers down her springy black hair, fluffing it around her face. Natalia had the skin tone of the gods—a deep, glorious brown that glowed freaking gold in the sun. "So don't bother trying on a hundred different things just to add to this pigsty."

She was the most powerful Seer at the Academy, and life was a hell of a lot easier with a Seer in your corner.

I smirked, opening the closet, and assessing myself in the mirror on the back of the door. The golden, henna-style, living tattoos on my arms swirled and flowed excitedly as if they knew we were about to hit a party. Natalia was right, of course. I already knew I was going to wear red.

I ran my fingers through my long, silver hair, sighing. "Do you think I should tie my hair up or leave it down?"

She shot me a flat glance before rummaging through the pile of makeup in front of her. "We both know you'll wear it down. Shit, where is Phoebe Cates?!"

"It's on my vanity," I told her, pointing toward the peachy nude lipstick she was referring to.

Twenty minutes later, we were ready to break necks.

I grabbed my blackmirror and scrolled through the plethora of notifications waiting for me. I held it out and snapped a few pictures of me and Natalia, posting to Magigram right away. Damn, we looked good. The likes and engagement started pouring in, so I locked my blackmirror and set it on silent. "Ready?" I asked.

Natalia stared off into space for a moment before she snapped back into reality and her brown eyes met mine. "Your sister is here..."

"What?" I hissed, blood instantly draining from my face.

"Your mother is bringing her early."

"What the fucking fuck?" I obsessively unlocked my blackmirror again and checked for missed calls or messages. Zero from my mother or my sister. So, they were just going to show up unannounced? Mother knew I would be out at the party tonight. It was tradition, after all. Every year all the students from all the LA Academies came together to end the summer with a bang—have some fun before we dove into another year of ruthless competition against each other. Did that mean they meant to miss me? A coldness settled in my chest, coiling into a pile like a snake preparing for sleep.

Whatever.

I schooled my features and tipped my chin up. "Well, good for them then. Emilia can get all settled in with her mommy's help. As if I'd expect anything less."

Natalia's expression became urgent. "Actually, they are coming he—"

Knock, knock.

My best friend and I shared a quick, horrified glance. I knew that cold, distant knock. Heard it outside my bedroom door a million times before I got lectured on what a waste of existence I was.

As if! I hadn't spoken to my mother or sister in weeks. Emilia wasn't set to arrive until next week when classes started. Seven hells, I was supposed to have seven more days of freedom. Luna Academy had been damn near empty since June, with everyone having lives and families to go back to. Natalia was estranged from her family, which worked out for me since I'd rather hurl myself off a mountain than go spend the summer with mine. She and I stuck around, utilizing all the free space to practice magic.

I did my best to assemble my face into a picture of ease and confidence before opening the door to find my family standing there apathetically. I don't think my mother's eyes even touched me before they darted instantly to the mess on the floor behind me. Like she expected it. Of course she did. I swallowed thickly and glanced behind me, gasping once I realized the room appeared immaculately clean.

Natalia bit her lip to hide her grin.

Oh, what a clever little fox! She'd cast glamour over the room to make it appear perfect to my mother.

I beamed at my mother and sister. "Why, to what do I owe this royal honor?"

It didn't matter that the room looked clean. Esmeralda Morningstar was not a pleasant woman, especially not to me. She was true to our family's nature—the fearsome, fire-blooded descendants of the last dragon riders. In the Old World, our ancestors were royalty. She carried that energy in every move she made, every word she ever spoke. Her elder sister, Sophia, who was four centuries older than my mother, had ridden one of the most glorious dragons in all of history. Niaxus, the sapphire beast of old. They were famous in our Celestial history. Their epic unified death was too.

We Morningstars, named after Venus in the sky at dawn, were a matriarchal bloodline. Every child born to us was female. We only took men to bed when we were ready to conceive an heir. *"Morningstar women don't ride men. We ride dragons."* Too bad this charming little catchphrase was beyond outdated—though I'd never tell my mother that. The dragons were gone, so I may have dabbled in some forbidden fruit here and there.

Our family was once one of the most highly regarded bloodlines in existence dating back to the times of Atlantis, but without dragons, our status waned.

My mother refused to accept that. In truth, so did I.

She held her sharp chin high, managing to look down the bridge of her nose at me even though we were the same height. She turned one hundred and eighty-three last month. Still young in the Celestial world —we lived for thousands of years if nothing took us out.

Her thick dark hair was tied back in a slasher ponytail that teased her tailbone. As always, she wore heavy eye makeup and dark red lips, looking like me in so many ways it made my skin crawl. Except the hair, of course. My mother and I held striking resemblance in our faces and body shape, but our hair put us worlds apart.

The tattoos running up and down the olive skin of her arms drew my attention right away. She'd gotten more. All runes and symbols and unsettling designs that had always made me feel uncomfortable as a kid. Even now. *Fixed* tattoos that never moved. So creepy.

If my mother was a blade incarnate, my sister was a fucking water lily. Emilia had a softness about her that I always secretly resented. Perfect, gentle, cooperative Emilia. She had the same olive skin as us, dark hair like my mother, but her eyes shone a twinkling, unfair blue. She'd grown about six inches taller than we could ever dream of being, too.

She offered me a hopeful smile which I didn't know how to receive so I just grimaced back and tossed her the rock n' roll sign. Not my finest moment.

"You think I can't detect an illusion, Nyx?" Mother drawled, flicking her wrist so the mess behind us reappeared.

My cheeks heated but I kept my head up and didn't bother looking back at the truth. I had grown accustomed to being the family's disappointment. I relished it. It made me who I was. I mean, what did she expect? She named me after the Goddess of Night and then acted shocked and disdained that I possessed a certain...darkness.

But it didn't matter what my mother thought of me anymore because I had come to Luna Academy, and I fucking *slayed*. Within my first year, I was top of the class and queen of the student body. The girls here practically worshiped me. There hadn't been a fireling as powerful as me in centuries, if not longer. I was heading into my second year totally on top. I didn't need my mother's validation.

"The Luminary will be out in the Sacred Temple, Mother. We are heading out now."

"*You* are bringing Emilia to the party tonight."

Natalia and I both stiffened. "What?" I stared at Esmeralda as if she'd just spoken to me in an alien tongue.

"She's nervous," my mother went on, making Emilia turn crimson. "Take her out and let her meet some of her classmates before the year starts."

Emilia had no business attending this party. She hadn't even Emerged yet.

I didn't bother trying to hide my incredulity. "Most of the Luna girls are still out of town," I spoke slowly, not believing I was having this conversation right now. "The party is going to be mostly people from other academies..."

"Bullshit, the Luna girls are all portalling in. Don't try to play me for a fool. All the noble young starseeds will be there and you are bringing your sister with you."

Noble young starseeds. Ha! Get a grip, woman. These people are terrible.

Looking at my mother now, I got the feeling this wasn't just about Emilia's nerves. This was a test. For me.

Goody. I loved failing my mother's tests.

"Fine," I quipped, folding my tanned arms over my exposed chest, golden tattoos swirling rapidly to match my thrashing heart. Esmeralda's eyes raked up and down my dress disapprovingly. It fit me sinfully, accenting every curve, separating in the middle so my midriff was on full show, not to mention the slit up to the thigh. The bust did little to hide my tits and as always, I wore no bra. I hadn't exactly expected to see my mother tonight.

She brought her eyes back up from my painted toes and they landed indefinitely on the silver jewel I had placed over my third eye.

I expected her to chastise me for dressing so explicitly, but no such lecture came. She merely shoved Emilia at me and turned away without another fucking word. I blinked at her, watching as she cast a sparkling white and violet portal in the middle of the hallway and disappeared in a vortex of spinning light.

"Jesus Christ," Natalia whispered.

"I'm sorry!" Emilia gushed immediately like the air expelling out of a balloon. "I told her we should just wait till next week, but you know how she can be–"

"It's fine," I put my hand up between us and let my eyes trail over her outfit. Tight jeans, sandals, hideous t-shirt. She looked horrendously mortal. I stalked over to my closet and pulled down a pale pink mini dress with a low neckline and peasant sleeves. I tossed it at my sister. "Put this on and we'll go."

Emilia smiled nervously. "Okay." She stared down at the dress, biting her bottom lip. "PS—I'm not nervous. Well, that's not the reason

Mom wants me here. She wants me away from my mortal friends. Says I'm too attached."

I noticed the way her cheeks pinked as she spoke, and how her fingers played with the material of the dress I gave her. I cocked a brow. "Not just friends. You got a boyfriend, don't you, sis!"

Emilia turned beetroot and shook her head. "It doesn't even matter. As soon as I Emerge, their Amnesia will kick in and they'll forget all about me."

A beat of sad silence passed between us.

"Well, this is where you belong anyways. And damn, little Morningstar," Natalia cawed as she checked out my sister. "You've grown up."

"I'm eighteen in two weeks," she replied excitedly, pleased about the subject change.

I stood back and watched my best friend fawn over Emilia, noting the way her body had changed since I last saw her. Yes, she was growing up. As she slid that ugly shirt off, revealing the impressive bust she hid underneath, all sorts of devilish ideas swarmed through my mind and a smile slithered its way across my lips. All I'd have to do was introduce her to some cute guys, and voila. Innocence lost. I'd prove to my mother that both her daughters were flawed, not just me.

She slid into the dress and adjusted it to perfection, looking to me for approval. I was smiling like a Cheshire cat at her, and she took that as a good sign.

CHAPTER 2

IN PLAIN SIGHT

NYX

Fuck, I loved this city.

I decided my sister needed a little tour.

The sun had officially set, turning the night sky the color of rich amethyst bleeding into onyx. She marveled over the dreamy aesthetic, the twinkling lights and the palm trees, and the beautiful people. I watched her taste the sin lurking around every corner and noticed as she felt drawn to all the wicked temptations the City of Angels had to offer.

Mother had had her cooped up in that small forest town for too long. She raised us in a quaint home up in Mosier, Oregon. Sure, I loved nature. We drew our power from the Earth. But all the big, famous cities of the world had been intentionally built on the most powerful ley lines —the energetic underground pathways that charged our magic. Natural power lines. We were strongest in places like this. This was why in LA alone, there were three Magical Academies. Luna, Veneficus, and San Gabriel. Though San Gabriel was up in the mountains, out of city limits.

I was ignoring all the looks Natalia tossed my way. She could sense my cruel intentions, but I didn't want to hear it. Emilia could use a rousting. Wasn't that why Mother had sent her here? Perhaps her second daughter's softness was starting to feel more like weakness. Why else send her off into the land of carnal sin with the likes of me?

We passed a lit-up restaurant bar pumping with music. The outside terrace was packed. I slowed as we passed on the sidewalk, smiling deviously as my focus zeroed in on a young couple sitting closest to the outskirts. A waitress dropped off their drinks. A glass of brown liquor for the guy and some fruity cocktail for the girl. They were too busy staring lovingly into each other's eyes to notice that their drinks suddenly vanished from in front of them.

With a single thought, I had the two glasses gliding into my waiting palms without spilling a drop.

"Holy shit!" Emilia breathed, astonished. She glanced around, wondering if anyone saw. I didn't give a shit. The streets were packed but the people in this city were way too self-absorbed to notice all the abnormal things that happened right in front of their damn noses. I offered the fruity drink to Emilia as I slammed the whiskey down my throat, reveling in the glorious burn.

"Amazing, right?" I grinned triumphantly.

"Are you sure you should do magic like that?" Emilia's voice became hushed as she leaned in. "We're in plain sight."

I smirked. "The best place to hide."

Natalia chuckled.

Emilia swigged the pink drink like she wanted to impress me. It worked, slightly. She handed the empty glass back to me just as the couple noticed their drinks had disappeared. I grinned wickedly as I sent a gust of energy back to their table, the glasses returning before them, empty.

We turned and hurried away as the couple started gasping in confusion. Goddess, I loved magic.

"That was so cool." Emilia gushed. "Hey—er, what's the difference between what you just did and air magic? I thought only airlings could move objects."

"What I did is telekinesis," I explained haughtily. "All of us possess the ability to use basic telekinesis. It's completely different from air magic. It's a psychic thing." I tapped my temple suggestively. "It's all about a magnetic connection between the mind and the object. It has nothing to do with air manipulation."

"Oh." Emilia nodded, pretending to understand. "Well, it was amazing."

"And we haven't even taken you to any of the Unseen Sites yet," Natalia said. "Not-so-little Morningstar, you know what an Unseen Site is right?"

"A Celestial place with a glamour spell placed over it so no mortals can see it."

"And what is another word for a glamour spell?"

"Er... A veil?"

"Yeah, girl!" Natalia whooped and I couldn't help but find their interaction heartwarming, meaning it made me queasy. I'd never seen my earthling roommate so doting.

"Little sister, you better be ready," I warned as we strutted down the lit-up sidewalk, taking the reins of the conversation. "Tonight is going to be wild. There are some things you should know, so listen close. Everyone is going to smell that you are fresh meat. In other words, trust fucking no one. Starseeds love to tease and test the newbies. It's a full moon which means everyone's crazy is going to be amplified. In the Celestial Society, everyone our age is fighting for our place. Power is everything to us. Being my sister will be a gift and a curse. Everyone at Luna worships me but the students from the other schools are threatened by me. Stick close to me and don't look anyone in the eyes unless I give you the okay."

"And do not, by any circumstances, accept a drink anyone tries to offer you," Natalia added.

"Right," I nodded in agreement.

I could practically hear Emilia's mind whirling and her heart racing. "Um... Okay. I mean, I think I'm ready. Mom has drilled it all into my head, the way things work."

I snorted an indignant laugh. "Trust me, Mother knows nothing of how we operate. Things have changed since she grew up. Honor has been replaced with ruthlessness. Hard work with bloodlines. Just watch and learn, little sis."

"Okay, Nyx," Emilia replied earnestly. "I trust you."

The color drained from my cheeks. Shit, why did she have to go saying something like that?

"Tour of the city is over," I muttered absently, hailing a cab, wishing I could outrun my vile nature.

The cab ride was agonizing.

Emilia wouldn't stop asking questions. Natalia was more than happy to answer. It seemed like Emilia was going to Emerge as a waterling. She'd been dreaming about water nonstop the last few months apparently, and that was the exact same thing that happened to me before I Emerged as a fireling. I dreamt of fire nearly every night leading up to my Emergence.

Wasn't that just peachy? Water elementals were my only real threat as a fireling. *Of course* my sister would Emerge as one.

Our Emergence was intended to be a joyous, celebratory affair. If you had a family who gave a shit about you.

Almost a year had passed since my Emergence as a fireling, and I'd conquered so much in just one solar revolution. I'd become queen of my school and one day I'd be the most powerful fucking fire bearer this world had ever seen.

We arrived at the beach at half past ten. Natalia uttered a simple Compulsion charm to the cabbie, and he ever so generously offered the ride for free. Funny how that always happened.

I gauged Emilia's expression as we led her onto the sand, the glorious scent and music of the ocean caressing our senses. The waves crashed in the distance, the sky a blanket of black velvet overhead. The wind whipped our hair around and Emilia fought to keep it out of her eyes as she looked around in confusion. "The beach is empty."

Emilia had not yet Emerged, which meant she couldn't access her Sight alone.

I reached out and took her hand. She jolted slightly as if this was so foreign and unexpected. She wasn't wrong. A bolt of electricity passed between us as our fingers locked. I tried not to let my face change, but my lips parted in betrayal as I gazed up at my little sister in awe. Her power was evident under her skin. My mouth immediately dried. I cleared my throat, remembering the point of this.

I nodded toward the empty beach. "Look again."

I glared intently at the sand where the waves crashed, breathing deeply, and casting all my energy against the Veil. It dissolved instantly, the heavy pounding bass erupting against the once peaceful night as the incredible party twinkled into view.

"Oh, my Goddess!" Emilia squealed as I allowed my power to extend to her, clearing the Veil from her eyes.

As expected, the party was off the fucking chain.

Fire dancers dressed in skimpy leather outfits put on a show while air ballerinas floated ten feet above the sand, twirling and whirling. Flaming lanterns hovered midair, the fire charmed to be all different neon colors. Over a hundred shimmery bodies were dancing together, every single one dressed ethereally as if we'd stepped back in time. A roaring bonfire blazed in the center of the party while a gigantic sculpture of sand forged by the earthlings loomed over the party. They'd carved it into the shape of a masculine god slaying a serpent. I rolled my eyes at that.

Biggie Smalls rapped that classical shit as the three of us stepped onto the scene.

"Oh my..." Emilia breathed, her jewel blue eyes huge and shining as she took it all in.

Natalia and I kept our faces apathetic as we moved through the crowd. Every set of eyes fell on us, and several people voiced their greetings but no one came too close. They parted for us and everything. Shit was biblical.

Okay, so maybe people feared me. Story of my life. My magic had always been chaotic, even before I Emerged.

As a child, I'd been a tiny bit...emotional. My temper tantrums and outbursts would often manifest outside of me as something destructive. A fire, a ground shake, an explosion of sorts. I never meant to do any of it. It was unheard of for children to be able to harness their magic before they came of age. It drew the attention of the High Council of the Society. When I was eight, they showed up on our doorstep, looking like magical Secret Service motherfuckers, demanding my mother bring me into the Institution to be tested.

They couldn't detect any magic in me, so we were eventually released but they kept tabs on us throughout the years which was a real hindrance for Esmeralda Morningstar. And she never let me forget it.

It also made me famous amongst our people.

"Nyx!" a chorus of shrill voices called in unison, and I didn't even need to turn around to see who it was.

Three girls with bleached hair, overly smoky makeup, red lips, and dresses cut in my favorite style came rushing over.

"Hello, girls," I said.

"You look gorgeous!" one of them gushed.

"Whoa," Emilia muttered in my ear. "Why do they look identical to you?"

"Identical to me!" I cried. "Please! They look nothing like me, despite how hard they try."

The three girls were not insulted in the least. They took pride in their position as my chosen minions, as they should. They were all firelings, of course. Not particularly powerful ones, either, but they came from highborn families and were wise enough to know serving me was the best they'd ever get.

Natalia grumbled something under her breath.

"So?" I demanded. "What do you have for me?"

One of the girls held up her blackmirror, her face splitting into a grin. "Maverick Madriu liked and commented on your recent photo!"

My face crumpled with disgust. "Do you really think I give a shit about what *some guy* did online? And Minion One, what did I tell you about wearing lipstick in that shade? That is my signature shade. You are much too docile to pull off such a bloody red. Go wash it off right now!"

"Yes, Nyx!" She scurried off, leaving the other two standing there with wide, fearful eyes.

I waited expectantly.

They fumbled with their blackmirrors, desperate to not make the other girl's mistake. One of them piped up. "A bunch of students from San Gabriel were out on a houseboat last weekend. Two firelings got into a fight and the whole boat went down in flames. All ten of them died. Including Missy Calista, who was the only fireling to ever come close to your rank of power."

I narrowed my brows. "Seriously? Why haven't I heard this news?"

"Apparently, they're keeping it hush-hush. San Gabriel doesn't want anyone to know they lost one of their top students."

"Hmm." I smirked, folding my arms over my chest. Competition eliminated? Perfect. "Alright, that wasn't totally useless. Now run along and fetch me a drink."

They beamed, proud to have somewhat pleased me before they darted away.

"Only you would be glad to hear about the tragic death of fellow starseeds," Natalia muttered, not bothering to hide the distaste in her tone.

I shot her a glare. "You don't seem too broken up about it either."

"Did you... Did you just call that girl *Minion One*?" Emilia asked, aghast.

"Of course. Minion One, Two, and Three."

My sister looked horrified. I had to laugh.

The whole 'Minion' thing had started as a joke. Last year, these three girls became obsessed with me after I saved one of them from being bullied. They followed me around dotingly, which was super annoying as I was not looking for any more friends. As a joke, I told them they could be my minions. They bloody well agreed. Right away! I named them Minion One, Two, and Three, and they did not oppose. So, I just rolled it with it. Really, I was waiting for them to get a fucking backbone and stand up to me. But no matter how much of a bossy raging bitch I was, they remained loyal.

I wasn't complaining.

"Nyx! Natalia!" a familiar voice chimed from our left. I turned just in time to see Faye Casanova, wearing a pair of silver fairy wings and stumbling over with her arms flung out. She collided right into me, smelling like liquor and flowers. Her golden blonde hair was full of feathers and leaves, sticking out in every direction which was always part of her charm. She squeezed me tightly then held me out at arm's length, green eyes smothered in glitter scathing from my toes to my face. "I've missed you! You look amazing!"

"It's so good to see you, you bitch!" I cawed. "You promised you'd come back before everyone else so we could catch up in the Sphere without having to hold back." I gave her a teasing smirk before pouting my bottom lip.

"Well, I'm coming back with you tonight!" she promised. "I can't wait to get back in the Sphere. I'm so done being with my family. Hey, Natalia! Oh—who's this?" Faye's emerald gaze snagged on Emilia and her eyes lit up. "Oh, shit! This is your little sister! Well, she's not so little." Faye giggled.

"Yep. Emilia, this is Faye. She's a third-year airling at Luna."

Emilia blushed as Faye gathered her into a sloppy, touchy hug. "You're going to love it at Luna! Have you Emerged already?"

"In two weeks," my sister answered proudly.

"Any guesses on your element? I guess fire, obviously?"

"I'm actually thinking water."

"Ohhhh!" Faye looked at me with mischievous, challenging eyes. "Fire and water sisters. That won't be competitive at all."

"I need a drink," Natalia interjected. I couldn't agree more. Where the hell were my minions?!

The waterlings had cast a mountain of crushed ice to keep all the drinks cold. An abundant assortment of colorful drinks peppered the enchanted ice and holy shit, with a liquor supply like this, tonight was bound to be level ten crazy.

My minions were here, arguing over which drink I would like the most.

I dismissed them for the night, not wanting to deal with their fussing.

I scanned my choices, from fruity bottles of mortal beer and ciders to psychedelic tinctures enchanted by magic. Higher up were the fancy hard liquors, both from the mortal and magical realms. I decided to be naughty and grab a bottle of witches vodka. Usually, alcohol, especially the hard stuff, would dilute our magic. Witches vodka didn't. In fact, it gives you the same buzz while *heightening* your magic. A terrible, wonderful concoction. Starseeds were forbidden from drinking it, so I didn't know how or why it was here, but I wasn't one to give up an opportunity like this.

Natalia glared at me as we made our way toward the bonfire, and I took a hefty slam from the bottle. "Witches vodka? Seriously?"

I narrowed my eyes at her. "What's up with you tonight? Why are you being such a mom?"

"Because your little sister who hasn't even Emerged is with us and I just think you should chill out."

"Duly noted," I answered sourly, turning away from her, glad Faye was here. Faye was always down to have a good time.

Emilia drank her green apple cider and danced to the music, seeming to adjust just fine. Her eyes were on the air dancers as they twirled and bounded overhead like they were straight out of a Peter Pan movie. They were majestic. No matter how many times I witnessed magic, the excitement never waned.

"Aren't you going to introduce me to more of your friends?" Emilia asked me, finishing off the last of her drink and making a face about it.

I blanched. My friends? I didn't have many of those. I had fans and foes.

"You've met them," I muttered, gesturing to Faye and Natalia.

Emilia's brows jumped, but she didn't say anything back.

My spine stiffened as my stare snagged on Jedidiah Stone standing across the fire. His two butt buddies, Raziel and Demitri, the tall ginger twins, stood behind him dotingly.

"The Mole Boys are here," I muttered to Natalia.

"They're going to come over to us," she said, giving me her I-saw-it-in-a-vision look.

From across the blaze, three entitled pricks who screamed of trust fund money had their eyes glued to us. Veneficus was the most pretentious masculine Academy in existence. An elite boy's school that operated from twenty stories beneath the surface of the earth, underneath a five-star hotel downtown. Hence, the nickname I gave them: The Mole Boys. They hated me for it. It was awesome. We'd had a war going on ever since I started it. I enjoyed getting under their skin almost as much as I enjoyed them getting under mine.

They each held a long, wooden staff at their side, a glowing crystal atop of each. That was the difference between masculine and feminine magic. Males needed a staff to express their power, whereas feminine magic was innate.

"Who are they?" Emilia wondered, twirling her goddamn hair.

I fought the urge to slap her upside the head. Sure, they were hot. Sublimely hot. In the mortal realm, such beauty was revered as a rare treasure. Emilia was still used to those standards. In the Celestial Society, though, beauty was the norm. We were born into magical bloodlines and therefore we were creatures of immaculate genetics. She'd get used to all the pretty, mythical faces.

"The tall one in the middle is Jedidiah. Earthling," Faye said. "He's the son of the High Lord. Meaning one day, he'll be the leader of the Celestial Society. The other two are twins who both wield fire. Nothing like your sister, though. But they are at the top of their Academy."

"And they're grade-A fucking assholes," I added, tipping back the bottle of witches vodka and letting a torrent of burning liquor annihilate my throat. "And Jedidiah will probably never inherit his father's position. They're practically estranged."

"Your sister and them hate each other. It's a power struggle." Faye giggled.

"There's no *struggle*," I quipped deviously.

"You talking about us, sweets?" Jedidiah moved in on us like he owned the entire beach and every person here. His dark blue eyes zeroed in on my sister, assessing her in a way that made me murderous. "Oh, goody. There's two of you." His glare landed on me. I smirked to mask my quaking fury, which didn't work on him.

Jedidiah stood tall, conventionally handsome, and traditionally arrogant. He wore a crisp white tunic that complimented his tanned skin and broad shoulders. He knew he was hot; he knew he was powerful, and he didn't bother to add even the slightest dash of humility to the mix.

The party around us was not so subtly paying attention to our interaction.

"What's your name, sweetheart?" Demitri or Raziel asked Emilia. I always had trouble telling them apart. They put the I in identical, especially right now while they rocked the same shaggy hairstyle. Whichever one he was, he reached out and took my sister's hand, leaning down chivalrously as he planted a kiss on the back of it. Her cheeks flushed with pink heat. I rolled my eyes. She was going to learn this lesson the hard way. I'd warned her.

"Emilia," she cooed. *Cooed!*

"Ah, this one's sweet, not bitter," the twin purred, raking his eyes up and down the length of my little sister.

"She's got doe eyes," his brother drawled.

"Not siren eyes, like our dear Nyx."

"So innocent, this one."

"Oh, to have two sisters, so similar..."

"And yet so different!"

"One so tall, legs for days..."

"The other, petite, with an ass that won't quit!"

"How spectacular!"

I didn't bother to hide my true feelings as I bared my teeth and let the burning in my chest unleash with an angry white-gold flame extending over my right palm. "Back off!" I told the twin, holding my hand out suggestively. That witches vodka had definitely kicked in.

The twins stared at me and then fell into hysterics before holding out their staffs, the crystals on top of them igniting with orange fire.

"What are you gonna do, Morningstar?" one of them taunted. "Fight our fire with your fire?"

Jedidiah's lips stretched into a cruel smirk.

"How comical!" I chimed jubilantly, holding out my other hand as it came alight with flame. "You think your little sticks stand a chance against *my* fire!" I laughed maniacally as I called upon every ounce of my power.

An explosion of white fire burst out of me and the whole party gasped and went flying back. The fire didn't just manifest over my hands, but from the sand in front of me as well. Tall, ravenous, sentient flames that did my bidding. Three heavy streams merged into one vein as it hurled towards the twins so quickly, they didn't have time to react, let alone fight back. They even squawked in surprise. I continued to laugh as I set off to chase them around the beach with my flames. People watched the show, completely invested, cheering, and laughing as they filmed us with their blackmirrors.

The twins gained their wits about them and stopped running, instead turning to face me. With their power merged and doubled, they released impressive streams of fire from their staffs that clashed with mine. I grit my teeth, putting all my energy into trying to break through their flames. Neither side would give, and the pressure began to build up where our magic met. We created a monstrous wall of fire. The whole party dispersed, moving out of our way, standing on the outskirts, and watching through wide eyes.

This was our way. This was the norm. Power versus power.

CHAPTER 3
THE NYX SHOW
EMILIA

I absolutely could not believe my life right now as I watched Nyx. She looked like a madwoman, standing there with her hands out, teeth bared, white-gold flames shooting from her without relent. The fox-haired twins fought back with all their might united, making it an even battle.

Everyone just stood around, hooting, and filming and cheering their favorite on. Just like if a regular fight broke out at a mortal party. *Crap*. I thought I was ready for all this but watching my sister now, I wasn't so sure anymore.

That could never be me.

I mean, why would I want that to be me? Nothing even happened. He kissed my hand, big whoop. Nyx was just being Nyx. An explosive over-reactor who took the bait anyone ever cast out before her. This was ridiculous, but apparently, it made for good entertainment. Considering everyone else seemed to be thoroughly enjoying this.

Mr. Tall, Dark, and Blue Eyes snarled from where he stood in front of me and slammed the bottom of his staff into the sand. I knew it wasn't a coincidence the earth began rumbling under Nyx's dainty feet. She looked down just as the ground split beneath her and I let out a ghastly scream as she fell into oblivion.

"No!" I cried, instinctively lurching forward. I ran stupidly right to the edge of the crack in the earth, relief washing over me when I realized it was just a small hole. Well, not exactly *small*. The crater was at least fifteen feet deep.

Faye and Natalia were quickly at my side as we peered into the hole at my sister who looked back up at us through wild eyes.

"Jedidiah!" she yelled callously, fire igniting from her clenched fists. "You always fight their battles! Face me now! One-on-one!"

Good Goddess—she was dead serious.

"We really shouldn't have let her drink that witches vodka," Natalia muttered.

Faye giggled.

"Someone get her out!" I hissed.

"No," that smooth, arrogant voice wrapped around me like an unwarranted caress as Jedidiah stepped to the edge of the hole. He looked down apathetically, pointing his staff down at her. "No one can help her. Come on, Luna Queen." He taunted her with more than his words. His eyes lit with an ominous light as he glared down. "Surely it'll be no sweat to get yourself out."

The party oooh'd as if they were a freaking live audience on some cheesy sitcom. I made a sound of disgust, my heart pounding as I prayed my sister would turn this around.

My first Celestial party and Nyx was drunk, stuck in a hole.

"Before it fills up with water," Jedidiah added sweetly.

The fury on her face waned and she became calculative. An eerie kind of silence fell over us as the music switched songs. The rising water was up to her knees. A new beat thrummed then, this one slower and more intense, the bass pounding in sync with my heavy heart.

Nyx bared her teeth once more. "This is cheap!"

"You're sexy when you're angry," he told her slyly, every single syllable laced with mockery.

At that, she grinned, but it was a dark, threatening grin. "You do get off on dangerous things, don't you, Jedidiah? Well, prepare to be really fucking turned on, because when I get up there, I'm going to murder you!"

Someone in the crowd whooped and others cheered her on in echo of that.

Jedidiah smirked, showing absolutely no sign of being shaken by her threat. He looked like she just told him she was going to come up here and blow him.

"Nyx," I pleaded, wishing she'd stop messing around already. *Get yourself out of there. Get yourself together.*

"You want to help me, little sis? Toss me the witches vodka!"

"Oh, fuck me." Natalia shook her head and scrubbed her face with her hand.

Faye bit her lip as she looked to see what I'd do.

Jedidiah didn't move but I swear he watched me from the corner of his eye as I hesitated. Nyx had dropped the bottle to fight the twins. I glanced back at where we'd been standing before and saw it lying there in the sand. My heart kicked into top gear.

Natalia thought the magical liquor was the problem here. I wished that was the case, but I knew my sister. This was *alllllll* Nyx.

I sighed, retrieving the glass bottle with the pretty pink label, and returned to my place at the edge of the hole she'd dug herself. I mean, this had to be symbolic, right?

"Beware," Natalia warned me. "That shit messes with our magic. Diviners used to drink it to talk to spirits."

What choice did I have?

The entire party had their eyes on me, waiting to see what I'd do. Chomping at the bit. Even those amazing dancers who had been twirling and floating in midair had stopped to focus on us.

Screw it.

I tossed the bottle down to my sister who caught it with a squeal of excitement. Everyone went crazy, moving closer to the hole. People fought and elbowed to get a front-row seat to see The Nyx Show. My sister did not disappoint. She chugged half the freaking bottle in one go. The party lost it. They were cheering her name and whistling like she was a freaking celebrity.

Nyx dropped the bottle into the sand and wiped her hand over her mouth. Her eyes watered, and her red lips flushed and swollen.

With a fierce, primal scream, my sister clenched her fists to her sides,

and they exploded with fire like out of a rocket ship. Yes, she quite literally *rocket-launched* herself out of the hole using the full force of her
fiery power. She went soaring overhead, way above the crowd, screaming
as she flew higher than she anticipated. I watched in panic, her life practically flashing before my eyes as she began plummeting toward the
sand. People hurled out of the way. Faye stepped forward and shot her
hands out, a gust of energy rippling across the sand. For a beat, I had no
clue what she'd done, but then Nyx's fall was broken by a soft shield of
air. She bounced on it a little as if there were an invisible mattress to
catch her fall. Then she stuck the bloody landing. Everyone went
berserk.

Including me.

She beat those guys, three on one, and looked damn good doing it.

Even Jedidiah and the twins were smirking as if they knew she'd
triumph.

I ran at Nyx as she collapsed to her knees, breathing heavily. Faye
and I helped her up, slinging her jelly arms over our shoulders. "Damn,
I'm pooped now. I need a drink!"

"You're cut off," Natalia barked, though there was love in her eyes.

"Waahhh!" Nyx whined like a small child. She looked over at me
as we pulled her away from the hole, and back through the main area
of the party. People still stared, but the moment had passed, and the
music ramped up again. The cue for everyone to get back to their
shit.

"Not bad, Morningstar," Jedidiah said with an impish twinkle in
his eye.

"Fuck you," Nyx shot back. "I'll murder you later, Mole Boy."

"Can't wait," he replied, saluting her.

I couldn't read the look in Nyx's eyes as her lids fluttered halfway
down. She was drunk, that was for sure. "I love you, little sister," she
said then. Okay—she was *really* drunk. "Do you know I love you?"

I laughed nervously, wondering why a fervent heat crawled up my
neck at that moment. "Sure, Nyx."

"That's a no," she quipped. "Well, I guess I can't blame you, I am a
real bitch. I was going to corrupt you tonight, but you know what? I
decided you're fine just the way you are. And it's okay if you're a water-

ling, I guess. Hey! Speaking of water! I want to go swimming! Take me to the ocean!"

I stared at her drunk face while those words settled in my gut. I never had any clue how to accurately perceive my sister. She was an enigma wrapped in black humor dunked in a riddle and stamped with a secret.

What did that mean? She was going to corrupt me? How?

Perhaps I didn't want to know.

Even now, drunk off her ass, Nyx was just so ethereal. It was no wonder she was the Queen of Luna Academy. How could she not be? Her long, *naturally* silver hair fell to her hips, like liquid moonlight. A striking contrast to her thick, dark brows which were nearly black. Her bronze skin was alive with living tattoos, her body voluptuous despite her small size. There was no one like her, no one even came close. She stuck out like a dragon among lambs. She had fire in her dark eyes, fire that burned inside of her at all times. She looked at everything and everyone like it was hers to conquer. Because it was. The world had always yielded to my sister.

For *me* to Emerge *after* her... How would I ever live up to the Morningstar name?

Having a place in Luna Academy was supposed to be a great honour. A gift. Something to be excited and passionate about. Yet every minute counting down filled me with more dread than the last. First, there was my element. I wanted to be a fireling like my mother and Nyx and the rest of our bloodline, but every fibre of my being sensed I would Emerge with the power of water.

Putting me in direct opposition to my family.

Fire and water aren't two elements that can simply go smoothly together. They are total cosmic opposites and when they are around each other in a magical sense, a magnetic pull begins. The two are drawn together, and there are only two ways the union can go. Either they battle to cancel the other one out, for one to be victorious and destroy the other, or they merge and alchemize into Aether, the fifth element.

It never went the way of the latter.

Would fate truly sentence me to a life in opposition with my own blood?

On top of my elemental conundrum, there was also the fact that I was: Me. Soft, pathetic, passive me. My mother and sister were flaming swords given human form. Me? I was more like a feather fluttering at the mercy of the wind. Tonight was beyond what I could ever imagine, and yet, everyone seemed unfazed. My pulse hadn't slowed down one bit but now we were sauntering off to the ocean for a whimsical swim like everything was fine. Nyx and Faye were gushing about freaking mermaids and sailors and shit.

Not to mention how much I missed Michael. *No, don't think of him,* I tried to tell myself. He'd probably forgotten all about me by now. We weren't even dating but he made my heart race, and he was all I could think about before I came here and—ugh. *Stop thinking about him. The Amnesia spell will make him forget you ever existed.*

Nyx tore her arm from its purchase around my shoulder and leaned over to projectile vomit on the sand. We all squealed and flew back to avoid her spewage. She laughed while she puked up straight vodka, and part of me was entirely relieved she got some of it out of her system. Without missing a beat, she straightened up, wiped her face, and began stripping off her red dress, letting it pool at her feet like spilled paint. In nothing but a gold thong, with her plethora of living tattoos going wild, she beelined it for the crashing waves. I gawked after her, knowing damn well I wasn't built for this fervent level of existence.

CHAPTER 4
PRETTY LITTLE DEATH THREATS

NYX

My little vomit session paired with the swim in the ocean sobered me up... a bit.

I emerged from the waves, water glistening down my naked, tattooed body as I strutted through the moody tide. The party had revved up considerably now that the air ballerinas were making the fire dancers float, so it was unlikely anyone would notice me now, though I didn't care much even if they did.

Emilia stood at the shore with my dress clutched in her hands. She watched me apprehensively. I bit back a giggle as I took in her expression. She looked like a startled owl. She'd looked like that for some time now.

"Here I am! Emilia Morningstar, Emerging as an all-powerful waterling!" I cawed theatrically, tossing my hands in the air, bearing my ocean-drenched body. "Here I am! Rock you like a hurricaaaane!" I splashed water over my head and cackled boisterously, though the girls didn't seem to find it funny. Tough crowd.

"Come on, Nyx," Emilia urged. "Let's go back to the Academy."

Always the buzzkill. I stalked back to the sand, pouting.

I snatched the silky red dress and slid it back over my wet body. "That's better," I sighed wistfully.

Natalia and Faye stood back a few paces, chatting while they both looked at Faye's blackmirror. Natalia was annoyed with me so she wouldn't look at me, but I knew we'd kiss and make up later.

"I spook you, little sis?" I asked teasingly.

Emilia blew out a breath and ran her fingers through her dark hair. "That was pretty crazy, Nyx."

I shrugged. "We haven't even gotten started yet, honey. Buckle up. It's wild around here. Get used to the rivalry and the random breakouts of song and dance." I laughed at my joke and Emilia struggled to chime in with me.

"You'll get used to it. You're a *Child of the Divine*," I spoke those ridiculous words with an accent and a puffed-out chest. "It's in your blood to survive here."

"I hope you're right," she breathed back, sincerity in her eyes.

Sheesh. She needed to settle down. Everything was fine. She looked ready to burst into tears.

I turned to move over to Natalia and Faye but they weren't there. A wall of misty black collided with my gaze, sending my heart into freefall.

What the—?

Everything

Just

Disappeared.

A sharp gasp tore through my lips as my chest exploded with splintered ice. An endless expanse of darkness splayed out around me, every which way I turned.

The balmy California night completely vanished, replaced with icy, pitch-black nothingness. I whirled around, wholeheartedly miffed, searching for evidence of sand or ocean or people. My breath puffed out before me in white clouds. Holy shit. I hadn't seen my breath in years. I panicked, spinning around like a broken windup doll, searching for a light or a sign, or a sound. Nothing.

Nothing but silence. Darkness. Coldness.

Like I'd been sucked into the void.

"Hey!" I called, my voice echoing repeatedly off the dark as if it were a tangible thing.

Someone must have been casting an illusion over me.

The fucking Mole Boys. *I swear to the Goddess, I'll smite them—*

A phantom chuckle sounded from all around me, halting me mid-thought. Goosebumps rose over every inch of my flesh like the army of the dead. My bones fossilized completely, eyes darting in search of the source of that strange voice.

It was as if a magnet were pulling on my heart space. I'd never felt anything quite like it. A strange, foreign magic called me from the depths of this void, beckoning my fire to play.

"Hello?" I bellowed, feeling beyond stupid. "Tell me who's there! Jedidiah, I swear—"

The creature who emerged from a swarm of shadows before me was *not* Jedidiah.

My breath hitched, my heart bombing against my ribs as if it meant to carve a path out of my chest.

A pair of impossibly bright silver eyes pinned me in place. I'd never seen eyes that color before, which was alarming, seeing as how the Celestial Society was full of bright, colorful eyes. Never eyes like that.

His eyes appeared first, and then the rest of him materialized into view like a fucking body rising to the surface of dark water. He stood tall, lithe, and—phantom-like. His hands were folded behind his back, expression neutral, skin smooth and flawless like polished stone. He looked not of this world, with those pointed, elven features and piercing eyes that shone like lights in the dark. A billowing mane of dark mahogany hair framed his face and settled far below his shoulders.

I didn't recognize him—not from around the city, anyway. He couldn't be from around here, that much was clear in the moon-colored complexion of his flesh. He looked like he'd burst into flames if he dared to step into the sun. Despite that, however, there was a certain, undeniable familiarity about him. Perhaps I'd seen him before in a dream. Or a nightmare.

In a strange, frightening way he was beautiful. The sharp, primal beauty of a viper before it lashes.

A pale hand adorned with chunky silver rings was suddenly reaching for my face. He—! This motherfucker thought he could *touch* me! I winced, swatting his hand away, beyond perturbed. When our skin made contact, he jolted. For a split second, his eyes widened, as if the occurrence seemed impossible. He schooled his features instantly, but I saw the reaction, undeniably.

"Who the hell are you?" I demanded, refusing to show fear.

His gaze had me crossing my arms over my chest. My damp dress did little to hide my bristled skin, and he damn well noticed.

He settled into an immutable force of apathy. I didn't like it. This calmness, this stillness, it was unnatural. "If I tell you, do you promise to whisper some of your pretty little death threats just for me?"

I bared my teeth instinctively, fire erupting from my clenched fists. I gasped at the sight of the flames writhing over my skin. They didn't look right. This shadowy realm made them ghostly and translucent. Almost silver. Feeble and see-through, rather than the white-hot rage they usually were.

Confused, I banished them, my chest heaving. "Return me at once, or I will—"

He leaned in closer, amusement dancing over his features as he waited for me to go on and deliver a threat. I clipped my jaw shut, too stubborn to give him what he wanted. He sighed, as if he figured as much, and straightened again.

"You are quite the destructive force," he mused casually. "Burdened with glorious power that you do not care to try and tame, nor understand fully."

I grimaced. "And you know that how? Are you one of my secret admirers who's obsessed with me? Get in line, buddy. If you know who I am then you know this will end badly for anyone who messes with me."

I internally rolled my eyes at myself. Me, unable to resist uttering threats.

He smirked infuriatingly. I couldn't stand the sight of it so I allowed my gaze to travel over the entirety of him. His long black jacket with ornate silver buttons hung almost to the ground, but the ground had been swallowed by smoky shadows. I tried to look down at my own feet but saw nothing. We stood in a sea of black, floating in the middle of actual nowhere.

This magic was unlike anything I'd ever known. Wrong, dark, inverted. Endless.

"What do you want from me?" I asked, hoping we could get to the bloody point.

I prepared myself for the worst and held my chin high, awaiting his response.

"I want you to do what you do best." The grin on his lips turned dark and kissed with malice. "Unleash yourself."

I stared at him, waiting for the joke. He was serious.

"I'm not giving you the satisfaction of a fight. I don't even know you. Trust me, dude. You don't want to do this. You must be new around here and I guess what happened tonight with the twins gave you some ideas but—"

"Please," he interrupted, waving me off. "Does this feel like juvenile magic to you?" He motioned toward the dark abyss around us.

No. No, it did fucking not.

I swallowed thickly and prayed to all the most merciful Goddesses that my face did not betray me.

"I'm not fighting you."

"No?" he quipped lightly. "Well, that's too bad. Seeing as how it's your only way out of here."

I narrowed my eyes while my heart plummeted into the pit of my gut. "Excuse me?"

"This is my pocket dimension," he supplied, looking around proudly.

I grimaced, folding my arms across my chest. "Well, no offense, but it's depressing and smells like a damp cave with a dying beast rotting in the corner. So, if you don't mind, I'd like to be on my way."

He appeared offended for half a second before he schooled his features once more, looking at me through vacant silver eyes. "Your opinion on my dimension doesn't matter. All that matters is that neither of us can leave until you initiate a battle with me."

I snorted impulsively, sure this was some sick joke but the look in his eyes killed that wishful thinking.

"But why?" I breathed, sounding more desperate than I intended. "I don't understand the point of this."

"The point? You clearly know not what you are and what everyone in your life probably works tirelessly to hide from you." He started circling me now, looking down the bridge of his nose at me, making me feel pathetic and small. Shadows whirled around him like they were attracted to the air he breathed.

"Each time a Celestial initiates a battle with another, our power grows or depletes depending on the outcome of the fight. You'd think that you won tonight, but you hold greater power than those twins, even combined, so the fact that they held their ground against you and did not back down means they will be the ones to grow in power."

"Bullshit!" I snapped. "They lost. They were losing before they had outside help. Jedidiah interjected and they didn't even finish what they started."

"What *you* started."

"How do you know? Were you there? I don't think I would have missed you."

The ominous stranger waved a dismissive hand. "Never mind how I know things. You are only stalling. We both know you can't turn down a challenge."

"So, you've dragged me into your stank-ass pocket dimension in hopes to best me in a fight and gain more power?"

"My motives wouldn't make sense to your unilluminated mind," he sneered.

"Well, where's your staff?" I quipped. "You're going to need one if you want to fight me."

He laughed. I didn't get it. What was funny?

"I have no need for some object medium."

My eyes widened at that. A male Celestial who didn't need a staff to do magic? Unheard of.

Thunder cracked in my heart as the power lust took hold of my senses. Who did this freak think he was? If I didn't know any better, I'd think he lived here. He looked like he hadn't seen sunlight in centuries. He was as hollow and empty as this dreadful place.

"You couldn't just challenge me at the party?" I spoke low, my voice husky as I dared to take a step closer to him. The scent of citrus and metal filled my nose in his proximity. Bizarre. But sort of enticing... No. "You have to drag me off into the shadows because you can't face me in the real world? Pathetic. I don't fight people who mean nothing to me.

As fun as it would be to drop you on your ass, I don't care enough about you to bother. The twins may be insufferable assholes but they are from a competing academy and so they are relevant enough. You are nothing to me. Send me back at once."

"I guess you didn't hear me before. You can't leave until you challenge me. Time doesn't exist here, darling. We could stay for all eternity, and it would be little more than a blip in the universe. If you'd like to take up permanent residence in the shadows you so despise, so be it."

A thickness gathered in my throat as I gawked around at the endless black. No, I didn't want to stay here another minute, let alone eternity.

And as ridiculous as this all sounded, I believed him. I couldn't leave, not until I did what he wanted. I felt it.

I sucked in a sharp breath.

Well, fuck me.

I couldn't deny the bloodlust filling my veins. The stranger's power thrummed in the air all around us, manifested as the darkness itself. Every fiber of my being wanted to unleash my chaos. My most innate instincts rose to the surface like a charging bull. Whatever his magic was, I'd never felt anything like it. A strange, heady magnetic pull drew me in, the fire inside me flicking aggressively. I almost had the mind to assume he was a waterling. Only water could beckon fire so wantonly. Yet, that didn't seem exactly right. I sensed water, yes, but something else, too... Something I couldn't quite pinpoint.

One thing remained clear: I was the one at a disadvantage. Several disadvantages. This was his realm, meaning his magic would be favored and amplified whereas mine had already been drained. I was exhausted after drinking heavily and battling the twins. My fire didn't even look right here. I'd never seen ghostly silver flames before.

But Celestials didn't sit around and cry about how unfair everything was.

We bossed up.

I lifted my chin, knowing my eyes smoldered as I made my decision. "I promise you will regret this."

A smile that made my insides heat up and tighten slithered across his lips while his silver gaze shone. He said nothing, he only waited.

I bared my teeth and groaned as I held my hands out and summoned my fire. I breathed deeply, calling upon the most potent energy from my heart space trying to bring my magic to full color and fruition. A grin tugged at the edges of my mouth as the flames over my palms appeared bright, brilliant white, and ready to spar. Time to make this shadow bitch regret ever laying eyes on the likes of me.

CHAPTER 5
SNATCHED

EMILIA

"Nyx! NYX!" I kept shaking her, but she wouldn't snap out of it. She wouldn't wake up. She just stood there on the sand, eyes half closed and rolling back while her lashes fluttered frantically. She wouldn't move or speak. She looked freaking possessed and I didn't like this at all. My entire body rattled with panic.

"Holy shit," Natalia breathed, shaking her head. "This is bad. This is fucking bad."

"What's happening to her?" I cried, shaking her shoulders still.

"It's like she's been Astral Snatched," Faye murmured, her eyes wide and full of severity.

"Astral Snatched?" I repeated sharply. "What is that?"

"Dark, dark magic," Natalia answered. "It's forbidden. Even for the Embodied. It's only for the High Council in extreme situations. It invades another person's Sovereignty. It's like her soul has been snatched from her body. Her consciousness has been taken somewhere else."

"Like where?" I rasped.

The girls both shrugged hopelessly.

"I have no idea who would do this," Natalia growled. "The fact that I didn't See this coming..." She stepped forward and went to touch her

38

palm to my sister's cheek but as soon as she did, she dropped to the ground and started convulsing.

"Oh, my Goddess!" Faye screamed. She dropped to her knees at her friend's side. "Natalia!"

"HELP!" I cried in dismay, my eyes burning with tears while my body brimmed to the top with terror. "Someone help us!"

Jedidiah appeared at my side in an instant. I had no idea how he could arrive so quickly but when his eyes landed on Nyx, I didn't like the look that bloomed over his features. Anger struck behind his eyes like lightning while his weighted glare dropped to me. "What the fuck did she do?"

My lips tore back over my teeth. "She did nothing! She was just standing there and suddenly this happened!"

We may have been several yards away from the party, down by the crashing waves, but people started noticing us now.

Raziel and Demitri came rushing over, halting mid-step as they laid eyes on my sister.

Jedidiah shook Nyx aggressively and I hollered in protest. "Get your hands off her!"

"You called for help."

"From someone who doesn't hate her!"

"Then I'm afraid there's no one to help you."

"You guys!" Faye's wail interjected. "Just help her or get lost, Jedidiah!"

The entire party ogled at us now, everyone dead silent while they gravitated over here to catch the latest episode of The Nyx Show. The music still blasted wrongly but the crowd hushed as they watched. This time, I saw no excitement in their eyes. Instead, I saw fear. That sure didn't stop some of them from filming. A foreign growl rumbled in my throat as I stepped in the way of their view of her.

"Please," I whispered, desperate. Natalia was still on the ground. She'd stopped convulsing now, but her stillness brought me no comfort. Faye was crying silently, streams of glittery tears splashing onto the sand.

To my horror, blood started pouring from my sister's nose and for the first time, I feared for her life.

I had zero recollection of when the dark storm clouds rolled in, but thunder and lightning began warring overhead. An unnatural storm that filled my veins with adrenaline and anxiety.

"Please!" I cried again.

Nyx collapsed in Jedidiah's waiting arms. A strangled sound left my throat as he instructed the twins to grab Natalia.

A crack of thunder boomed from the dense clouds. Dark blue eyes landed on me, and my body lit up with goosebumps at the look he gave me. "Reach into my pocket," he instructed.

I blanched. "Excuse me?"

Jedidiah rolled his eyes as lightning flashed. "Reach into my pocket and grab the crystal sphere."

I didn't understand but I was in no position to argue. I did as he said, feeling ridiculous as heat crawled up my spine at his closeness. I slid my hand into the pocket of his trousers, heart pounding as my fingers brushed a small, smooth sphere no bigger than my thumbnail.

Just as I pulled my hand back, Nyx roused awake.

"What the hell?" she croaked groggily, blinking up at Jedidiah with horror blossoming over every inch of her face.

"Nyx!" I wailed, thrusting myself at her. "Are you okay?"

Natalia groaned awake in either Raziel or Demitri's arms. I'd never be able to tell them apart. She glanced around in alarm, shoving out of the twin's arms as soon as she registered that's where she was.

"Put me down, you menace!" Nyx growled at Jedidiah, thrashing out of his arms at once. She swayed on her feet, her lips and chin stained with blood. I caught her desperately as she toppled over. I'd never seen her look so weak. Her breaths escaped her in short, rapid huffs while her body trembled against my skin. She was freezing.

"Fuck you," Jedidiah snapped, offended. "You possessed bitch. Come on, boys." He snatched the crystal I forgot I was holding and turned without another word while the twins followed him.

Natalia stood stone still, looking at Nyx with a fathomless expression. Faye seemed ready to pass out as she fawned over my sister, wiping the blood from her face.

"What the hell was that?" I breathed.

Nyx shrugged casually, though cold darkness swarmed in her stare.

She glanced at the party, giving everyone a death glare until they got the message and turned away. With a stumble in her step, my sister started trudging off the beach. "Let's go."

LUNA ACADEMY STOOD TALL AND POWERFUL BEHIND A SET of iron gates in the hills overlooking the city. Even with the glamour, the place was ginormous. On the outside, to the mortal world, it appeared to be a modern LA mansion, drenched with opulence, screaming filthy rich. Once we were behind the gates, though, and the glamour dropped, the true face of the Academy showed itself.

A giant, medieval castle made of lava rock and quartz, with dozens of windows, balconies, and extravagant turrets that climbed to the sky. Towering evergreens, twisting oaks, and weeping willows guarded the property, whispering their secrets to the wind. The rich scent of earth and moss caressed my senses, reminding me of home. The famous Elemental Sphere shone from behind the Academy, a massive structure built in the image of the moon where all the elemental magic took place.

We arrived here out of a freaking cab. Like this was all so normal.

Nyx didn't say two words the entire ride back from the beach. Neither did Natalia. I didn't want to push them but—what the hell? That was the scariest thing I'd ever seen, and I knew I wasn't being overly sensitive about it because Faye was in the same boat as me. We'd all been rocked by what just happened.

Nyx led the way along the stone path, up the staircase to the giant double doors which magically opened for her.

The place was huge but narrow, adorned with feminine oil paintings, symbolic art pieces, tapestries, and statues. A spiral staircase with red velvet carpet led us up two stories. Floating candles and lanterns glowed from every which way. I was too distracted to really take it all in. My heart was in my throat as we ascended and followed my sister down a long hallway to her room.

"Aren't there...any staff here?" I wondered quietly as we stepped into my sister's dorm room which was an absolute pigsty.

"There are two Priestesses here right now, but they're not exactly helicopter guardians," Natalia muttered flatly. "We're all adults here."

I swallowed. "Right."

Nyx stripped out of her dress without a word and disappeared into the bathroom, slamming the door behind her. The shower turned on seconds later and the three of us stood awkwardly, not knowing what to do with ourselves.

"You guys are slobs," Faye scolded, holding her hands out at the mess. The destruction became buoyant, all items floating midair as she guided it with her magic. She straightened everything while it hovered, her hands moving as if she were the conductor of an orchestra. The clothes magically folded, the books stacked themselves and all the makeup gravitated back to the vanity drawers. It seemed so effortless for her as she cleaned the entire room without touching anything. The objects shot back into their rightful place and my lips parted in awe.

I now understood the difference between air magic and telekinesis.

Faye yawned when she was done. "Well, it's nice to be back but tonight was screwed up and I'm beat. I'm going back to my room. Will you guys be okay?"

Natalia and I nodded and said our farewells.

The silence that draped over the room seemed to wrap its fingers around my throat.

"Are you okay?" Natalia asked me.

"Are *you*?"

She released a shaky breath as she sat down on her bed under the window. Natalia was pretty, with her glowing melanin skin, bouncy black ringlets, and doe eyes. Her golden septum piercing made her look badass like you wouldn't want to mess with her. Aside from that, though, she had very calm energy. She took her bottom lip between her teeth and chewed on it before she answered. "I didn't See anything."

For a beat, I didn't understand what she meant. *Right, Natalia's a Seer.* "You didn't see anything when you were unconscious? What do you think that means?" My voice came out slow and quiet as if the words were scared to escape my tongue.

"I don't know," she answered. "It was like... Whoever did that to her did not want me to See. I was blocked. I should have been able to See where she was when I touched her cheek. Instead, I met a wall that dumped me on my ass." Her eyes strayed far away as she spoke, her fists clenched. "I may not be able to See but I still feel. Whatever just happened... It was bad."

My heart knocked against my ribs like I had a demolition crew in there. "It's Nyx," I said, trying to make myself feel better. "She can survive anything."

"True," Natalia muttered, though she didn't seem entirely convinced.

She helped me make a bed on the floor and by the time I had a cozy little nest, Nyx emerged from the bathroom in a cloud of steam. Her dark eyes were shadowed and bloodshot. If I didn't know any better, I'd think she'd been crying. Natalia and I fell silent as she stalked over to her bed on the opposite wall of Natalia's. She didn't even acknowledge that the room had been cleaned. She didn't acknowledge anything. She let her towel fall to the ground and slid into bed naked. She tucked herself deeply under the covers and turned away from us.

Natalia and I shared a glance.

"Nyx..." I breathed. "We have to talk about what just—"

"No, we don't. Nothing happened, alright? It was just some prank. Stop being pussies and just shut up because I need to sleep."

Rage bubbled into view from deep in Natalia's eyes. I watched her throat bob, and I was sure she had an argument ready to burst out of her but at the last second, she clipped her jaw shut. She climbed into her bed without another word.

I always knew my first night in the Academy would be beyond my wildest dreams, but I never thought it would be a page straight out of a nightmare.

CHAPTER 6
LIGHTLESS
NYX

"Fuck," I whispered shakily, staring down at my useless trembling palms. Phantom ice in my throat made it nearly impossible to breathe. The hole of darkness inside me stretched through the map of my veins, spreading emptiness throughout my entire being. I didn't dare glance in the mirror. I was still traumatized from the last time I had made that mistake. Whoever I'd seen in the glass, she wasn't me.

I was beautiful. Vibrant.

The creature staring back at me in the glass had been gaunt and pale and lightless. Sickly, drained. Her eyes were ringed with shadow, her cheeks sunken in and her lips dry. Drab, pale hair fell to her hips, knotted and stringy.

Almost a week had passed.

Emilia returned home the morning after the party when my mother had portalled in and whisked her away without a word. The look in my sister's eyes before she vanished in a poof of light would be ingrained in my memory forever. She didn't just look terrified or worried. She looked... She looked like she *pitied* me, and I didn't need anyone's pity. Least of all hers.

My ass went numb from sitting on the toilet this long. This was the only place I knew I wouldn't be interrupted. I sat on the closed lid and stared down at my shaky hands. Trying repeatedly to get them to produce a spark without killing my fucking self.

Tears slid soundlessly down my cheeks, blurring my vision. My heartbeat could be compared to the drums of war in a battle I was destined to lose.

My head exploded with blinding pain as I forced myself to produce a flame. A tiny, pitiful flame. The agony behind my eyes as I did so was staggering, and my nose instantly started bleeding. Same as the last time I tried to do magic. Blood dripped over my lips, but I refused to let the white flame die.

"Come on," I growled, gritting my teeth through the pain. I glared at the small, writhing flame over my palm. "Grow!"

It obeyed, but for a price.

The pain in my head spiked along with the fire. My vision went dark as my muscles spasmed.

I blacked out.

Woke up minutes later. On the bathroom floor.

This couldn't be happening. I was Nyx Morningstar, the most powerful starseed the Society had ever seen. Nobody could beat me, no one could even come close. I'd proved myself again and again.

"How could this happen?" I breathed to myself as I shakily rose to my feet. My head spun and ached something fierce. I kept thinking I'd wake up from this nightmare. Half a thought from me and I should've been able to burn an entire city to the ground if I wanted. Not now. Not anymore.

Natalia and I had barely spoken all week. I'd pissed her off with my reckless behavior in front of my sister, but she needed to get the hell over it. Though, part of me was glad to have her mad at me. It meant I had an excuse to withdraw into myself and hide the truth. I couldn't bear to tell anyone, even her.

I had no idea how it happened, that was the worst part.

All I remembered were the musty, endless shadows and those bright silver eyes that shone with the promise of ruining my goddamn life.

He convinced me to challenge him. I did. For a beat, it seemed so simple. My fire had exploded out of me, filling the shadow realm with living light. Blinding light. It seemed to consume the shadows effortlessly. I had already been internally celebrating my victory when out of nowhere the shadows engulfed *me*. Sentient, heavy darkness gobbled me up and I couldn't remember anything after that. I'd woken up on the beach in Jedidiah Stone's Goddess-forsaken arms. I'd never been so tired in all my life. I'd thought I just needed to sleep it off.

I slept. And slept. And slept. Each time, I prayed I'd wake up back to normal. Each time, I woke up like this. Pitiful. Drained. Stripped and abandoned by the Divine.

What had that shadow prick done to me?

It couldn't be a curse. A curse or a hex would leave some kind of mark on my body, a rune or a scar or a brand. I had searched every inch of my skin and found none.

So how had he managed to steal my power?

My hands balled into fists as my molars ground together. A low growl rumbled through my lips, but my rage was laughable. My rage should have been the most lethal weapon nature ever created and yet here I was, fuming without proper fumes.

I could still produce fire, but each time I tried, the repercussions got worse. I feared that one of these times, doing magic would kill me.

"Fuck!" I cried, grabbing whatever was close to me and hurling it at the back of the door.

Natalia's paperweight shattered on the bathroom floor. I bit my lip to stifle my sobs as I stared down at the broken glass.

"Nyx?"

I straightened up, fingers instinctively rising to wipe the evidence of tears and blood from my face. Not that I could wipe away my bloodshot eyes or swollen face.

"Are you okay?" Faye asked through the door, her voice quiet and gentle. It made me sick.

What was she even doing in my room? "I'm fine," I rasped. "Go away."

A beat of silence.

Ice and fire battled up my spine as the bathroom doorknob jiggled as she willed her air magic to unlock it. A protest got stuck in my throat.

Faye pushed the door open with a gust of warm wind and gasped as she took me in.

"Oh, my Goddess—Nyx!" She couldn't decide what to be the most horrified about. The mess of glass or the mess of me.

With a few simple gestures of her hand, she had the shards of glass rising off the floor, orchestrating them back into place and fixing the paperweight. Good as new, easy as pie. She commanded the air to place it back in its rightful spot on the shelf beside me and then paused to give me another once-over. Faye's magic was so fucking benevolent. She fixed broken things. My magic had never done anything but destroy, and there was no repairing the damage I caused.

Glossy emerald eyes assessed me as if I were a rabid animal, bidding whether she should approach me.

She decided to be brave. She moved across the marble floor and knelt before me. I chewed my lip bloody to refrain from crying. "Nyx, please, tell me what's going on."

I shook my head as my vision turned to watery smudges of color.

"Are you sick? Did someone hex you?"

I said nothing back and made no gestures. I looked down through my hot tears, fidgeting with my fingers.

"Please tell me who Astral Snatched you. I won't tell anyone, Nyx. Not if you don't want me to. But you can't let this shit eat you up all alone. Tell me."

Even if I wanted to... I had no idea who that freak was.

"It doesn't matter. It's over now."

"It doesn't look over."

My lip curled back. "I just want to be alone, Faye."

"Bullshit, girl. I've never seen you like this before. Something is seriously wrong and if you're going to be too proud to ask for help—I'll tell the Luminary."

"It's none of your guys' goddamn business!" I shot to my feet with my fists balled at my sides which couldn't have been intimidating in the least since I also had tears running down my cheeks. "You're seriously threatening to *tattle* on me? I'm an adult, Faye."

"Tattle on you? No. But you are trying to play off what happened at the beach like it was nothing when clearly something terrible happened.

You look half alive, Nyx. I'm not going to sit around and let your stubbornness be the death of you. Astral snatching is dark, dark magic. Whoever did this... The Luminary needs to know. It could happen again to someone else. It's not just about you."

"I'll tell Delphyne after the Inauguration Ceremony tonight." I lied through my teeth with perfect ease. "I will, okay?"

Faye searched my face wordlessly.

"Today is the first day everyone's back and the Priestesses are busy getting everything ready for tonight. The first years are all getting settled in. I promise I will tell the Luminary after today, alright? I'm not going to go and ruin everything for everyone."

Faye's green eyes swam with sorrow. "Nyx... If you're really in trouble, asking for help is not ruining anything for anyone... We are all sisters here. We stand by our sisters whenever we are needed, not just when it's convenient."

A small smile crept its way across my lips. "I appreciate that, but I'm fine. I look like shit, I know. I haven't been sleeping well but I promise I'll get my shit together, okay? Just don't tell Delphyne. I will do it myself."

She gathered me into a tight hug, and I avoided our reflection in the mirror beside us. Faye's skin radiated heat like the sun, smelling of flowers and sage. Her magic thrummed under her flesh, vibrant and abundant. My chest filled with sand as we pulled apart and she squeezed my hand for encouragement. I heard the words she didn't say. My skin felt cold and clammy, and it worried her.

I followed her out of the bathroom into my bedroom, walking her to the door. Excited chatter and scurrying footsteps sounded from out in the hall. I swallowed thickly, trying not to let the horror show on my face. Faye turned to me before she opened the door to leave. "Your sister got here an hour ago. She's officially got her room in the first-year wing. Her roommate looks... interesting."

I nodded. "Good. Good."

"I'll see you in the Sphere tonight. Text me if you need me."

I nodded hollowly again as she left.

I wondered where Natalia was. Mingling with the other girls, most likely. Happy to see faces that weren't mine. We had a good summer, us two. That was over now, though.

I released a heavy sigh as I sat down at my vanity and faced the monster in the mirror. Not even makeup could save me. I slathered my skin in foundation and concealer and bronzer but there was nothing I could do about those dark, dead eyes. My skin evened out slightly, but underneath; the truth pulsed.

"Seven hells," I barked as I grabbed my blackmirror and texted Faye. A low moment for me. I felt way too needy, but I couldn't handle the idea of showing up to the Inauguration looking like this.

She burst through my door thirty seconds later. "What do you need?"

"Close the door," I murmured.

She did.

"I need you to glamour me."

Her blonde brows furrowed slightly. "Why?"

"Because I look like shit. Please just make me look vibrant and powerful. I can't show up at the Ceremony looking 'half alive' as you said."

"You can't do it yourself?" The shock in her eyes and her tone hit like two slaps in the face.

With a heavy, dry tongue, I managed to say, "I'm trying not to use my magic right now. I'm more tired than usual and I'm saving up for when we start training in the Sphere."

Faye could smell my bullshit from a mile away but decided to let it slide. We sat on my bed together and she did a simple glamour charm on me. Made me look the way I usually looked. She brought the glow of my skin back to life, dashed the light back into my eyes, and filled my cheeks out. An illusion, but still better than facing the Academy looking like a corpse.

"Thank you," I told her with a sigh. "I'll get ya back for this."

"I'm holding you to your word, Nyx. That's how you can get me back. By talking to the Luminary."

I felt way more confident in my fake smile now that I'd been glamoured. "Of course."

"Okay." Faye believed me. "Now I'm going to get ready. See you tonight."

"See you tonight."

I waited until she was gone before fully checking myself out in the mirror. I didn't care that the reflection was a total lie. At least on the outside, I was back to my proper, powerful, gorgeous self. Perhaps my insides would follow suit. As within, so without, right?

CHAPTER 7
LUNA ACADEMY
EMILIA

With a sigh of satisfaction, I stepped back and drank it all in. My things were officially put away. My crystals, knick-knacks, pictures, and tapestries were all hung. This room felt like... me.

My roommate, Destiny Martinez, got here before me so she'd claimed the bed by the window but that was fine with me. I had more wall space, and Goddess knew I needed it. Destiny had already lined her windowsill with succulents and plants with long, hanging vines. She seemed to have a lot of plants and I wondered if that was a sign she'd be Emerging as an earthling. We had both squealed in delight to learn neither of us were Emerged yet. Her birthday hit a week after mine. I was stoked to not be the only girl here unEmerged.

I had met her only an hour ago and yet I knew we'd be fast friends. Our roommates were chosen by a magical algorithm that studied each of our files and paired us with who it deemed was our most compatible match. So far, so good.

Destiny stepped out of our attached bathroom. She was an odd little thing, but pretty. She had her head clean-shaven, just a dusting of dark hair to cover her scalp. An impish look always brightened her amber eyes, it seemed. She had deep brown skin and plump lips. Before when she had no makeup on, she looked quite young but now that she'd applied thick, dark eyeliner and painted her lips red, adding silver hoops to her ears, she could have passed for twenty-five. "How do I look?" she asked, striking a pose.

"You look hot," I told her honestly.

"Thanks," she beamed, striding over to her bed. She wore high-waisted denim shorts with a thick belt, a black crop top, and tall boots. Casual yet effective. "Are you nervous about the Ceremony?"

I shrugged. "Not really. I'm excited to finally get to see the Elemental Sphere."

"Me too!" She checked her blackmirror and then moved over to the closet, fishing through her side of the hangers. She slid a black Stevie Nicks-style shawl over her shoulders. Wow. From casual to witchy chic.

She saw the way I ogled at her and grinned. "Want to borrow one?" She pulled another shawl from a hanger and offered it to me, brows wiggling.

"Really?" I smiled, taking it from her and slipping it on over my simple black dress. I had no idea what to wear, but you could never go wrong with a little black dress, right? The Stevie shawl tied the look together as I noted my reflection in the wall mirror. A flush of heat hit my cheeks as reality sunk in. I was here. A student at Luna Academy. In a week, I'd Emerge. I would have magic.

"Have you gotten a blackmirror yet?" my new roommate asked me.

"Yup." I grabbed the device off the bed and held it up suggestively. "For some reason I expected it to be different. It's almost identical to the mortal smartphone I had before. Except it's made from obsidian."

"Of course, it is," Destiny replied. "Smartphones are a gimmick of blackmirrors. Except they're powered by brain-frying frequency waves that literally deteriorate DNA. Our blackmirrors are crystals, powered by ether—the energy that exists all around us. And we have those crystal towers to help power our technology. It's all totally natural and divine."

"Huh," I muttered, angling the device around to get a better look at it.

"Ready to head down?" Destiny asked and my body lit up as I nodded.

We left our room together. Chatter and laughter and whimsical musings filled the hallway as we made our way toward the spiral stairs. Everyone had their dorm doors open, girls scurrying from one room to the other, gushing over this incredible place.

Down on the main level, activity buzzed in the common room, so we went in there before heading out to the Sphere. We were early, anyway.

Damn, I thought as we stepped through the extravagant archway. It was like a throne room, minus the throne. Dozens of beautiful girls of all shapes and sizes peppered the marble floor. Floating candles overhead cast a warm glow upon us.

Joining the Celestial Society was like stepping back in time. Back to an ancient time of gilded gowns and candlelight, romance, and danger. Everywhere I looked I saw striking, mythical faces and magic flying from manicured fingertips. The air itself was laced with a heady magic that made it hard to breathe. But beyond the initial essence of a resurrected ancient world, was something undeniably modern... futuristic, even. Everyone's bright, graphic makeup, their living tattoos that whirled and reacted based on their heart rates—it all came from a time that had not yet been. The Celestial future made manifest.

I was overwhelmed. With marvel and desire and *fear*. Fear unlike anything I'd ever felt, fear that this place would eat me alive. My magic had yet to Emerge, and they could all smell that. Countless colorful eyes flicked my way, sizing me up, and comparing me to my notorious, all-powerful sister. I had a lot to live up to.

I looked around for Nyx but didn't see her.

My heart rate instantly spiked at just the thought of her. She hadn't talked to me since the night of the party. I had no idea how she was doing or what had even freaking happened. She shut me out like she always did. I decided I wouldn't let it eat away at me. This was my first week at the Academy and I wouldn't let The Nyx Show ruin that.

"Emilia!" Natalia floated into view, a wide smile across her brown lips. She wore an earth-tone halter dress that fell loosely to the floor, a crown of sticks and thorns resting over her ebony ringlets.

"Hey, Natalia," I beamed as she pulled me in for a quick hug. "This is my roommate, Destiny."

"Hey," the girls greeted each other in unison and then shared a laugh.

"Nyx with you?" I wondered quietly, feeling the way her name instantly densified the mood.

Natalia kept her face even, but I sensed the tension as she shook her head. "No."

I swallowed, turning to Destiny. "Nyx is my sister."

A wry expression swathed my roommate's features. "Er, I know. I know who you are."

"You do?"

"Yeah. I think everyone does." She gestured at the room, all eyes on us. On me. "Your sister is famous around here and I saw you in some of those videos from the end-of-summer party."

My cheeks heated. "Oh..."

"Faye and I were just about to head out to the Sphere," Natalia interjected. "Come with?"

"Sure," I breathed.

We linked up with Faye, clad in a baby blue two-piece outfit that clung to her curves and then fell to the ground like liquid silk. Her eyelids were coated in silver glitter, as well as her shoulders. White and gray feathers hung from her loose, golden locks, fluttering as she moved. I fought the urge to gape at her in wonder.

Destiny and I sure weren't dressed as enchantingly as them, but it didn't seem to matter.

Together, we ascended out into the fresh air just as the sun slid below the shoulders of the horizon.

Luna Academy sat on fifteen acres of a magical land, glamoured and hidden in the Hollywood Hills. We had our own forest, a natural mineral pool, rows and rows of gardens, the Sacred Stone Temple where the Priestesses stayed, and of course, the Elemental Sphere.

It really did look like someone had lassoed the moon and gifted it to us. Against the darkening sky, The Elemental Sphere stood bright and round, a massive sphere emitting a calming white glow. As if the moon had fallen. Mortals would be baffled by this magical architecture. The quartz glimmered under the twilight sky. I stared up in awe as we strode along the cobblestone path. A yoni-shaped door allowed the sound of music and voices out into the fresh night. Excitement filled the air around us, warming my skin. My heart slammed harder as we made our way towards it and stepped through the blue velvet curtain.

My breath caught.

The interior had been set up for a show. An elevated stage area in the middle with rows of seats all around it. A couple of dozen girls scattered about, clustering together in their favored groups. Behind us, more began filing in. Destiny and I followed Faye and Natalia through the room. I couldn't help but notice all the eyes on us, the way the girls hushed and stared as we passed by. We sat in the front row on the far side of the room.

"Looks pretty now, but usually this is a magical boxing ring of ass kickery." Faye giggled, gesturing all around us.

Destiny and I shared a grin.

Girls kept filing in and yet I did not see my sister.

"She'll be here," Natalia murmured. I hadn't noticed she'd been looking at me. "Don't worry."

I breathed a nervous laugh. "I know."

I counted over fifty girls. For Luna, that was a high count. We were known for our small but powerful student body. Big numbers had never been a concern for us like it was for the other Academies. We had the Original Goddess teachings. This was the home of the most powerful feminine starseeds. We didn't need numbers.

The giant moon roof over us darkened, the pink dimming into a molten glow. The chattering quieted at once. Music stopped.

I held my breath, my heart thudding slowly. The Ceremony was officially starting, and Nyx Morningstar had yet to show up.

The Priestesses appeared in the center of the slightly elevated stage in an eruption of spinning light.

Five of them. Lovely, ethereal women, drenched head to toe in flowing, layered robes that looked from a different time. Red for fire. Blue for water. Green for the earth. Silver for air. Each Priestess was a master of her element. The woman in the middle, their leader, and our Luminary, wore glittering robes of bright gold. Her element—Aether. The Fifth Element. No one living possessed it but her. Another thing that set Luna apart from everyone else.

Delphyne Rae Augustus, Luminary of High Magic, Bearer of Aether, and Interpreter of the Mother Goddess.

I knew allllll about her. But seeing her in person for the first time... My body felt light and airy. The entire sphere was filled with magical energy, unlike anything I'd ever felt.

The Luminary's long, pearl-white hair cascaded down her body, nearly reaching her knees. Her skin shone, golden yet translucent, her eyes a bright turquoise, even from here.

She lifted her hands gracefully above her head, casting silver and gold fireworks throughout the Sphere, earning wistful praises from all of us.

"Welcome, sacred sisters," she cooed, her voice amplified by magic. "It is an honor to see each and every one of you here tonight. I look around and I see the faces of young, powerful women who are on this Earth to do miraculous things."

I swallowed the thickness at the back of my throat, trying to enjoy this rather than worrying about my damned sister.

"We are Celestials," she continued, eyes scanning over all of us evenly. "Being a Celestial on Earth is not always easy. It's one of the most challenging things your soul could ever experience. Which is exactly why we are here. We may come from the stars, but we are here to be on Earth. Our existence, in a nutshell, is a delicate balance. Having one foot in the stars and one foot firmly planted on the ground, while knowing the truth that they are one and the same."

The Priestess in the green robe stepped forward. The stage burst to life with plants, vines, moss, and ornamental trees blooming out of thin air. She didn't even wave her hand. Earth manifested all around her as she smiled. Her long dark hair hung below her shoulders, shaping her square face and hooded dark eyes.

"The Earth is our foundation," the Priestess said, holding her palms out as a handful of smooth stones appeared over her skin. "She is, literally, our rock. Whether or not you are an earth elemental, you must get to know this foundation as if it's your closest loved one. Because trust me, she is."

The Earth Priestess tossed the rocks into the air and with a quick flick of her wrist, they morphed into gray doves. The beautiful birds flew all around the Sphere before dissolving back into dust.

"Thank you, Priestess Thea," The Luminary chimed.

Priestess Thea bowed deeply and stepped back.

The Luminary introduced the remaining Priestesses for all of us new students.

Priestess Adria, water. Her wiry black hair floated around her head as if we were under the sea. Her dark skin had a dewy shine to it, giving her that just-emerged-from-a-midnight-swim look. With a swift gesture of her hands, she unleashed a stampede of water animals. The crowd gasped. Wolves, deer, eagles, rabbits, lions, and even dragons. All made of water. I watched in awe, smiling giddily as a water rabbit dashed right in front of my nose. When she was finished, she turned them all to mist which hung in the air and smelt like heaven.

Priestess Bridget, fire. She had long orangey-red hair and a hard look in her eyes. She performed no magical act to impress us. She merely glared at each one of us, exuding a don't-mess-with-me-or-I'll-destroy-you expression. Noted.

The Air Priestess's hair matched the silver of her robes. She smiled warmly, looking like the eldest of them all, with charming crow's feet around her blue eyes. She introduced herself as Eliza. She held her hands in the air as the most enchanting shamanic music began to play, coming from nowhere yet everywhere.

"This is the natural rhythm of the Earth tonight," she explained with a smile. "All around you, there is music, if only you can tune in. Air magic is much more than whirlwinds and moving objects. With the power of the air, one can harness all the natural frequencies around us and amplify them." She pointed her fingers at one of the ornamental trees the Earth Priestess had grown on stage. The tree began to sing.

"Wow," Destiny breathed beside me.

"I know," I replied, voice barely audible.

The Air Priestess bowed and stepped back, handing the spotlight back to our Luminary.

"At Luna Academy, we highlight a few different key forms of mysticism: esoteric symbolism, element wielding, the power of intuition, and of course, astrology. Here, we follow a different astrology system than what you are used to in the mortal realm. We go by the original thirteen-sign astrological calendar, which features a sign that has long been hidden from the collective. The serpent bearer, Ophiuchus. Those born on the last days of November and the first half of December fall under this sign. We have one student here who bears this constellation as their sun sign. Though I don't see her tonight..."

A swooping sound caught my attention and before I even had time to look, the click-clacking of heels echoed off the floor.

Nyx. Luna Academy's notorious serpent bearer.

Clad in fighting leathers, she strutted in like she owned the place. My cheeks instantly filled with heat as I gulped up the sight of her. A swell of low murmurs rippled through the Sphere. Her silver hair fell loose down her back, dancing over her tailbone as she stalked forward with a face of stone.

Wait—where the hell were all her tattoos? Her arms were freaking bare!

She took the empty seat between her doppelgänger minions, sitting down casually, crossing one leg over the other and folding her hands in her lap.

The Fire Priestess's lip curled back over her teeth. Her fingers curled inward, and fire erupted from the stage, making everyone squeal in alarm. The flames licked fervently, coating all the plants and trees yet not burning them. Bridget's scorching stare focused solely on my sister who gazed back, expressionless.

The girls and I shared a series of loaded looks. My heart slammed against my ribs, sweat beads forming down my back.

The Luminary acted as if she didn't even notice the disrespectful occurrence.

Bridget withdrew her flames, but she didn't take her eyes off Nyx.

"Here at Luna," the Luminary began again, "you may be younglings in the magic world but in the grand scheme of things, you are all still adults. This is not a nursery school. You are all entitled to come and go as you please. If you do not put our Academy at risk of being discovered by the mortals, we do not care what you choose to do. This means, there will be no one to coddle you. You don't want to show up? You don't want to put in the work? No one will force you. Your place in this

Academy is entirely up to you. If you do not put in the effort, you will be banished. It is as simple as that."

My sister's face didn't change, not even slightly.

"You all grew up attending mortal schools. Luna Academy is nothing like those places. Here, we do not have a strict regime. Every day, the Priestesses and I will host different classes, lectures, and activities, and you are welcome to join as you see fit. You each have an inner compass inside of you, pointing to your own true north. Here, we teach Sovereignty. We encourage you to navigate by yourselves and follow your intuition. Our Goddess is inside of all of you, and She will guide you.

"Look around, see each other," the Luminary murmured. "Look at each and every face in this room and understand that you are looking at your soul sisters. Daughters of the Great Mother. We may not have the numbers of the other academies, but we have something greater. We have a small, connected coven of powerful women. Do not underestimate the magic of sisterhood. The Goddess created each of us uniquely, fitting together like a perfect puzzle. Alone, we are powerful. Together, we are indestructible."

The Ceremony went on. The Priestesses spoke of the elements and the stars and the challenges of being a Celestial among mortals. They talked about how each of us has our own Star Lineage, and everyone got excited about that.

I hated that I could hardly hear any of it. My focus had been stolen by The Nyx Show. I couldn't take my eyes off her, sitting over there haughtily, not giving a damn about anything. She looked like she'd rather be anywhere else, and it made me want to slap her. Just because she was powerful didn't mean she was above any of this. She was a second-year fireling. Big freaking whoop.

We were in there for another hour but all of it went over my head. I barely even registered as the Luminary closed the Ceremony and encouraged us to go celebrate. We filed out of the Elemental Sphere, the joyous chatter from all the girls playing in the background of my mind like white noise.

"Dude, you okay?" Destiny asked me as we exited through the velvet curtain. "You look like someone pissed in your cereal and then dumped it on your head."

I folded my arms over my chest, forcing out a laugh. "I'm fine. Just a lot on my mind."

Some girls went back to their rooms, and some of us stayed down in the common room. Faye, Natalia, Destiny, and I stood next to the giant fireplace on the far wall under the ginormous portrait of a dragon goddess.

"Watch this," Faye grinned as she held her hands out toward the fire. "Ever heard the music of flames before?"

Destiny and I shared a look, shaking our heads.

"Okay, I don't know if I can do this because I've never tried before but here goes nothing." Faye squeezed her eyes shut, focusing so hard sweat manifested over her glittery temples.

For a long stretch of heartbeats, nothing happened.

Just when it looked like she was going to give up, the most enticing and peculiar tune began to play.

My lips parted as the unearthly music wrapped around me like a phantom embrace. It... was indescribable. Nothing like the music that had come from the air or the trees in the Elemental Sphere. Those had been traditional shamanic tunes, like binaural beats. But the music of the fire... Haunting. Alluring. Moody. Aggressive. Notes low and high, writhing together like serpents of dark and light. Almost like...

"This is what rock n' roll was inspired by," Faye stated proudly.

"No fucking way!" Destiny exclaimed.

Clusters of girls gravitated this way, drawn in by the melody. Faye kept her hands out proudly coaxing the music from the flames.

Girls started dancing, some started singing. Airlings allowed themselves to stop fighting gravity, their feet leaving the ground as they levitated above our heads, twirling and swaying.

The music of fire and the most powerful fireling in the Society wasn't here to enjoy it.

A hard lump manifested at the back of my throat while tears pricked behind my eyes. Why was she like this? She should have been standing right next to me experiencing this with us. She gave me all those lengthy, ominous speeches about "what this world is like" and how screwed up and ruthless and unpredictable it is but so far, the only thing that had been any of those things was *her*. She was the one to initiate a destructive battle at the party. She was the one who made a spectacle of herself. She was the one who ended up getting freaking possessed. Maybe it wasn't the Celestial Society at all. Maybe it was just Nyx.

A strange sensation buzzed on the side of my cheek. Hot, prickly energy. Instinctively, I turned toward the feeling, my heart dropping slightly at what I found. Outside the archway of the common room in the middle of the spiral stairs, sitting alone in the dark watching us, was Nyx.

CHAPTER 8

DARKNESS & FIRE

NYX

Fucking Emilia and her spidey senses spotted me sitting here pathetically like some loner and my entire body flushed with the worst kind of heat. I held her eyes only briefly before rising to my feet and stalking back to my room.

Wasn't that so cute? All the girls bonding and dancing and embracing my sister? Good for her. Good for Faye, too. Amplifying the music of the elements was no joke. Her power was growing. My best fucking wishes went out to all of them.

The hallways threatened to close in on me. I had every intention to pack my bags and get the hell out of Dodge. I couldn't be here, not like this. I needed to get my true magic back or crawl under a rock and die, whichever one came first. I couldn't keep facing everyone with a glamour to make me look alive. I had to figure this out. That meant I needed to find that shadow bitch and demand to know what he'd done to me.

I slammed my dorm room door shut with a backward kick and growled a series of colorful profanities.

Someone chuckled.

My heart stopped beating.

He was *here*. In my room. The universe was mocking me.

I couldn't help the way my jaw went slack. He stood by the window, watching me. His eyes were just as bright as I remembered. He'd cut his hair. Left it longish, framing his face in a lustrous mop of mahogany that fell loosely just above his shoulders. He wore a long dark jacket, standing with his hands folded behind his back. His skin had more color now, his cheeks less sunken but still sharp.

"Hello again," he said, voice thick with amusement. His eyes practically sparkled as they scathed me up and down.

The instinct to detonate nearly consumed me.

I wanted to charge him. Scream at him. Turn him to a pile of ash at my feet. My most primordial feminine instincts rose to the surface, and I longed to embody the black widow and devour him.

But I couldn't. My rage was not backed up by the justice of fire.

Perhaps I could have done something, but I still felt so empty of magic, and I didn't trust my abilities right now. The last thing I wanted to do was pass out in front of this asshole.

So, I swallowed my violent cravings and poised myself. I squared my shoulders and looked him dead in the eye as I slowly strolled closer to where he stood. He watched me approach him, taking in every detail as if I were a painting.

I had other powers besides fire. I was still a beautiful woman with dark, entrancing siren eyes.

I came and stood right next to him at the window, inhaling his bizarre scent of citrus and metal. There was a new element to it now, something more earthy that I couldn't think of a name for.

"I knew I would see you again," I said, keeping my voice low and husky. "It's a dirty little game you've started, I must say."

He glared at me. "You think this is a game?"

"I know it is. And clearly, you won the first round. Interfering with my magic is quite...advanced. You have my attention, as you wish." I kept my tone light as if I weren't imagining what it would be like to gut him.

"It is not your attention I am interested in."

I cocked a brow. "No? Well, it's not just my magic you're after... Or else you would have driven off into the sunset by now. But here you are, coming back for more. So, what else do you desire?"

"My intentions will become clearer over time."

I peered up at him through my thick dark lashes, noting the way his throat worked in response to my closeness. I might have been hallucinating but he almost looked nervous. I decided to take advantage of that idea.

"Who are you? Where did you come from?" I kept my voice even because my curiosity was genuine. I wanted to know who in the seven realms he was. Remaining calm and collected was beyond difficult, though, especially with him this close. I cursed myself for not having a weapon on my person. He was close enough to stick a dagger through his heart...

His silver gaze gravitated to the window. He took in the expanse of twinkling lights splayed out below Luna Academy, considering my questions. As if his name and origin were a mystery.

I awaited his response, my heart pounding. His magic was a tangible creature in the room, densifying the air. I fought to breathe without panting.

"It doesn't matter who I am," he murmured, finally.

I saw red. He was so smug and aloof, thinking I was at his complete mercy. In a way, I was.

With every fiber of strength I had, I remained calm. "It matters to me. You stole from me, and I know not even who you are. Why are you hiding?"

"I'm not hiding," he snapped. "I'm right here."

"Hiding in plain sight is the Celestial way. Be straight. What do you want from me?"

He scoffed, leaning down to be closer to my face. I winced but didn't move backward. The unnatural shade of his eyes made me feel winded. His towering, lithe frame made me feel small. He seemed to see these truths in my eyes. A sly, cruel smirk slithered across his lips. "I want so many things, and all of them I will get through you."

My heart thundered wildly.

He opened his mouth to say something else, but he didn't get the chance because my forehead smashed into his nose. A glorious, wet crunch filled my veins with adrenaline as he reeled backward. I'd never head-butted anyone before but, *shit*, it felt good. I didn't have magic, no, but I had the element of surprise and a history of running with a bad crowd. Not to mention combat training in the Sphere. I knew how to fight.

Only half a second had passed when I pulled back to see his nose pissing blood—a magnificent sight that made my stomach erupt with butterflies. The fervent shock in his wide silver eyes made me snap a dark laugh while I wound my arm back to hit him right in the—

The ground disappeared under my feet, and I released a yelp, the world spinning around me. A moment of whirling confusion was followed up by my back hitting the bed. Something cool and silken wrapped around my wrists and ankles, locking tightly so that I couldn't move my limbs.

"What the–?" I hissed, lifting my head as horror filled my veins like wet concrete. My heart was already in turbo gear, and it still managed to accelerate. Shadows writhed around my wrists and ankles, tethering me to the bedposts.

He—he was—the shadows, they—

"Yes, the shadows are mine," he mused, watching me catch on. He stood beside the bed, staring down at me as I struggled against the bonds. Angry red blood poured from his nose, over his lips, and stained his teeth as he revealed them with a smile at me.

My chest rose and fell incessantly. I wanted him dead. Right now. *Goddess, smite him!*

"Stop thrashing. It won't work. They will hold you in place until I am done with you, so I suggest you just listen."

I stared through wide eyes at the impossible occurrence. Sentient shadows curled around my skin like black snakes. I'd never seen anything like it. No matter how I moved or yanked or pulled, they didn't falter in the slightest. Yet they were little more than smoke. Smoke with the strength of steel.

"No," I murmured, but in all honesty, it sounded more like a whine. "No, please—"

"Ugh." His pointed features angled with disgust. He didn't bother to wipe away the blood as it drizzled down his chin, splattering onto his immaculate jacket. I was sure I broke his nose, but it had healed already. "You're not going to beg, are you? I didn't take you for a beggar."

I bared my teeth at him, anger pulsing through my body so intensely I could pass out. "Get your creepy magic off me right the fuck now!"

"Calm down or I will shove them down your throat, too."

That made me go stone still. I didn't even breathe. I swore we could both hear my heart crashing.

I glared at my hands bound up behind my head, leaving me so open and vulnerable. I couldn't hold my tongue as the words "Usually I make a guy buy me dinner first," hissed through my lips, earning me a dark chuckle from my torturer.

He leaned down, bringing his face only inches from mine. This time, with me completely disarmed.

"I underestimated you," he voiced roughly. "Your will is even more relentless than I thought. What a wonderful and necessary revelation, Firefly."

His closeness made it damn near impossible to stay still. His blood dripped onto me, peppering my collarbone with red blots. I wanted to cry out in outrage and disgust. My fight or flight instinct kicked in and it took every fiber of my strength to not thrash around. He searched my face as if it had long-lost answers he'd been searching lifetimes for written on it.

"Yes, I do like you like this," he murmured, eyeing me like I was some prize he'd won. He trailed a finger along my collarbone, tracing a line of ice over my flesh. His eyes lit up as he watched my skin react with goosebumps. "I much prefer you without all those ridiculous tattoos. They were too distracting. Though something still isn't quite right, now, is it?" He waved a hand in front of me, and I gasped, wincing, bracing myself for whatever devilish magic he cast upon me. Yet I felt nothing.

"Ah, that's better. Your true face." He grinned blackly. Shit. He'd dismantled my glamour. "Firefly, you look dreadful. Whatever is the matter?"

"Fuck you," I ground out, longing to thrash against the shadow bonds. I was not a creature built to be confined. It went against everything that made me, me. "Whatever you did to me, I promise it won't last. You have no idea who I am, what I'm truly capable of—"

66

"Trust me, I know exactly who you are, and I know exactly what you are capable of."

"You prick!" I growled defiantly. "You think you know me because you stalk Magigram and Celestial Tea, well let me just tell you—"

His laughter cut me off. A laughing man with humorless eyes and a nose pissing blood was a truly terrifying sight. "I have no interest in social media or gossip blogs. Please." He reached into the breast pocket of his warlock jacket and pulled out a gaudy red medallion that hung from a chunky silver chain. He dangled it above me mockingly. The glass medallion glowed with pulsing crimson light that got brighter as he held it over me.

"Your taste in jewelry is as terrible as your taste in fashion and pocket dimensions," I told him.

"This, little Firefly, is dragonglass."

My spine turned to stone.

"And don't lie. My taste in fashion is immaculate."

"Dragonglass doesn't exist anymore," I bit back.

"Right, right," he muttered, looming over me like a storm cloud. "Just like it's natural to wield only one element and the Celestial Society isn't entirely corrupt from the inside out."

I narrowed my eyes in disdain and confusion.

"This particular medallion was forged over a century ago, with one sole purpose. Do you know what that might be?"

"Just tell me. Stop playing with me."

A smile that flashed all his blood-stained teeth slashed across his face and sent my heart plummeting. "As you wish. Once upon a time, the US government started a neat little program called the Star-Cross Project. They kidnapped Celestial children and raised them in underground military bases. The purpose of this project was to try to understand— scientifically—how magic worked. And how to replicate it with science and technology. They brainwashed the children against their own kind, experimented on them, got them to forge all sorts of weapons to use against Celestials. This is one of them. This little number here was forged to sense when high magic is being used. Once it picks up the signal of magic, it latches onto the Celestial's energetic signature like a parasite and siphons their power."

A cold, cold sweat pooled at the back of my neck while my mouth went completely dry.

"No," I said stiffly. "You're lying. Celestial children can't even do magic."

He raised his brows, amused. "Like you couldn't?"

My lips parted. "How do you know I did?"

"Remember what I said before, never mind how I know things."

A beat of heavy silence passed. "Are you trying to say you stole my magic with a *necklace*?"

He grinned smugly down at me.

"My magic could never be contained by something so insignificant."

"Tsk, tsk." He shook his head, glaring at me with those penetrating silver eyes that had my doom reflecting in them. "Your ego will be the death of you. An entire universe can fit inside a single human cell, and yet you think a bit of fiery woo-woo can't be held in this generously sized medallion?"

My own vulnerability made me sick. Here I was, on my back, hands tied above my head by shadows. Not only magicless, but utterly, entirely defenseless, at this psychopathic stranger's mercy. I hated the way my chest rose and fell, gleaming with a sheen of sweat, evidence of my fear.

The worst part was, he was enjoying every second of this. His eyes kept raking over my body, lingering in places that made my stomach knot. He seemed to favor my throat and thighs. The number of times I mentally cursed him became uncountable.

Could any of this be true? Did that medallion hold my magic? I knew Celestial children had been targeted by certain factions of mortals, but I'd never heard of them being experimented on. I didn't want to believe a word he said... But... I was professional at smelling bullshit, and I couldn't scent any on him. I didn't trust him as far as I could throw him but about this one thing, he was telling the truth. I felt it.

"Well, you should know," I hissed through clenched teeth, "that your precious medallion is shotty. I can still do magic."

His eyes lit up at that, genuine surprise washing over his features. "You are tenacious. This is good. In truth, this medallion would kill most Celestials once it latches onto them. It siphons all magic and then eventually, life-force. But you are not like the others, are you, Firefly?"

I breathed heavily but said nothing.

"But let me guess. Accessing your power now comes with a dangerous and painful cost? Why else wouldn't you incinerate me on the spot tonight?" He smirked, knowing he was right.

I couldn't stop the furious cry that howled through my lips. "Just tell me what you want from me and get on with it!"

"I want everything from you," he muttered softly, seduction laced in the shadows of his words. Silver flames lit behind his eyes and my stomach hollowed out, sensing I wasn't going to like what he had to say. "For now, I want you to remember that *I own you*. I want you to remember that the fate of you and your magic lies in my hands. In the events of the upcoming days, you should be wise when choosing sides. Cross me, Firefly, and I will toss this medallion into the shadows where it, along with your power, will be gone forever."

My body reacted without my mind's consent, thrashing against the shadow bonds as a string of vulgar curses shot from my lips. This pleased him.

"So that's it?" I hissed, hardly able to get the regular words out beyond the filter of my rage. "You're just going to keep dangling my magic in front of my nose without telling if there's even a chance I'll ever get it back?"

"You'll get your magic back. When I decide you're ready. I'll enjoy stringing you along until then. But when the time comes, you should expect to adhere to my terms and conditions, of course.".

I spat a derisive laugh that was full of venom. "Your idiocy is astounding. I am the queen of this school and I have about fifty powerful females who would looove to help me get this—"

"Go ahead and summon your army of clucking hens." He waved me off dismissively. "Of course, the second you tell them you've had your power stolen, and they see you for what you are—weak, powerless—you will no longer be queen. They may help you, but their entire image of you will be shattered. The next girl will rise in your place, and so on. And darling, when I hide in the shadows, I can't be found, not even if your Luminary herself tried to find me. But go ahead and try with this little feminist vendetta if you wish. I'm sure it will be most entertaining."

I opened my mouth to clap back but he was right on the money and the fact of that had me sinking.

I could have told the girls right away. I could have assembled my army against him and yet I didn't because he was right. As soon as I told the girls what happened, my position as queen would be abolished. Queens didn't have their magic stolen. Queens weren't helpless in the face of an adversary.

My breathing labored as I glared up into his metallic stare. This man came into my life as little more than a ghost and took everything from me without even lifting a finger. Right now, parts of me were breaking. Entire internal foundations crumbling. There was no point in denying that, not even to myself. But I wouldn't stay like this. I wouldn't stay defeated and chained and shattered. I would rise from the ashes like I always did. I already had a series of revenge fantasies blooming in my mind's eye and acting them out would be a glorious affair. It had felt good to headbutt him, and it would feel even better to swipe his head clean off. I held onto that visual. His head on a flaming fucking spike.

"Ah, yes, stoke your flame," he whispered as if he heard my thoughts. He watched my face while his head cocked curiously. "You don't think I'm all bad, do you?"

"Of course I do," I spat.

He sat on the edge of my bed and my entire body seized with an electric charge. His closeness stirred the strangest and most blasphemous sensations in my traitorous body. Why did the evil ones always have to be so beautiful? Even with—especially with—blood staining his lips, chin, and jacket, he was stunning. A cosmic mockery. I'd never seen a face like his before. So damn pretty, yet wholly masculine and intimidating. The Goddess was feeling depraved and satirical when she dreamed up this one. Not to mention his magic, the way it called to me...

That alluring, magnetic pull made my teeth clench in defiance. "You are a water bearer," I spoke the words as if they were a criminal accusation. It had to be the case. Why else would my body react this way?

He chuckled. "Amongst other things." He held his hand above me and summoned a swirl of shadow over his palm. My lips parted at the sight. "Darkness is an element, too, you know," he informed me as he banished it.

"Darkness is just darkness."

"Fire is just fire."

"No," I argued fiercely. "Fire is heat and light and passion and life-force. Fire is fury and power and fucking vengeance and destruction!"

At that, his lips twitched into an impish grin. "And darkness is the womb from which we all came, and where we will all return when this cosmic play meets its end."

"Get off my bed," I demanded, wishing my voice had more conviction.

"But you haven't even accepted my kindness yet," he argued, leaning closer to me as he tightened the shadows around my wrists. His face lingered mere inches from mine as he held the medallion over my heaving chest, angling it a certain way so I saw it had an opening. Where the chain connected to the red glass, it opened like a potion vile.

"Your kindness?" I breathed indignantly, wishing my head would stop spinning. He was loving my body's ridiculous reactions to his close-ness. That biting smile that kept tugging on his lips made me want to spit in his face. He needed to get a grip. I couldn't help that danger and darkness turned me on. It meant nothing except I was sick in the head and had a thirst for twisted fucking thrills. If he thought he could manipulate me using seduction he was sorely mistaken. "You are inca-pable of kindness. I sensed that from the moment you pulled me into your pit of endless misery and darkness."

He opened his mouth to respond, eyes lit, but the doorknob turning shut him up. Someone tried to come inside but he shot his hand out and locked the door shut with a gust of darkness.

"What the hell?" Natalia voiced indignantly from outside. She tried again, rattling the doorknob aggressively. "Nyx? What's going on? Open up!"

The stranger turned his face to mine, curious to see what I'd do. "Are you going to scream for help, Firefly?"

I fought the urge to squirm. I squared my shoulders as best I could despite being on my back with my hands tied above my head. I leveled him with a look, and he chuckled under his breath.

"Open that pretty mouth of yours," he murmured, so quiet I almost thought I'd imagined it.

My heart performed an Olympic dive in my chest, soaring sound-lessly into my gut. My lips popped open in disdain, brows narrowing together. "I will do no such thing."

He brought the glowing red medallion to my lips. "I would not be so cruel as to deprive you of all your power on your first day tomorrow. Not when you have such a character-defining challenge awaiting you. As fun as it is to see you squirm, you are of no use to me completely powerless."

I just stared at the sadistic motherfucker, wondering how in the hell I'd ended up in this situation.

"Nyx!" Natalia shouted from outside. She tried to get in using magic, but the shadow prick's power was immutable.

The stranger tipped the medallion slightly over my mouth, and that's when I realized the glowing light pulsing inside was actual liquid.

My power... It was a tangible *thing*.

"Open your mouth," he whispered, voice grated.

My chest rose and fell so intensely that I thought I would burst.

"It will be *just* enough," he warned, his eyes holding mine. "You will be able to access your magic without pain... but show off too much and you'll drain yourself in front of everyone. Be wise. You'll need every drop I'm giving you for your moment in the Sphere tomorrow. But whether you've used all you've been given; your magic will be gone again tomorrow by sunset."

"Wha–?" When I opened my mouth to protest, he tipped the medallion and a single drop of warm, lustrous liquid hit my tongue.

No more than a raindrop, yet it ignited my energy instantly, spreading through my body like wildfire. Burning that emptiness away, filling me once more with light. I gasped, my back arching. I saw stars while the effects swam through my veins as if he'd injected me with the magical equivalent of heroin.

"Until next time," he said, his voice like that of a phantom. With a whirl of shadows, he was gone.

Natalia burst into the room half a second later to find me laying on my bed, panting wantonly, high off a dose of my own bloody magic.

"What in Goddess's name are you doing?"

I breathed heavily, palms sweaty, staring up at the ceiling. A sigh of relief escaped me, followed by a maniacal laugh. My power and I, reunited. If only for a short time. I welcomed her back, feeling the fire returning to its rightful place in my heart. I didn't care that I looked ridiculous. At least I was ridiculous and powerful.

"Nyx!" Natalia growled, moving to stand over me as her dark eyes raked over me, trying to figure me out. "Seriously, what the hell? Why did you lock me out?"

I met her scathing glare and shrugged, rising to my feet nonchalantly. I could feel how rattled I appeared, but I played it off like nothing. "I was Astral traveling. Sorry. Didn't mean to lock you out."

"Astral traveling?" She gaped incredulously at me. "You're not supposed to do that shit alone. You're always supposed to have someone guarding your body and we are only second years. You aren't fully initiated into Astral—"

"I was looking for the person who snatched me on the beach."

That shut her up.

I hadn't told her a single detail of what happened, and it was killing her. She couldn't See. Natalia, the greatest Seer at Luna Academy, could not perceive a thing beyond those shadows. She seemed to not be able to See anything involving my torturer. She should have been able to See I was trapped in my room with him, yet she sensed nothing. Alarming, to say the least.

"Did you find them?" she breathed; eyes wide.

I moved toward the ensuite bathroom. "I did, yes."

"And?"

"And...this is the kind of prey you stalk before you attack. I'm going to savor this hunt."

CHAPTER 9
DEATH BY HOLLYWOOD
NYX

The magic flowing through my veins had a limit. I felt that now, unlike last night when I'd been distracted by the euphoria of reuniting with my power. It thrummed inside me, sure, but not with the same eternal flow as before. Before, my magic had been like an internal waterfall that would never run dry. A waterfall that enchanted the blood in my veins. Now, that waterfall was reduced to little more than a babbling brook under the hot sun bound to dry up in the relentless heat.

It was almost worse than not having my power at all.

Okay, not worse than that. Nothing was worse than that.

It meant I couldn't be a reckless instigator. For me, that would be difficult. I thrived in chaos. I needed to start shit to function properly. Biting my tongue and holding my fire would be a challenge, to say the least. Based on the amount of power I sensed humming inside me, I'd have to stick to the basics and pace myself. *Fuck my life.*

I dressed in black leather tights and a matching sports bra, my silver hair tied up high, Ariana Grande style. I looked plain as hell without all my gold tattoos, but I couldn't waste any magic on bearing them.

The first day of classes meant the top-ranking students of last year would compete in the Sphere. Great timing, seeing as how I was low on power, and this was one of the most defining moments of the entire year. Goody.

The first years would be off with the Luminary getting a tour of our land and learning the different portals and sacred spots. Everyone else would be in the Sphere watching the competition.

Whoever came out on top would be awarded with being the Keeper of the Baton for the next three moon cycles.

The Sacred Baton, an ancient celestial object forged thousands of years ago by a nameless goddess. A peculiar thing. The sharp, pointed ends made it look more like a fancy vampire stake, but who was I to judge? Made of angel oak, blue obsidian, and pure silver. It wielded the power of divine justice and authority. It possessed a psychic sentience and bonded to its Keeper. It was designed to detect deception and all sorts of ill intentions. Whoever became Keeper, instantly held a higher authority amongst the student body. If any dark riffraff went on, the Keeper would know, and justice would be swift.

For most of last year, the position had belonged to me. Laughable, seeing as how it was usually me who was up to no good. The Sacred Baton hardly ever objected to my shenanigans though, so I guess that meant I wasn't totally evil.

It would be mine again.

The shadow prick wanted me to have it. Unsettling, but whatever. Why else would he give me some magic for this "character-defining challenge" and tell me I was no use to him completely powerless?

I hated not knowing his true motives but swallowed that notion down like a jagged stone and left my room.

The common room was lit. I wondered what all the commotion was as I descended the spiral stairs. Excited chatter and exclaims echoed off the towering, gilded walls. The dragon, snake, and owl carvings looked particularly amused. The floating candles overhead trembled slightly from the excess squealing. Nobody even noticed me as I entered the room. Over by the fireplace, the girls clustered. Even my minions.

Emilia stood back with Natalia, Faye, and that weird bald girl that dressed like she was sneaking out of her bedroom window to meet up with some boys and smoke weed out of a can. Emilia sensed me right away, her eyes locking with mine as her brows raised. I beckoned her over with a nod and she came right away.

"What's going on?"

Emilia opened her mouth to speak but as she did, the crowd parted enough for me to see what all the fuss was about.

Who the fuss was all about.

"Holy shit, is that–?"

"Venus St. Claire, yeah," Emilia interjected wistfully.

"You're kidding." I deadpanned. At the same moment, a weighted, menacing glare met and locked with mine.

Venus St. fucking Claire.

Movie star.

Not just some little actress who'd been in a few films here and there. She was full-blown A-list-Oscar-winning-known-all-over-the-world famous. Beloved in the mortal realm and the Celestial Society. And there she stood, staring right at me, a mischievous grin tugging at her lush, crimson-painted lips. Lips the color of murder. A color I knew as Wrath. My fucking color.

My heart leaped in my chest, but I remained stoic as I drank her in. Long, shiny locks of red hair tumbled over her chest and down her back. Even from where I stood, I could see the warm honey color of her eyes, and the cruel intentions they hid within them. She was tall and curvy, clad in a set of red training leathers, cropped to show off her midriff. *Red. Leathers.* Sinful, just sinful. I fought the urge to look down at my outfit in comparison. Her grin widened as if she sensed that. She tossed a lock of fiery hair over her shoulder, dismissing me with her eyes.

"Shit," I breathed, miffed.

Natalia, Faye, and the hairless wonder gravitated over to us. My minions were already behind me, though I hardly noticed them. A group of other girls known for being loyal to (and borderline obsessed with) me followed as well. I probably should have known their names but oh well. I couldn't even remember my minions' names. Without so much as a glance in their direction, I spun on a heel and headed out of the Academy toward the Sphere.

The girls followed.

"What's her element?" I asked curtly.

"Earth," Faye answered.

My shoulders relaxed as a laugh tumbled through my lips. "Perfect." Earth was no match for fire.

"What's she doing here?" I inquired next, stalking fiercely out into the morning sun.

I was well aware that Hollywood was crawling with Celestials. It was their sneaky way of being worshipped by mortals in the twenty-first century. Most celebrities were not human. But I never expected one of them to join our school. Hollywood Celestials didn't care for education. They enjoyed basking in the limelight and being adored by the world.

"She enrolled as a third year," Minion Two informed me. "She was going to some fancy Academy in Paris but decided to come here to be closer to work."

My face scrunched. "So, she's staying?"

"Yes," about seven girls answered together.

The sun beat down on my silver hair as I crossed the path toward the Sphere with a gaggle of females on my heel. My ponytail lashed behind me like a whip and I swore I burnt footprints in the cobblestone.

Judging by the way Venus was dressed, she planned on competing today.

"Great," I chirped, feigning cheerfulness. "Can't wait to kick her ass."

$$) \,) \, \bullet \, (\, ($$

BY HALF PAST EIGHT, THE SPHERE WAS FULL. EVEN THE FIRST years were here. Usually, they went off on their tour, but I guessed today was something special because of our new Hollywood starlet. Peachy.

The girls and I finished stretching and warming up. I showed Emilia the basic stretches which she was having a hard time with, but she'd become more flexible over time. I pretended not to care about the fact that Venus St. Claire already had her own flock of followers. My group was bigger, but still. It was absolutely crucial I put her on her ass today to re-establish the natural order.

Inside, the Sphere looked incredible. Vines grew up the moon-shaped architecture while ornamental trees grew around the edges. Floating candles lingered overhead, more for aesthetics than lighting. The obsidian floor gobbled up the sunlight rather than reflecting it. In the center of the space, an elevated boxing ring had been set up. My favorite place in the world. About three times the size of a mortal boxing ring and shaped like a circle rather than a square. The ring was enchanted to keep all magical activity inside to protect everyone on the outside.

"Oh shit," the bald girl (Why was she always here?) said. "She's coming over here."

My neck snapped in the direction she was pointing. Lo and behold, Venus St. Claire and her new band of traitorous little bitches were sauntering right this way. Venus's amber eyes locked with mine as a dark grin tugged at her ruby lips.

I straightened up, flicking my silver pony over my shoulder.

The girls stood behind me, a united front.

"Well, well, well," Venus chimed. "So, this is the famous Nyx Morningstar." She stood right in front of me, eyes raking me up and down. Slowly. "I thought you'd be taller."

I snorted. "And you are...?"

"Baby girl, it's cute you wanna play indifferent. Though I may not look like one, I am an empath. I can sense your intimidation from a mile away." The words slipped from her lips like she was whispering sweet nothings in a lover's ear. She glanced behind me at the girls, her eyes then traveling over the entirety of the Sphere. "I think I'm going to like it here. Nice to meet you!"

Her posse laughed like she'd told the world's funniest joke before they turned and went back to where they'd been stretching on the other side of the ring.

Underwhelming. Just like her movies.

Yet suddenly this horrible future flashed before my eyes. A future where I was nothing, and Venus was queen. The girls of Luna Academy, flocked around her, hanging on her every word. They had all forgotten about me, the girl who lost her magic and disappeared from the Celestial Society without a trace. No one missed me. No one remembered me.

I shook my head to clear this abhorrent vision.

I glared after them, noting each face that chose to follow her. An unsurprised laugh escaped me. Of course. Most of them were fourth and fifth-year girls. Figured. Last year left them insanely bitter to be bested by a wee little first-year like me.

A fire lit in my heart as I thought of all the delicious ways I could put them in their place. Venus St. Claire had done nothing to prove her power. Coming from Hollywood didn't mean anything. How petty of them to back her as if she had earned her place here. None of them could rise to the occasion and go against me themselves so they had to look for the next girl to stand behind. Pathetic.

I turned back to my group, grinning impishly. About thirty girls stood behind me, waiting to see what I would say or do. Admittedly, the split was almost even, and all my girls were younger. It didn't matter. Age meant nothing to Celestials. Power was power. Girls who'd had five years of training ahead of me still ended up mercilessly at my untrained feet.

"Venus has posted all over her Magigram that she's fighting you today," Faye told me. "The entire Society is placing bets on who will win."

A scoff escaped me. "Is that so?"

My focus dashed over to the girl in red who was already staring over here with fire in her eyes. She waved sweetly.

"She's saying some pretty crazy things about you." Natalia voiced while I continued holding eye contact with Venus. "Talking all sorts of shit, saying you aren't as powerful as everyone thinks and she's going to prove it today."

I turned back to my girls, my heart pounding in my throat.

Shit. I didn't even have my full power running through my veins. I had but a drop of it to spare. I guessed this was the "character-defining challenge" my torturer had mentioned. He gifted me with a dose of my magic so I could face her today. I could only pray it would be enough.

All eyes were on me, and I was at a total disadvantage.

As I should be. This was the only real way Celestials truly grew.

Natalia turned to me, a severe look in her eyes. "Nyx, you should know that Venus St. Claire is no ordinary earthling. She can manifest crystals. Meaning, she can manifest power that is immune to fire. You're going to have to play smart rather than play hard."

Shit. She could summon *crystals*? I'd only ever heard of one or two Exalted Priestesses being able to do that. I'd never had an earthling come close to beating me.

I swallowed thickly, keeping my chin high. "Anything else I need to know?"

"She fights dirty," Minion One informed me.

"So do I," I clapped back with a smirk.

"Fighting firelings is her specialty," Minion Three said. "She's never been beaten by one."

Wow. Okay. The stars weren't playing today.

"She's getting someone to film the live stream of your battle," Minion Two added. "It'll be streamed on her Magigram."

"Yeah, the whole Society is going to be watching." Faye supplied as she scrolled on her blackmirror. "Celestial Tea is running a poll to see which one of you everyone thinks will win. Right now, it's fifty-fifty." She turned the screen to me so I could see the webpage.

Yes, the poll she showed me was exactly that. Fifty-fifty.

In the last week, I'd been Astral Snatched, had my magic stolen, and then given back with a ticking countdown like I was Cinder-fucking-ella, and now a Hollywood movie star had moved in on my school and was challenging me as queen.

Faye stepped closer to me, a grave look in her eye. "Are you sure you're up for this, Nyx?" she murmured low enough that only I could hear. The last time she'd seen me, I'd been a mess asking her for a damn glamour spell. I couldn't stand the way she was looking at me now.

"Time to tip those scales," I growled.

CHAPTER 10
TO RIVAL & EXCEL
EMILIA

We gathered around the ring, listening diligently as the Luminary dished out all the rules. Which were minimal. There didn't seem to be rules at all, but more like suggestions. *Don't be cheap. Try not to kill each other.* The end.

"At the beginning of each year, and every third moon cycle after that, we hold these competitions to not only push you but inspire you. Competition is healthy and it is what motivates us, to not just reach our goals but to soar past them into the great unknown where all the greatest magic happens. For the first competition, all competitors are selected based on their rankings from last year. But next time you will be able to sign up, despite your level of power. Everyone should get a chance to compete and prove themselves." Our Luminary smiled brightly, her white hair shining under the twinkling dome. "That said, these competitions are ruthless and not for the faint of heart."

"Or perhaps exactly what the faint of heart needs," Priestess Bridget supplied through a dark grin. Murmurs of agreement rippled after her.

The Priestesses sat in elevated throne-style chairs in the back, watching from above. In fact, their chairs weren't just elevated. They were levitating. Nearly twelve feet off the ground, floating mid-air to watch the show from the best seats in the house. Each throne had its element symbol engraved on the top. Their long, flowing, translucent robes cascaded down like silken waterfalls. Majestic as hell.

My heart slammed as I turned to assess my sister, desperate to read her face. A lost cause. She remained stoic and unbothered. Though at times I thought I saw her jaw clench and her throat bob. Was she nervous? I had no clue. Those freaky girls who looked like dollar-store versions of her stood behind her. Her minions, as she called them.

"We have decided to spice things up a little this year..." the Luminary purred mischievously.

Curious whispers spread at that, and for an instant, it seemed like Nyx paled but I couldn't be sure because that girl always had walls of steel up around her.

"Come on in, boys," the Luminary sang.

The velvet curtain didn't just open. It flew off its rack and went flying through the Sphere in a ferocious gust of howling wind. Seconds later, it burst into flames and rained black sand over the lot of us. Girls gasped in wonder and then erupted with both excitement and disdain as a pack of young, good-looking men poured through the yoni-shaped entrance looking like they owned the place.

"No. Way," Faye breathed.

"Oh, my God!" Destiny squeaked beside me.

Nyx didn't move an inch. My sister had turned to stone.

I didn't understand. Why would there be—

I locked eyes with Jedidiah Stone and my thoughts were snuffed out like a candle in the wind. He was cruelly gorgeous under the brightness of the quartz dome. My heart felt as if he had his fist around it. He had a knowing, mocking look in his navy eyes as he led his group of guys to the ring like it was no big deal. The twins stood behind him like ginger pillars and I wondered if the three of them ever went anywhere without each other. One of the twins spotted me and winked, blowing me a freaking kiss. A waft of heat hit my skin and it didn't take long to realize it came from Nyx. She all but had smoke coming from her nose and ears.

Venus St. Claire stood across from us on the other side of the ring, grinning smugly. I got the idea she may have had something to do with this. Pulling those Hollywood strings already.

"We thought we would add a bit of extra oomph to the competition this year," Eliza, the Air Priestess, said from her floating throne. "We have invited some of Veneficus's finest to watch."

"Okay, but why are they permitted in our sacred Sphere?" Nyx spat. "No men were allowed in Goddess Diana's temple. Why the hell are they allowed here? Did they even cleanse themselves before stepping their musty ass feet in here?"

Jedidiah snorted. "It's the twenty-first century, babe. Being a sexist bigot is not a good look."

His boys sniggered. She shot daggers from her eyes at them, folding her tanned arms over her pushed-out chest.

I noticed none of the guys had their staffs. Most likely because they weren't permitted to do any magic here in the Sphere.

Destiny and I shared a quick, weighted glance. "This is so insane!" she mouthed, and I nodded fervently.

The Luminary stood in the ring, grinning with bright eyes as she watched us react. "Veneficus will be holding a similar competition amongst their own student body, as well as San Gabriel. The top-ranking starseeds will be offered the chance to compete in the Clash of Spirits!"

"What's that?" someone asked.

"The Clash of Spirits is an exciting event held only every thirty-three years, on Hallows Eve when the veil between our world and the spirit realms is the thinnest," Bridget explained proudly. "It is a glorious affair. Performances, music, dancing, battles of the elements! Celestials come from all over the world to attend. It's not only for us but all those who came before us. A tribute for those watching from behind the veil."

"Whoa," Destiny breathed. My thoughts exactly.

"For today, ladies, you are competing to be Keeper of the Baton." The Luminary went on. "A great honor. A great a responsibility. The Baton is an ancient, divine object with its own powerful sentience. Its Keeper will be psychically bonded to it, sharing its drive to seek out deception and lies."

"Let's get on with it, then," Bridget cawed.

The Luminary splayed her hands out in front of her, her golden robes shimmering in the sunlight that spilled through the quartz roof.

Eliza held out her hands, casting a gust of wind that whirled around our Luminary and lifted her from the ground, flying her to her hovering throne.

"Let the competition begin!" the Luminary declared, clapping her hands and the sound amplified by magic, booming like a loose cannon.

"First in the ring will be Amy Rose, earthling," announced the Water Priestess, "versus Camilla Gomez, airling."

The first few rounds were intense to say the freaking least.

Girls morphed into ruthless beasts, battling their hearts out. Gusts of wind met spears of wood. Fire met waves of water, canceling each other out to make steam. The girls weren't just trained in magic but combat as well. They moved like warriors, ducking and dodging and kicking and lunging. I couldn't take my eyes off them.

The rounds didn't last long. The battle of elements proved to be a swift, relentless affair. Earth beat air, air beat water, water beat fire, and fire beat them all. I got the idea they were saving the best for last. Nyx versus Venus would be the grand finale.

As the second to last round finished up, my sister went and stood at the edge of the ring, waiting for her turn to kick some ass. Natalia went with her, murmuring her endless moral support.

Pathetically, I found myself looking for Jedidiah to gauge his reaction. My heart beat some type of way when I didn't spot him.

"Looking for someone?"

I jumped out of my skin, my entire body flushing as his chest brushed against the back of my shoulder. I whirled around, swallowed by his shadow as those stormy dark blue eyes bored into mine. A cocky grin tugged the edges of his lips.

"Don't do that," I hissed.

"Do what?" he wondered innocently.

"Sneak up on me like that."

"You were looking for me."

"I was not."

"You were." His smile should have been illegal. His face should have been illegal. The way he was looking at me right now in a room full of people should have been goddamn illegal. I fought the urge to adjust my shirt to make sure it was sitting properly.

The round finished. I had no clue who won. I turned back to the ring, cheeks warm, mind frazzled.

"Your sister's going to lose," Jedidiah promised, leaning down to speak near my ear. He stood right behind me. Close. Too close. I peeked over my shoulder at him, finding his gaze awaiting mine. His eyes darkened while he watched my flesh betray me and erupt with goosebumps.

"Never," I growled back.

He scoffed. "Don't tell me you share her inflatable ego."

"I share the common knowledge that my sister is the most powerful person in the room aside from the Priestesses."

"Oh, come on," he snorted mockingly. "She ain't all that. Has she ever told you about the time I buried her alive?"

I winced, my cheeks going cold. "Excuse me?"

He smiled menacingly. "Yeah, last year at a bonfire party, she started shit with me and I finished it. She thinks she's such hot shit with her fire, but earth will always be superior. I buried that girl six feet under and—"

"And she clawed her way to the surface like a fucking queen!" Destiny interjected defensively.

Jedidiah made a noise of annoyance, dismissing my friend.

"That didn't happen," I said, shaking my head, and looking up into his blustery eyes. How could Destiny know about this and not me?!

He shook his head, clicking his tongue at me. The way all eyes flocked to us was not lost on me. Venus St. Claire's gaze nearly burned a hole through my head. "Rumor has it, your sister's got a dirty little secret," Jedidiah told me. "You should ask her what really happened on the beach that night."

"I know what happened," I argued. "She was Astral Snatched."

"Yeah, but by who? And what happened? Are you telling me you haven't noticed a change in her since that night? I mean, just look at her. No tattoos? Living tattoos can only be borne by those who possess high magic. And your dear sister went from bearing them on every inch of her flesh.... to having none. Strange, isn't it?"

My heart pounded. Of course, I had noticed a difference in her—but Nyx kept me at arm's length. If that. She didn't tell me anything that went on with her. She didn't tell anyone.

My eyes went downcast while my throat worked. I hated how easily this prick could get to me and I didn't even know him.

"That's what I thought," he chuckled smoothly.

Something hot touched my shoulder out of nowhere, making me gasp. Jedidiah's fingers trailed a line of fire along my collarbone as he stood too close behind me. I stood there like a senseless mute as he leaned his lips down to my ear. "You are going to be more powerful than her, I can sense it."

The hairs on the back of my neck rose while a tremor ran down my spine.

"Emilia," he murmured and I physically winced. The way he said my name made my thighs clench. So slow and savoring, like he wanted to taste each letter. "You know what Emilia means? It means to rival. To excel." A sharp but quiet laugh escaped his lips. "It's your purpose in this life. To rival your sister. And excel."

Dear Goddess, please open a portal to the Underworld and swallow me whole.

Every person in the Sphere seemed to be watching but the only face I saw was my sister's. She glared over here with disgust and fury swarming behind her striking features. My heart pounded like he was holding me over the edge of a cliff, and the way Nyx looked at us, it felt like he was.

"She knows it, too," he went on casually as if he and I were close familiars. "She senses the threat in you and guess what? If you are a threat to Nyx Morningstar, you better watch your back."

"She's my sister," I retorted, wishing my voice had more vigor behind it.

"You're lying to yourself if you think that means anything to her." Why was he still touching me? More importantly, why was I letting him? His fingers brushed along my throat as he pushed a piece of my brown hair behind my ear.

Something about those words made my insides turn to granite, sinking me into the ground. Jedidiah chuckled in my ear, straightening back up so he towered over me once more. "I love how responsive you are. Even more than your sister." He offered me a dark smile before heading back to his friends.

Nyx was gaping at me, her eyes demanding *what the hell?*

I just shrugged impossibly. I had no clue what that was.

You'd think I'd just returned from space with a blue alien sitting on my shoulder, the way Destiny gawked at me. "Dude, that was Jedidiah St–"

Destiny's words were cut off by the Luminary introducing Nyx and Venus as they stepped into the ring. Nyx looked rattled. Oops. My chest filled with guilt. I swallowed the lump of glass at the back of my throat, wishing I hadn't just stood there and let him grope me. He just did that to piss her off. Used me to get under her skin and I allowed it. It was so obvious he had some sort of demented hard-on for her. He pretended to hate her but apparently hate and lust weren't as different as I thought.

"Nyx Morningstar, the highest ranking fireling our Academy has seen since her mother attended centuries ago." The Luminary spoke proudly as Nyx stood with her chin held high, eyes forward and strangely empty. "Versus Venus St. Claire, an exceptional earthling who just transferred here from La Magie Academy in Paris."

Venus grinned, her eyes sparkling with malice as she assessed my sister. "Luminary, with all due respect, I do prefer to be referred to as a crystalling."

Nyx's face crumpled with a grimace.

"If you can prove yourself as such today, you can bear that title," Bridget said from her floating throne, her tone dismissive.

Venus appeared insulted but said nothing back.

"Let the final battle commence!" Priestess Adria declared.

Nyx and Venus stared at each other. Neither one made a first move.

Everyone in the Sphere seemed to be holding their breath.

They began circling like two alley cats preparing to attack. Nyx's expression remained unreadable while Venus looked thrilled, eyes glittering with triumph as if she already won.

A few girls cheered Nyx on. She didn't show any signs of hearing them.

"Come on, all-powerful fireling," Venus taunted. "You scared?"

"Of your shiny rocks?" Nyx laughed apathetically and no light touched her eyes. "Give me a break, Hollywood." My sister sucked in a sharp breath before summoning fire over her hands. Bright white licking flames crawled up her arms to her elbows, turning her into a human candle wick.

Venus's eyes lit up. A second later, she manifested a spear that looked like it was made of ice, but I knew it was crystal. She hurled it at my sister and my heart dropped. Nyx dodged the death crystal and tossed a ball of fire at Venus. Venus ducked out of the way, summoning two more crystal spears, and shooting them one by one at my sister's heart. Nyx whirled out of the way, letting the crystals crash against the invisible shield around the ring where they shattered like glass. The shards evaporated into thin air.

"So, what if she gets hit by one of those spears?" I gasped to no one in particular.

"Once we Emerge, we heal almost instantly. Even so, just in case, we have healers on deck." Faye informed me, pointing to a trio of women dressed in green on the other side of the ring.

Nyx yelled wordlessly and stomped her foot, a line of furious fire erupting from the ground before her, charging toward Venus. Venus grunted and a vine descended from above her, out of thin air, which she gripped onto and used it to swing away from the fire like freaking Tarzan.

This went on for some time. We all stood on edge, watching, and gasping and wincing as the two females in the ring shot their shots and missed each other every time. Nyx looked annoyed and Venus seemed surprised.

"Nyx finally has some competition," a girl I didn't know muttered and a few girls laughed.

My mouth went dry.

Across the ring, Jedidiah smirked at me, mouthing the words "Your sister's going to lose."

I grit my teeth but forced myself to ignore him.

"I could fill this ring with fire, and it would be bye-bye Hollywood," Nyx warned, chest heaving.

Venus growled and manifested a spear three times longer than all the ones previous. She brought her arm back to launch it at Nyx, who twirled out of the way in response. But Venus had been bluffing. She waited for Nyx to move a certain way, and then she let the spear fly, for real this time. Nyx hadn't expected it, and as a result, it impaled her right through the shoulder.

Everyone gasped.

Nyx's dark eyes went wide, blood instantly flowing down her arm. The spear went right *through* her. In one side, out the other.

Venus beamed.

My heart hammered. A dizzying sense of worry swamped me. But Nyx just looked down at the crystal impaling her shoulder and grinned. She gripped the front end, and slowly, ever so slowly, yanked it out of herself. It dripped with blood—her blood. She smirked at Venus as she held it up and ran her tongue along the sharp end, tasting her own blood. She made a show of it, her eyes hooded and seductive.

A few of the guys from Veneficus cheered.

Then my sister twirled the spear like a baton, summoned a white flame over the pointy end, and threw it at Venus, who barely moved out of the way in time.

Nyx grinned broadly, pearl-colored flames writhing up and down her arms.

Vines burst through the ground at my sister's feet, wrapping around her ankles and chaining her in place. "I favor crystals, but I still hold the power of earth!" Venus exclaimed.

"Oh, I'm so scared." Nyx giggled as she scorched the vines immediately, dancing her way toward Venus. She brought her hands out in front of her, a cluster of flames manifesting into the shape of a bow and arrow. My heart pounded as Nyx created the weapon of fire and aimed the beaming arrow right at Venus, pulling back the string and letting it fly.

The crowd went wild. Venus swerved out of the way, but the arrow skimmed her arm. She screamed in surprise and pain, eyes turning feral as she glanced down at the burn on her arm.

"You bitch!" Venus exclaimed. A crystal spear materialized over each of her hands, and she threw them viciously toward my sister. Nyx evaded each one. Venus didn't stop. She manifested spear after spear, sending them flying at my sister. They shattered against the shield around the ring while Nyx danced out of the way, an impish grin tugging at her lips.

"Two minutes!" the Luminary declared loudly.

Nyx's grin turned into a cruel smile.

Venus's fury grew a life of its own. Her face had gone as red as her hair. She screamed fervently, sweat dripping down her temples while she held her hands out, fingers curling inward. Nyx yelped as a wall of crystal formed at her feet, rising from the ground impossibly all around her. Enclosing her in a cage of glimmering crystal that looked more like ice. Venus was still screaming as she guided the crystal to completely close over my sister, trapping her in a rock-solid enclosure.

The Sphere went silent.

Venus stood there, chest rising and falling, expression unreadable.

The Priestesses exchanged peculiar looks.

My heart threatened to burst through the cage of my ribs.

The crystal enclosure around Nyx was shaped like a bullet. A thin tube with a pointed top. Her own personal prison. It shimmered in the sunlight that poured through the quartz dome, thick enough so all I could see of my sister was a shadow figure.

"Is...is that it?" Destiny breathed. "Did she lose?"

"Just wait," Natalia whispered.

I felt like I was going to faint.

Nyx pressed her hands against the crystal wall and the entire enclosure filled with flames. Faintly, I could hear her yelling. The fire blazed behind the opaque walls of her entrapment, literally swallowing her whole. Was that okay? Was she going to burn off all her hair? How immune was she to her fire?

A crack split through the crystal. And then another, and another. Until the entire thing shattered like glass, shards flying every which way, ricocheting off the shield.

Nyx emerged in a whirlwind of flames that died as soon as she was free. She stood there, stark naked, clothes burned away, skin covered in ash and soot. Her hair remained intact on her head, thank the Goddess. Her chest heaved as she collapsed to her knees, exhausted but free.

Wait—why was her nose bleeding?

Venus St. Claire glared at her with those red brows narrowed as she took a step nearer. "What's the matter, fireling? Are you tired or something? You look unwell."

Nyx did look beyond drained. Was that normal?

My sister's chest continued to rise and fall as she looked up at Venus who zeroed in on her menacingly. Venus manifested a crystal spear, pointing it at my sister's throat. "You can't fight me off, can you?"

Nyx bared her teeth. "I escaped your ridiculous little cage," she hissed. "We're done here."

"I don't think we are," Venus taunted. "I'm still standing. And here you are, on your knees before me. Bowing to your new queen, are you?"

Nyx attempted to rise to her feet. Venus kicked her down and mounted on top of her with the crystal spear pressed to her exposed throat. "Yield."

Nyx had fire in her eyes. I expected her to explode but she didn't.

Murmurs broke out through the crowd.

Jedidiah smirked at me, an I-told-you-so look swathing his annoyingly handsome features.

No, this couldn't be right. Nyx was bluffing. Stalling. She was going to fight back, she had to. She wouldn't be beaten.

"Shit," Destiny breathed. "Is she really going to yield?"

Venus pressed the crystal spear harder into Nyx's flesh, drawing blood. A sharp gasp escaped me. My sister clenched her teeth defiantly.

"Yield!" Venus hollered.

Nyx opened her mouth and holy shit she had a defeated look in her eye. She looked like she was about to—

A swirling vortex of light erupted in the center of the ring. A portal. What the–? Two cloaked figures materialized from the vortex. I knew those deep purple cloaks. My heart fell into the pit of my gut as two High Council members stepped into the ring. They wore gold-plated, horned masks, disguising their faces. The identities of the High Council members, aside from the High Lord, were top secret. My mother said that it was in our best interest as a Society to not know who ruled behind the scenes.

"Nyx Morningstar," a male's voice boomed through the Sphere. "You are coming with us."

"Uh, we're a little busy here," Venus argued stupidly.

With a flick of his wrist, Venus went flying, smashing into the shield of the ring, and crumpling to the ground in a heap of limbs.

Nyx stared up at the two cloaked Celestials, her eyes wide and confused.

One of them reached a hand out to my sister, helping her to her feet. They wrapped a thin, black cloak around her naked body before the three of them disappeared in a spinning vortex of light.

CHAPTER II
ARIES VANDERBILT
NYX

"Y ou can't just keep me in here like some criminal!" I shouted, banging furiously on the glass of the enchanted two-way mirror.

Five hours. Five fucking hours I'd been sitting in here alone, not knowing why in the seven realms I was here in the first place.

I was no stranger to the Institution. My first time here was when I accidentally lit my mortal classroom on fire after the teacher singled me out and embarrassed me for no reason. That was merely the first of many instances that wound me up in this Goddess-forsaken interrogation room. It looked exactly like the mortal ones. A small box of a room with a two-way mirror, one table, and a couple of chairs.

On the outside, the Institute was a massive stone castle built into the Rocky Mountains. Veiled, of course. Mortals would never see it, but to those with the Sight, the thing stuck out like a sore thumb. Creepy place, bad vibes. I hated it here.

I had no interest in acting a fool and pounding on the glass like some lunatic, but they'd left me in here for too long. No one had spoken a word to me. I was portalled in here and left to my damn thoughts, with nothing but my reflection to keep me company. Not a good time.

I became more drained by the minute. I'd used all the power my shadow torturer had given me to battle Venus St. Claire. The visible effects of my lack of magic settled in swiftly. My eyes were ringed with shadow, my irises lightless. My cheeks even sunk in a little, and my dark olive skin went pale. The only upside was that this room naturally dismantled the magic of whoever was trapped inside, so my being powerless wouldn't be a red flag.

When the door finally opened, I jolted up from my seat, a snarl tearing through my cracked lips.

Aries Vanderbilt, High Lord of the Celestial Society himself, entered the room with a smooth stride and a smug face, carrying his long wizard staff at his side. The bright blue crystal on top sizzled with electric power.

He was the last living Celestial to bear a Divine trait. From his temples grew two curling ram horns. He looked like a cruel, vindictive god. Standing tall and broad, clad in a billowing dark purple cloak with hair the color of merlot to match his ominous horns.

At the dawn of the Age of Amnesia, Celestials needed to choose a new leader. When the world was split, all our monarchies and political systems were abolished so they could create a new order. To find a new leader, they held an event called The Divine Rite. Thirteen powerful Celestials from all over the world competed through the lengthy challenges, including my mother's sister, Sophia Morningstar. Somehow, in some Goddess-forsaken way, it was Aries Vanderbilt who won the Divine Rite, and so here we were.

It should have been *my* bloodline in power.

Honestly, the whole situation was ironic as hell, because of this small truth that existed in the background of our reality—one that hardly anyone ever spoke out loud.

Male Celestials were not as powerful as females.

It was just nature. Men held more power in the physical world. But women? Our wombs gave us a direct, immediate connection into the ethereal realms, and therefore, when it came to magic and spirituality, we were superior.

Aries Vanderbilt was the only male in centuries to make it to High Magician level. Not even the Chancellors at Veneficus bore this title. So, despite there being thousands of Priestesses, and only one High Magician, Aries got to be king, all because of some stupid competition that happened centuries ago.

It was bullshit.

I knew his dirty little secret, though.

Last year when I'd been Keeper of the Baton, he visited Luna Academy, and the Baton had sensed his deception. I learned his real name was not Aries. The Baton couldn't detect what his real true name was, but I liked to play around with it. Randel. Simon. Pete. Craig. Something mundane and forgettable, I was sure. I never told anyone, though. It was my own little inside joke.

His eyes locked with mine and it felt like a knife to the heart. His face was all hard lines and smooth planes. Handsome in a threatening way. He was over eight hundred years old, and it showed in his eyes. Celestials didn't prune up like mortals do but our age showed in other ways. Aries carried his years in his hardened glare.

He was Jedidiah's father. Jedidiah took his mother's last name, and I always secretly wished I knew why.

"Miss Morningstar," he greeted me evenly, taking a seat in the chair across from me.

I folded my arms over my chest. "What am I doing here, Aries?"

We were familiars. He interrogated me several times as a child.

"You will address me as High Lord."

"What am I doing here, High Lord?"

He smiled coldly, gesturing for me to sit down.

With a harumph, I did. I knew the deal. If I refused to cooperate, it just meant I had to stay here even longer.

He waved a hand over the metal table and a file folder appeared. "It's been a while. How are things?" he asked.

I didn't bother fighting the scowl that took place over my features. "Small talk? Seriously?"

"You don't look well, Miss Morningstar."

"That's rude."

"It's also alarming. As a young Celestial, you should be vibrant with health and vitality. What happened to all your tattoos?"

I shrugged, leaning back in my chair. "I grew bored of that look. Trying something new. Cleaner."

He didn't look convinced. "We've been watching you."

"I'm sure you have. You're the Celestial CIA with your nose in everyone's shit. So what? What did I do now?"

"Why don't you tell me?" Aries challenged.

I rolled my eyes, pointing to the file. "Whatever it is, looks like you already know."

He inhaled deeply, folding his large hands over the folder, leveling me with a look. He angled his head slightly, so his horns were pointing ominously my way. "Are you sure there's nothing you want to tell me before I get into it?"

"I'm sure."

"Fine." He opened the file, and my heart performed a long jump in my chest as he pulled out a photo and slid it in front of me. "Do you know him?"

Of course, Aries noted the way I winced as I took in the bright silver eyes glaring at me from the old, black-and-white photo. Bad quality or not, I'd recognize that face anywhere. Sharp, angled, striking, young. The shadow prick looked different. His head was shaved. The photo almost looked like a mugshot.

"No." I lied. Poorly.

"No?"

"No."

"You know what happens when you lie to us, Miss Morningstar."

I swallowed thickly. But then I realized I wasn't even lying. I didn't know this person. To me, he was a ghost. A ghost in the night. I knew nothing about him, not even his name.

"I don't know him, Ar—er, High Lord," I said, with more conviction.

He searched my face for a moment. "His name is Solaris Adder. He was kidnapped by mortals at the age of three. He was raised in a deep underground military base. The entire purpose of the organization was to experiment on him and his magic and eventually turn him into a weapon against us. He was one of many children subjected to these horrors."

My mouth dried, my skin breaking out in nervous beads of sweat as I fought to remain calm. So, he *had* been telling me the truth last night.

But he never said he had been a part of this 'project'. My heart thudded painfully.

"You don't learn of this history until your fifth year. It's heavy stuff. We don't wish to burden our starseeds with these truths until they have learned how to properly harness their power and navigate their emotions."

"How valiant," I retorted dryly while my pulse thundered in my temples.

Aries pushed the photo closer to me as if that would suddenly make me see it differently.

"Wait," I said, straightening in my chair. "You know, maybe I have heard of this before. The Star-Cross project, wasn't it? So, that would have been, like, over a hundred years ago?"

Aries tried to hide the shock on his face while he nodded curtly.

I battled my body's instincts to physically react to this news. "So why does this concern me?"

"Solaris Adder has recently been released from his prison realm."

My entire body turned to ice, the breath halting in my lungs. My lips popped open. Aries scrutinized my body language, and I knew for a damn fact I was giving myself away but holy shit.

He *had* been living in that Goddess-forsaken shadow realm. My skin erupted with goosebumps. An entire century in those shadows...

Aries reached into the file and pulled out more pictures. This time, he was showing me different angles of a horrendous murder scene. Blood everywhere. Bodies everywhere. A bunch of lab workers were quite literally torn apart and left to rot.

I grimaced, leaning away.

"He didn't have to kill them this way," Aries said, his tone grave. "Solaris possesses a very...unique power. He can kill swiftly and cleanly, but he chose to torture these mortals."

"Weren't they experimenting on him?" I rasped. "Didn't these people kidnap him and subject him to 'horrors' as you put it?"

"True," Aries admitted, eyes holding mine. "But he didn't stop there. Solaris blamed us, the Celestials, for what happened to him. His vendetta didn't stop with this massacre. This was just the beginning. He broke out of the underground base and carried out unspeakable crimes against his own people. We were forced to imprison him in a realm of his own making. He was successfully contained until about a week ago."

I was almost positive Aries could hear my heart slamming wildly against my ribs.

He waved a hand and a holographic screen appeared between us. A video of me down by the ocean the night of the beach party played on the magical 3D hologram. I stood there, eyes rolling back while my sister and Jedidiah Stone tried to rouse me. Thunder and lightning crashed in the background.

He banished the hologram and looked to me for answers.

I said nothing.

"You were Astral Snatched at the same time Solaris Adder was released from his prison realm. Am I supposed to believe this is a coincidence?"

I shrugged lamely, afraid that if I talked, my voice would crack and betray me.

Aries's eyes flicked to the two-way mirror which he could probably see through before leaning in closer to me. "Nyx, listen. Nobody blames you for what happened. We are all aware of Solaris's power and manipulation. Whatever he made you do, it isn't your fault. We can help you. We just need you to tell us the truth."

Tempting. But bullshit.

"I have no idea about any of this," I told him, managing to keep my tone even. "You said Solaris was only one of the children subjected to these 'horrors'. What happened to all the others? Where are they?"

"I will be the one asking questions!" the High Lord bellowed venomously. He reached out rapidly and grabbed my wrist from across the table. His sudden movement made me yelp. With a blur of movement, he pricked my wrist with a needle and drew blood.

"Hey!" I growled and he brought the needle to his lips and tasted my blood like a goddamn vampire.

I breathed hard and ragged, hugging my wrist against my chest like a wounded child.

"Your magic is drained." Aries deadpanned. "Your blood is nearly mortal."

"Lies!" I shouted furiously. "How dare you cross my boundaries like that! Send me back to my Academy at once! I know nothing of your prisoner!"

"When Solaris Adder was locked away, he possessed one, single object. A medallion capable of draining the magic out of another Celestial."

"Great," I replied, feigning indifference. "You are wasting your time with me. Even if I had seen him before, which I'm not saying I have, I know nothing about him. I will be of no help to you or the rest of the High Council."

Small bolts of lightning crackled over Aries's staff. I fought the instinct to wince away from him. "Are you sure you want to lie to me, Miss Morningstar?"

"Go ahead and tase me, Lord Vanderbilt," I spoke the words with acid on my tongue, tipping my chin up to show him I wouldn't cower in fear. "Like I said. You will get nothing out of me."

He eyed me with those fathomless black portals to his weary soul. Crackles of lightning bolted up and down his curling ram horns.

My chest rose and fell but I remained stoic.

"How do you think the girls at Luna will react when they find out you are powerless?"

A fucking threat. A threat to my reputation, my place as queen. Low, even for an elitist like himself. Celestials acted like we were so much better than mortals, yet we were just like them. Mortals were corrupt. Well, so were we. Aries Vanderbilt tortured me as a child, trying to figure out how I could use magic before Emerging. My mother allowed it. He electrocuted me ruthlessly trying to shock the truth out of me. It didn't work then, and it wouldn't work now.

One day, when my power reached its maximum potential, I'd burn all this shit down. I'd build a new world and then I'd reign over it with a crown of fire atop my pretty little head. No more of this High Lord and his secret High Council bullshit. We'd go back to the old way—where the rulers were kings and queens. Our courts would be out in the open. My subjects would be Celestial and mortal alike. I wouldn't be so prejudiced. I'd rule them all. And I'd keep them all in line.

"I don't know what you're talking about," I chirped. "My power is as abundant as ever. Sure, I'm a little tired after battling a crystal-wielding hothead, but I'm fine. I'll bounce back. Now, if you don't mind, I'd like to get back—AHH!"

A lightning bolt to the heart had me flying out of my chair, writhing on the ground in agony as our reigning High Lord showed me the consequences of not being a fucking snitch.

THEY LET ME GO AT SUNDOWN. AFTER ARIES GOT HIS FILL of seeing me on the ground at his mercy, he portalled me back to the Academy. I burst through my dorm room door trying so hard not to cry it felt as though my face was going to explode. Natalia jumped up from her bed instantly, shooting toward me as she breathed my name.

"Oh, my Goddess," she whispered. "Nyx... What the hell did they do to you?"

I pushed past her as she came in for a hug. I'd never been so exhausted in my entire life. I needed to sleep for a few years.

Natalia watched me, her dark eyes teeming with concern. I stripped out of the dark cloak they'd given me, revealing the swollen flesh on my neck, arms, stomach, and shoulders. Electrical burns covered my skin, bearing the truth. I put on panties and a bra before I grabbed my silken housecoat, wrapping it around myself. I wasn't healing. Red flag. I couldn't handle it—the way she looked at me. As if I were some poor, defenseless animal in need of being taken to the shelter and put down. I needed to deflect. Anything but this.

"Why didn't you tell me about Venus?" I croaked indignantly. I plopped down on my bed and released a long sigh.

"What?" she retorted, thrown off. She sat at the edge of my bed, her melanin features swathed with worry.

I met her gaze, swallowing hard. "You must have Seen her coming. I mean, you must have Seen all of that. The fucking Mole Boys showing up this morning. Why didn't you warn me of any of it?"

Her turn to swallow hard. Her shoulder slumped guiltily. She pushed a thick, black ringlet from her face and blew out a breath. "Nyx, you haven't been telling me anything. You never told me what happened at the beach. You haven't told me why you look so tired and sick. And I bet if I ask you what just happened with the High Council, you won't tell me that either. So why should I tell you anything?"

"Because I am queen!" I hissed, sitting upright.

"Do not mistake me for one of your little fan girls, Nyx. I am your friend. I am your equal. Don't pull your queen bee bullshit with me right now. This goes beyond all that."

"My equal?" I scoffed. "Seriously?"

Her glare darkened, rightfully so. That was low of me, but I couldn't control my tongue. "You're right. Perhaps we're not equals. Perhaps I am much more powerful than you are now." She whooshed her hand over me, manifesting a rope of vines that wrapped around my wrists and cuffed them together. "Burn your way free, queenie."

A challenge.

Fuck.

A pitiful seedling of rage bloomed in my belly. This was the fourth time in less than twenty-four hours that I'd been magically confined. Shadow bonds, a crystal cage, Institute interrogation room, and now handcuffs made of vines.

"Release me," I growled.

"So, you admit you can't get yourself out of this."

I glared at my best friend, hating her so much in this moment, even though she wasn't the one in the wrong. My temples started beading with sweat as I shut my eyes and focused on the tiny thrum of power inside me. The power that nearly killed me if I dared to try and access it.

Blinding pain ignited behind my eyes as I willed my white flames to crackle over my skin. They were small and pitiful, not even powerful enough to burn away the vines, yet my nose instantly gushed blood.

Natalia yelped, startling me, and in the same instant, she flew off my bed, crashing horribly into the wall and crumpling to the floor, unconscious.

I gasped in shock and horror, shooting to the edge of my bed just as Solaris Adder appeared in a whirl of shadows.

I froze.

He loomed over me, hands folded behind his back. Silver eyes impaled me. He wore a new long dark jacket with ornate silver buttons and polished boots, having no business looking so fucking bewitching.

His gaze slid from my face down to my cuffed wrists. "How wonderful to find you like this, Firefly. I quite enjoy you all tied up on your bed. Is this our thing now?" He reached out with one hand, his long silver-ringed finger brushing the skin under my nose, wiping away the blood.

"You—!" I snarled but my words cut off as he flicked his wrist and the vines wrapped around my flesh disintegrated.

"You can utter your death threats later," he said dismissively. "Get dressed."

"Excuse me?"

"You and I are going out. We have much to discuss."

I blinked, miffed. A beat of silence passed between us. "Are you on glue? I'm not going anywhere with you. You just assaulted my best friend!"

Solaris didn't even glance at Natalia's unconscious body on the floor. "I saved you. She was about to find out the truth. If you insist on being difficult, I will leash you up and pull you along like a dog." A coldness touched my throat and to my horror, I realized it was a shadow coiling around my neck like a collar. "Or you can come willingly."

"I know who you are." I ground out.

"I'm aware," he replied lightly, banishing the shadow at my throat. "I'm also aware you didn't tell that crustacean Aries Vanderbilt anything despite the way he tortured you." Solaris's bright eyes darkened as his attention skimmed over the electrical burns covering my skin. If I didn't know any better, I'd think the wounds enraged him, the way he seemed to clench his jaw as he assessed the damage. Probably just because these were wounds he didn't cause himself. I tightened my silk housecoat over my throat, trying to hide. "For that, I have decided to offer your power back ahead of schedule."

I felt my face pale as it dropped. My lips parted, though no air escaped through them. I stared up at him, hating the vulnerability I sensed crawling across my expression.

His lips twitched into a grin. "Now, be a good girl and get dressed. Wear something jaw-dropping."

"You are fucking psychotic."

He shrugged. "*Stand up.*"

Like an obedient soldier, I rose to my feet without meaning to. Compulsion! I'd learned how to shield Compulsion within my first week of attending Luna and now it worked effortlessly on me as if I were mortal. I really, really hated this no-magic thing.

"*Don't move. Don't argue,*" Solaris commanded, and I stilled into place like a porcelain doll, lips clamped shut. My heart thundered erratically as he brought his hand up, peeling the silken fabric away from my throat and shoulders, brushing his fingers lightly along my tender skin, summoning goosebumps. His eyes shone with unreadable emotions as he caressed my wounds, healing my burns. My basic instincts screamed at me to fight back. I was too proud for this. But no matter how wild and potent my primal instincts were, the Compulsion kept me in chains.

His cool, healing touch felt...exquisite. A truth I'd take to the grave.

"There," he murmured as he finished. "Good as new."

He leaned back a little to get a better look at his work. His eyes darted side to side and his throat worked in a way that told me he was nervous. Perhaps because the last time he was this close to me, I broke his nose. He was safe this time, though, keeping me under Compulsion. Rendering me a statue as his eyes roved over my skin, moving up to my face. He pulled his bottom lip between his teeth, an idea lighting behind his eyes. "You should look your best tonight," he muttered, sounding more like he was talking to himself.

He leaned in—Goddess, this psychopath leaned in as if...as if he meant to kiss me! I couldn't move, but internally I was writhing and fighting. I watched in horror as his mouth moved in on mine. My head spun like crazy, my heart morphing into a large bird desperately trying to escape the cage of my ribs. He paused, his face only an inch from mine.

"*Part your lips.*"

I did. *Fuck my life.*

His magic thrummed in the air, shadows wafting around us enticingly. The shadows...they called to me. In a way I couldn't explain or make sense of it. The pull was even more magnetic than that of water.

His magic ignited something deep in my soul, even in my powerless state. I couldn't help the way my breathing labored, the way my eyelids half shut as he closed in on me.

Solaris brought his lips to mine. I felt like I was going to pass out. He paused a hair away from my mouth. Confusion, along with a plethora of other feelings I was too ashamed to acknowledge, swam through my veins as he stopped right before our mouths met.

He didn't kiss me. He *breathed* into me.

I gasped, hot energy surging through my veins instantly, lighting me up like a Christmas tree. My skin went from pale to deep olive. I could feel the life force scorching through my body once more.

AS IF he possesses the Breath of Life! Goddess, why are you cruel?

I couldn't help but tremble at the profundity. The Breath of Life could raise the dead. Heal the sick. It was a rare, highly benevolent power that very few Celestials possessed. The fact that this creature before me possessed it made me question my entire reality.

"Better than a glamour spell," he whispered as he stepped back. He grabbed my shoulders and whirled me to face the mirror.

I looked...stunning. Vibrant, alive, powerful. Better than a glamour spell, indeed.

Not to mention the way we looked standing together like this. Him at my back, looming behind me like the shadow he was. My stomach pooled with a dishonorable heat. Solaris moved away, going to stand by the window, his back to me. "*Get dressed.*"

CHAPTER 12
THE SERPENT'S WOOD

EMILIA

The tour of the Academy grounds was *amazing*. I could hardly grasp the depth of the magic. Such a vast property concealed by a Veil, hidden in the hills. It didn't feel like LA here though. It felt as if we were thousands of miles away from civilization, thriving in our own realm of enchantment. In a way, that was true.

The tall, medieval castle that was Luna Academy rose high and triumphant, watching over the land which it inhabited. Crystal towers were planted here and there, standing tall, catching the sunlight as they beamed and sizzled with energy. They helped us channel our magic, as well as powering our technology. Lush, green grass lined with cobblestone paths, floating lanterns, and ornate trees led you to the Elemental Sphere, which paralleled the Sacred Temple where the Priestesses stayed.

The Temple was made of stone, with high pillars and pointed turrets. Inside, the Eternal Flame blazed in the center of the stone floor. A ginormous stone statue of the triple Goddess loomed on the back wall, guarding the flame, each of her three faces left blank. The magical fire needed no wood or fuel, it rose from the ground and remained self-sustaining.

The Stone Gardens were my favorite place so far. They seemed to go on forever, different winding paths taking you this way and that. Every plant, flower, ornate tree, and shrub existed here. Statues of goddesses and dragons watched over us as we meandered through. The Luminary said that at night, many of these plants emitted a Celestial glow. She led us through the gardens until we reached the pond in the middle, which she referred to as the Reflection Pool.

The Water Priestess, Adria, stood waiting by the water. She smiled in greeting and beckoned all of us girls over to her.

"It is time for you first years to learn your Star Lineage!" Adria informed us proudly. "To discover your Celestial ancestry, and which star systems your soul originates from. Come, come, girls! Close to the water's edge."

We listened, approaching the edge of the water, peering over to see our reflections in the clear pool. Koi fish swam below the surface, making some girls point and squeal.

Priestess Adria pulled a small silver blade out of her robe. "To learn your Star Lineage, you must use this blade to draw blood from your left hand and let the blood drip into the Reflection Pool. Like reading tea leaves, I will then interpret your blood in the water and tell you your Lineage."

Destiny and I shared a wide-eyed glance. I'd never done blood magic before.

"What's the difference between our Star Lineage and our zodiac sign?" a girl asked, a murmur of agreeing echoes rippling through the group.

"Why, what a wonderful question!" The Priestess beamed. "Your zodiac sign is the cosmic archetype you take on during this life. So, sort of like an energetic uniform your soul puts on when you incarnate here. Your Star Lineage, however, is the Celestial energies you naturally carry in your soul. It's the true essence of who you are and where you came from. You see, Earth is a young planet. She is still evolving, and Celestials are seeded here to anchor higher cosmic frequencies from solar systems and constellations that are already spiritually evolved. Each of us is unique. For example, my soul carries energies from the Pleiades, as well as Sirius, and Eridanus."

Wow.

I wondered, almost nervously, where this curious soul of mine had come from.

"Priestess?" Another girl spoke up, a little nervously. "Since we now go by a different astrology system...with thirteen signs...does that mean the one we used before is false?"

Again, Priestess Adria seemed enthralled with the question. "Well, pop culture has sure done a number on the tropical system. But no, I would not say it is *false*." She held out her hands and summoned two zodiac wheels made of water. One slightly bigger than the other, and it spun faster. The one with thirteen signs. "Think of them as mirrors," the Priestess said. "One reflection is slightly more...developed than the other."

Destiny and I shared a glance. I didn't really get it, but I was intrigued.

"Now! Back to Star Lineages. Emilia Morningstar, would you like to go first?" the Priestess asked me, smiling.

I swallowed, a little shocked to be singled out. I cleared my throat and nodded. "Sure."

Adria passed me the blade. I stared at it for a moment, attempting to build up the courage to cut myself with it.

"Just slide it along your left palm and hold your hand over the water," the Priestess urged.

"Okay," I murmured. After a moment of preparing myself, I did just that. It stung and I winced. Blood flowed immediately from the slice over my palm. I held my hand out over the Reflection Pool and let the blood drop into the water, watching the strange patterns and formations it made as it dispersed.

All the girls huddled around and watched while Adria interpreted my blood in the water.

"Oh my," Adria breathed. "Different than I expected..."

My heart raced as I waited for her to disclose more. The Priestess stared hard at the water, seeing things we could not.

"Your sister and mother both originate from the constellation of Draco, with soul ties to Venus as well... But you... Your dominant origin is the constellation Lyra... Most notably, the Vega star. Oh, how enticing! Yes... You are a Lyran starseed, through and through. Lyrans are ascended feline beings, meaning you have a cat-like nature about you. This makes you emotionally strong but misunderstood. You are curious yet serious and born to walk your own path. You do have Venusian energy within you too, Miss Morningstar, but your strongest Lineage is of Lyra. Ah... How interesting..."

I shouldn't have been surprised I had a different Star Lineage than my mother and sister. But still...much like the blade on my palm, it stung.

I stepped back and let the rest of the girls learn their Lineage.

Destiny went after me, and it sure did seem like she had more in common with my family than I did. Her dominant constellation was Draco, with ties to Orion and the Serpens star. I smiled when she turned to gauge my reaction, hoping it was convincing enough.

After every girl had their blood interpreted by the Water Priestess, the Luminary led us out of the gardens.

Behind the Elemental Sphere and the Sacred Temple was a cluster of giant oak trees known as the Serpent's Wood, where we headed now.

"The Divine Feminine needs the forest," the Luminary chimed, leading the way as all of us first years followed her diligently. "There is one vital reason why this Academy is in Los Angeles rather than somewhere far off in the mountains, hidden in nature. Does anyone know why?"

Destiny piped up right away. "LA is built on the most ancient, powerful ley lines that feed our magic."

"Right," the Luminary beamed. She wore her flowing golden robes that swished and glowed under the sunlight. Her long platinum hair fell down her back like a stream of sunlight. She stopped walking, turning to us on the cobblestone path with the backdrop of trees making her look even more mythic. "And what is another word for ley lines?"

"Dragon lines?" I answered hopefully.

"Yes. Once, long ago, dragons were our most powerful allies. Benevolent sages that bonded with us on a soul level and assisted us in our journey of evolution. Though not all bloodlines were permitted the gift of being trusted enough to mount these creatures. The Morningstars are the last living lineage of dragon riders. Emilia here is the descendant of them. Does anyone know what happened to the dragons?"

I swallowed, my blood pumping something fierce. Nyx and I hardly knew any details about our bloodline. We were famous, in a way, but entirely enigmatic. Most of our family records were destroyed in the Burning Times, though the tales of our glory still existed as campfire or bedtime stories. My mother would sometimes tell us about our ancestor, Alexandria Morningstar, who was supposedly a powerful and beloved queen in the Old World.

Sometimes, I was quite sure the reason my mother was so cruel and bitter was because of the fall of our bloodline. We were once queens and dragon riders, but we lost all of that to the Age of Amnesia. My mother would never get over Sophia losing the Divine Rite to Aries Vanderbilt.

The Luminary waited for me to answer her question, but I had nothing.

"The dragons went extinct," a cute girl with dark hair sheepishly offered.

"Not exactly," the Luminary sighed. "When the mortals began turning against our kind, the dragons tried to intervene to keep the peace and order. Humanity felt threatened by these magical creatures. They didn't understand them. They feared them. And so, they did what mortals always do when they fear something—they sought to eradicate them. Their churches demonized the dragons and cast a hunt against them, rewarding warriors who slayed them. The dragons were no longer safe here, and so, many of them left this realm and returned to the higher dimensions."

"Many of them, Luminary?" Destiny peeped. "As in, some of them stayed?"

The Luminary smiled knowingly. "One day, the dragons will return and bring back that balance and harmony once more. Though, I'm afraid that day is far off."

My heart raced. Instinctively, I looked up to the sky, imagining what it would look like to see it alive with the flight of dragons.

"In the last couple of decades, mortal technology has grown into a threat against magic," the Luminary said. "They have wrapped the earth in an artificial energy field with all their cell towers and their satellites. All these radio waves interfere with the natural energy waves of the earth, from which we draw power. Eventually, this city will no longer support our existence."

"Why don't we just destroy all the mortal technology?" Destiny wondered.

"The treaty made between our kind and theirs prevents us from disrupting their affairs. We must allow it to play out. It is all finite, and will not sustain itself long and as Celestials, we will be here to rebuild from the fallout. Now, come along, ladies." The Luminary turned and continued toward the line of trees. "The Serpent's Wood may be but a small cluster of trees, but inside, it holds a great and wondrous secret."

We followed her until the rising oak trees nearly swallowed us whole. Luminary turned back to us and said, "Take off your shoes."

Without question, we did. There were thirteen first years, which apparently was a lot. I liked that. Thirteen. The Goddess' number. We obeyed our Luminary and kicked off our shoes and sandals, following her into the Serpent's Wood barefoot.

Being enclosed in trees always brought me peace. The rough, soil floor felt like home. I breathed deeply, inhaling the earthy scent, letting it fill my being.

The Luminary led us to a grassy knoll. A round hill that protruded out of the otherwise flat ground. As we rounded it, my breath hitched. A door nestled into the rising knoll, radiating an unseen thrum of power. We all murmured in surprise and wonder.

The Luminary waved her hand, urging the heavy wooden door open. It groaned in slight protest but widened for her, revealing nothing but darkness behind it. "This is the fairy door. Who will be brave enough to go first?"

A beat of silence passed.

"I will," Destiny announced boldly, moving forward.

The Luminary grinned, her turquoise eyes bright. "I knew it." She gestured encouragingly toward the mysterious door, her gold robe shimmering with the movement.

I swallowed hard, watching my new friend strut towards the dark entrance. She looked back at me, smirking mischievously. "See you on the other side."

My heart sped up as she turned and walked through, disappearing instantly. The way the Luminary's eyes fell on me expectantly was not lost on me.

Screw it. I moved forward, heart in my throat, laughing nervously as I stood before the opening. I couldn't see a damn thing beyond the door. Only darkness. Unsettling, but I trusted the Luminary didn't bring us out here to do anything nefarious. I had faith. So, I stepped through the threshold and let the shadows gobble me up.

CHAPTER 13

RAGE WITHOUT FIRE

NYX

"You've got to be fucking kidding me," I said as a gust of shadows dropped me and my torturer off in front of a trendy restaurant in downtown LA.

Solaris Adder grinned at me in a way that made my stomach fall like when you hit the drop of a rollercoaster. The city streets were lit up and bustling, music, and chatter harassing my senses. Los Angelians, as always, remained too self-absorbed to notice the magic occurring around them. We appeared in a whirlwind of shadows, and no one blinked an eye, despite the sidewalk being packed.

I mean, really? I expected him to take me to some haunted house or an insidious underground cave or perhaps another dimension altogether. I was not expecting to emerge outside of a mortal bar & grill with a Rihanna song blasting from inside.

He offered his hand out to me to escort me into the restaurant. I grimaced and folded my arms over my chest.

"I could continue to Compel you," he reminded me lightly.

I rolled my eyes. "What are we doing here?"

"We're going to have a conversation. I decided it would be best if we are in a mortal, public setting."

I scowled at the enigmatic man who lived to ruin me.

He wasn't bothered by my attitude in the least. He seemed to thoroughly enjoy it. Same as he clearly enjoyed my outfit. I thought I was being clever and defiant when I chose this fit. He had Compelled me to wear something jaw-dropping, so I chose my edgiest black training leathers with combat boots. The shorts did little to hide anything, putting my legs on full show, the leather crop top flaunting my toned midriff. I tied my hair back in a sleek, slasher ponytail, resembling Tomb Raider rather than someone on a dinner date.

If I'd had my way, I would have dressed in a garbage bag and rubbed mud on my face.

Solaris put a hand on my back to lead me inside. My skin erupted with ice and fire. With the last, pitiful morsel of sovereignty I had, I swatted him away with a feral hiss. "Don't touch me."

He chuckled, unoffended, and together we entered the establishment. The music was loud, the lights low, tables packed. I should have been scouring the place for exit points, thinking about the right time to make a run for it. I couldn't deny it, though, something told me to stay put. Perhaps it was just a morbid sense of curiosity, but part of me wanted to have this 'conversation.' Solaris Adder was imprisoned for nearly a century, and apparently, I had freed him. I had some questions.

A gorgeous blonde hostess awaited us inside, leading us promptly to a private table in the back. She couldn't hide the bewilderment on her face when she noticed the way we were dressed. Solaris and his warlock jacket, me in skimpy combat leathers. Her expression was comical.

"Are you guys in that movie they're filming down the street?" she asked, smiling at us with her too-white teeth.

"Yup," I answered brightly. "He plays the insidious villain and I'm the fearless heroine who gets to kill him in the end."

"Oh," she replied, laughing a little nervously. "Sounds cool. Can I bring you something to drink?"

"I'll have a bottle of the most expensive wine you have, please," I chirped.

Solaris waved her off. "Nothing for me."

The hostess gave us a strange look before heading away to fetch the alcohol I desperately needed if I was going to make it through this Goddess-forsaken affair.

A pregnant silence passed between us. My clothes felt too tight, my lungs too tight, and the pressure between my eyes too tight. Being in this close of quarters, with the low lights and the enticing music playing in the background... Ugh. I tried not to feel totally and completely abandoned by the Goddess.

"Give me my magic back, you psycho." Worth a shot, right?

"From what I saw back in your room tonight, you do have power."

I glared flatly at him. "You know what I fucking mean. I'd like to be able to do magic without having a brain hemorrhage."

He smirked. "You'll have your full power back, so long as you agree to my terms and conditions, Firefly."

"Your *terms and conditions*?" I spat, rolling my eyes into another dimension. "What are you, a software update?"

The hostess returned with my wine, pouring me a glass, and leaving the bottle. "Your waitress will be right with you," she promised before she turned away.

Solaris reached out and grabbed her wrist. The girl and I both jumped at his unexpected gesture. She looked down at him in confusion and his metallic eyes held her in place as he commanded, "*Tell the waitress to stay away. We need privacy.*"

With a blank stare, the hostess nodded, turned, and left me here with him.

"This is so fucked up," I muttered. I took a greedy slam of the dark red liquid, praying for it to take a bit of the edge off.

"Why didn't you tell Aries what you know?" Solaris asked, genuinely curious.

I narrowed my eyes. The way he addressed him by his first name and not as High Lord was not lost on me. "Not because I'm loyal to you. I hope they catch your ass with a giant net and toss you back into your musty-ass prison realm ASAP. I didn't tell Aries anything because I'm not a snitch. I don't owe him or the High Council shit."

His brows raised slightly at that. He said nothing.

"He told me you were imprisoned in that shadow realm and that I released you. How the hell does that work?"

Even though the music boomed through heavy bass speakers, his silence was deafening. The way he looked at me made me feel as though I would melt into a puddle of nothingness. Those fucking eyes. So clear and bright, an impossible shade of silver, yet possessing unimaginable darkness. His irises were like silver snakes coiling around the black void of his large pupils. I'd never seen eyes like that, not even in the most powerful sects of Celestials. Ouroboros embodied. I couldn't fathom it.

"Did you just bring me here to stare at me, or...?"

Solaris scoffed; his hands folded under the table as he leaned in slightly. "I could see you in the shadows."

A coldness slithered down my spine as it instinctively stiffened, those words making my arm hairs rise on edge for reasons unknown to me. "What?"

"For decades I roamed through that realm of nothingness. Until one day I saw a light. A small, flickering light in the distance. It took eons to reach the light. I began to think I'd never catch up to it. But eventually, I did... And when I did, I realized the light was a girl. A small, furious girl whose emotional outburst birthed fire and destruction. It was fleeting. You ebbed in and out. But you were there—a part of you, anyway. That was just the first time. You were only a child, not yet Emerged. I saw you countless times after that."

My mouth had gone dry, my hand trembling while I gripped my wine glass as if it could steady me. "That doesn't make any sense."

"Sure, it does," Solaris cut back. "The brighter the light, the darker the shadow."

I shook my head while my brain failed to compute. "Goddess, you are cliche." I rubbed my temples, trying to process. "No... What you're saying is impossible. I'd never been in the shadows before the night you Astral Snatched me off the beach."

"Maybe you never consciously perceived it, but you were there. I watched you erupt with ridiculous power countless times. Such a tiny thing, even all grown up like you are now. Each time you expressed the full capacity of your magic, a fragment of your soul manifested in the shadows. Soon, I started seeing you even when you weren't using magic. You became this...bridge. A bridge back into the living world."

"This is a load of bullshit," I growled, hating the way my body was lighting up with all kinds of chills and electrical surges.

His words were resonating deep inside me, and I could not understand why. I clung to denial as if my life depended on it.

"You were trapped because you're an evil prick who enjoys a good, bloody massacre and somehow you managed to snatch me into your jail cell and use my power to break you out. And as if that wasn't enough! You then steal my magic like the heinous criminal you are and now you have me forced to sit here and listen to you talk some bullshit!"

"It must be so infuriating to feel rage without your fire, hmm?" he mused tantalizingly, grinning as he took in the heat of my cheeks and the grit of my jaw. "You can think whatever you want of me, Firefly. It doesn't matter. What matters is, a part of your power linked you with my shadows and so, you bridged me back onto this plane. You drank witches vodka, which was invented by diviners who used it to transcend the physical realm and talk to spirits. With that in your system, your astral body manifested wholly in the shadows. I managed to anchor you there and talk to you. It was only a guess that your power would destroy the wards and set me free. It worked, and here we are. Now, we have more important matters to discuss."

I folded my arms across my chest, leaning back in my chair. "Like how you're going to be a good little psycho and give me my magic back out of the kindness of your tar-black heart?"

"I know you secretly despise the Society and the way it operates." Solaris deadpanned, silver fire dancing in his eyes. "And I know you enjoy the mortal realm." He waved a hand, gesturing at the restaurant and all its patrons around us. I had always enjoyed the mortal realm, and mortals themselves could be pretty badass when they had a rebellious spirit. He seemed to enjoy it himself. The lights, the music, the laughter. "You want to merge the two again. Go back to what it was before the Age of Amnesia. To bring back the glory from before the worlds were split, back when your bloodline was royalty."

The slow, knock-knock beat of my heart thudded at the back of my throat. Instead of denying the truth, I remained silent.

"I know something else about you," he continued wryly. "You want to be queen. As your ancestors were."

"I am queen."

"Of a school," he scoffed indignantly. "And who knows how long that will last now that Venus St. Claire has transferred to Luna." I blanched and he noticed. Dammit. "Even if you did manage to keep your position, what will happen after you graduate and become Embodied along with the rest of your classmates? Will they still follow you?"

"What's the point of all this psychobabble?" I hissed.

"Aside from sharing a common goal, you and I also share a common enemy," he replied, and I rolled my eyes.

"*You* are my enemy."

"Am I?"

"You tricked me into breaking you out of your mystical prison and then to say thanks, you stole my magic. Not to mention how you snuck into my dorm like some stalker and tied me up with your creepy shadows. Or how you Compelled me to get dressed in front of you and forced me to come here. Yeah, I think you're my enemy. You'll have to get in the back of the line, though."

"Because you already have a plethora of enemies," he pointed out as if it should have meant something grave to me.

I shrugged. "People love me or hate me, there's usually no in-between."

"Meaning many of them will align with Venus St. Claire just to spite you. Many of them are dying to see your downfall."

"I can fight my own battles, thanks."

"Can you?" he quipped, grinning blackly. "With no magic?"

I sucked in a sharp breath, willing myself to remain calm, even though I wanted to grab the bottle of wine and smash it over his arrogant head. "That's the part I don't understand. Not only were you imprisoned in those shadows for over a century, but before that, you were confined in an underground base. Against your will. And now that you've finally broken free—you come after *me*. Someone who has nothing to do with anything that happened to you. I don't understand. Don't you have someone more important to torment?"

He just stared at me, the ghost of a smile whispering over his lips. "You'd think so, wouldn't you?"

This. Motherfucker.

"And those objects you told me about. Like the one you stole my magic with. You said Celestial children forged those. I'm guessing you forged the dragonglass medallion?"

"I did, yes."

A straight answer. Wow.

"What else did you create?"

He grinned. "Wouldn't you love to know? Unfortunately, we aren't here to play twenty questions. We are here to strike a deal."

I released an aggravated sigh. "Fine. Just get to the bloody point then, Solaris Adder. What do you want from me? I mean, you've gone to great lengths to get me in your claws so tell me what it is you really want." I brought the wine glass to my lips, knowing damn well I should have been keeping a clear head, but this man drove me to drink.

"Your allegiance."

I spat the wine out, choking ineptly as he remained unfazed, watching me. "Excuse me?" I managed to say between coughs. The people sitting at the tables near us all turned to glare at me.

"I want you to pledge your allegiance to me. Simple as that. Once you do, I shall return your magic to you."

He was dead serious.

I sat up straight, looking him in the eye, searching for...I had no clue what I was searching for. Something. Something to make this all make sense.

"You spent a lot of time alone in the dark and it shows," I muttered dryly as I blotted my chin with the napkin and tried to tame my thrashing heart. "Why would I ever *pledge my allegiance* to *you*?"

"Because a war is coming, and you strike me as the kind of girl who wants to be on the winning side."

"A war?"

"Yes, Firefly. A war. You might hate me right now but one day you will realize this was necessary. You needed this. You would have run yourself into the ground and gone out in a blaze of premature glory before you ever reached the full potential of your magic. It would have been the world's biggest waste. One day, you'll thank me. You and I are not so different from each other, but we are entirely different from the rest of our kind. We both want to remake the world. Together, we will—"

"*Together?*" I spat, fury rising like bile up my throat. "I've heard enough." I pushed back out of my seat, rising to my feet. I could hardly breathe or think. I needed to get out of here. Away from him. "I don't know what they did to you down in the bunker you were raised in but whatever happened seriously fucked you up. To think I would ever, EVER, pledge my allegiance to you—I mean, come on, that sounds so fucking pretentious, I can't even. You're insane. I'd rather live my life as a mortal than swear loyalty to you."

He stared up at me, his expression unreadable.

"We're done here," I snarled.

While I turned harshly on my heel to leave, the world went dark. Just like the night on the beach. Reality vanished. All the sounds and lights and people and voices—gone. Like someone pulled the plug on the entire universe. I sucked in a sharp breath and when I blew it out, it puffed before me in a thick, white cloud. The frigid air wrapped around me in the most unsettling greeting.

No, no, no, no...not back here. No.

Something cool wrapped around my wrist and jerked me around. Solaris towered over me, his shadows binding my wrists behind my back. I struggled against them, but it was no use. His eyes shone in the darkness, planting me in place as I glared up at him defiantly.

"I thought my magic destroyed this place," I ground out, wishing my chest would stop rising and falling and giving me away.

"You were right, before." He spoke low, his voice husky. "I did spend a lot of time alone in the dark. So long that the darkness became mine." He brought his hand up, shadows writhing between his fingers.

"Your firelight burned me free, and for that, I will be eternally grateful. So, I'll grant you this one mercy. Three days to decide if you want your power back or not. There is only one way to get it, and I have disclosed my terms already. If you choose to be my enemy, so be it. But soon you will see it's pointless to stand against me. The next time we speak, I won't take your disrespect so lightly."

I bared my teeth, my pulse going wild. "I'll tell my closest girls and we will find a way to get my magic back—"

"You might be able to figure it out eventually," he cut me off casually, a smug grin tugging at his full lips. "If you had time on your side. Which you don't. When the three days are up, your power will either be transferred back into you... Or into the shadows. Where it will be gone forever. Not just gone but erased. To have never existed. It's all up to you."

I shook my head, tears burning the backs of my eyes. "No." I kept shaking my head. "You can't do this."

"Oh, Firefly, I can. You can't even begin to fathom the true devastation I'm capable of, but soon you will know. The power of shadows is far more personal than you could imagine. To be haunted by your own ghosts is the most merciless of fates, for the demons that belong to us are the ones that will eat us alive."

"You're insane."

"Maybe so. It's my wish to see you in your full glory, but I can't have that be the case if you are to stand against me. So, you must decide."

A sick, deranged laugh tumbled from my lips. "I've already decided. I'll be mortal. I'll be a cutthroat rock n' roll mortal and I'll enjoy my life of freedom away from all this bullshit. Fuck you. Fuck the Celestial Society."

He smiled, eyes alight with marvel. "There it is. Our common enemy."

My stomach leapt.

"They've hidden the truth from you. On purpose. A true enemy is rising all around us, and they know of it. Eventually, they plan on having you fight it. You can fight for them, Firefly. Or you can fight for the truth."

We stared at each other with loaded gazes, a thousand unsaid words riding the breath through my lips. Alone in the endless darkness, my demise was given the form of a cunning man with silver eyes. I saw my life flash across the smooth planes of his face. Who was he really? How could someone turn the world off as if it'd never been there in the first place? How could someone look so young and ancient at the same time?

How could he speak to me so smoothly as he plucked all my petals and turned me into nothing?

"Three days, Firefly. Choose wisely. You say you'll enjoy a life of freedom but there is no freedom without magic. To be mortal is to be in chains."

I opened my mouth to counter, but he flicked his wrist, and the shadows dropped me off back in my room.

CHAPTER 14

FORBIDDEN

EMILIA

T he strangest sensation of falling hit my guts but before I could even gasp, a new world materialized into view.

My skin prickled with pins and needles. I blinked incessantly, taking in the new ambiance.

Destiny frolicked through the trees, giggling with glee.

All I saw was green.

Dense, moist, vibrant earth surrounded me at every angle, a light mist floating throughout. Trees like emerald towers rose to the sky, their trunks thicker than cars. I knew right away we weren't in California anymore. We were deep, deep, deep in the most luscious forest I'd ever seen.

I ran forward to explore with Destiny. The soft, mossy ground beneath the soles of my feet felt like walking on a damn cloud.

Soon, more girls spilled through the door which disappeared into a massive tree when the Luminary came through.

"What is this place!" a girl with blonde hair gasped wistfully.

"An old-growth forest in British Columbia," the Luminary replied. "As I said before, the Divine Feminine needs the forest. Therefore, the Priestesses and I created a doorway here. Our Academy may be built over a powerful ley line, but the forest holds primordial magic on its own, with or without ley lines streaming under it."

That rang true. As I leaned against a gigantic evergreen tree, I sensed the etheric power coursing behind the bark. Ancient wisdom resided here.

"As beautiful as it is, we did not come to merely frolic. You have an important task to complete today before you can return to the Academy. Listen closely."

Destiny and I shared an intrigued look before our focus fell on the Luminary.

"Hidden along this vast forest floor is a rare, magical fungus called witches cauldron. It looks exactly as described. A round, brown base with a black center, making it identical to a cauldron. You will pair up into teams of two."

Destiny's fingers instinctively locked with mine. "Partner?"

"Of course," I chimed back, grinning.

"There's thirteen of you, so one group will have to be of three. Assemble yourselves now and get started. The door will not appear for you until you find a witches cauldron." The Luminary spoke gravely, though her eyes stayed light.

"So, we could potentially be here forever if we don't find one?" a dark-haired girl squeaked. Shit, I'd have to start learning names soon.

The Luminary shrugged. "Relax your senses and let your intuition guide you. It is your divine birthright as female Celestials to communicate with the spirits of the forest. Hear their whispers."

Destiny and I began our search as the other girls paired off. Scouring the forest floor was second nature to me. Mom raised us in a small, mountainous town with woods very similar to this. While Nyx had been busy running with all the delinquents, starting fires in junkyards or whatever the hell they did, I kept mostly to myself, spending time in the trees of our backyard. Until last year, when Michael... *No, don't go there. Focus. Witches cauldron.*

My flesh tingled with memories despite my effort.

He was just so...ugh. Different. Interesting. Cute. That curly brown hair fell over his forehead, framing his deep brown eyes. The full lips he always had a cigarette between. The lip ring he chewed on when he was lost in thought. The dimple that appeared on his left cheek when he smiled. The way he always talked about his vivid dreams, discussing them as if they were real.

No. Don't think of him.

But I couldn't help it. Something about the deep forest brought out the truth in me.

He tried to kiss me once. I ran away. Ran. Away.

Of course, it was never the same between us after that, but he never seemed to hold it against me. He was just so—

"Whoa," Destiny blurted, startling me from my reverie. "What are you thinking about?"

"Nothing," I answered too quickly.

"Girl. Your eyes were all hooded, lashes fluttering while you bit your damn lip. Spill! Who is he?"

Was I that transparent?

I sighed heavily as we walked through the thick brush. "His name's Michael. He's mortal. It's hopeless."

"Forbidden love," Destiny giggled. "Sounds hot."

I swallowed, eyes downcast. "It's not. He'll forget about me after I Emerge. If he hasn't already."

Destiny put a warm hand on my shoulder. "My granny always said love is the most powerful force in existence and it trumps all. She said in the end, those who are meant to be together will always find a way to defy cruel fates."

"It's not love, though," I argued sadly. "We weren't together or anything. He just... We were... I don't know. Nothing. It's done now, and it never even started."

"Doesn't sound done to me."

"Even if it weren't, my mother would kill me. I could never go down that road. She said the reason my Aunt Sophia lost the Divine Rite was because she was in love with a mortal. Not focused on her divine path."

Destiny's brows shot up. "Sophia Morningstar was in love with a *mortal*?"

"Yup," I replied, gazing off into the forest, feeling defeated.

"Well, Jedidiah Stone seemed to take an interest in you in the Sphere. Maybe he can be your sexy, magical rebound."

"No!" I wailed, hand flying to my heart. "That asshole? No way. He was only all over me to piss off Nyx and it freaking worked. I will be steering clear of him, and his Mole Boy friends. Hey—speaking of Jedidiah. Was it true what he said to me in the Sphere? Did he bury Nyx underground?"

"Yes," Destiny answered, nodding her head. "Most Celestials aren't allowed blackmirrors before they Emerge, but my mom gave me one the year I turned thirteen. I've been keeping up with all the Celestial gossip blogs since then. Last year, at a bonfire party, your sister started messing with Jedidiah and he split the earth open under her, kind of like what he did to her that night on the beach. Only this time, he sealed the ground back over her. It was a huge scene—everyone was freaking out. Then Nyx burst through the surface of the dirt with her hands flaming! It was insane! She was famous after that."

My brows had risen into my hairline halfway through her story. "Jesus Christ," I muttered, though I shouldn't have been surprised.

"Yeah, she literally clawed her way up from Hell," Destiny laughed. "Your sister is iconic, dude. Alright, let's find these damn mushrooms."

Destiny and I started following a stream that cut through the brush. We followed the twinkling vein of gurgling water, searching the ground vigorously. Destiny was telling me about her life growing up. She sounded a lot like Nyx, though I didn't bother pointing that out. She was raised in a small town outside of Seattle and all her mortal friends were badasses who enjoyed setting teacher's desks on fire and jumping cars in coal pits. It made sense, especially with the way she carried herself. Her shaved head, big hoops, thick eyeliner, the whole I-don't-give-a-shit-what-you-think-of-me demeanour. She had three serious boyfriends throughout high school but was ready to "upgrade to some magical D".

"Oh, shit, look! A waterfall!" Destiny pointed excitedly through the woods. Sure enough, the quaint stream we'd set out to follow evolved into a thicker torrent that funnelled into a wide swimming hole with a waterfall hurling over a set of rocky bluffs. She wiggled her brows at me. "Care for a swim?"

I laughed nervously. "We're supposed to be looking for—"

"I know what we're supposed to be doing. But Emilia! We just traveled through a magical door that spat us out a thousand miles away from the Academy. We're in the middle of the oldest, densest woods and we just found a freaking waterfall swimming hole! Seize the moment and all that..."

I sucked in a sharp breath, hiking over the thick ferns. "Okay."

She squealed and clapped before taking off like a bullet through the trees.

I followed Destiny to the clearing of the swimming hole, wondering why she stopped dead in her tracks as she reached the tree line.

"What is it?" I murmured, coming to stand beside her. I followed where her eyes went, and my heart sank into the furthest depths of my stomach.

Down at the water's edge, sitting crumpled up on the pebbled little beach, was Nyx. What the—?

She was *sobbing*.

Rough, gut-wrenching sobs tore out of her without mercy. The sounds were devoured by the raging waterfall. She clung her knees to her chest, her face red and stained with tears. Her silver hair fell all around her like a pale shroud.

"Oh my gosh," Destiny breathed, making a move as if she meant to go to her.

I grabbed her wrist and pulled her back, shaking my head.

Her eyes narrowed in confusion.

"My sister will kill us if we find her like this," I warned honestly, though it brought me physical pain not to go down there right now and wrap her in my arms. "She came out here for solitude. Trust me. If she sees us, we're dead."

"But she looks so—"

"I know," I rasped, gripping her wrist tighter as I pulled her away from the clearing. "But Nyx is a complex creature who sees emotion as a weakness and if she knew someone was watching her... She'd reduce us to ash. Let's just head back. We'll look for the witches' cauldron closer to the door back to the Academy."

"Emilia... She's your sister. She looks like something terrible happened to her."

"Yeah." My heart shattered behind my ribs. "I know. But you don't know her. She won't tell me anything. She doesn't tell anyone anything. Ever since that night on the beach, she's been different." We trudged through the thick, green forest floor. "Maybe... Maybe this emotional purge will be good for her. I'll check on her later tonight. I promise."

Destiny seemed entirely uncomfortable with leaving her like that. I loved her for it but she just didn't understand Nyx Morningstar.

CHAPTER 15
THE BITTER TRUTH
NYX

Venus St. Claire won the fucking Sacred Baton.

Apparently, my being taken away by the High Council was equivalent to forfeiting. Complete and utter bullshit. She paraded around, bragging about how I'd been on my knees before her, bowing to the true queen.

Many girls thought it was cheap. Some even demanded a rematch but that was sore loser behavior. I had to play my cards right.

I had to adapt to my circumstances. Remaining unbothered was key. Venus winning by default was not queenly. She did not beat me fair and square. Enough girls realized that. The split between groups remained even. She had her posse of fourth and fifth years who'd secretly hated my guts for the last year. I had my loyal band of younger girls who looked at me as if I'd birthed the sun itself.

The problem was... Venus had the Baton. It was created to detect deception.

I'd become a living, breathing, walking deception. I had no magic and yet I strutted around the Academy as if I were the most powerful girl here. So far, that strategy worked. My girls followed me, and Venus's girls followed her, but no one baited any conflict between us so I wasn't forced to reveal I had no magic. I anticipated that moment may come, though.

I had two more days to decide what to do about Solaris Adder. Pledge allegiance to him or lose my magic forever.

After spending most of yesterday crying in the forest like some pathetic sissy, today I was back on track, attending classes and bossing up. So far, no one suspected anything. I made it through Divination and Feminine Mysteries, but when it came to Firebending, I skipped. No big deal. Like our Luminary said during the Inauguration Ceremony, Luna Academy was not a daycare. Skipping was my choice.

I used this period to scour the Athena Library, desperately seeking a way out of the current mess I was in.

The library was massive and etheric, four stories high, decked out in golds and browns, the place designed as a freaking labyrinth. Delphyne's logic. *"Knowledge should always be sought by the perceiver, not handed over in alphabetical order."* I guessed I sort of understood the concept but right now it did nothing but set me back and piss me off. We were supposed to use our intuition to guide us to what we needed. I tried, I did—but the ability to slow down and focus escaped me.

"Dammit," I ground out. I stood in a winding aisle of books, heart thumping in my temples. I forced myself to breathe deeply and evenly as my eyelids fluttered shut. *Focus. Focus, dammit.*

An hour later, I found one old leather book that seemed promising. The Dark Art of Siphoning. I sat my ass right down in the aisle, leaning back against the wall of books, and went to town.

I learned a few things. Things that didn't help.

Siphoning was dark, inverted magic and thus, difficult to fight against. The siphoner had their victim by the balls. Solaris possessed my magic and therefore he held a piece of my soul. I wouldn't be able to combat him alone, and the option of telling the girls what happened was not possible. I couldn't. Simple as that. Even if I only confided in Natalia, Faye, and Emilia, that would immediately threaten my position as queen and my entire future as a Celestial. Sure, they were my friends and sisters, but the Celestial dynamic was fixed. If my closest confidants knew I was a moot, powerless shell, my entire foundation would crumble. Natural Law and all that.

I *had* to fight this alone. Even if it meant losing my magic forever. I'd rather disappear into the mortal realm than live for eternity in the Celestial Society having them all know I'd been so easily power drained. I'd be a joke. A nobody.

I shut the book harshly, releasing a groan before tilting my head back and glaring up at the ceiling as if it had personally wronged me.

"Fuck my life," I muttered.

A burst of warm light beside me had me jumping out of my skin. A small dragon made of fire manifested in the aisle just a few feet from me. I stared at it in confusion, looking around to see who was there. I didn't see anyone. The fire dragon hissed and began spitting flames at me.

I screamed, shooting to my feet. "Hey! Who's there? Who's doing this!"

The dragon of fire flapped its flaming, smoking wings and then shot right at me.

I hurled out of the way, another scream escaping my throat. The thing did not relent. I had no choice but to beeline it out of the Athena Library. My heart slammed erratically as I tore down the narrow hallway, knowing the fire creature was right on my heels. Whoever was casting this magic was powerful as hell. I could feel the heat on my back and hear the whoosh of its flaming wings.

"I swear to the Goddess when I find out who's doing this, I will—"

"You'll what, Nyx?"

I stopped short in the mouth of the common room. Priestess Bridget stood there with a gaggle of firelings at her back. She banished the dragon she'd made with her fire magic just before it bulldozed into me.

I stood there under the archway, chest heaving. "What in the seven realms was that for?"

"Why are you skipping out?" Bridget challenged. She wasn't clad in her red robes. No, she was dressed for battle as she always did when teaching Firebending. Tight black leathers and boots, her hair tied back neatly. Her eyes blazed furiously at me. Bridget was always angry, that much I was used to. But something about the way she looked at me now made the hairs on the back of my neck rise.

I shrugged arrogantly, checking my nails. "I had more important business to attend to."

"Is that so?" Bridget cocked a brow. Her nostrils flared then. "It is unlike you to miss Firebending. I can smell your bullshit from a mile away, Miss Morningstar."

I scoffed but said nothing.

"Why didn't you fight off my dragon?" she asked, her voice thick with accusation.

I fought the urge to blanch. "Because I thought maybe it was leading me somewhere important but clearly, I was wrong."

"Lies," chimed a different voice.

Venus St. Claire, followed by her circus of girls, flooded in from outside. Two girls stuck out from her crowd. Bianca Star and Cassiopeia Black. Two fifth-years who had secretly despised me all last year but couldn't do shit about it because they weren't powerful enough. Now they had a new queen to follow, and their cruel intentions stunk up the goddamn room.

Venus twirled the shiny Baton casually, her amber eyes finding me at once. She clicked her tongue and shook her head. "Nyx Morningstar is lying to your face, Priestess."

"I know," Bridget replied, sounding somewhat irritated at the arrival of our Hollywood starlet.

"She's been lying to everyone. Isn't that right?" Venus strolled closer, still twirling the glowing Baton, putting on a show. She eyed me like a predator playing with its prey and every fiber of my being longed to turn her into a pile of ash.

"St. Claire, I can handle my student, thank you," Bridget snapped. The firelings behind her were looking back and forth between the three of us, their eyes wide with anticipation.

"I am the Keeper of the Baton and I have a right to speak the truth," Venus retorted. She wore her red training leathers, looking like a freaking Bond girl as she made her way over to me.

A squeal escaped my throat without my mind's consent as a vine burst from the ground and wrapped around my throat. It squeezed the breath from my lungs as it pulled me down. I was on my knees as Venus stood over me, glaring down through wicked eyes and a grin dripping with malice. I clawed at the thick vine. It was no use. She tightened it mercilessly, looking pleased to see me struggle.

Fuck fuck fuck fuck fuck

Over thirty girls were watching me get dominated. Bianca and Cassiopeia beamed with jubilance. Bridget did nothing. She stared at me incredulously, wondering why the hell I wasn't fighting back.

"I can't tell exactly what she's hiding," Venus announced. "Not even the Baton can sense it. Do you know what that means, girls? Black magic. She's drenched in it."

"You wish," I wheezed.

"Aren't you going to use some of your flashy fire powers to burn your way free?" Venus wondered innocently. "Or...or can you not access your power right now?"

Bridget blanched. A chorus of murmurs rippled through the crowd of girls.

"Something terrible happened to you that night on the beach, didn't it, little fireling?" Venus continued to taunt me, circling me as well. Her vine around my throat remained tight but loose enough for me to breathe weakly. "Perhaps it was your wrath of karma. Something tells me you are unable to call upon your magic. I don't understand why, but can you truly tell me I'm wrong?"

I just scowled at her, refusing to be baited into an argument. Which confused everyone.

"*Tell us what you're hiding,*" Venus spoke the words thick with Compulsion.

No. No, please, Goddess, no.

But I could feel it, the magic taking the reins of my tongue, about to parade the bitter truth to the entire room of girls. I felt myself gearing up to tell them all what happened and how I was now the weakest student at Luna Academy.

Venus's glare brightened as she realized the Compulsion was working. I'd never seen a face I wanted to punch in more. My lips popped open, and the words began flying off my tongue, only to be cut off instantly by a deafening crack of thunder.

The Luminary followed by the rest of the Priestesses appeared in the doorway that led outside. "Everyone in the Sphere—NOW!" Delphyne commanded.

A beat of ominous silence skipped by.

Reluctantly, Venus released me.

I gasped in a breath, hands flying to my throat.

"Get on your feet, Morningstar," Bridget snapped, eyeing me like she didn't know me anymore.

The crowd of girls stared at me a moment longer before filing out of the common room, out toward the Sphere.

I rose to my feet, wishing I'd catch my breath faster. Bridget zeroed in on me, her eyes intense and searching my face like it was the surface of my soul. Perhaps it was. I avoided eye contact with her as I made my way toward the exit.

"Nyx," she called after me.

"Didn't you hear?" I shot back without turning around. "We're wanted in the Sphere. Luminary's orders."

Just as I was about to step through the doorway outside, a wall of fire manifested on the threshold. I stopped short, rolling my eyes. "Seriously?"

Bridget appeared at my side. "What is going on with you? Why don't you feel like you can come to me? To any of us, for that matter?"

"You're not going to give me a ridiculous super-sisterhood speech, are you? Because come on, we all know that's bullshit." I waved a hand, motioning to where I'd just been on my knees on the floor. "This has never been a sisterhood. This is a chicken coop with a ruthless pecking order."

"I'm not talking about your classmates," Bridget replied. "I'm talking about your Priestesses. Why don't you come to us? What do you think we are here for?"

"Nothing's going on," I lied smoothly. "I made a bet with someone that I could go a full twenty-four hours without using magic. If I lose, I'll grow a fox tail that will last a whole moon cycle! Though I'm sure I'd look cute as hell with a tail, I'm a winner by nature. So, I must endure. Plus, screw Venus. I'm not giving her the satisfaction of a fight. She won the Baton like a cheat. Everyone knows the battle wasn't over. I'm going to let her self-implode before I finish the job and wipe the floor with her."

"How easily and elaborately you lie," Bridget breathed, her gaze raking me up and down. "Your stubbornness will be the end of you. You better think hard before pursuing the path you are on. This will be my only warning." The Fire Priestess banished the flames in the doorway and stalked outside, her red ponytail slashing behind her.

My eyes burned. I swallowed hard, tipped my chin up and strutted toward the Sphere.

Inside was set up like a stadium, like the Inauguration. I spotted Emilia next to her hairless friend but chose to go sit with Faye and Natalia and the other second years. As always, I was the last one inside.

The Priestesses stood in the center on the elevated platform, surrounding the Luminary. Delphyne's expression made my skin erupt with goosebumps. I'd never seen her so...serious.

Delphyne looked around, her eyes scanning over each face until she was sure this was everyone. "Something terrible has happened."

Faye, Natalia, and I shared a loaded three-way glance. I narrowed my eyes at Natalia, a silent question, wondering if she'd Seen anything. She shook her head sadly. What was up with that? It seemed like she wasn't Seeing anything lately. Could...could that night on the beach have affected her magic too? She had no problem wielding the earth element, but so far, she hadn't spoken of any premonitions.

"There was an attack on San Gabriel Academy," Delphyne declared, her voice loud and grave.

A gasp escaped me, echoed by the rest of the girls in the Sphere.

Lord Aries Vanderbilt strode through the yoni-shaped entrance of the Sphere, striding toward the center of the room without so much as glancing at the crowd.

My heart instantly raced.

He wore his long, dark purple cloak that flowed behind him like dark water. His dark eyes found me briefly, and as our gazes met, the phantom pain of electrical burns harassed my skin.

"Our High Lord Aries Vanderbilt is here to disclose the information to you," our Luminary announced.

He joined them in the center of the plateau. "Greetings, Children of the Divine. I wish brighter circumstances brought me here today. Unfortunately, I come bearing terrible news. Please take a moment to breathe deeply and ground yourselves for what I'm about to tell you."

Like good little soldiers, the girls of Luna Academy obeyed. Me, on the other hand? I glared at Aries without releasing a breath.

A moment later, he sighed deeply. "Recently, an extremely dangerous Celestial has broken out of their prison realm."

Cue the chorus of gasps and murmurs.

"As you all know, the Celestial Society is a free society. We do not persecute our people for every little discrepancy like mortals do. If one of us is imprisoned, it is for good reason. We do not know exactly how this prisoner was released, or who is responsible for freeing him, but we do know he is free, and he is extremely dangerous. We hoped we could handle this ourselves and not cause fear in our Society. Due to recent events, this is no longer possible."

I didn't like the way the Priestesses all stood behind Aries with their eyes downcast. All of this felt wrong. My mouth completely dried, the air feeling like it had been sucked from my lungs. Why was Aries here relaying this message? Why couldn't Delphyne tell us herself?

"San Gabriel Academy, along with the students and faculty inside, has been wiped out of existence." Aries deadpanned.

My heart sank.

A strange, heady silence tolled by.

"What?" Venus hissed sharply. "What in the seven realms does that mean?"

Aries shot daggers from his eyes at her outburst. "The prisoner who has been released possesses the element of shadows. A rare, insidious power that corrupts the Celestial from the inside out. While fire can destroy matter and turn it into ash and dust, the shadows can do the same, except the matter turns into nothing. It is not burned but swallowed. Consumed. Erased. Made to have never existed in the first place."

I was shaking my head. That didn't make sense. That wasn't possible.

Silver eyes harassed my mind. I'd seen Solaris Adder erase the world...turn it black...send me into the endless shadows. But the world always came back. He didn't—he couldn't—could he?

"Soon, you will all forget San Gabriel ever existed. Shocking, I know. At the Institution of the High Council, we have ways of permanently storing this data to ensure our inner circle doesn't forget. But we cannot pass this on to all of you—not at this time. Anyone who knew anyone from San Gabriel will forget about that person. If you have pictures and videos of this person, they will be erased as well. Shadow magic is something we can hardly even grasp. It is not even in the realm of Creation-Destruction, a concept you are all familiar with. Shadows go beyond creation and far beyond destruction. They erase and leave holes, holes that are magnetic to dark forces. The land in which San Gabriel once occupied will now be a prime site for a gateway into a lower realm."

Panic rippled through the Sphere. My face felt ice cold and I couldn't take my eyes off Aries. He was so...calm.

"Will the same happen to us?" a young-looking girl cried.

"What do we do?" another yelped.

"If we are just going to forget this happened, why are you telling us?" Venus St. Claire demanded to know. Murmurs of agreement followed her question.

"It is Divine Law that we disclose the full truth to our people, even if they will fall into Amnesia. Somewhere in your subconscious, this information will exist." Aries explained. "It is Law to disclose the truth, always. In one way or another."

"Why can't you just film this assembly and show us tomorrow?" Venus continued to challenge. "Then we will all know."

"You cannot just inform someone they are under Amnesia. It doesn't work that way. Just like you cannot tell a person under mind control that they are under mind control. It will quite literally make you go insane. You will lose your mind and be a danger to yourself and others."

Fearful chatter erupted and the Luminary stepped forward. "Silence!"

Silence fell.

"We have put wards all around the perimeter of the Academy. Impenetrable wards. Any magic cast against it will be returned to sender, times three." Delphyne's eyes were full of scattered emotions. "It pains me to tell you all, but at this time, no one should leave the Academy. For your safety."

I sucked in a sharp breath and murmured, "What the hell?"

"As you all know, this is no prison. You are all Sovereign beings. If you do choose to leave, the wards will not permit you back inside. Not unless you enter your original, sacred energy signature into our database to detect who you truly are when you try to return. We must take these precautions at this time."

I glared at the Luminary disbelievingly before glancing around at the other girls to see if they sensed the same shadiness as me. What was this, a police state? Why would I ever give them my sacred energy signature? That shit was to be kept to yourself, for it was the direct imprint of your soul essence, and if it fell into the wrong hands, it could be used for all sorts of nefarious magic.

"We do not know what to expect next," Aries admitted, his voice boosted by magic. "My own, personal intuition tells me this attack was a statement and a warning. I do not believe another strike will occur...for now. Still, both Luna and Veneficus will be on lockdown until further notice. Being erased from existence is no small thing. Please choose your actions wisely. The force of power that has been released back into our world is unfathomable. Shadows are self-amplifiers. Only a trained army of Embodied will be able to stand against this being. What we are facing is nothing short of war."

"Who is this psychotic jailbreaker?" Venus St. Claire snarled; her amber eyes lit with some desire I couldn't quite detect. "You clearly know who it is, and we all have a right to know as well."

Girls echoed in agreement. Even I had to nod along to that. Aries needed to come clean with everyone and lift this weight off my chest. I couldn't be the only one haunted by those silver eyes.

"If I tell you who he is, if I show you his face, he will officially exist in your mind," Aries replied grimly. "If he exists in your mind, he has a thread into you. For now, his identity must remain confidential. Until we get a reign on things."

"Tomorrow, you will fall under Amnesia," the Luminary told us grimly, but I barely heard her. "The Priestesses and I will alert you of a new threat in the city and advise you to stay within the Academy. We will get through this. Together."

If he exists in your mind, he has a thread into you...

I fought the urge to scream FUCK as loud as I could, rising to my feet with a hot head and a stomp in my step as I stalked out of the Sphere.

I couldn't hear another word. Couldn't look at Aries's face a second longer.

All of that—all of that felt so, so wrong. I couldn't quite pinpoint why or how. Solaris Adder was a threat, I knew that to be true. Especially now. I believed Aries about the shadows and the permanent erasing they were capable of. I didn't doubt the true potential of Solaris's power. What I did doubt were Aries's intentions. Him and his pretentious, shady, corrupt High Council being the only ones to retain the memories of all that was lost?! Screw. That.

I needed to find a way to remember. And I wouldn't stay locked up in here like some animal. Nor would I be giving them my sacred energy signature. I'd sooner die.

As soon as I stepped out into the starry night, the Goddess spoke to me. Or, rather, showed me something. I saw the vision in my mind, clear as day. Where I needed to go.

It made no sense, but at this point, I was down to try anything.

CHAPTER 16
CHAINS OF GOLD
JEDIDIAH

The news hit me right in the fucking gut, turning my insides to stone. The flames in the giant fireplace roared behind Veneficus's top Chancellor, Aro, casting ominous shadows along the walls that fit the terrible mood.

The lounge was full but had gone dead quiet. Each of us processed the information wordlessly.

Aro stood tall and thin, face paler than usual, his long black cloak pooling at his feet as his eyes traveled over each of us. He'd just dropped a massive bomb, and now he was gauging the damage.

A shadow-casting psychopath had escaped his prison realm and was now wreaking havoc within our Society, seeking revenge for his imprisonment.

I had buddies at San Gabriel. Sure, I always thought their Academy was fucking whack with the way they mixed the genders and let it be a free for all for everyone. They dabbled in lesser magic and tarnished the Celestial name but damn, some of them were my friends. Adam. Christian. Saskia. Wiped out of existence—soon to leave my memory altogether.

I scrubbed my hand over my face, sighing heavily, sinking back into the black leather sofa. The lounge was the shape of a circle, with sacred geometry patterning the floors. A balcony on the second level lined the whole room. A few guys stood up there, looking down, looking lost. The walls were tall and windowless, painted deep espresso, displaying countless portraits of old farts who were legendary in our Society. Floating lanterns gave the room a low, muted orange ambiance.

Our Chancellor remained standing in front of the huge fireplace; his hands folded together like a church steeple. Someone needed to say something already.

"So, what does this mean for us, then?" Raziel broke the crippling silence, his voice shaky. My fox-haired best friends sat on either side of me, literally mirroring each other's painful expressions. "Are we next? What about Luna? Have you spoken to the Priestesses?"

"We have been in contact with the Luminary, yes," Aro answered. He was a peculiar man with a thin face, all hard lines and years carried in the permanent frown of his eyebrows. He kept his dark hair long, and his skin reminded me of aged paper. Guy looked like a vampire if I was being honest. "Luna Academy is now protected by impenetrable wards. We will be doing the same very soon."

"What about my father?" I asked sourly, hating the fact that I was bringing him up. "He obviously knows about all of this."

"Indeed," Aro answered a bit reluctantly. "The High Lord is at Luna now, relaying the information to the students himself."

I scoffed. Of course.

I glanced around the room, gauging everyone's expressions. Veneficus used to be a bigger Academy, as in we used to have more students. When this Academy first opened, my father said, over three hundred boys attended this school. Which, in retrospect, seemed sickening since we were stuffed in an underground bunker with no fresh air, all farts and coughs and sneezes just trapped inside forever. Perhaps if you ignored the whole no windows thing, you might not be able to tell right away that we were twenty stories underground. The Vault was designed to mirror the opulent hotel above us. Everything gleamed, rich in a dark color, gilded with gold. A king's lair, my father would say. Yeah right.

I gripped my staff with white knuckles, the emerald crystal on top of it glowing with the fervent need to unleash some chaos. I withheld, for now.

"So, as of right now, there are no wards up?" I clarified.

"Not yet," Aro answered. "The other Chancellors are visiting the Institution to gather as much intel as they can. As soon as they return, we will install the wards."

A storm of shadows erupted beside Aro with a *whoosh*. A man appeared out of thin air, a grin tugging at his lips. "A little late for that," he said.

Aro's face turned chalk white.

An iron fist squeezed around my lungs, forbidding me to breathe.

Demitri and Raziel stiffened beside me, but no one made a single sound.

"Hello," the shadow man said to the lot of us. He looked young and boyish, like he could be the same age as me, yet somehow ancient at the same time. His eyes shone with an unnatural shade of silver, his reddish-black hair wavy, framing his face. His face—I'd never seen bone structure quite like that. Or eyes that freakishly bright. The shadows he'd emerged in waned a bit, but some remained around his hands.

"Judging by the looks on your faces, you've all heard of me by now."

"We heard what you did," I growled back, refusing to show any sign of fear. I rose from the sofa. Raziel and Demitri stood behind me, my twin pillars, as always. A few others stood up as well.

"Boys," Aro warned. "Do not—"

The shadow man flicked a wrist at Aro, sending him flying and crashing into the wall, rendering him unconscious before he even hit the floor.

My stomach sank. This shadow freak had no staff. I'd never known of a male Celestial who could do magic without one.

"My apologies," the stranger mused, so casually it made my head spin. "This is a private matter. Please, sit down. Relax. I am not here to hurt any of you. I am here with an offering."

My spine turned into a rod of steel. The new energy in the room came from another world. A darker world. I could feel it in every breath I drew—the creature standing before us was like nothing we'd ever known. That truth was obvious, just looking at him. Though he did possess this alluring, snakish charm, that might seduce some. Not me.

Glancing around at my brothers, though, I could see the effect of power already clouding their judgment.

"An offering?" I retorted, trying to sound bored. "What could you possibly offer us?"

"To be on the winning side of the coming war."

"You dare come here!" a guy called Victor Rathbone spat, his face etched with vehement disdain while his eyes welled with tears. He held up his staff, conjuring hectic wind magic. "My girlfriend went to San Gabriel; you piece of shit! What you did is abhorrent! You should be—"

With a bored, unimpressed look, the invader made a vague hand gesture and muttered something under his breath, instantly shutting Victor up. No, not just shutting him up, but... His mouth was *gone*. Victor's brown eyes bulged out of his skull while he dropped his staff to the ground and desperately ran his hands over the smooth skin where his mouth should have been.

I blanched, everyone around me intaking sharp breaths. A defensive nature lit up in my belly and shot to my fingertips, but something had me refraining from using magic.

"Who can tell me what spell I used to silence this lovesick fool?"

No one made a peep.

The stranger rolled his eyes and sighed, displeased. "*Verum silentium*," he said. "I make it look easy, I wouldn't expect any of you to be able to do it, but still, you should at least know what I did to rid this buffoon of one of his main bodily orifices. But you do not. I wonder why that is? Why aren't they teaching the most powerful male heirs in the Celestial Society important dynamic spell work?"

The truth of silence. I knew that spell. But I didn't learn it here, at Veneficus. I learned it during my independent studies in my father's grand library back home. I wouldn't give him the satisfaction of answering.

"What spell did you use to wipe out an entire academy of us?" I hissed, my heart pumping wildly. I knew the flush of my skin was giving away my distress, but I still did my best to feign the image of being stoic.

Silver eyes clashed with mine and I felt it, tangibly. What was it about this guy? My nerves raced around on high alert, yet I refused to be the one to break eye contact.

"No spell work needed for that, I'm afraid," he mused. "And you should know that."

My fists clenched at my sides.

"To hell with this guy!" my buddy Jason Lovett cried, summoning fire from his staff and releasing a war cry as he propelled it forward.

Before I could even blink, nearly every guy in the room had their staffs pointed at the shadow man. A fury of elements blazed through the lounge as they launched their attack on the intruder. The intruder who remained motionless, standing with his hands folded behind his back, not concerned in the least. For good reason, too. I watched as every magical attack was blocked by shields of shadows that manifested on their own, protecting their master, returning every blow to the sender.

Chaos ensued. Elements ricocheted backward, knocking into people, furniture, and the walls.

Stupid fucking idiots.

As if the man who just wiped-out hundreds of our people like nothing would come to stand before us and be so easily taken down.

My jaw clenched while I slammed the bottom of my staff onto the floor, willing the earth under our feet to tremble. It started slow, going unnoticed by most, while boisterous elements flew and crashed around us. Until the trembling turned into violent shaking that had the foundation of the entire Vault threatening to crumble upon us. Boys shouted and moved to the walls, knowing the length my power could go. I could split this room in two and send us all into the Underworld if I fucking saw fit.

The shadow man's eyes lit up with excitement as he watched me. The walls trembled, portraits crashing to the floor, furniture uprooting from their spots.

"Ah, yes, there you are, Groundshaker," the shadow man said, his voice thick with passion and adoration which only made me a hundred times madder. He gazed at me as if we were familiars. I growled something fierce as I willed my magic to its full potential. The black marble floor beneath him began to crack and groan.

The stranger's face changed. An impish grin tugged at the corner of his lips. "Fine," he murmured. "If you wish for it to go this way..."

A piercing alarm punched my eardrums, and it took me a beat too long to realize it was Demitri and Raziel, screaming. I turned in horror, my stomach hollowing out as I watched the shadows ravaging my best friends. Swirling around their faces, their hands, going into their eyes, their noses, their mouths—choking them, blinding them, maybe even killing them.

My heart threatened to burst through my ribs as I banished my magic and shouted, "Fine! Fine! STOP!"

He didn't.

Silver eyes glared mockingly at me, a lethal promise hiding within them.

"Stop!" I cried. "We'll listen to whatever you have to say! Just fucking stop!"

The lounge was destroyed. Water damage was already eating at the walls and the floors. An armchair had caught fire. All the portraits of super important old farts had fallen and smashed. All this destruction, and yet the invader had not even lifted a finger. Sweat formed on my temples, my hands shaking as the shadow wielder glared at me suggestively. The panic in the room became a tangible, living thing.

After an agonizing moment of proving his point, he banished the horrible shadows and freed the twins.

They collapsed onto the sofa, gasping for dear life, their hands roaming over their faces as if they expected to find the shadows still there.

The shadow man's silver eyes skimmed over everyone else, who remained plastered against the wall, in fear. "*In somnos,*" he declared, his voice like the crack of a whip.

Everyone in the room fell to the ground, unconscious.

Including the twins, who sagged against the sofa behind me.

I waited for the spell to take effect on me, but nothing happened.

"I understand your trepidation," the shadow man said as he took a few steps over the carnage to come closer to me. He remained as poised and casual as ever. As if this were the most normal affair. "What I did to San Gabriel is alarming. But I had my reasons."

I just stared at him, unable to come up with a coherent sentence. He was almost as tall as me, which was a rarity. Almost, though. I still got to look down on him and it felt good.

"I'm Solaris Adder," he informed me, his tone wry. "The only Celestial alive to possess the element of shadows."

I blinked. "What, do you want me to clap?"

He chuckled, amused. "You remind me of someone."

My face crumpled. Was he seriously trying to make small talk with me right now?

"Yes, you remind me of our mutual friend," he went on, a menacing glint in his creepy silver eyes. "She's about yay tall." He held his hand out at chest level, to show the petite height of whoever he was talking about. "Eyes blacker than coal, hair like moonlight, a bad attitude, fire hotter and brighter than the sun itself."

My stomach fell out of my ass while my eyes widened. He was not standing there talking about—

"You are the son of the High Lord," Solaris continued before my brain could process anything. "And from what I've gathered, you are not a fan of your father. You're estranged, are you not?"

How do you know? I glared at him with loathing burning in my eyes, my chest rising and falling. Every primal instinct I had screamed inside me, urging me to crack open the earth and send this motherfucker back down to hell.

"You know better than anyone, the true corruption of this regime. The High Lord and his band of anonymous mummers. They try to teach you to believe the Celestial Society is a noble, honest empire that is ruled by freedom and sovereignty. And while you are given luxuries, privileges, and benefits that inspire you to believe this lie, most have been blinded from the truth." He glanced around at the demolished room, noting the opulence under the destruction. "Chains made of gold are still chains, after all."

"What do you want?"

"I'm surprised you even still attend this mockery of a school."

I could not shake the way he seemed to know me. Maybe he was just trying to get under my skin...but the way he spoke, the way he looked at me, it was as if we were long-lost friends. Like he was expecting me to suddenly remember who he was.

"You must know, deep down, that these schools are a masquerade. They focus solely on elemental magic, which *is* a powerful tool, but in the face of true adversity, one must know the right spells. Look how easy it was for me to put your entire academy to sleep. None of you even know any dark arts defense! Do you ever wonder why you're only taught elemental power?"

"We learn some spell work," I argued.

He rolled his eyes.

"What do you want from me?" I forced myself to ask again. His eyes quickly flashed to my throat, as if he could hear my raging pulse.

"I wasn't always this way," he murmured, holding up his hand as a whirl of shadows danced over his palm. "I was born a waterling. Somewhere along the line, I learned how to alchemize my power into something...greater." He made the shadow grow bigger before he banished it. "A Celestial that can wield multiple elements is a threat to a regime that seeks to keep its populace pliant. Have you ever heard of the Star-Cross project?"

I swallowed, reluctantly recalling the program started by mortals. An underground military project, where Celestials were kidnapped and experimented on. Another thing I learned about in my independent studies.

I shrugged, being purposely vague.

"My parents sold me out to this program because of my unique power. They feared me, and so, they locked me away. I was experimented on and treated like a lab rat. They tried to control me and my power and use me as a weapon. When they couldn't control me, they imprisoned me in a realm of my own making.

"But their efforts were in vain, and as you can see, I am free now. And while the attempt against me by your brothers was *okay*, it's going to take a lot more than messy elemental magic to affect the likes of me. Currently, you have nothing to fear from me. I came here to offer you a chance at—"

"Oh, let me guess. You have come to make an offering of liberation." I snapped a laugh. "Liberation or extermination, is it? Typical dictator shit. San Gabriel didn't bend the knee, so you killed them off. And now you're here to see if we will join you. Well, you can shove that up your—"

"You are being raised as pigs to slaughter. They want to keep you under control, for now, teaching you half-truths and dogmatic magic. They pit you against each other, in an endless fight for power. You all stay cooped up in these schools, learning nothing of importance while mortals run amuck, destroying the world. Your superiors know of the coming war, Groundshaker. They have been training you all as elemental soldiers. They want to use you to fight their ancient battle. What I'm offering is the chance to fight on your own side."

I was shaking my head halfway through his speech. How the fuck could someone who spent his life underground and then in a prison realm know anything about our world?

"You expect me to believe the guy who emerged from a prison of shadows and instantly committed mass murder is a better choice than the current powers that be? There haven't been any Celestial wars since the Age of Amnesia. You are the first one to speak of it. You declared war when you vanquished an entire academy of us. I think it's clear you are the problem here."

"My strategies may seem harsh, but it was necessary to show you what devastations I am capable of. Plus, there are things you do not know about San Gabriel. One day, you'll understand why I've done what I've done. It's not important now, though."

My brows lowered. "Who were your parents? Were they from San Gabriel? Is that why you did what you did?"

He grinned, only slightly, and it did not touch his eyes. "You'd think that, wouldn't you? It might seem like going straight for the throat of your enemies makes the most sense, but, in my opinion, it's much more satisfying to go after everything they've built first. Dismantle their empire brick by brick and make them watch. If you kill a king, he dies a king. But if you collapse his castle, turn his kingdom against him, strip him of his crown and titles, and render him a peasant, well, then, he dies as nothing. And that, dear Groundshaker, would be far more satisfying."

Every word settled in my stomach, resonating far deeper than I would ever admit. I swallowed, though my mouth felt dry. "Sounds like you've given this a lot of thought."

"I would imagine, so have you."

"So...it's my father you're after?"

A heavy silence hung in the air.

"Let me give you a piece of advice. The root of the problem never lies in the most obvious place. True monsters have many limbs, and it can be tempting to cut them off, but you mustn't bother with anything but the head. Limbs can grow back. Cut the head off the monster and the entire body dies. Unfortunately, the head is always in the last place you look."

I grimaced, perturbed. "Do you always talk like this?"

He shrugged.

"Everything you just said contradicts itself. First, you say to dismantle the empire. Then you say fuck that go for the head. You make no sense."

He cocked a brow. "Don't I? Or are you just not keeping up? The only way to lure out a monster that's hiding in plain sight is to destroy the territory to which it has camouflaged itself."

"So, you're not after a king, then. You're after a monster."

"Can they not be the same thing?"

I raised my hands in mock surrender, a snap of a laugh escaping me. "Jesus Christ, man. I don't know why I'm bothering to try and understand the mental workings of a deranged sociopath. You committed mass murder. You're the monster. I'll never join you."

Solaris Adder stepped back, and I felt dismissed. "Very well. I'll return later to see if you've changed your mind."

In a storm of shadows, he vanished.

For a moment, I just stood there.

What in the seven hells was that?

"FUCK!" I bellowed, picking up a chair in front of me, hurling it across the room, and breaking it against the wall. My chest rose and fell, my fists clenched.

Aro groaned from the floor, fighting to gain consciousness. I stalked over to him immediately, my raging pulse making it hard to see straight.

I grabbed Aro by the cloak and hurled him up to his feet. He blinked rapidly, barely conscious as his eyes attempted to focus on me.

"You better fix this!" I shouted at him, gesturing to the plethora of bodies scattered on the demolished floor. "You are supposed to be our Chancellor, our leader, our fucking protector! You were taken out like nothing! FIX THIS, ARO." All I heard in my voice was the cruelty of my father. I shoved Aro backward, his back hitting the wall while he gaped at me. Useless idiot.

I had to get out of this stuffy, pretentious bunker. After taking a long look at all the unconscious bodies littering the floor of the destroyed lounge, I stalked out of there, not bothering to help clean the mess. The ground shook under my feet as I trekked through the windy hallways to the elevator. Aro didn't dare try and stop me.

The elevator took forever like it always did. I felt numb. Eventually, I was spat into the immaculate foyer of the Sun & Moon Hotel. Soothing music caressed my senses as life went on like normal up here.

I stepped onto the glossy floor and stopped short, my body going cold when I saw who stood at the front desk.

Leaning against the wood, showcasing her cleavage to poor old Mort who didn't stand a chance against the reigning she-devil of LA. Her eyes were hooded, her lips full and tempting as she muttered huskily, no doubt trying to manipulate Mort into doing something for her. She wore tight black ripped jeans which hugged the generous curve of her round ass. Were those *Converse* shoes on her feet? What the fuck? She dressed like a mortal, though her etheric beauty couldn't be tamed by tattered pants and a too-big concert tank top. Metallica, of course. She'd tied it up at the front, so it was a belly shirt.

Her eyes gravitated over to me. Like she sensed me here. Even though I stood unmoving, staring at her. Which now seemed creepy as a grin played at the corners of her lips.

"Nyx Morningstar," I growled, finding my legs, and forcing them to move me toward her.

CHAPTER 17
THE WILD SIDE
JEDIDIAH

Mort's face shone beet red. He was our front desk clerk, an old mortal whose family had long ago sworn allegiance to the founding bloodlines of Veneficus. He was useful in the sense that he had no life outside of this. He spent his every waking moment being the eyes and ears of this hotel. The Vault could only be reached through Mort. Quite a big, important job for a mortal but he never let us down.

Something about the look on his face right now, though, told me he was about to do just that.

Nyx had that effect on people.

"Well, if it isn't just the Mole Boy I came here to see." She flashed me her most dazzling smile, all those white teeth on full show behind her crimson lips. That girl always had lips painted the color of murder. And a look in her eyes that said she could back those intentions up.

"What's she asking of you, Mort?" I demanded.

"She–she wanted–she wanted the key card to the Vault."

Nyx feigned a look of betrayal at the old man. "Mort!" she cried, her hand flying over her heart.

"I–I'm sorry, my lady."

"Don't be sorry and she is no lady," I snapped, reaching out to grab her by the arm. She gasped which sent heat all through my body. I towed her away from the front desk. She didn't fight me off. Fucking weird. Something was seriously up with her lately. I'd thought her magic had been drained or something that night on the beach, but after I watched her battle Venus St. Claire with my own eyes, I figured that couldn't be true.

I dragged her to a private corner behind a massive ficus and shoved her against the wall, caging her in. Her sweet, smoky scent wafted up at me, making my abdomen light on fire. She smelt like cherry incense, rich and burning and sweeter than anything I'd ever known. I always felt so on edge and engaged around her, like walking through a field of land-mines. This devious silver-haired creature with big black eyes and a look on her face that could lure any man to his death.

I pressed the crystal of my staff to the base of her throat. "What in the seven realms are you doing here, Nyx?"

"Oooh," she crooned, licking her lips, her gaze locked with mine. She wrapped her fingers around my staff suggestively, grinning as she watched my face react to that. "Are you trying to threaten me with a good time?"

The crystal at the end of my staff pulsed with emerald light, mimic-king what was going on in my pants. Gods, this girl knew how to fuck with me. I feigned indifference, though it was hard to breathe. I pressed the crystal harder into her flesh. "*Talk*. Why are you here?"

She shrugged, unwrapping her fingers to check her nails. "I came to speak to my buddy Mort. He's good shit." Her voice was as smoky as her scent, evidence of the fire that burned inside her.

"Nyx," I snarled. "Cut the shit. Am I supposed to believe after everything that just went down in the Vault that your visit is an unre-lated coincidence?"

She paled. Authentically, which humbled me. Her spine straight-ened as she looked up at me. Her eyes bored into mine and I momen-tarily felt like I was falling into them. "What happened?" she breathed.

"I take it you already heard about San Gabriel. From my father, no less." I didn't bother hiding the bitterness from my tone. I lowered my staff, assessing her body language.

She nodded once. "Yeah. I heard."

"The Celestial who did it just showed up down in the Vault."

I nearly heard her heart drop. "He did?"

My eyes narrowed as I scrutinized her expression. A familiarity lit behind her eyes, there was no mistaking that. "You know him," I snarled accusingly. "He suggested that we had a 'mutual friend'. How the fuck do you know him, Nyx? Who is he to you?"

She swallowed as her misty stare went downcast. "Jedidiah, please. I came here to see you. I know we hate each other and I'm probably having a manic episode by even coming here but I need a favor from you. A no-bullshit favor. I'll do whatever you want in return but I neeeeed you to lend me your portal globe. I know you have one. I know you were going to use it that night on the beach to get us back to Luna after...after what happened. Please."

The fathomless depths of her black eyes stole the breath from my lungs as she looked up at me with so much raw need. For a terrifying, fleeting moment I felt like doing anything she asked of me. I felt like destroying whoever or whatever was responsible for her grief. But instead, I laughed in her face and shook my head. "You're right. You must be having a manic episode to think I'd ever do a favor for you."

"Jedidiah." My name whispering through her full, red lips made my dick ache. This girl confused the hell out of me and my body. She always had that infuriating resting bitch face that made me want to fight her or fuck her or bury her or lift her up and spin her around. But now she had a different look on that mythical face. I hardly saw any pieces of the furious, fiery girl I'd once known. Something about her now was so... broken. She even had shadows under her eyes and now that I looked at her closer, her cheeks were gaunt too.

Something terrible must have happened to her. It would take *a lot* to knock a Draco starseed down. I would never admit it out loud to her, but I knew how powerful she was. Not just because of that bright, golden fire that coursed through her veins. Draco, the constellation of dragons, was one of the most ancient star systems, making her Star Lineage not just the rarest, but the most formidable. She was like a dragon in human form.

"What?" I snapped.

"He can erase the world," she said, so low I barely caught the words.

"I've seen it. He—he's more dangerous than we can even fathom. He—"

"He's the one who Astral Snatched you on the beach." I interrupted, deadpan.

Her eyes darted back and forth between mine. "Yes," she croaked.

That made my heart switch into turbo gear, relentlessly ramming against my ribs to drive a hole out of me. "Why do you want the portal globe?"

"I need to visit my hometown," she said desperately. "I was going to take a train, but I don't have time. Please, Jedidiah."

I shook my head incredulously. "Why in the seven realms do you need to go back to your mortal hometown? That makes no sense."

Her lips parted as if she were going to say something, but nothing came out. She continued to gaze up at me with that expression that made my heart squeeze. I simultaneously wanted to do anything to make her feel better while also wanting to drive her further into madness by toying with her. I'd never seen her so vulnerable before. I hardly knew how to contain myself. This girl may have had the spirit of a dragon, but she was the size of a church mouse. And now, that dragon fire had been smothered out, leaving her as no more than that fragile little mouse in the palm of my hand. Mine to crush if I wanted.

Or mine to keep safe.

It was a staggering pendulum swing.

"I can't explain it," she whispered. "Something is just calling me there. I need... I need to go back. There's something there that can help us. I feel it."

My face scrunched up. "Nyx, you're insane. Nothing in your mortal hometown is going to help us. This is a real, Celestial threat. The element of shadows hasn't been possessed by one of our people in over a thousand years. The power is unlike anything we've ever known. We need to stay and figure out—"

"So *stay*!" she hissed venomously. That familiar fury bubbled to the surface of her obsidian eyes. "I'm not asking you to come. I'm telling you *I* must go. I know you probably have a raging boner at the fact that I'm here, at your mercy, needing your fucking help. Trust me, it wasn't easy to get myself here. You could mess with me until the cows come home and ruin this opportunity. Or you could just swallow your damn pride and help me out."

I scoffed. "You're unbelievable, you know that? A Celestial who can destroy the world as we know it has declared war on our Society, and you want to go to your mortal hometown."

"Come on, Jed," she purred, stepping closer, making me freeze. Her smoky scent rose off her shiny, silver hair, threatening to send me into oblivion. Every cell of my being became urgently aware of her closeness. Of the heat radiating from her curvy little figure. "You can come with me if you want," she offered, placing her hand on her hip. "It's Saturday night. I know exactly where everyone will be. Taking a night away from all this Celestial shit might be exactly what we both need. Let's go drink some shitty beer and watch mortals be ridiculous and find what the Goddess is urging me to find. I know there's something, Jed. I know it."

I opened my mouth to protest but damn. I must have been suffering from a severe case of shock after what just went down in the Vault because what she was saying didn't sound so bad. I remembered what mortals were like on Saturday nights. I'd heard the stories of Nyx growing up, too. Part of me was curious to see this creature in her original habitat.

"Your friends won't remember you," I told her lamely. "Their Amnesia is in effect now that you're Emerged. So, if you're expecting a warm welcome or homecoming, you're way off base."

"I'm not," she replied sharply. Her dark eyes lit with defiance as she squared her shoulders and tipped her chin up at me. "Don't be a pussy. I know you grew up in a mortal country club where everyone had summer homes and trust funds. Me? I grew up in a place we called The Cut, where everyone had tattoos by age fifteen and siphoned gas from their neighbors' cars to be able to go wheeling in a stolen Jeep." A smile that gutted me slid across her lips as she watched my face. "Come take a walk on the wild side."

"You're crazy," I told her honestly and she laughed. A sound that echoed through my being and made tension gather in all kinds of terrible places. I was shaking my head in disbelief—at myself—while I reached into my pants pocket and pulled out the small, clear globe.

My brothers were unconscious down in the destroyed Vault, and yet, here I was, about to comply with the ridiculous desire of my nemesis.

"You're going to have to throw it," I said, ignoring how stupid it was for me to trust her with this. I had this mini-portal globe made last year. It was the same as having a fake ID. We weren't allowed to use portal magic until our fifth year, but that was bullshit. This globe was hardly bigger than a marble, smaller than most, and unable to transport me to the other side of the world but it worked for locations in the country. "All you do is—"

"Hold it, envision where I want to go, and throw it." Nyx beamed up at me smugly, a dark brow cocked.

"Right," I grunted. "And we have to hold hands."

She rolled her eyes. "What a dream come true for you. Give me your big hand then, you giant."

The laugh that escaped me was pathetic, but not as pathetic as the way my entire body lit up as she laced her small, soft fingers with mine. Swallowing the stone in my throat, I reluctantly passed her the crystal globe. She grinned down at it before shutting her eyes, concentrating deeply. The little furrow in her brows and the pout of her lips as she focused made my stomach flutter. Butterflies? Fucking butterflies? Disgusted with myself, I shut my eyes too. Seconds later, a vortex of glowing light sucked us into oblivion.

CHAPTER 18

ANARCHY

NYX

My mind whirled like someone had flushed my consciousness down the toilet. Jedidiah's portal globe was *not* a smooth ride. We were sucked into the ether and jolted around on a turbulent flight through nothingness before we were spat violently onto hard, unforgiving cement. We landed in a tangle of limbs and groans. The familiar scent of burning tires and dank weed filled my nostrils though, and I knew I was home.

"What is that heinous smell?" Jedidiah complained as he pried himself off me, sitting up and taking in our new surroundings.

A Cheshire smile crept across my lips. We'd arrived exactly where I wanted to. Right outside the old, abandoned warehouse where everyone came to party. Amid a junkyard, scattered with old cars, smoldering tires piled to the sky. The heavy bass music blasted through the night, disrupting the peace. A blanket of twinkling stars dotted the velvet sky, and I couldn't help but sigh deeply. Home sweet home.

Jedidiah's expression was comical. "You didn't focus hard enough, and now we're—"

"We are exactly where we need to be," I cut him off, rising to my feet, and dusting myself off.

He stared up at me as if I'd just spoken gibberish. "You can't be serious."

I gave him an impish grin before turning on a heel and strutting toward the massive old warehouse. Black Sabbath played from inside, the windows lit up with changing neon lights. Like clockwork. Nothing had changed since I left. Everyone was still on their bullshit, coming out here to escape their shitty lives for a night.

"Come on, pretty boy," I called over my shoulder. "You don't want to be left out here alone. Especially not dressed how you are. The heathens lurking around here will eat you alive."

He caught up to me quickly. Him and his long, effortless strides. "What's wrong with what I'm wearing?" he asked bitterly, still dusting himself off.

"Er, mortals don't usually wear skin-tight shirts threaded with real gold," I teased, allowing myself to steal a glance at him. Jedidiah may have been an arrogant, self-serving asshole but damn, the Goddess wasn't playing when she made him. He wore leather pants and a metallic gold t-shirt that clung to his muscular frame, putting it on full show. The Celestial norm, sure, but he was way out of his element here and I couldn't wait to watch him squirm. "Not to mention the freaking wizard's staff."

"Of course, they don't," he clapped back indignantly. "They wear cheap, fake fabrics laced with poison that corrupts their DNA and destroys their magnetic field. Why would I give a *fuck* what any of them think of me?"

I scoffed, my eyes narrowing at him instinctively. He was so hard on them all the time. So full of revulsion. "They know not what they do."

He made a face. "Clearly."

We stood right in front of the old warehouse now. I reached out to grab the door handle, but he jerked me backward, stealing my breath away as he wrapped his hand around my throat and forced me to look up at him. "If you're bullshitting me, Morningstar—if this is just some pointless game, you and I are going to have a real problem."

"You and I already have problems," I hissed, baring my teeth at him. But he was onto something. Was this just a game? Was this bullshit? Sure, I saw that vision and I felt an intuitive call to return to my hometown but that could have just been my fear disguising itself as intuition. To be honest, I didn't know if I was bullshitting him or not. There could have been something here to find, but maybe not. Maybe I was just here because my power had been stolen and my entire world was being threatened by a shadow monster who could erase people, places, and things from existence. Maybe I was just here to try and hide.

His deep blue eyes searched my face and for a moment I worried he could hear my thoughts. He released me, though. Reluctantly. My skin tingled where his hand had been. I lightly massaged my throat, glaring up at him. "You done?"

"We'll see," he muttered blackly.

"Why did you come?" I blurted. Surely this wasn't the time to push him, but curiosity took the reins of my tongue before I could think twice.

"To drink cheap beer and watch mortals be ridiculous and forget about all the Celestial bullshit for a night," he replied evenly, taking me by surprise.

I couldn't help but grin. "Alright, then."

"Don't get the wrong idea," he added. "I still despise you, Morningstar."

"I love it when you talk dirty to me," I quipped, and he rolled his eyes.

But despite him helping me tonight, I wouldn't forget what we were. The first time I ever met Jedidiah, I had embarrassed the shit out of him and sealed our fate. I'd heard everything about him, of course, the infamous heir of the High Lord. He thought he was such hot shit, and he was. He walked right up to me at a party at Lucifer's Playground, the hottest Celestial club in LA. The crowd parted for him biblically, and he looked devastating in the low, red light. He came right up to me and asked me if I wanted to dance.

So, naturally, I made *him* dance.

I set his shoes on fire, making him hop and jolt around, trying to put out my relentless flames. It was hilarious. He became enraged so I singed off his eyebrows and declared him a Mole Boy. The entire thing was caught on several different cameras and went viral on Celestial Tea.

Ever since we'd been in a vicious back-and-forth feud. I loved it.

So, of course, I was skeptical about his true intentions tonight. I couldn't focus on that, though. We'd cross that bridge when we came to it.

Inside the warehouse was a dream. Black lights lit up all the psychedelic posters on the old, decrepit walls. A massive fire roared in the middle of the large, square space; the yawning roof overhead having been burnt away years ago. A large vintage stereo was set up on the back wall, enormous speakers lining all four corners. Neon lights shone upon the crowd, changing colors, and pulsing to the bass. And of course, the people. The crazy ass punks with their colored hair and mohawks and chains and eyeliner. Dozens of bodies moved with the music, hollering, and rioting.

As soon as we stepped onto the scene, the music changed and *Anarchy in the UK* by the Sex Pistols started playing, making everyone go crazy. I couldn't help but feel like it was a Divine moment. Perfect. Just perfect. I started jumping and dancing around, screaming along to the lyrics like I was just another delinquent from the Cut.

"Mother and Father above, you're insane," Jedidiah breathed, staring incredulously.

"I wanna beeeeee anarchyyyyy!!!" I sang in response.

"What are we looking for, again?"

I shrugged. "I have no idea. For now, let's go find the keg and loosen all that tension in your shoulders."

"I'm not tense," he bit back, totally tense. The stars of Capricorn had this boy by the balls, but he was in constant denial of his overly serious, grumpy, and immutable nature.

I scoffed and grabbed his big hand in mine, so warm and calloused, ignoring the heat that scorched between us as I dragged him through the crowd.

Okay. So maybe it was depressing that no one remembered me. Jedidiah and I stuck out like sore thumbs, getting side eyed as we poured ourselves a beer. Trying to blend in was a moot plan. Mr. Gold Shirt beside me looked like a fucking trumpeter swan amongst an unkindness of ravens.

"You need to loosen up!" I whisper-yelled over the music. We stood on the outskirts with our red cups, and he couldn't have looked any more uncomfortable if he tried. I stood on my tiptoes and reached up, rustling my fingers through his thick, auburn hair, messing it up. He snarled and swatted my hand away but not before I got the job done. I grinned up at him, reaching into my black jeans. "Oh, my Goddess! That girl has her tits out!" I pointed in the opposite direction of myself, and his eyes followed quickly. I pulled the switchblade from my pocket and swiftly slashed the front of his pretentious gold shirt. Three times to resemble claw marks.

"What the fuck!" he roared, grabbing my wrist, and staring at my knife in disbelief. His eyes fell on his newly slashed shirt, nearly bulging out of his head. I didn't bother holding in my giggles.

"There," I chirped innocently. "Now you look sort of metal."

"I'm going to kill you." Though he made no move at me. He didn't take his eyes off the blade until I officially stuffed it back in my pocket. "Why do you have a knife?"

I frowned. "Why wouldn't I?" Though, he was right. Normally I would never carry such a pathetic excuse of a weapon, but this old thing had sentimental value. I used to carry it around, back in my mortal punk days. It may not have been much but it sure was satisfying to slash something, even if it was just Jedidiah's shirt.

"What's going on with you, Nyx? Seriously."

If I didn't know any better, I'd think that was genuine concern shining in his eyes. That couldn't be right, so I shook the ridiculous notion from my head.

"You haven't even tried to burn off my eyebrows or spell my shoelaces to tie themselves together. I grabbed your throat, and you did nothing to fight me off."

"Dude, shut up and drink your beer." I slammed the rest of mine, letting the fizzy burn cloud my mind. I stalked away from Jedidiah, going to dance by the fire. That beer hit me right in the goods, making me want to merge with the music and transcend this dimension.

I danced, letting myself zone out in the movements. I could feel Jedidiah watching me and it only pushed me to move more fluidly, letting Pink Floyd affect me on a soul level as I became one with the song.

Time stopped as my attention snagged on my old group of friends.

The sight of them impaled my heart. Danica, Marvel, Layton, and Maria. Oh, my Goddess—all the memories we shared played like a montage in my mind's eye, stealing the breath from my lungs. We were wild, man. Judging by the looks of them now, they hadn't changed. Marvel still rocked his platinum blond mohawk that contrasted wickedly against his dark skin. Maria still repped her Mexican culture, her face painted into a sugar skull. Her signature party look. Danica had dyed her brown hair purple, her eyeliner more excessive than the last time I saw her. Layton looked stoned out of his tree, his dreadlocks long, still rocking his beanie and ripped jeans.

Marvel spotted me then, standing here beside the fire, gawking at them. His brows knit together, only slightly, a strange look flashing across his face. For a fleeting moment, hope dug its talons into my soul. Did he remember me? But then he looked away, back to Maria, leaving me hanging like the ghost I was.

I cursed under my breath, shoving through the crowd of sweaty bodies. I fetched myself another beer, slammed it in one go, and poured another. Slammed it and poured another. Went to slam that, but the cup was plucked from my fingers and a very annoyed-looking Jedidiah glared down at me. The neon lights made his face glow pink, and I couldn't help but giggle.

"I saw your sad little moment out there," he informed me dauntingly. "I told you they wouldn't remember you and you still look like a kicked puppy over it."

"Beat it," I hissed, snatching my beer back from him and tossing the contents down my throat as he shook his head at me.

"You played me," he accused, pulling me away from the keg which was swarming with people. He towed me through the bodies until we reached a wall. Jedidiah's new favorite thing, apparently, was caging me against a wall. I hiccupped as he leaned down so his face was freakishly close to mine. He smelt like earth and smoke and man, which to my newly intoxicated brain, seemed enticing. Like I wanted to move closer. "You're here for a miserable stroll down memory lane, not because your Goddess urged you here."

"Maybe," I admitted lazily. "But that doesn't explain why you're here. I came to you in a moment of seriously embarrassing desperation, and honestly, Jed, I expected you to laugh in my face. But you helped me out, without even giving me that much flack. So, what's up with you, huh?"

"No. No, you're not going to deflect like that. Something has changed in you ever since that night on the beach. You haven't even used your magic once since we've been together tonight. I've had my suspicions...but...I didn't think they could be real. Looking at you now, I think they might be."

I shoved his chest which did nothing but make him grunt and close in on me even more. "Get away from me," I warned.

"Oh yeah?" he mocked, his beautiful face lit with cruel intentions. "What are you going to do to me if I don't?"

My heart galloped like a herd of wild horses behind my ribs, the alcohol making me woozy. Jedidiah's closeness made my head spin even more. Bloody hell, what was I thinking asking him to come with me? I wasn't safe around him without magic. Now his eyes blazed into mine as he read the truth in the windows to my soul. *Fuck my life.*

"He took your magic." Jedidiah spoke low, each syllable hitting me like a bullet. "That's how he escaped his prison realm, isn't it?" His eyes brightened with realization, though the expression on his features remained grave. "Somehow, he siphoned your magic and used it to break the wards. You—*that's* why you're here tonight, isn't it? Scoping out your old life? Seeing if it still has appeal now that you're powerless?"

I shoved him again, but he didn't move. "Stop."

"But how? How could he Astral Snatch you like that? How could he have access to you?"

"Stop!" I shouted, slamming my palms into his hard chest.

"So, it's true." His hand found my throat once more and I watched as the revelations settled behind his eyes. "You can't fight me off."

"So what?" I spat. "You're going to hurt me, Jedidiah? Now that I'm defenseless, you're going to be cheap and dirty like that? Go ahead."

I went to reach into my pocket and grab the switchblade, but he caught onto me and suddenly my hands were bound behind my back by thick, rough vines. I let out an angry cry, wishing I could light him up. The lack of magic in my veins turned into a gaping hole inside my being.

Agonizing and ever-expanding. I hated this. I fucking hated this so much.

His warm hand tightened around my neck and his lips tore into a snarl. The music got louder, Led Zeppelin singing about the souls of women being made down below. I'd never seen his face like this before. His deep blue irises were stormy and furious, his breath leaving him in heaves. He pressed me into the wall, hard, my heart slamming like crazy. "After everything you've done, you'd deserve it," he growled in my ear.

"You're probably right," I wheezed.

"What does Solaris Adder want from you, huh?" he pressed, his brows knit together, teeth grinding. "I can see it on your face. You're being blackmailed."

"Fuck you," I managed, feeling my face go red.

"Nobody knows, do they?" he continued. "Not your friends or your sister. How did you manage to face Venus in the Sphere?"

Why was he asking me questions? I couldn't breathe, let alone speak. And I didn't give a shit, either. Jedidiah squeezed my throat, cutting my lungs off from the air they craved. But fuck it. I let my eyes flutter closed, basking in the sensation of the consciousness tingling out of my body. Pain and pleasure were the same to me. If he killed me, so be it. All my problems would be put to rest. Probably just to follow me into the next life, but screw it, I'd cross that bridge when I came to it.

He growled and released me. Air hurled back into my lungs, my eyes popping open, slightly disappointed he was yielding so soon. "Whatever bullshit is between you and me, there's no denying that we both face a common threat now. Solaris Adder emerged in the Vault in a poof of shadows and tried to threaten me into joining him in a war he said is coming. He overpowered Aro like nothing. Countless starseeds stood up to fight him off and no one could get their magic close to hitting him. His shadows have a mind of their own. So, if he's got something on you—whatever's going on, Nyx—you have to tell me. This is no fucking joke. Everything we are is at stake."

I rasped a weak laugh, shaking my head up at him. Everything he said caused an electric stream of panic through the map of my veins, but I forced myself to play it cool. "Only you, Jedidiah. Only you would choke someone out and then hint at an alliance and ask for answers. You're a real piece of work."

"Nyx—"

"Get away from me!" I kicked against his enormous, solid body with all my might. "Stop caging me in like I'm some stray animal whose fate is in your hands."

"But your fate is in my hands, isn't it?" he jeered, tightening the vines around my wrists. "I know your dirty little secret now. What will the girls at Luna think, hmm? Venus St. Claire is more than ready to take your place as—"

"STOP!" I shouted desperately, hating the truth spewing from his lips.

Jedidiah's eyes lit with a brand-new idea that made the hairs on the back of my neck stand on end. "*Tell me the truth.*"

Goddess damn me. I immediately felt the tethers of Compulsion wrapping around my tongue, urging the truth from the depths of my soul. My lips popped open, prepared to betray me. "He—"

"What's going on here?" a new voice laced with a British accent interrupted from behind us.

Jedidiah turned his head, and with the new distraction, he dropped his focus on both the Compulsion and the earth magic binding me, giving me a window of opportunity. I tore my wrists free and ducked under his arm, away from him.

I did not expect to collide chest-to-chest with an extremely cute guy whose face was painted with disdain and concern.

He caught me by the arms, a set of deep brown bloodshot eyes scathing me up and down. He rocked a faded black eye, his right brow busted with a deep cut. "Are you okay?" he asked, drawing my focus to his full lips, his bottom one pierced with a silver hoop. Dark, tousled hair fell over his brows, and holy shit—I knew him. Michael. Michael Hawkins—Danica's little brother. Well. Not so little anymore. If I remembered correctly, he was the same age as Emilia. Clad in a black leather jacket and heavy Doc Martens. He looked... dare I say...hot. The last time I saw him, he was awkward and skinny and did not look like the revival of punk rock.

I was too busy appreciating his glow up, I missed the critical way he was staring at me. "Nyx?" he breathed.

My stomach hollowed out. "You *remember* me?" I gasped.

His brows knitted together. He looked drunk and high on Goddess knows what, but he still managed to level me with a stare. "Why would I forget you? Where the hell have you been?"

I opened my mouth, but nothing came out.

The thorn in my side otherwise known as Jedidiah Stone appeared beside me and gave Michael a warning glare. "*Leave us.*" He spoke the Compulsion firmly and Michael's eyes widened a bit before his face reassembled into a frown.

"Why would I do that? It looked like you were hurting her. Who even are you, mate?"

Jed and I stared at Michael in pure shock.

He remembered me. Compulsion didn't work on him.

"Holy shit," I said. Jedidiah and I shared a loaded, incredulous glance.

"Is your sister with you?" Michael asked hopefully, looking around.

I scowled. "Um, no?"

"Who the hell is this kid?" Jedidiah demanded, annoyed.

A grin pulled at the corners of my lips as I reached out and trailed my finger down the center of the navy-blue t-shirt underneath Michael's jacket. "This is who the Goddess sent me to find."

CHAPTER 19
SUN & MOON

EMILIA

"This should work," Faye announced, her nose still in that old, leather grimoire. "I found a rune that should keep our memories intact. But, you guys, runes are forbidden to be used by starseeds. We're going to have to conceal them on our bodies somewhere no one will see."

"Whatever it takes," Destiny said firmly.

My focus was on Natalia as she sat on the floor, her eyes covered by a thick black blindfold. She had the flat-screen TV on the wall behind her displaying static because apparently, the white noise helped her focus. A piece of my sister's clothing was clutched in her hands. She was looking for Nyx, who left the academy two seconds after the Luminary warned us that we shouldn't leave. Of course. Natalia hadn't been able to psychically see anything involving my sister since that night on the beach. Something was blocking her out. Something bad.

The four of us were splayed out in Natalia and Nyx's room, grimoires open, searching for answers. Answers Faye had just found.

"This is the rune," Faye announced, turning the leather grimoire so we could see the page. "It has to be tattooed on our body somewhere close to our heart and there has to be silver in the ink or it won't work."

The strange, curving, and looping symbol depicted on the page rang a bell for me. "I think my mother has that tattooed on her."

"I'm in," Destiny offered without hesitation.

"You two haven't Emerged yet," Faye murmured, her blonde brows furrowing together slightly. "I don't even know if it will work on you."

"Well, we can try," I suggested lightly, though most of my attention remained on Natalia. She hadn't spoken in a long time.

"See anything yet?" Faye asked her.

Natalia shook her head, not bothering to speak an answer.

"So, who do you know that will tattoo this on for us?" Destiny asked excitedly, laying on her stomach on my sister's bed with her feet in the air behind her. Nyx would freak out that the "hairless wonder" was lounging all over her space.

Faye grinned mischievously. "Oh, girl. I got you. I'll be right back." The little blonde, who was covered in fairy glitter, rose and bounded out of the room like a fawn.

A beat of silence passed by. Destiny and I did our best to help look through the grimoires, but as brand new first years who hadn't Emerged yet, our help was useless.

Natalia gasped, drawing all eyes on herself.

"What is it?" I wondered breathily, inching closer to her from where I sat on the floor. "Do you See her?"

"No... But... I See... Jedidiah."

My heart dropped. Destiny and I shared a quick, confused glance.

"I think... I think he's with her."

"Where are they?" I pressed.

"I... I'm not sure. It seems... It seems like they are surrounded by mortals. Sweaty mortals? It's loud...music. Rock n' roll? There's someone else... A face I've never seen. They're talking to someone."

"How do you know Nyx is there if you can't see her?" I had to ask.

Natalia shrugged, her eyes still hidden behind the blindfold. "I don't know exactly. I just feel her. Why else would I find Jedidiah while searching for Nyx?"

"Why would she be with him?" I muttered darkly.

"Because he's mega hot and insanely tall," Destiny gushed, snickering at herself.

I remained unmoved and unimpressed, staying focused on Natalia.

"Oh!" Natalia cried. "They just portalled! I lost them." She tore the blindfold from her eyes, her chest rising and falling. Her brown eyes were wide and wild, confusion lacing her features.

Not even thirty seconds later, my blackmirror started blowing up with texts.

Nyx: **GET HERE NOW. Sun & Moon hotel. Room 2777.**

"She's texting me!" I exclaimed, unable to believe my eyes. She never texted me. Like, ever.

"What did she say?" Natalia demanded.

"She wants us to come to the Sun & Moon hotel."

Both Destiny and Natalia grimaced incredulously at that. "Leave the Academy? We can't," Destiny protested.

"Just like we can't have rune tattoos?" I shot back, somewhat icily even though I hadn't meant to snap.

My blackmirror buzzed again.

Nyx: **Seriously, I can feel y'all overthinking this. Trust me. You need to get here ASAP. Leave the others behind if they won't come, Emilia.**

My heart raced. "She sounds adamant."

"When isn't she adamant?" Natalia grumbled. "We haven't given our energy signatures yet. We won't be able to get back into the Academy."

Nyx: **Please tell me you haven't given them your energy signature yet. And answer me asshole. I know you're reading these.**

Me: **We haven't given our signatures yet!! Where have you been!!! How are we supposed to come there when we won't be allowed back in the Academy????**

Nyx: **They'll let us in. Get here now. I wouldn't demand it if it wasn't crucial.**

"Shit," I murmured, having no clue what I should do. Every fiber of my being wanted to go to my sister. But the timing... A psychotic shadowling was on the loose who had the power to erase you from existence. The Academy promised safety...

Faye returned then, holding an ornate feather pen between her dainty fingers. "Who's ready to get tatted? My brother gave me this on my last birthday. It's a tattoo pen!" She held out her wrist, showing the small heart tattoo. "I did this myself. It's the only time I ever used it. I never really had the desire to cover my skin in fixed tattoos, but for this, I'll make an exception."

Natalia rose to her feet. "Bring it. We're going to the Sun & Moon hotel."

Faye blanched. "Seriously? Why?"

"Nyx texted and wanted us to meet her there," Natalia explained. Faye's brows jumped.

Destiny and I stood up too, the four of us standing in a circle in the center of the room. Natalia's expression was fixed and serious, her shoulders squared. I had no idea what changed in her in the last two seconds, but I wasn't going to argue. I was with her. We needed to go.

"You don't have to come if you don't want to," I told Destiny softly.

"No." She tipped her chin up, her silver hoops catching the light of the floating candles over our heads. "I'm coming. I'm with you guys."

I grinned.

"Faye?" Natalia pressed. "Are you coming?"

She shrugged, glancing down at her feather pen. "Fuck it."

ASIDE FROM BEING EXTREMELY OPULENT AND OUT OF MY league, the Sun & Moon hotel appeared normal. Nothing like Luna Academy, the castle hidden behind a glamour. I found it interesting, Veneficus's strategy. Rather than using magic to hide their establishment, they hid in plain sight under a mortal hotel. Genius, really.

The four of us hustled inside, leaving the nightlife on the streets behind. The foyer of the Sun & Moon took my breath away. Everything was glossy, either black or gold, a glorious aesthetic that made the planted ornamental trees and hanging vines more endearing. I could feel it—the magic. The Celestial touches.

We skittered past a grumpy old man seated behind the front desk. He had a shiny bald head and a knowing look in those beady eyes. Just by the way he glared at us, I could tell—he knew what we were.

"Hello," Destiny chirped at him.

"I'm watching you, starseeds," he grunted back.

We each shared an incredulous look before spilling into a fit of giggles, waiting for the elevator.

"His name tag said Mort," Faye said through a snort. "Imagine spending your life being called Mort?"

"Shh," Natalia hissed, though a playful smile played on her lips. "Mort might hear you."

"Mort does hear you," Mort confirmed flatly. "Mort hears all."

We erupted with laughter as the elevator dinged and I swore grumpy old Mort bit back a grin as well.

Natalia punched in the number for the 27th floor and we ascended, the humor dying now that shit was getting real.

My heart was thudding in my throat by the time we finally reached our floor. Natalia led the way into the hall, the pillar of strength and determination. I tried to steady my breathing but *Goddess damn me*, I was nervous. What could be so 'crucial'? It seemed entirely reckless to leave the Academy right now. Our Luminary advised us to stay. I hadn't even had two full days of classes yet, and already I was rebelling. Damn, I really was my sister's sister through and through.

"Here it is," Natalia announced quietly, looking back at us with her brows raised. We stood in front of room 2777 and nobody made a move.

"What are we waiting for?" Destiny whispered.

A second later, the door swung open. Nyx appeared, her silver hair a wild mess, her eyes no better. She wore a tied-up Metallica tank top, ripped black jeans, and—were those *Converse* shoes on her feet? I gaped incredulously at the way she was dressed. Like a mortal. The way she used to dress back home...

"Get in here!" she demanded, stepping aside. "Hurry!"

"What in the seven realms are you wearing?" Faye gasped as we filed into the room.

It was more like an apartment than a hotel, which shouldn't have surprised me. Nyx led us through the entryway of the suite, into the great room where Jedidiah and the twins lounged across the luxurious black furniture. A fire roared under an enormous mantle, casting low orange light through the space. The entire west wall was made of glass, the city of LA twinkling below like a sea of colorful, fallen stars.

"What's going on?" I inquired firmly. My eyes grazed over the Mole Boys, wondering why my sister was here with them.

"I found something," Nyx announced. "And I think you're going to like it, sis."

My heart somersaulted in my chest before it kicked into top gear. Usually, my sister's words possessed dualistic meanings.

The twins stared at me wryly from the sofa. I couldn't help but notice they looked...shaken up. Both had shadows under their eyes, their fox hair disheveled. Jedidiah sat in an armchair, looking unimpressed like he'd rather be anywhere else. His tight gold shirt was ripped three times across the chest, resembling claw slashes. Something told me the shirt didn't come like that. The way he kept glancing at my sister with fire in his eyes was not lost on me. What had they been doing?

"Come out, mystery boy!" Nyx sang.

Destiny and I shared a confused glance while Natalia glared at my sister. A moment later, a door clicked open, and someone stepped out of the attached bedroom.

"Michael." I gasped, hand flying to my throat in surprise.

"He's mortal?" Faye squawked.

"Tell me about it," Jedidiah grumbled.

I blinked but he was standing there. Really standing there, right in front of me, in this hotel room. Here. In Los Angeles.

He looked achingly handsome in his leather jacket, his dark hair tousled and hanging over his brows. Those familiar, endless brown eyes drank me in from across the room. Both of us just stood there. Everyone bickered in the background, but their voices melted into white noise. He had a deep cut through his right brow, and his eye and cheek were bruised slightly. Michael was always getting into fights. He chewed his lip ring as he gazed at me wordlessly. His eyes were red, evidence of the drinking and smoking, but he appeared entirely lucid as he looked at me.

Even with an entire room separating us, an electrical current ignited between us, becoming a tangible thing in the room. I swore everyone else could feel it too. Their bickering died out. I could feel the scorch of their attention on us, but I didn't dare look away from him.

"I bet this is the boyfriend Mom wanted to keep you away from," Nyx stated obnoxiously, moving to stand beside me. "I approve. He is cute. And a little dangerous, as he should be."

"Nyx!" I hissed, a furious heat rising on the back of my neck, coloring my cheeks.

"Where have you been?" Michael asked me. His lazy accent made my abdomen pool with liquid heat. He looked at me and only me as if we were the only two people in the room. Even though we had an audience. "Your mom told me you went to a fancy university in Europe, but I knew that was bullshit."

I gaped at him, unable to form a coherent sentence.

My attention slowly turned to glare down at my sister questioningly. The mischievous look on her face lit a fire inside me. "You went back home?"

She shrugged. "I felt this, you know, call type thing."

Jedidiah rolled his eyes. "Here we go."

"Why would you bring him back here?" I demanded hoarsely. "Right after everything that just happened? Why would you put him in danger—"

"Why are you talking about me like I'm not standing right in front of you?" Michael's sharp voice cut me off and made my heart burst into a thousand pieces.

I stared at him like a mindless mute.

"Who is this mortal?" Faye demanded to know. Destiny nodded in agreement.

Natalia was staring at him, almost blankly, so I knew she was using her inner Sight to truly See into him.

Jedidiah stood up from his armchair harshly, a snarl ripping through his lips. "He's no one. He's some kid from Nyx's hometown and she's using him to fuel her current manic episode. He needs to be mind-wiped and sent back—"

"Seriously?" Michael snapped. "All of this coming from the guy I just caught choking Nyx Morningstar in the back of a party? You should shut the fuck up about me and her, right now, mate."

Before I could even react to that, Jedidiah's face contorted with fury as he lunged at Michael. He made a sharp gesture with his staff and my heart plummeted out of my ass. I knew that action—we just learned it the other day in the Sphere. It was a telekinesis move. He meant to send Michael flying.

The gust of telekinetic power cracked against an invisible shield in front of Michael, ricocheting off and hurling back at Jedidiah. It hit him right in the chest—*hard*. He dropped his staff, and I watched through a scream as his massive body was tossed backward, shattering through the glass wall. Right out the freaking window of the twenty-seventh floor.

The twins were up in half a second, screaming in horror as they rushed to the window.

"MOVE!" Faye shrieked, darting toward the window at top speed.

My heart threatened to burst through my flesh and splatter on the floor before us. I'd never felt such a raw, cold fear coursing through my veins.

Jedidiah Stone just went flying out the window. Did I seriously just witness one of the most powerful starseeds in the Society die?

Faye held her arms out and grunted with fierce power. Her hands were strained, fingers splayed, and her magic became a palpable whirl-wind that filled the room. She called upon every ounce of her air magic. Her body shook and her temples beaded with sweat. Her wild, golden hair whipped around her face. She released a callous, primal scream that sent shivers across every inch of my skin.

"It's working!" one of the twins shouted, his head out the window. "Keep going!"

No one said a word as Faye cried out one final time, jerking her arms dramatically as Jedidiah floated into view from outside, his face painted with a shock that might have been funny if this wasn't so terrifying. His long limbs were spread wide as he desperately tried to find the purchase of something other than air. Faye successfully guided him through the shattered window on a blanket of wind, plopping him down on the glossy floor with a grunt.

Demitri and Raziel started throwing a conniption fit as they crowded their rattled friend on the floor. Jedidiah's hair was a wind-blown mess, his eyes still wider than wide as he sat there, still in complete shock.

Faye wiped her brow and then sucked in another sharp breath, now focused on the carnage of shattered glass all over the place. She splayed her arms once more and used her air magic to levitate the shards. Once they were all afloat, she began...repairing the entire sheet of glass. I watched in awe. She looked so focused and sound as she fixed something that should have remained destroyed forever, putting the window back in place.

That kind of power seemed... underrated.

"What in the seven realms just happened?" Destiny breathed beside me.

Nyx watched through an expression I couldn't read.

My heart jolted as I remembered Michael. I turned to him, catching the way he was looking down at his hands in dismay.

"Tell me again how he's no one, Jed," Nyx taunted, her dark eyes lit with something that made my stomach churn.

"How did you do that?" Faye asked Michael, her voice high with adrenaline.

"I-I don't know. I didn't. I didn't do anything."

"Bullshit," Jedidiah cursed venomously.

"He's Divinely Marked," Natalia whispered, her eyes still focused solely on Michael.

"What does that mean?" every single one of us retorted in unison.

"I don't know," Natalia replied, staring deeply at Michael—or rather, into Michael. Seeing his spirit, his essence, his entire life. In return, he regarded her.

"Bloody hell," one of the twins groaned.

"He remembers me," Nyx said to me. "He's not under Amnesia. Compulsion doesn't work on him. Now it seems he has a built-in shield that protects him from magical attacks. Whatever he is... The Goddess wanted me to find him."

"So, what then?" Faye said. "He's Enlightened?"

"What's Enlightened?" I asked right away.

"Some mortals have the ability to perceive magic—they can see into our world. Like old Mort down at the front desk."

Jedidiah made a sound of disgust. "Enlightenment takes a series of lengthy rituals. This kid does not strike me as an occultist. Are you an occultist, man? You do blood rituals?"

Michael blanched. "Er, no—"

"See." Jedidiah rolled his eyes.

Each word settled into my gut, planting seeds of something undiscovered inside my being. I inched closer to Michael instinctively and his breath hitched. A whole room remained between us, but I felt his presence in every cell of my body. I could even smell him—that familiar scent of cedar and cigarettes and something musky, unique to him. Before my mind could catch up with my feet, I was flying towards him, and his arms opened instinctively as if to catch me.

Nyx caught my wrist. "Er, I don't think you want to go bulldozing into him just yet. After what just happened."

"I would never hurt Emilia," Michael growled, trudging forward, and closing the space between us. I gasped as his big, warm body enveloped me. I breathed in his heady, masculine scent while I shut my eyes, shutting the rest of the world out. He was a perfect head taller than me, which made my ear level with his heart. It thrashed behind his shirt, hurling itself against my cheek while he wrapped his arms around me, locking tightly. I clung to him too, my mind whirling, wondering how this could be real.

I left him behind. I came to Emerge at Luna Academy, to officially take my place in the Celestial Society. He was supposed to forget about me.

I'd trained my mind every night for the last year to let him go.

"Can you explain to me where I am and how I got here through a circle of spinning light?"

A breathy laugh escaped me. We pulled apart, only slightly. He held me at arm's length, looking me up and down as if to make sure I was in one piece.

"No time to explain," Nyx cawed. "We're Celestials. It means we're magical and badass."

Michael's brows jumped.

"Wait—so you *know* this mortal?" Faye asked, her brows narrowed as she tried to figure this out.

"Oh yeah?" Jedidiah challenged, rising to his feet with malice in his eyes. "Is that true for you, Nyx? Are *you* magical?"

Nyx's face fell. "Jedidiah, stop. Now isn't the time."

"What's he talking about?" Natalia demanded.

"I'm so lost," Destiny admitted.

"Oh, I think it's a perfect time." There was acid in Jedidiah's voice. "Nyx has been keeping a dirty little secret from all of you. She's using this mortal as a distraction." Jedidiah strode across the room until he was in front of my sister, towering over her, a menacing gleam in his stormy eyes. "*Tell us the truth.*"

She glared up at him defiantly, but her lips popped open. Which made no sense because there was no way Compulsion should have worked on my sister. We all watched in disbelief as it appeared she was going to obey his magical command.

I regarded my sister dubiously as she trembled, trying with all her might to fight it. Her teeth ground together but the worlds slid out. "The shadow summoner is named Solaris Adder—he's the one who Astral Snatched me on the beach. I'm the one who released him from his prison realm by accident. He stole my magic and is blackmailing me with it. He will only give it back to me if I agree to pledge my allegiance to him. I have till tomorrow night to decide."

All the oxygen in my body was sucked out violently, leaving me a dried-up shell who couldn't process anything she said.

Nyx released a sigh, almost of relief, as if a weight lifted off her chest.

An agonizing moment of silence thrummed by.

Natalia detonated, making us all jump out of our skin. She released a wanton, angry sound as she thrust a bout of earth magic at my sister, knocking her across the room until her ass planted itself in a chair. Vines grew all around her legs, tying her to the chair, while more of them wrapped around her wrists, binding her in place. Nyx's eyes were wide and fearful as Natalia approached her. "You..." she breathed darkly, "are going to tell us everything."

CHAPTER 20
QUEEN OF ROCK BOTTOM

NYX

My friends and sister just fucking *stood there*. No one made a move to help me. Jedidiah knelt before me cockily and interrogated the truth out of me while I sat against my will, bound to the chair. *Goddess damn me*—I was *so sick* of being chained. By shadows. By vines. By life itself. What happened to me? How had I fallen so far in such a short period of time? Two weeks ago, I was the reigning Queen of Luna Academy, the most powerful fireling the Celestial Society had ever seen. Now I was nothing. Even the mortal in the room held more power and significance than me.

Jedidiah was getting off on this, that much was clear. In that way, he was just like his father.

They all stood around me like I was some criminal. Looking down at me, expressions bleak and full of judgment.

"Why didn't you *tell us*, Nyx?" Emilia wondered, aghast. Her ocean eyes searched mine from where she stood next to her mortal boyfriend.

"*Why didn't you tell anyone?*" Jedidiah demanded.

"Because," I spat, my chest rising and falling. Attempting to fight the Compulsion made me work up a sweat. "Because I didn't want anyone to know I was powerless."

Natalia's unrelenting glare remained hard, but Faye and that random bald girl softened a bit.

Jedidiah sneered mockingly.

Demitri and Raziel stood behind him, their arms folded, expressions amused. "And how'd that work out for you, princess?" Raziel taunted me. He pulled out his blackmirror and *snapped a picture* of me. Me, Nyx Morningstar, tied helplessly to the chair with Jedidiah kneeling in front of me menacingly.

I bared my teeth at them and thrashed uselessly against the vines. "Fuck you!"

Faye shot a gust of wind at the ginger, sending him flying and crashing into the sofa. His blackmirror was knocked from his hand, smashing on the marble floor. "No flash photography," she muttered as he pulled himself up to his feet, dusting himself off and trying to act cool.

I grinned and Jedidiah made a sound of annoyance.

"Honestly," I said through heavy breaths, "I can still do magic if I really force myself. But..." I gulped, suddenly wishing I hadn't said anything. This part just made it all worse.

"*But what?*" Jedidiah sneered.

"But it hurts. Feels like an aneurism or something. My nose bleeds and I pass out if I try too hard."

"Jesus!" Faye cried.

"You wasted so much time." Natalia growled, shaking her head. "You could have told us right away. We could have found a way out of this. We could have found a way to get your magic back without complying with Solaris. Shit, in only a few hours, Faye found a rune that will protect us from falling under Amnesia. We could have worked together and helped you."

"Yeah," Faye nodded. "I should have done something the moment I found you in the bathroom that day." Her green eyes lined with silver and her bottom lip quivered. "I knew," she whispered. "I knew something terrible had happened to you and—"

"Hey, fairy girl, cool it on the waterworks," Jedidiah snapped.

The twins scoffed.

Faye frowned and wiped away the single tear that escaped her eyes.

Michael stood there looking absolutely confused and out of his element while he incessantly chewed his lip ring. My sister stayed beside him, and it was the weirdest thing ever because they looked so natural together, like they *belonged*. Even the way they stood; their bodies aligned perfectly next to each other. They just fit. With everything going on, I managed to notice this, and I knew in my soul this peculiar mortal would come in handy. At least I could say I helped with that.

"And it's not just about *you*, Nyx!" Natalia went on, growing angrier by the second. "This Solaris person has wiped out an entire fucking academy of Celestials! Didn't you stop to think maybe *you* wouldn't be the only one he assaulted? Your pride clouds your judgment so bad! This attack could have potentially been prevented if you had just *told someone* what happened to you."

I swallowed hard, feeling my eyes line with burning tears. I said nothing.

"Solaris Adder showed up down in the Vault today," Jedidiah informed the others, earning himself a gasp from the girls.

"He wants me to join him, too." Jedidiah continued. The twins looked shaky and nervous as he spoke. "He did a sleep spell on everyone but me. He gave me all these speeches about a coming war and how corrupt the Society is and how our schools are designed to oppress us."

"What?!" I hissed, horrified. "He wants *you*! And you didn't tell me this?"

"I *did*, you idiot. You're too self-absorbed to hear words when they're not about you." Jedidiah smirked darkly in my face. "What's wrong, baby? You mad that you're not the only one he wants on his team? You're not that special."

"But what does he want you guys to *join him* in, though?" the hairless girl wearing the massive silver hoops asked. "Is there going to be a war? What does that mean? Does he have an army? Does the Society? Is he just going to erase anyone who defies him?"

Nothing but ringing silence followed her little outburst.

"He wants to remake the world," I offered on my own merit. *Fuck it.* Everything was out in the open now. "Whatever that means."

"He said his parents sold him to an underground military faction of mortals who experimented on him as a child," Jedidiah said. "He's

180

clearly driven by revenge, but he's acting indirectly. He's not targeting his true enemy, not yet anyway. He spoke to me in weird ass parables and story metaphors. He kept saying all these contradicting things...but whatever he meant, he's after someone. Or something. Seems like he's willing to destroy whatever gets in his way, too."

"Aries told me he was *kidnapped* by mortals," I voiced.

Jedidiah scoffed. "Well, my father has been known to tell a lie or two in his day."

"But who do we believe?" Faye wondered. "The shadow terrorist or the High Lord?"

No one replied because the answer was a bloody mystery.

"Who are his parents?" Emilia asked me.

I shrugged. "I have no clue. He never mentioned them to me."

Natalia shook her head, scrubbing a hand over her face. "Jesus Christ."

"Whatever his villain origin story is, he's dangerous," I declared. "More than dangerous. He... He can erase the world. I don't know how he does it. I thought he was just Astral Snatching me like on the beach but... I don't know. One minute you're there, in the real world, and the next, everything's gone and there's only shadows. Only an endless sea of darkness. It's cold and lonely and every second there shaves off a piece of your soul. The shit he said to me...straight diabolical. We can't underestimate him."

"It seems like he doesn't even have to consciously control the shadows at all times," Raziel mentioned. "Countless guys down in the Vault tried to fight him but no magic even got close to him. The shadows wielded themselves—like they formed on their own to shield and defend him."

"Aries said the shadows are self-amplifiers," Natalia muttered, her brows furrowed thoughtfully.

"It's like they worship him," I added with a grumble.

"Well, we have to be smart about this." Jedidiah snapped. "We can't set him off. We must focus and regroup and find a real way to stand against him or it's hopeless. I don't know about the rest of you, but I really don't want to be wiped out of existence. My soul is too fire. We're eternal and he isn't going to fucking take that."

My heart picked up into top speed, his words resonating within every particle of me.

The others seemed to agree as well.

"I dreamed of this…" Michael breathed then, his eyes far away.

We all blanched, focusing our attention on him.

"Go on, mortal," the twins urged together.

Emilia's jewel blue eyes fixed on Michael as he stared off into space, seemingly reliving a memory. "Ever since I was little, I dreamt of this… shadow. A shadow in the shape of a scorpion, who turned into a man— he emerged out of dark water in the sky and brought all sorts of monsters and devastation with him. He haunted my nightmares for years as a kid, him and all his monsters."

We each stared at this peculiar mortal boy wordlessly.

"And sometimes…" Michael went on, fidgeting with his fingers. "Sometimes there was a woman with him. A woman who looked half dragon or something. Part of her skin was scales, and she had—"

"So your parents read you too many bedtime stories," Jedidiah said dismissively. "Your little dream doesn't mean shit."

Emilia's expression contorted with defensive rage, and I watched as a lightbulb went off in her head. "Wait. Didn't you say he was choking my sister?" she asked Michael who nodded instantly, his face darkening.

"What the hell!" Emilia cried, lunging at Jedidiah who still knelt in front of me. She slapped him across the face, so hard his head jerked to the side and a handprint immediately materialized on his cheek.

Whoa, Emilia!

A shit-eating grin took its place on my lips. Impressive. I'd never seen my sister boss up before.

"Ow!" Jedidiah roared. For a split second, his expression was all Aries. Vicious. Reactive. It looked like he had the mind to strike back at my sister but, unlike his father, he refrained. He nursed his cheek with his palm. "Big whoop," he grumbled, irritated. "She liked it."

Emilia's rage only grew at that. "You—!"

"*Tell them the truth. Do you like it when I choke you?*" Jedidiah asked me, his voice thick with the pull of Compulsion.

Fuck fuck fuck fuck my life.

"Yes," I gritted out reluctantly, wishing the floor would open up and swallow me whole.

Natalia rolled her eyes. "Bloody hell."

Faye and the bald girl bit back giggles while my sister stared at me like she didn't know me.

Jedidiah and the twins grinned smugly.

"See?" Jedidiah gibed, looking deep into my eyes, making my stomach flip. "I would never touch her in any way she doesn't want me to."

"Can we focus on what really matters, please?" I hissed. "You know, the impending shadow threat that haunts us all."

Emilia glared down at me in a way that made my stomach tighten with shame. This new little revelation of how fucked up her sister truly was changed her mood considerably. "How could you let this happen, Nyx? You and your insufferable pride! Look at where it's gotten you!"

I snorted, shaking my head at her. "You still don't fucking get it, do you? Wake up! This is how our universe works, Emilia! You want to level up? You want a purpose? Then you gotta walk through your own personal hell and come out the queen of it. Otherwise, you might as well just be a clueless mortal, living in stagnant comfort."

Her blue eyes filled with disdain. "How you manage to sit at rock bottom and still go off about *being queen* is beyond me."

I laughed, genuinely. "I'm flattered you think *this* is my rock bottom."

"Wait a minute," Jedidiah interjected, a new light flashing in his blue eyes. "You told us that Solaris initiated a battle with you, and then you blacked out, but that's supposedly how he was released, right? By you unleashing your fire in his prison realm?"

I nodded.

"And then he siphons your magic, only offering it back if you pledge your allegiance to him? Which, in translation, means you wouldn't be using your magic *against* him..."

"Where are you going with this?" I demanded.

"He's scared of you," Jedidiah deadpanned. I scoffed. "No, think about it. He wants to be in *control* of your power. The power which released him from a shadow prison. Your magic must be a key factor in how to fight him."

"Or a key factor in how to help him be successful," I shot back. "He could have just thrown my magic into the void and left me powerless. Shit, he could have just killed me. Why go to all this trouble to keep me alive and give me a choice in the matter?"

"You're right, Jedidiah." Natalia said, nodding slowly. "Nyx, your power is a key factor here. I don't know how or why—ever since he took you on the beach, the shadows surrounding you block my Sight. But I know in every fiber of my soul that your magic is absolutely crucial in all of this. You need to get it back."

"I'm just a fireling," I croaked, sounding more defeated than I would have liked.

"No," Natalia said. "No. Your fire is different. Brighter, hotter..."

"Celestial Fire," Jedidiah offered reluctantly. "My father has told me about it. Your bloodline was once known for possessing a higher caliber fire, the fire of the sun and stars themselves."

"Shouldn't we be telling the Luminary and the Priestesses all of this?" the hairless girl asked, her voice breathy and laced with concern.

"They would have us *forget* about everything," I snarled. "I'm sure they know a lot more than they let on. Instead of offering us a way to stay out of Amnesia, they want us to give away our sacred energy signatures and remain on lockdown. Sounds suspicious if you ask me."

"Speaking of forgetting," Faye piped up. "I found a rune we can tattoo on ourselves that will prevent us from forgetting. It's forbidden for starseeds, though."

"Why didn't you say so!" the twins exclaimed in unison.

"Can I be released now?" I grumbled.

Hesitantly, Natalia banished the vines that bound me in place. I shot to my feet, rubbing my wrists, glaring hatefully at Jedidiah as I walked away from him.

Faye had apparently brought a magical feather pen to give us tattoos. The whole concept felt ridiculous to me but ridiculous seemed to be the theme of everything lately.

"Shit!" Faye gasped. "I forgot—we need silver."

"Silver?" I retorted. "Why?"

She shrugged. "It was written in the grimoire."

A beat of silence passed.

"My earrings are pure silver," Emilia's friend said. "I... If you can find a way to melt them down, you can use them." She removed the hoops from her ears and placed them in her palm, offering them up to whoever.

"Well, this pen is enchanted," Faye supplied, staring at it in her hand. "It already has its own endless supply of ink. So, I don't know how that would work... Unless... I guess we could melt down the silver and I could dip the pen into it to add to the original ink."

"Nyx, would you do the honors of melting down the silver?" Jedidiah taunted. "Oh, right. You can't."

I shot him a dirty look.

AN HOUR LATER, WE ALL HAD MATCHING TATTOOS. HOW cute.

Placed right under our hearts, Faye showed off her freestyling skills, giving us each an identical protection rune, which gleamed with silver under the light.

We hardly spoke the entire time. We were all processing in our own minds. Michael and Emilia gravitated toward the corner, whispering amongst themselves, looking way too cute for my liking. Natalia sat on the sofa and stared into space, clearly perceiving different visions and timelines. She informed us that someone was trying to remote view us right now—though she couldn't perceive who it was, so we assumed it was Solaris. The Mole Boys lurked in the kitchen where they drank beer and bro'd out, so they didn't have to succumb to the dark truth which was settling in more by the minute. I stood by the massive glass window Faye had repaired, glaring out at the twinkling city lights below.

We wouldn't forget San Gabriel. We wouldn't forget what that sadistic motherfucker had done.

Now what?

"So, what are we going to do about Nyxxy's little no-magic situation?" Raziel asked. "If her magic is crucial, but she only gets it back if she swears allegiance to the ever-consuming darkness, what—?"

The front door opening made him shut his mouth and we all fell still from our different spots in the suite.

My body froze over, and my heart plummeted as the Luminary strode into the room with Priestess Bridget at her back. The Chancellors of Veneficus, Aro and Tiberius trailed behind them.

Oh shit.

We each stood there like startled rabbits.

"As inspiring as it is to see the lot of you attempting to work together for once," the Luminary drawled, "this little vigilante rendezvous is over."

Bridget's fiery eyes were dead set on me. I had the feeling it was them who Natalia sensed watching us. Meaning they knew everything.

CHAPTER 21

ASCENSION

NYX

I'd been right about one thing: we were allowed back in Luna Academy without the stupid energy signatures. The Luminary portalled us into the Sacred Temple where the rest of the Priestesses awaited us. Michael came with us. He was immediately whisked away by the Water Priestess, Adria, who was going to give him an in-depth psychic evaluation. We girls were asked a series of lengthy questions. After a while, the other girls were dismissed, as well as the Priestesses, leaving me alone with Delphyne, our reigning, all-knowing, perfect, superior in all ways, Luminary.

I sat awkwardly on the stone floor with my legs crossed, staring blankly into the writhing Eternal Flame. The triple Goddess loomed over me, casting her judgment upon me, times three.

For what could have been hours, neither of us spoke.

Finally, I decided to break the silence. "So, am I in huge shit, or what?" Classy, as always.

"How could I possibly give you more shit than you are already in?" she quipped back, raising a pale brow.

"Fair," I muttered, fidgeting with my fingers. "You're mad, though."

"I'm not mad," she replied with a sigh. "I'm...sad. I'm sad you didn't feel like you could come to me about this. I'm sad that you have suspicions of our intentions here at Luna Academy... Have I done something to betray your trust, Nyx?"

I swallowed the stone in my throat, my cheeks heating as I shook my head. "No. Not really. I'm just suspicious by nature. I trust no one. Probably the lack of parental love growing up, ha." I laughed dryly and it only painted more hurt in the Luminary's expression. "I don't like the idea of giving our sacred energy signatures, though, if I'm being honest."

The Luminary nodded as if she expected as much.

"Nyx," she murmured, eyes soft. "Your mother has always been... rough around the edges. She takes after her mother...and her mother before that. Your bloodline has always been known for its stoic nature. But I know deep down, she loves you. After all, she named you after the Goddess of Night—she clearly knew how powerful you would grow up to be. You are named after the night and yet, you hold the power of the sun and bear a family name that references the dawn. That is profound, full spectrum alchemy."

The fact that she completely dodged the topic of the energy signatures was not lost on me. For now, I decided to let it go.

I scoffed. "Yeah? Look at me now." I stared down at my flat palms, tears burning the back of my eyes as no magic manifested over my flesh. "Either I agree to pledge my allegiance to the psychopath who wants to erase and remake our world—or I give up my magic forever and be forgotten about by our people. Either way, I'm fucked."

"It's not like you to go down without a fight," the Luminary jibed. "Since when do you give up so easily?"

I looked up at her curiously. "What could I do?"

"You overestimate Solaris, and I understand why. But remember, Nyx. He is little more than a child. He may be over a century old, but that century was spent in prison. He was no older than you when he was sentenced there."

My heart thudded dully in my chest while the Luminary's stare glazed over as if she were reliving a memory.

"I remember when all of this went down." Delphyne spoke grimly, her turquoise eyes lost in the flame. "I admit... I was abhorred by the way it was handled. Solaris, and all the others involved, deserved better.

That doesn't excuse what he's done, but the High Council handled the situation poorly, and we're all paying for that now."

"What do you mean?" I asked, my voice dry. "You were there when this all happened?"

"Not exactly, but I was aware of what was going on in my own way." She tapped her temple suggestively, her expression sorrowful. "I have to say, this all reminds me of an old prophecy passed down in my family. When I was a little girl...which was a long time ago..." She smiled half-heartedly. "My grandmother told me a story. A story that her grand-mother had told her, about how the entire collective unconscious was stored in the deep, dark waters of Scorpio. All our fears and nightmares and discords lived there, and from them, grew monsters. She said one day, the Goddess would take all this darkness from the stars of Scorpio and fold it into one form, allowing it to incarnate, perhaps in the form of a man. He would be the personification of the shadow. My grand-mother called him the Scorpio rising. She said he would bring all that had been kept hidden into the light. He would be the catalyst of great and terrible change."

My eyes narrowed, pulse thundering. Instantly, I recalled Michael's dream. "So, you are suggesting Solaris is this Scorpio...?"

The Luminary lifted a shoulder. "A little over a century ago, I remember hearing whispers of a baby born in triple Scorpio. Sun, moon and rising. This is inexplicably rare. I would bet my last penny, it was Solaris. Nyx, you are born under Ophiuchus, the star sign that was purposely hidden from the collective. The serpent bearer. This energy has been cast out, demonized... That innate rage you carry inside you, is not just yours. It belongs to all those who came before you. Celestial and mortal alike. Women, witches, even goddesses. The Earth herself. Every female that was hunted, persecuted, and tortured for her magic. They live in your blood.

"You and Solaris bear archetypes that have been excessively feared and denied within the collective. And I'm not talking about fire and shadow. I mean the serpent and the scorpion. Both are wildly misun-derstood and vilified, by all factions, mystical and mundane alike. The serpent has been framed as the devil. The scorpion is used as a metaphor for poison and pain. And perhaps the danger they carry is real... But do you know what else these Celestial archetypes have in common?"

I shook my head, gnawing on my lip.

"Ascension," the Luminary breathed, and my heart skipped a beat. "The serpent becomes the dragon. And the scorpion... In ancient astrology, Scorpio has three phases. The scorpion, the eagle, and finally, the phoenix. Both of your archetypes have the potential to ascend into the highest, most divine embodiments, and here you are, together at the eye of the storm."

I was shaking my head, denial coursing through my veins like wildfire. But the Luminary ignored me and went on.

"What Solaris has done to you and San Gabriel is inexcusable, Nyx. But as Celestials, we must not see things as black and white, even when that's how they appear to be at first. Writing Solaris Adder off as nothing more than a psychopath blocks you from truly understanding him, and therefore understanding how to neutralize him. He seeks to control and spark fear in others but deep down, there is more to him. He spent his childhood underground, only to break free and be instantly locked in another prison. If that was you, what would you want most in the world now that you were truly free?"

"Um...revenge?"

She chuckled humorlessly. "Perhaps... But what else?"

I stared at her while she sat next to me, her translucent gold robes settled around her like a pool of sunlight. The Eternal Flame flickered high and mighty, whispering prophecies I couldn't quite catch.

"I'm not picking up what you're putting down," I admitted wryly.

She cracked a small smile. "Solaris has been isolated from the world his entire life. Don't you think he may want to...experience some of it? Live a little?"

I blanched. That was not what I expected her to say.

"He doesn't strike me as..." I trailed off mid-sentence, my eyes traveling to the fire as I remembered the look on his face as he brought me to that bar. I hadn't thought much of it at the time, but thinking back now, he did seem quite taken by the place. By the people, the nightlife... "Even if he did, what am I supposed to do?"

"Remember who you are," Delphyne declared, her tone rich with passion and encouragement. "He chose the most beautiful and powerful starseed to try and fit in his pocket. I think he's looking for more than just your allegiance. You have more power than just fire or spells. You *are* magic, Nyx. Use what the Goddess gave you."

I laughed nervously, my heart rate accelerating. "Luminary, are you... are you suggesting I try and *charm* him?"

She shrugged innocently. "Amongst other things."

"He wants me to pledge my allegiance to him, though. Even if I did try and work my feminine magic on him, how do I get out of that?"

"Oh, there's no getting out of that," Delphyne sighed.

"So I'm just supposed to choose?"

"Not exactly. You will present a counteroffer. This is a negotiation, after all, is it not? Every deal in existence, mortal, and Celestial alike, can be wagered and bartered. You will present a slightly altered offering."

My brows jumped, a tiny seed of hope blooming within me for the first time since all of this shit started. "Go on."

CHAPTER 22
THE BOY IN THE TOWER
EMILIA

The next day was.... weird, to say the least.

All the girls at Luna Academy fell into Amnesia and had no recollection of the events from yesterday. No recollection of the shadow bringer, no recollection of San Gabriel...

Everyone was summoned into the common room where the Luminary gave a short announcement regarding a new threat that was passing through the city. She told us a coven of vampires from Romania had come to the city and it was unsafe for us to leave the Academy at this time.

Up until that moment, I had no clue vampires even existed. Every day it became a little clearer to me how much I didn't know about this world.

The news stirred some uneasiness, sure. But mostly? Life went on.

The really weird thing was everyone except our group had given their sacred energy signatures. But now they had no recollection of doing so, and it was never brought up again.

I couldn't focus on anything academic. How was I just supposed to go about my day like it was normal? I still hadn't heard from Michael— I had no idea where he'd been taken. My sister had vanished off the face of the earth as well, but Natalia assured me she was safe in the Sacred Temple. I wasn't allowed to see her. Of course.

"Hey," Destiny's voice in my ear made me jump. "You okay?"

We walked together down the long, narrow hall, looking for the Feminine Mysteries classroom. I shrugged lamely. "Not really."

"I have this weird, crazy feeling that everything is going to somehow be okay."

I scoffed. "Seriously?"

She lifted a shoulder, a small smile playing on her berry-colored lips. "Yeah. I know everything seems seriously bleak right now but... I don't know. I have faith. The Goddess will take care of us. Of Michael, and your sister too."

"I hope you're right."

"I am," Destiny chirped.

"There's just something I don't understand..." I admitted, biting my lip. "Solaris Adder was supposedly kept underground and experimented on by mortals...over a hundred years ago. I mean, did they even have the technology to do that back then?"

Destiny gave me a flat look. "Sis, artificial intelligence and all that tech have been around since Atlantis. It ain't new. It's ancient as fuck."

"But even for mortals?" I pressed, still skeptical.

"The elite ones, yeah."

I sighed, still feeling beyond weird about everything, but I decided to let it go for now.

We filed into Feminine Mysteries, along with a variety of other students ranging from first years to third years. The Air Priestess, Eliza, stood at the front of the class with a bright smile. The room was free of desks. Instead, there were big, comfy-looking meditation pillows set up in a giant circle. I snagged a spot next to Destiny, watching as the other girls chattered and chose their spots. No one ever seemed to talk to us. Destiny said it was because we were unEmerged but I thought it was something more. I couldn't bring myself to care, though. I liked it like this. Destiny was all I needed.

I didn't hear a word Priestess Eliza said to the entire class. Which sucked because this subject normally interested me. My mind was far,

far away. Thoughts of my sister and shadows and ultimatums and... Michael. Michael, Michael, Michael.

How could he be immune to magic? Not just immune, but somehow shielded? Jedidiah flew out the window to his death after trying to smite Michael with telekinesis. And the fact that he remembered Nyx even though she'd been Emerged for over a year was beyond profound.

I knew in my heart that he was just a human boy. Well, not *just* a human boy. What did that even mean, anyway? Why did Celestials see themselves as superior to mortals? Sure, mortals didn't possess high magic and they didn't live for thousands of years but they had divine traits of their own. They were creative, funny, and daring. They made glorious art and wrote fantastic stories and knew how to live in the moment. They built this city, the city we called home.

By the time we were dismissed from Feminine Mysteries, my mind was so far gone, I didn't even make it to the Sphere. Destiny and I were still unEmerged, so the rest of our classes would consist of watching other girls in the Sphere and learning some stretches and stances. As if I could focus on any of that right now. I gave Destiny some bullshit story about how I needed to go call my mom and discuss my Emergence party and I'd meet her there. Shit—that was soon. Soon, soon. Though that wasn't the pressing issue that had turned my brain into a hive of bees.

I needed to see my sister. Or Michael.

After the girls had all filed into the Sphere and the Academy grounds were quiet, I snuck out to the Sacred Temple.

I kicked off my shoes as soon as I hit the cobblestone path, slinking soundlessly until I reached the steps of the Temple. I swallowed the jagged stone in my throat and dared to ascend the stairs. The Luminary had told me my sister needed to be alone right now but screw that. She'd been alone all this time, suffering in silence, not letting anyone in. As always. She was Astral Snatched, and power drained and yet she remained a stubborn bull, fighting her battles alone. It broke my heart, how closed off she was. She'd always been this way and it never got easier. Especially now, after this.

My skin prickled as a familiar voice floated out from inside the Temple. No, that couldn't be right... She wouldn't be here, would she?

"Once again, you have brought GREAT SHAME upon our house! Does your recklessness know no bounds? Do you have ANY idea what you've done!"

"Our house?! You are delusional! Our bloodline has fizzled out to nothing. You, me, and Emilia are the last Morningstars. We are not a hou—"

"Do not finish that sentence! You have no respect, no dignity! What you have done is unforgivable. I truly hope you never get your magic back, Nyx. The Society is better off without you."

I conquered the stone steps and stood in the open archway of the Temple, peering in just in time to see my mother stalk across the stone floor and slap Nyx across the face—hard. So hard my sister fell to the floor, hitting the unforgiving ground with an awful splat. The Eternal Flame roared in response, the licking fire reaching higher, whipping rapidly. My heart sunk, my eyes darting from side to side, hoping to find the Luminary rushing to defend my sister. But Nyx and my mother were alone in here.

Nyx spotted me standing here at the same time as my mother did.

Esmeralda Morningstar had eyes of fire, literally. Flames roared in her dark irises, her face painted with fury and disdain. All this ferocity was now directed at me.

"What are you doing here?" she hissed at me. She straightened up, flicking her long black ponytail over her shoulder. "It is a disrespect to the Goddess to come to the Sacred Temple without an invitation! Leave at once, ignorant daughter!"

And it's not disrespectful to the Goddess to slap your daughter in Her Sacred Temple?

But those words did not manage to escape my tongue. I stood there, mute, and frozen, my lips popped open.

Nyx wiped the blood from her swelling lips, glaring at me as she rose to her feet. "Get out of here," she growled at me.

We'd been here a thousand times before. Time and time again I found them like this. But something about right now was different. Esmeralda had come completely unhinged, her fists balled and alight with wicked flame.

"GO!" Nyx shrieked, her facial expression drenched with desperation.

I stood unmoving on wobbly knees for a handful of heartbeats before I turned and quite literally ran away.

I beelined it across the cobblestone path, into the Academy, down the narrow halls until I found a small alcove and sat my useless ass down. My chest rose and fell, tears pricking my eyes as they threatened to spill down my cheeks. I couldn't catch my breath. Soon my vision turned into a watery mirage. No wonder my sister never let anyone in. No wonder she didn't ask for help. I just stood there and watched Mother attack her. I did nothing. Same old story.

But what was I supposed to do?

"Emilia?"

I jumped, looking up through hot tears as Priestess Adria materialized into view. She stood by the alcove, looking down at me with a soft expression. Her long, ice-blue robes flowed around her like liquid silk, pooling at her feet. Her eyes were somehow light blue despite her dark skin. Her black, tightly ringleted hair seemed to float around her as if we were underwater. She offered me a smile. A calmness washed over me, lightening the tension in my shoulders, willing me to relax. Breathe. The soothing effects of water magic. I couldn't complain.

"Yes?" I rasped, wiping tears from the corner of my eyes awkwardly.

"Come with me," Adria purred.

The magnetic pull of water magic had me rising to my feet in no time. Her voice was luxurious and enticing, reminding me of a siren's song. I trusted her fully as I followed her down the hallways. Those silken robes cascaded behind her in a train of heavenly blue, swishing along the polished floor.

She brought me to the doorway of one of the towering turrets. We climbed a narrow, spiral staircase, dimly lit by floating candles. No windows allowed any sunlight in. I trailed along behind the blue-robed woman, my heart thumping erratically in my chest. When we reached the top, she encouraged me to go through the door alone. "I will be waiting at the bottom for you."

I swallowed thickly, the hairs on the back of my neck rising.

I stepped into the low-lit circular room. A peculiar space, free of clutter, but with books stacked to the ceiling along half the wall space. One small, round window let the light in through blue and red painted stained glass. There was a chair and a desk, a few floating candles, and a mattress on the floor. Michael stood there beside the mattress, a vision that cast a blade through my heart.

"Hey," he said.

"Hi." I didn't move from where I was planted in the doorway. I took in the small space, and him standing in it.

"Like my new pad?" He laughed nervously and it took me a moment to register that he was attempting to make a light joke. Like right now was the time for jokes. "It's an upgrade from my mom's basement if you ask me."

"Michael," I breathed. "Are you okay? What's been going on?"

"I'm fine," he answered, shoving his hands into his jeans pockets. Those endless brown eyes had me pinned in place, heat traveling up my spine as our eyes stayed locked and he chewed the silver ring through his lip. "I'm Marked by your Goddess, apparently."

My heart skipped a beat. "What?"

"Fuck if I know what that means, Emilia. Yesterday I was just living my boring, normal life. Then your sister shows up at the warehouse with that angry giant. She freaks out because I can remember her and the next thing I know I'm being sucked into a portal made of spinning light which brought me to Los Angeles. All that shit in the hotel goes down and now I'm here, being 'psychically evaluated' by a lady who controls water. She didn't tell me much, except that I am somehow chosen by the deity you all worship at this hidden magical school. No big deal."

I just stood there. My signature response: nothing.

Eventually, I started shaking my head. "But you are mortal."

He rolled his eyes to play off the way those words stung him. "So I keep hearing."

"W–what I mean is, she didn't say you are somehow Celestial?"

"No."

"Okay," I said stupidly. I still hadn't moved from my spot in the doorway. He hadn't moved either.

"What I do know is: magic doesn't work on me. Any supernatural weapon formed against me will bounce right back to the sender, times three. That's why that huge guy went flying out the window. Pretty fucking epic if I'm being honest."

My heart hammered slowly in my chest, thudding dangerously against the cage of my ribs.

"You seem weirdly unfazed by all of this," I stated suspiciously.

He shrugged, taking one single step closer to me which still left the whole room between us, yet my body stiffened in anticipation. "Your mother said some weird shit to me last week. Ever since I knew something was up. I've been dreaming of you... I..."

"What did my mother say?" I demanded, bitterness lacing every syllable.

"You stopped replying to my texts, so I went to your house, asked to see you... She said you weren't there, and you wouldn't be back. She said you went to Europe for school! I knew that was bullshit and when I demanded to know how to contact you, she reached out and grabbed my arm. Harshly. She looked into my eyes, and it was the weirdest thing. I felt this...an unexplainable, um, I don't know, a magnetic pull or something. She spoke to me in tongues—in Latin—and I felt the power of the words. I was so freaked out, I just left. I went and Googled the words she said to me and, Emilia, she was trying to make me forget you! She tried to put a spell on me!"

My heart thrashed painfully, my legs turning to hot jelly. "But it didn't work?" I whispered.

"No," he growled. "It didn't work. After that, I've been going fucking crazy. Trying to research witchcraft and magic—trying to figure out what happened to you." He moved even closer to me, brown eyes wide and teeming with tidal waves of emotion that threatened to swallow me whole. "Now I see it's a lot deeper than shit like that." His masculine scent filled the air around me and finally, I found my legs and managed to step closer to him. Only a few feet stood between us now.

My eyes raked him up and down. His black shirt, blue jeans, tousled hair... My attention snagged on the tattoo on his inner forearm. Scripted writing, **Rebel Army**. A tattoo I'd admired a thousand times but something about it felt entirely new now. My tongue dried, my heart still racing. "So, what now? Are you going to stay here?"

"I guess," he replied softly. "That woman—the water woman—"

"She is a Priestess," I told him gently.

"Er, right. That Priestess said I can stay here for a while." He motioned around the circular room. "She said I should read some of these books and I should start journaling all my dreams."

"What about your mother?"

"It's taken care of," Michael said, a hint of dubiousness in his tone. "Whatever that means."

I nodded. As if any of this made sense.

Michael was staying at Luna Academy.

Our Goddess chose him.

"I'm supposed to stay a secret, though," he added, gnawing his lip ring, gauging my reaction. "Only you and your sister and those other three girls can know I'm here. I'll be working with the one who...who has those psychic, seeing powers or whatever."

"Natalia," I breathed.

"Yeah, her."

"Are you...are you okay with all of this?" My body trembled as the words tumbled out ineptly. "Do you want to go back? If you don't want to be here, I swear, I'll have them let you go—"

"Emilia," he interrupted me, his tone making my breath hitch. *Goddess save me.* I loved the way my name sounded on his tongue. It was like a different word when he spoke it with his dazzling accent. Intensity burned in his stare as he shook his head slowly at me.

There was something undeniably different between us now. Something evolved, something that went far beyond the tension and temptation that always danced between us.

We shared a secret now. A deeper understanding.

Michael had never failed to make my heart race; we'd been drawn together over and over but I'd always kept him at a distance. The way I wanted him terrified me. I couldn't have him. He'd forget me. I made sure he knew not to cross that line with me—until he stopped giving a shit and tried to kiss me that night at the carnival. Fireworks exploded in the sky, and he leaned in, his eyes so lit and determined and mesmerizing. I'd fantasized about it a thousand times but the idea of it coming true had ignited my fight-or-flight instincts.

So I ran.

Just like I ran from my mother.

The way he was looking at me, part of me wanted to run away right now too. I fought to keep my weak knees from trembling visibly.

"I want to be where you are," Michael told me, his voice even, but his throat worked, and he shifted on his feet. "I didn't know if I'd ever seen you again. Do you know what that fucking felt like?"

"Uh, yes," I answered breathily.

"I realized how much time I wasted with you. Letting you keep me at arm's length, never letting me get close even though I know you wanted me to. Now I know why. You're some special, magical angel person and, Emilia, believe me, it makes sense. I mean, it doesn't make sense, but at the same time—it does. I always knew there was something different about you. Emilia Morningstar. Now that everything's out in the open, you don't have to keep pushing me away."

His words ricocheted through my being, making my ears ring. Was he right? Did all this mean we could be together?

I stepped back, shaking my head. "Weren't you paying attention yesterday? There is an escaped Celestial prisoner wreaking havoc on our Society. It's not safe, Michael. You shouldn't—you should be back home, with your family, away from all of this bullshit."

"Emilia."

There he went, saying my name like that, threatening to be my undoing. I released a breathy sound as the intensity in his eyes spiked even more.

"Look at me." He gestured to his split brow and faded black eye. "Last week, Malcolm and his buddies fucking jumped me over some he-said-she-said bullshit that wasn't even true. He pulled a knife on me and if a cop hadn't driven by right then and there—I might not be here right now."

My heart sank and then took off in an Olympic race. The thought of someone hurting Michael made me see red. I opened my mouth to speak but he kept going.

"A few nights ago, Rachel Stevens overdosed and died in Ricky's basement. My mom's cousin recently got into a terrible car accident and she's in a wheelchair now and may never walk again. The point is,

Emilia, the world itself is not safe. Every single day, you wake up and are at risk by simply being alive. The sky could always fall. Shit happens. I don't care what shit that may be as long as I get to be around you."

My stomach knotted. Rachel was dead? I knew that girl. Not well, but I'd seen her around school. Funny, pretty, and full of potential. Michael stared at me, searching my face, trying to see into me while I processed all of this. I opened my mouth, but nothing came out.

He took another step closer. "Stay with me for a bit. Help me go through some of these books and see what they say."

My breathing accelerated at the idea of that. Be alone with Michael, hidden away in a turret of the academy...

"Okay," I murmured.

CHAPTER 23
SUNSET HYSTERIA
NYX

I came to the beach to watch the sunset. I figured he'd find me here. I couldn't imagine there was a single place on this earth where he wouldn't find me.

Moments away from my cursed fate, I let the ocean wind gust over me, praying internally to the Goddess. Our primordial, inconceivable, great, and terrible Goddess. The Mother of All. Mortals, Celestials, gods, and monsters alike. All came from Her and would return to Her in the end. Nameless, ageless, unknowable. She'd had many titles over the ages, but no name could encapsulate Her entirety.

I saw no signs that She heard me.

The beach was busy, but I didn't mind the hum and chatter of mortals. Peculiar creatures, they were. Their children were wild and primal, but they were always scorned by their parents for it. I watched as a few kids played in the crashing waves, their parents lingering on the shoreline, calling out for them to be careful. Eventually, their wildness would be snuffed out. Pity.

The sky melted into a canvas of deep orange that merged into rich amethyst at the horizon. Gorgeous, yet I found not a drop of enjoyment in it.

I was fucking exhausted.

Physically, spiritually, mentally—*wholly* exhausted. I knew I looked like absolute shit despite wearing my best leathers. I was thin, gaunt, and drained. Plus, I had a busted lip from my mom's wonderful slap earlier. Fucking bitch. Portalled in just to give me an earful and a smack. Then left. Part of me was angrier at Delphyne than Esmeralda. The Luminary and I had chatted for hours last night, and she never mentioned that she'd be telling my mother. Fuck it, though. My mother detested my existence anyways. I couldn't care less what she thought of me now. Maybe she'd officially disown me forever and I'd never have to see her again.

Faye and Natalia had visited me in the Temple after that, but they weren't allowed to stay long. Faye offered to glamour me so I looked vibrant and healthy, but I'd declined. I decided to wear the bitter truth, right on my face.

I stood in the sand with my bare feet, feeling the lick of the tide caress my toes. Hot tears burned the backs of my eyes, but I bit them back, refusing to let them free. "Feeling sentimental tonight, Firefly?"

Solaris Adder appeared at my side, quite literally manifesting out of thin air. No whirl of shadows, no grand entrance. He didn't even look at me. His sharp, ethereal profile was illuminated by the golden hour as he stared out and took in the sunset. Like always, he wore a long black jacket, his mahogany mop windblown and glossy. The sight of him stabbed me, dead center. The breath halted in my lungs while my eyes traveled over him, my pulse accelerating.

"My name is Nyx," I said dryly.

"Have you made your decision?"

My stomach hollowed out. So we were getting right to it. Worked for me.

"Yes."

He turned to me now. My mind clouded over with sunset hysteria, confusing me, making him one of the most beautiful things I'd ever seen. The sharpness of his features, the otherworldly bone structure... Shit. The melted purple sky was messing with me.

Solaris's attention snagged on my lips, and I swore I saw lightning flash behind his eyes. "Who did this to you?" He reached out to brush his thumb along my bottom lip and I swatted him away indignantly.

"That's none of your concern."

"Tell me who it was, and I will give you the pleasure of watching me kill them ever so brutally."

I barked a cold laugh. "Oh, okay, hotshot. It was my mother."

His brows narrowed as if that information confused him.

Heat spilled across my cheeks. "And despite her being a miserable bitch, I don't really want to see her murdered. Anyway... We're not here to talk about my mommy issues, are we?"

"I suppose not," he replied reluctantly, those magnetic silver portals to his soul still focused on my mouth. For a moment I thought he wasn't going to let it go, but then his attention snapped back up to my eyes. "Tell me what you choose, then."

Eye contact with Solaris felt like freefall. It intoxicated me, giving my tongue a mind of its own. "I heard about your little visit to Veneficus. I must say, I'm a bit offended. I thought this little thing between us was special. But apparently, you're trying to force everyone into allegiance with you."

He stared at me as if I'd spoken in a foreign language. Then his face split into a dazzling smile that made my heart do a backflip behind my ribs. "Not to worry, Firefly. Every chessboard needs an army of pawns. But there is only one queen."

Goddess damn me.

"Jedidiah Stone is no pawn," I told him.

"Perhaps not," he mused quietly, his eyes far away for a moment as if the mention of Jedidiah sent him into a distracting train of thought.

My stupid heart was racing, and my stupid knees felt weak. I needed to deflect. I cleared my throat and reached into the mesh bag at my side, pulling out a small scroll. "Here."

He took it, curiosity blooming behind his elvan features. Solaris's eyes jumped from me to the scroll a couple of times before he dared to unroll it. He read it silently and I watched him while pressure built up in my chest. His face stayed unreadable.

He scoffed darkly. "You assume this is a negotiation? I made my terms crystal clear."

"I am a daughter of the Original Goddess! I am the descendant of Alexandria Morningstar, one of the greatest queens of the Old World! I have fire in my blood and dragon rider instincts! I have a right to make a counteroffer. You have not honored my Sovereignty, not once. I—"

"No." Solaris deadpanned. "Don't think I don't know these are the words of your Luminary. You talk about Sovereignty, and yet, you didn't even write these words yourself." His silver eyes skimmed over the scroll once more. "Pathetic. Did you think I would agree to this?"

I shrugged, my heart sinking at the look on his face. He showed zero signs of agreeing to my attempted bargain. Desperation ignited in my veins. I cleared my throat and prayed my face didn't betray me. "Why are you so hasty to start a war, Solaris?" The way he stiffened as his name slid out of my lips was not lost on me. Perhaps I was speaking in a huskier tone than usual. I stepped closer to him, making his brows lower. Delphyne said I should try and charm him...

"You've just broken free from a lifetime prison. Thanks to me, remember. You vanquished San Gabriel. You have all the Priestesses and Chancellors on their toes. Even the High Lord and his Council are afraid. They know they stand no chance against your power. You have them by the balls. But the rest of the Society has forgotten your horrific crime. They don't know anything about you. The Luminary gave a warning to the girls of Luna Academy about vampires. There's no heat on you. You don't have to start a war with the Society. Isn't there another way you'd like to spend your time now that you are free?"

He glared down at me, clearly thrown off. "Firefly, I—"

"There's so much you haven't experienced," I went on, my voice hardly more than a whisper as I looked up at him through my lashes. My pulse thrashed erratically, the sunset glow affecting us both on a soul level. "Do you truly crave more violence and conflict? Is that the real reason why you chose to target *me*? Or is there something else you want?"

His lips parted slightly at my subliminal message.

And then his expression bloomed with something like...desire. As if my words woke up a part of him that had been dormant forever. I didn't expect to move him, but when I saw the heat spring behind his eyes, my fight-or-flight instincts kicked in. The way he looked at me, like...like I was offering salvation. His gaze stayed locked with mine, a thousand unsaid words coursing between us. That was perfect, right? That was what Delphyne told me to do. Work my feminine charm and soften him. Looking upon his face now, it was working.

There was just one problem. One terrible, terrible problem. If I went there... If I unleashed my femininity at Solaris, if I dared to charm him...that would be a web only I would get trapped in. He was the black widow here. I was just the foolish, curious firefly dancing with danger.

His eyes left mine, traveling down to my mouth. He reached out instinctively and brushed the pad of his thumb along the angered skin of my lips. I sucked in a sharp breath but didn't swat him away this time. The emotion in his expression as he healed the wound my mother left on me made my mind whirl out of control. The coolness of his fingers against my sore, hot flesh did unspeakable things to me.

Yeah, no.

I couldn't do this.

I stepped back and hardened my expression, cutting the heady cord of intimacy that had formed between us. "You want my allegiance? You'll have to truly earn it."

The emotion in his eyes snuffed out immediately. He stepped back too, his guard flying back up.

I pointed to the scroll he still held. My skin vibrated with nervous chills. "Battle me. For real. One-on-one, with an audience, both of us conscious and coherent. If you win, I will pledge allegiance to you in whatever wars you wish to drum up. If I win, though... You have to leave. And swear to never use your malevolent shadow magic on anyone or anything ever again."

He stared down at me, searching my face wordlessly. My heart was thrashing behind my ribs. I was sure he could hear it.

Mortals bustled around the beach, living their simple, carefree lives, while Solaris and I stood at the shoreline in a face-off.

"Give me my power tonight and I swear to you, on the Goddess and the stars and the sacred animal kingdom, that I will not use my power against you except in allotted times. That's what you fear, isn't it? My power against yours? I am the only thing that could stand in your way, aren't I?"

His eyes widened and his brows narrowed. "Do you *really* have that much confidence in your power? Haven't I proved that it is pointless to stand against me? I'm offering you your magic back. All you must do is—"

"Of course I'm confident in my power." My heart slammed so hard, I felt it on my tongue. "And even if I wasn't, I would still risk my life for a chance at dangerous freedom, rather than yield to your deranged promise of power and safety. What you're offering me, Solaris, is a gilded cage. I would rather be powerless than bound to you, but I won't go down without a proper fucking fight."

I couldn't read the expression that polluted his features. All I knew was that my words changed something inside him.

"Come on, big bad shadowling," I went on, "don't tell me you are afraid to fight me fair and square?"

For a moment, he only stared at me, his expression grim but unreadable. And then, ever so fucking slowly, a smile that made my stomach drop crept across his full lips. An insidious smile that didn't touch those unrelenting silver eyes.

The sky darkened overhead, the orange and amethyst fading to blackish gray. He summoned storm clouds that boomed thunder over the beach—instantly. Mortals started crying out in shock and confusion at the rapid weather change.

I tried to stay calm, keeping my chin tipped up as I held his gaze.

A full-on storm commenced in the sky above. The mortals began to flee.

He splayed his arms then, sending snakes of shadows across the sand, where they began to hunt. It all happened so impossibly fast—my brain hardly registered that this was real. A scream got stuck in my throat as I watched the shadows writhe their way to the humans, dozens, and dozens of humans all over the long beach, snaking around their ankles, traveling up their legs, and—devouring them.

"NO!" I cried.

Thunder crashed, and lightning struck. It was impossible, what was happening. I'd never seen anything like it, not in my darkest nightmares, not in the scariest horror films. People screamed and cried as the tethers of darkness swirled around them, entering their mouths and eyes and noses, wrapping around them completely. Shadows feasted on them and drained them and made them small, until they were gone, leaving not even a dust pile behind. Solaris willed his shadows to consume each and every person on the beach before they could make it off the sand.

Soon the beach was empty and silent, save for the thundering storm overhead.

My chest rose and fell while hot, furious tears stained my cheeks.

No.

"You fucking monster!" I screamed. "They were innocent! How could you! Women! *Children!*" My voice broke on the last word, my knees buckling as I hit the sand, sobs ripping from my chest.

"It is mercy," Solaris quipped roughly, glaring down at me as lightning struck behind him. "Their pathetic, meaningless, mortal lives are nothing more than enslavement and suffering. Not even death is an escape for them. After they die, their souls are recycled back into this world via the reincarnation trap set up in the Astral Realm. Do you learn about that, in your elite academies, hm? Do you learn about the soul net that encompasses the Earth and traps every single mortal soul that tries to leave this place? Forcing them to come back again and again, to feed the beast machine, each life weaker and more agonizing than the last until their soul burns out completely!

"Don't you see? I freed them. I sent them back to the nothingness from which we all came. They are whole again. They are no longer bound by the light."

I shook my head at him, words escaping me. He was insane.

He believed the words he was saying.

"You didn't free them—you ravaged them!! You—that was horrifying! They were eaten by shadows!"

He grinned like a psychopath. "Tomato, tom-ah-to."

All I could do was shake my head.

"I told you that I am capable of unfathomable devastation, and yet still you test me. You treat me as if I am one of your lowly little classmates who can be manipulated and molded. Now you know what happens when you try to go against me, Firefly."

I sobbed silently in the sand, wishing the Goddess would materialize on the beach and send *him* back to the nothingness from which we all came.

"You are a coward," I ground out. My vision was little more than a blurry, watery screen of gray and black. "A fucking coward. You want to start a war? Go ahead. You might win for a while but eventually, my people will figure out how to defeat you. You are alone. The Celestial Society may not be perfect but at least we have each other. You stand no chance in the long run, Solaris Adder. I think you know that, or else you wouldn't be trying to force my allegiance. Well, you can shove that idea up your ass. I will never stand by you."

"*Rise*," Solaris demanded, his voice thick with Compulsion that gave me no choice but to stand up and face him.

I blinked away the tears, wishing they would just fuck off already.

I wept silently, standing in front of him while endless silver eyes pierced my soul. I decided at that moment that I hated his eyes more than anything. That unnatural, demonic color. The way they snared me like a fish on a hook. I couldn't look away, couldn't see anything else.

"You have a fierce spirit," he said. "I knew you would be a challenge, even with all the advantages I have. If you truly choose to give up your magic, I will honor that choice. But once you make it, there is no going back."

The tears dried, leaving sticky, tight-feeling stains on my cheeks.

"Your Society won't be able to defeat me without you." Solaris mused casually. "Either way, I will triumph. With you by my side, or you out of the picture completely—either one works in my favor. Don't you see?"

My breath came out hard and ragged, my fists clenched at my sides. Thunder rang down from the heavens, making the waves of the ocean furious. Wind whipped through my hair, the smell of rain descending from the clouds. Lightning brightened Solaris's face, casting ominous shadows under his sharpened cheekbones. He looked like a storm given form. Darkness, terror, and destruction incarnate.

It dawned on me at that moment... Jedidiah was right. Solaris feared my power. Which was why his first move out of prison was either ridding me of it or assuring it would be used on his side. Perhaps I'd always known I wasn't just your average fireling. My fire was different. Brighter, hotter. Celestial. Everything they'd said in the hotel was true.

We stared at each other while the thunder and lightning danced violently above. Solaris stood perfectly still, a face of stone while the wind made his hair thrash wildly. I got lost in his gaze, a series of tele-pathic images hitting my mind's eye so abruptly I gasped. *A small, cold, white room. Metal bed frame, uncomfortable mattress. Always cold. Dim hallways. Razer. Shaved head. Wires. Screens. Tests. Pain. Animals in cages. Demands. Men in white coats. Probed. Pain. Tests failed. Shock. Pain. Endless days. Darkness. Pain.*

The images fled as quickly as they came, leaving me even more breathless than before. I blinked up at Solaris while he glared down at me, showing no sign that he knew I'd seen anything. His eyes searched my face, but he spoke no words.

I was no Seer. So what the fuck was that?

I turned away from him, covering my face in my hands. No. No, I didn't want to see any of it. I didn't want to know about his life. I could have asked the Luminary to tell me the full story of what happened to him, but I didn't. I had no interest in learning about Solaris's past. I had no interest in finding reasons to empathize with him. He was a monster and he needed to stay that way.

"Don't you turn your back on me!" he roared, grabbing my shoul-der, and whirling me around to face him.

The intensity of his stare threatened to be my undoing.

"Solaris," I breathed. His name on my lips again seemed to stir him. "You spent a century in prison. A lifetime before that, underground. Don't you want to fucking live? Don't you want to experience the world before you...before you remake it?"

His brows narrowed.

"Maybe you will triumph in your war," I rasped, the revelation of that making me scoff darkly. "If that's truly what you want. If there's truly no part of you that is curious about what it's like to—live. Walk the lit-up streets at night, meet people, experience the sunrise, dive into the waves headfirst. Fall in love, read a good book, pet a dog—climb a mountain. The world is literally at your feet, and you want to destroy it. You want to make enemies and build an army of forced soldiers. You choose to ruin a perfectly divine sunset by annihilating a beach full of innocent people. Do you think any of this violence and terror will offer you solace? Do you think it will make your past any less—"

"How dare you speak of my life as if you have a clue!" he snarled, rage lighting like a firecracker behind those bright eyes. "You don't know the first thing about me."

I snatched the scroll from his hand, startling him with my audacity. I read the words aloud. "I, Nyx Morningstar, swear to pledge my allegiance to Solaris Adder if he can defeat me in a battle of our elements. I swear to not use my power against him except for at allotted times. If Solaris Adder fails to triumph against me, he must abandon his quest for war, flee Los Angeles and swear he will never use his power for malevolent purposes."

"I can read," he retorted dryly as thunder crashed.

"It's an official Celestial Oath. Once we both sign this, the deal is sealed by the stars themselves. If you want my allegiance, this is how you get it. By truly beating me. Not by luring me into the shadows to exploit me in the dark. Not by dangling my magic in front of my nose, giving me ultimatums."

I stepped closer, trying not to notice the way his breath caught as I did so. I tipped my chin up and leveled him with a stare. "Face. Me. One-on-one. Both lucid, both coherent, both unleashing our full power. If you win, you have me."

"You just don't give up, do you?" Solaris grumbled icily, his metallic eyes flashing with a look I could only describe as demonic. "You know what, Firefly? I'll humor you." He reached out and I jumped as he gripped me by the top of the arms, pulling me into his chest. I opened my mouth to protest but the shadows erupted around us, swallowing us into a black hole.

My body exploded with pins and needles, my vision turning to black lace as we traveled through the ether. The shadows dropped us off outside of a painfully familiar little white house.

"No," I breathed, my flesh rising with goosebumps.

Solaris kept his hands on my arms as he guided me toward the house. The night was dark and moonless, the stars blinking down upon us. My heart hammered in every inch of my body as he guided me to the back window of the quaint little character home tucked in the woods. He made me look inside.

There they were. My heart tore out of my chest for a thousand different reasons. My old friends, who had forgotten me. Marvel,

Danica, Maria, Layton. Sitting around in Marvel's father's basement, smoking out of bongs, and drinking cheap beer while the Sex Pistols raged on in the background. Laughing and bullshitting.

I assumed they couldn't see us. Marvel glanced out the window as he took a haul of his beer. He looked right through me.

"Why are we here?" I breathed shakily. Solaris stood at my back, his hand perched on my shoulder, casting traitorous surges of electricity through my being.

"You care for these strange creatures," he explained lightly. "In fact, you care for several strange creatures. That is one of your many weaknesses. Do you want to battle me one on one, little Firefly? Fine." He brushed the back of his fingers along my cheekbone, making me shiver. "You failed to become Keeper of the Baton. You must correct that error. Demand a rematch with Venus St. Claire. Beat her and get the Baton in your possession. If you fail to achieve this by tomorrow at sundown, I will erase these mortals from existence. And I will do it slowly. They will suffer in my shadows for hours before they are consumed."

My blood roared in my ears. The words he spoke deflated me. "I would need magic for that."

"Yes, I suppose you would." He gripped my shoulder and turned me around to face him. He was so close, leaning down, his regal face becoming my only reality. "I will give you another drop of your magic. You will face Venus St. Claire again—this time, you will win. Once you bring me the Sacred Baton, I will agree to your deal. You'll have your power back as long as you swear not to use it against me until we face off on Hallows Eve. If you fail tomorrow, all bets are off and I will feed your magic to the shadows, as well as everyone you've ever loved."

I sucked in a sharp breath, letting that all settle in.

"You can still go with the original offer, you know," he added through a smirk.

"If I beat Venus and bring you the Sacred Baton, you will give me my full power back? You will fight me one-on-one, and if you lose, you will swear to give up your plans of war, and leave us alone?"

He stared at me for a moment. Then nodded. Once.

My body lit up with energy that manifested as goosebumps.

"I will take your advice," he told me slowly, his voice floating in the air around me like a condescending caress. "I will put my war with the Society on hold for a while. You're right, after all, Firefly. Perhaps I do want to experience this world before I remake it."

He grabbed my face, aggressively, forcing me to look up into his glaring eyes. "I gave you a chance. I offered you the world and instead you tried to make a fool of me. You tried to tug at my heartstrings and weave me in your web. You will regret this. You will not beat me, Firefly. And when you lose, you will be mine. We could have been a harmonious pair, but I must say, you have succeeded in pissing me off. So, when you lose and become mine, you will pay for the trouble you've caused me."

He whirled me around so quickly I didn't even have time to gasp. He wrapped one long, strong arm around my throat in a choke hold and pulled me into his body, locking me in place. My flesh ignited with electric shocks as he forced my head back. I looked into his silver eyes. I saw the fury and pain in them. With his free hand, he held the crimson medallion that glowed with my magic. "Open your mouth for me, Firefly."

Goddess damn me.

I stared up at this creature, my heart beating a dent into my ribcage. He thought he had me. At his mercy. He thought he was the master of puppets here.

He still underestimated me. Even after everything, he was still so sure of his superiority over me. Arrogance would be his downfall, just as it had been mine.

He didn't realize the hold he held me in gave my pointy little elbow perfect access to his solar plexus.

I popped my lips open as if to obey him. My open mouth so close to his face proved to be a perfect distraction. I jammed my elbow into his solar plexus hard enough to make him grunt. I moved like lightning, knowing it was now or never. His face contorted with shock and rage as I winded him and he relaxed his hold on me. I whirled around and punched him right in the nose—hard. Once again, Solaris Adder was bleeding for me. I wound my arm back to hit him again, but he caught my wrist, a furious snarl tearing from his throat as he shoved me against the side of the house.

"You wicked little cricket," he hissed, though there was something like admiration hiding behind the rage in his eyes. He pressed his body against mine, earning himself a startled gasp out of me. "You really do enjoy it, don't you?"

"What, hurting you?" I spat. "Of course I fucking do."

"No." He shook his head, eyes burning. "Not just me. Anyone. You showed up tonight with a bruised ego and a busted lip. You want to pay it forward, don't you? You desire to inflict pain upon others, so they hurt like you hurt. You can't tell me I'm wrong, can you, Firefly? I'm just your excuse. I give you a safe, justified target. But that urge lives within you on its own. You feel most comfortable with your boot on someone's neck, don't you?"

I opened my mouth but *fuck my life*, nothing came out.

He gave me a bloody, taunting grin. "But the tables have turned, and the universe has given your karma a wicked form. Now it's my boot on your neck, and I shall not relent until you give me what I want. Now open your goddamn mouth."

My chest rose and fell, my body sparking with all kinds of despicable reactions to his closeness. Was he right?

I opened my mouth for him, and my stomach hollowed out at the soft sound he made when I did so. He brought the medallion to my lips and fed me a few drops of the glorious, sweet, and smoky substance.

I fucking moaned as the orgasmic glowing liquid power hit my insides and made the entire map of my veins light up like a Christmas tree. He looked so lovely covered in blood, the result of my violent little delight. I sank into him, my legs giving out. Euphoria possessed me. He felt so good with his arms around me, holding me up. I was delusional off my own magic, cackling as I admired his insidious beauty. His bloody lips looked good enough to kiss.

Pleasure and power consumed me but so did shadows. I could hardly even grasp what was happening as they tore me through the ether and dropped me back off in my dorm room.

CHAPTER 24
MOONRISE BLVD
JEDIDIAH

The last couple of days were straight out of an episode of *the Twilight Zone*. So I did what I always did when my head was all screwed up. I worked out. Down in the gym with my boys, I focused on sweat, screaming muscles, and pushing myself beyond all limits. The better shape your physical body was in, the stronger your magic would be. Which was one of the many reasons I worked out like a goddamn juice head.

I was a huge motherfucker—not beefy, but I stood at a whopping six-four, all lean muscle. I glared into my own eyes in the reflection of the wall mirror as I lifted my last set. My veins protruded as I pushed myself, refusing to give in to the strain in my arms. I crashed the dumbbells down with a grunt once I beat my record.

I looked like my father. I saw him every time I looked at myself. Which was why I fought the urge to spit at the glass every time I was in front of a mirror.

The gym down here in the Vault was just like a mortal gym except for the fact that everything was black and there were no windows.

I slammed the rest of the water from my glass bottle and wiped the sweat from my brow, breathing heavily. Raziel and Demitri finished on the machines behind me, our eyes all meeting in the mirror.

215

"That Faye girl texted me," Raziel said. "Nyx made a new deal with Solaris."

My chest tightened while I fought to keep my face neutral. I hadn't stopped thinking about that girl since we parted ways from the hotel. I knew she was set to meet him last night. At the same time as an unnatural storm occurred over the ocean after sunset. It was them—it had to be.

"What deal?"

"I don't know. But she hasn't sworn allegiance to him yet."

I scoffed. Of course she found a way to stall a tyrant. But obviously, she had to offer him something else to get him to change his mind. That was unsettling.

"Which means she's still on our side," Demitri noted with a grin.

"She's power drained." I snapped, fury rising from my solar plexus. "What good is she to us when she's practically mortal?"

"Faye said she has some of her power back," Raziel offered.

"Some?" I spat. "What the fuck does that mean?"

"I don't know, man," Raziel put his hands up defensively. "I'm surprised they're even keeping us in the loop at all."

"Did she say anything else?"

"No. Not really. She asked how I like my tattoo, and if I—"

"I don't give a shit about any of that," I muttered dryly, heading off to shower and get changed.

By the time I left the gym, I was ravenous. I'd been in here working out since sunrise. I needed to eat a twelve-course meal and drink a barrel of coffee. The twins had buggered off without showering, probably just to avoid me and my foul mood. Good. I needed to be alone. I needed to think.

When I arrived in the dining hall, I found it fully occupied. The long, black tables were fully seated with the eager students of Veneficus, whose attention was fixed on a startling face.

Solaris Adder sat at the far end of the middle table. Aro sat at the head of it, right beside him, and Mother and Father above—Aro was smiling.

Time moved slowly as I took in the scene. Solaris had a mug in front of him, an ominous grin tugging at his lips as he listened to whatever bullshit Aro was spewing. On the other side of Aro, sat Tiberius, our second Chancellor.

Aro caught sight of me standing in the archway and smiled brightly, waving me over.

What the fucking fuck?

I moved mechanically, gripping my staff at my side, almost hard enough to snap it in two. Part of me wanted to turn around and bolt out of there but a twisted sense of curiosity got me. I wanted to know what in the devil's dick was going on here.

Aro urged a few boys to scoot their chairs down and make room for me. I glared wordlessly, remaining standing. Solaris Adder had his silver snake eyes all over me, practically salivating at my tense stance.

"Come, join us," Aro insisted, motioning to a chair that had recently freed up. "We have much to discuss. Where have you been hiding, Jedidiah?"

"What is going on?" I deadpanned, staring straight into Aro's soul, trying to figure out if it was really him or if I was dreaming. Only one night ago, he had been crunched like a biscuit and tossed to the ground by the man who he now sat merrily beside.

"We are showing our esteemed guest a proper welcome," Aro explained through a smile that made me homicidal.

"*Esteemed guest*?" The words tasted like acid on my tongue. I swear the inside of my chest had completely iced over. I glanced around the room, at all the other guys. I didn't see the twins in here. Where the hell were they?

"Now, Jedidiah," Tiberius drawled, his tone laced with warning. He was a dark-skinned man with long dreadlocks and dead eyes. His finger-nails were disgustingly long. His air magic was shotty. He always wore the same black cloak that smelt like mothballs. "Have a seat, will you?"

"You can explain to me while I stand."

"We are the home of the most powerful male heirs in the entire Celestial Society," Aro said, his tone wry and shady. "Solaris Adder has recently Emerged as a shadowling. Where else would he belong, but here?"

Solaris watched my face the entire time.

I opened my mouth, but nothing came out.

Every single set of eyes in the room were fixed on me.

"Aro." My voice was hard but fractured. My heart thrashed as my glare darted between the two Chancellors.

"Yes, Jedidiah?" His gaze looked slightly glassy, his smile forced.

"After what he did to us?" I stated through gritted teeth. All the eyes that were fixed on me widened. Solaris kept his silver stare on me, unrelenting. I focused on Aro. "He assaulted you."

"Now, now! What are you talking about?" Aro cried, rising from his seat. He moved over to me, putting his hand on my shoulder as he led me aside, to speak only to me in a hushed voice. "What are you doing, boy? Don't be so difficult. You know how things work around here."

"He destroyed San Gabriel." I kept going, loudly, so everyone could hear despite us being off in a corner. *Fuck it.* They deserved to know the truth. "Hundreds of students, over a dozen Priestesses and Chancellors. Gone. Wiped out. Like nothing."

Students started murmuring in befuddlement, looking at me as if I were crazy.

A fist clenched around my heart as I scanned their faces, noting how docile and lost they looked. They had no recollection of San Gabriel, or Solaris showing up and putting them all on their asses.

I snapped my focus to Aro, then Tiberius.

Did they remember?

They should have. But something about the foggy looks on their faces told me otherwise.

I couldn't even find it within myself to be angry. I was just numb.

And *why* was this silver-eyed creep looking at me like that? Like I was one of his science experiments gone wrong, but the results turned out even more incredible than originally hypothesized. He didn't say a single word, he just stared at me.

A grin tugged at the corners of his lips.

"Fuck this," I growled, turning on a heel and stalking out of there, low murmurs rippling in my wake. I slammed my staff to the floor, leaving an earth shake behind as I left the Vault with zero intentions of ever coming back.

THE LA STREETS WERE BUSTLING AS ALWAYS, THE MORTAL rat race doing little to distract me. Sometimes I envied them. Their lives were so...fleeting. Every moment counted for them. Each decision weighed greatly on the unfolding of their brief timeline in this realm. They didn't bear the burden of magic and immortality.

My father always preached to me that Celestials were naturally above mortals. I used to believe him. Until I realized that we were no better--we were worse. Celestials judged mortals for their discord and their apathy, but where did they learn it from?

We were once like gods, and now we were just like men.

We fucking failed as a Divine race and no one in the Society wanted to acknowledge that truth. With each generation, we grew weaker, just like the mortals.

This world may have been split in two, but it was still on a one-way road to Hell.

I stalked down the bustling sidewalk, towering over the crowd, making the females stop and stare. Sometimes when I was feeling like shit, I'd seduce a few mortal girls and fuck their brains out. They were wild little things, great for a distraction, but not today. There was only one female on my mind right now. I was going crazy not talking to her, which was ridiculous seeing as how my life and the Celestial Society as a whole were imploding. Yet all my stupid brain could think of was Nyx Morningstar.

I hated that Solaris Adder had his claws in her. I might have even hated it more than him having his claws in my academy. I couldn't stand that he was bending her to his will. Manipulating her. Controlling her. Just thinking about it had my hands clenching into fists. She'd looked so broken when she came to me at the Sun & Moon. I'd buried that girl alive, and she clawed her way out with fire at her fingers, rising from the dirt like a soldier in the army of the dead, her eyes wild and determined. Nothing ever broke her. Nothing, until that shadow fucker emerged from his realm of misery.

I grabbed my blackmirror from my pocket and couldn't stop myself from texting her.

Me: **hey we need to talk ASAP**
Nyx: **who is this?**
Me: **oh fuck off**
Nyx: **oh hi mole boy ;)**
Me: **nyx i mean it. meet me at lucifer's playground right now**
Nyx: **boy are you serious?!? you want me to meet you at a celestial strip club at ten am?? should i be worried about u**
Me: **it's only a strip club on friday nights. trust me, you'll wanna hear what i have to say. meet me there. I'll buy you breakfast**
Nyx: **do they even serve breakfast? lol**
Me: **they will for us. come on.**
Nyx: **fine. but this BETTER be good.**

Lucifer's Playground was the most popular Celestial club in LA. It was where I met Nyx, the night I asked her to dance and she lit my fucking feet on fire, making *me* dance, thinking it was a real hoot. She'd been so cocky and rightfully so. That girl held a fierce, original power that put her above everyone else, and she damn well knew it. It had made her the most infuriating and desirable thing in the city.

I arrived at Sunset Blvd and stopped. I glanced around quickly, making sure no mortals were paying me any attention. Once I was sure there were no eyes on me, I reached out and wrapped my fingers around the pole of the Sunset and Vine Street sign. With a deep inhale, I lifted myself into the next layer of consciousness. The Celestial overlay that was Moonrise Blvd materialized into view.

The Sunset Strip, transformed into a street far more enticing.

Hidden behind a veil, the miraculous Celestial version of the famous street splayed out before me. On Moonrise Blvd, it was eternal night. Gone was the bright morning sky, thank fuck. I was not in the mood for sunshine. The light pollution from the mortal realm didn't exist here, either. The velvet blanket of stars always loomed over the magical strip, showing every single galaxy and constellation as if you were in the farthest corner of the earth with no cities for eons. Street-lights were replaced with floating lanterns, aglow with colorful, enchanted flames. Crystal towers stood tall and abundant, glowing with power. Celestial shops, bars, theaters, and other attractions lined the lit-up street, each one emitting music and voices.

Despite being a weekday morning, the club was bumping. Celestials dressed to the nines danced and laughed. Fire dancers twirled on the floating platforms. The stage was empty today, but the bar was fully staffed with pixie-looking women who gave me the fuck-me eyes as I strode through the crowd of colorful, glittery bodies.

I stalked into the back, behind the thick velvet curtain which was enchanted to keep out the noise. This was the quiet smoking lounge, adorned with tables that were distanced from each other. I slid into a booth in the far corner. A floating chandelier lit with low red lights hovered above me, creating an intimate ambiance. All the waitresses wore colorful hair that glowed in the dark. I waved the pink-haired woman off when she offered to take my drink order.

It didn't take Nyx long to show up, which was a huge shocker. Despite her snarky attitude over text, the girl looked rattled as she strutted over to my table. The sight of her instantly shot a dart into my nerves, my fingers drumming against the table as I tried not to let my eyes rove over her too blatantly.

Her long, silver hair was a chaotic mess, her eye makeup dark and smudged, as if she'd been in a rush while getting ready. Her curvy little frame was scantily covered by her famous training leathers, the ones that made my mouth go dry.

"This better be worth my while, Mole Boy," she grunted as she slid into the seat across from me. Her obsidian eyes were ringed with shadow as they snared me, but she didn't look as gaunt and pale as the last time I saw her.

"You look less like a corpse," I mused.

"Gee, thanks." She rolled her eyes. "Where's the breakfast you promised me, asshole? Do they even serve food here? I mean, really. Why are we *here*, Jedidiah?" She gestured at the low-lit ambiance. "Out of all places?"

"Because," I snapped. "Lucifer's is a haven of debauchery where

Celestials of all kinds come to experience their darkest desires... Meaning, there are impenetrable psychic wards in place, blocking anyone from Astral-spying on us. I wanted some real, good old fashion privacy."

Nyx's brows jumped but she didn't argue.

The pink-haired waitress returned and this time I listed off what I wanted. Two of every breakfast food imaginable. She tried to say they didn't sell breakfast, but I pulled my High Lord's Son card, and she had no choice but to fulfill my ridiculous desire. Nyx watched me through raised brows as I recited our order. She looked as if she didn't know whether to be disgusted or impressed.

"No wonder you're so enormous," she muttered as the befuddled waitress left us. "Must be nice to get whatever you want, whenever you want."

I scoffed. "As if you've ever had a problem getting what you want."

Her eyes immediately went downcast. "You'd be surprised."

I kept my hands under the table so she wouldn't see the way they balled into fists. I tried to keep the rage off my face as I assessed her pathetic demeanor. Gods, I wanted to crush Solaris Adder. I wanted to snap him like a goddamn twig and present his corpse to her as a pile of broken, bloody bones. What he was doing to her—I couldn't stand it. Nyx may have been cruel and spoiled and all things infuriating, but she was not meant to be the little bird trapped in some psycho's cage.

"Why are we here, Jed?"

"Solaris came back to the Vault today," I told her, and her face immediately went white. "Aro called him our *esteemed guest*. I honestly can't tell whether the Chancellors are under Amnesia. They're acting like they are—but they shouldn't be, right?"

She tossed her hands in the air, exasperated. Her fingers crackled with white flame, smoke seeping from her nose as her innate rage took over. "How should I know?"

My eyes popped. So the twins had been right. She did have her magic back.

She banished her fire and took a deep breath. "I have a lot going on, Jed. So, if you just brought me here to complain about—"

"I think we could find a way to cut Solaris off from his shadows," I deadpanned.

That shut her up.

She stared at me from across the table, assessing me like I was mad. "Cut him off from the shadows? How do you expect to do that? You can't just cut a Celestial off from their element."

"That's the thing," I quipped with a grin. "He was originally a waterling. He told me the night he first came to Veneficus. He somehow managed to harness shadows... That means he is not the source of them. Something else is. If he has an outside source that allows him to harness shadows, that means—"

"No." Nyx's tone was absolute. "It's not like that. I can see why you would think that, but you're wrong."

Three waitresses arrived at our table, placing the umpteen plates before us.

The food smelled delicious. Bacon, pancakes, hash browns, fruit, desserts, sandwiches, everything I could want. I didn't even wait until they were gone to start digging in. I gnawed on a piece of bacon while Nyx stared at me like she didn't know me.

"Eat," I ordered her. "You need some calories."

She folded her arms over her chest, leaning back, stubborn as hell. "I have more important shit to worry about than calories."

"Like what?"

She glared at me for a moment, and I was sure that wall of hers was about to fly up. She blew out a long breath. "Solaris wants me to challenge Venus St. Claire for a rematch. He wants me to get the Sacred Baton."

I froze, mid-chew, the bacon in my mouth suddenly tasting like ash. "A rematch? You can't. That's taboo. It's so...mortal."

"Yeah, I fucking know. Thanks. But what choice do I have? Solaris has—"

"I never took you for a little puppet, Nyx Morningstar." Rage burned in my chest as I stared at her and the defeated look that bled across her beautiful features. "You're stronger than this. At least you used to be. If Solaris wants you to get the Baton it means *he* wants the Baton. Fuck, Nyx! We can't give him anything that's going to help him grow in power. Are you serious right now?"

"Beat it, Jed! You don't know shit. Your little idea to cut Solaris off from his shadows is ridiculous, at best. Haven't you seen his magic in action? He is one with the fucking darkness, there's no cutting him off from it. He *is* it. If all you brought me here for was to discuss your dead-end hero's journey, I'm leaving."

She rose to her feet, ready to leave me high and dry. I reached across the table and grabbed her wrist, the contact sending a jolt of electricity up my arm. I yanked her back down, her eyes growing wide and feral as her lips tore back over her teeth. "Sit your ass down. We aren't finished here."

That familiar, white-hot fury lit behind her eyes and before I could even take another breath, she conjured a ball of bright fire and shot it at me, square in the fucking chest. I howled in surprise, throwing up a shield just a beat too late. My chest exploded with searing agony, my shirt burning away as blisters instantly bubbled on my newly exposed skin. I patted the fire out frantically. It died right away, but it left its mark.

"What the fuck!" I roared. I grabbed my staff off the seat and pointed the glowing emerald crystal at her threateningly.

All sets of eyes in the far corners of the club were on us.

Nyx breathed heavily across the table, the disdain still swathing her features. She remained unfazed by the staff pointed at her. "You don't get to order me around."

"So you almost burn me to death!"

"Seems like you've forgotten who I am!" she rallied back, slamming her fist down on the table. "I already have one insufferable man trying to control me at every turn. I will *not* tolerate another."

Her blackmirror buzzed on the table. We stared at each other for a moment before I finally lowered my staff and leaned back, trying not to show my wounded ego.

She grabbed the device and tapped it awake, reading whatever message awaited her. I watched as her features crumpled into a grimace.

"Natalia says we have to meet her at the Sun & Moon. She says it's urgent."

CHAPTER 25

EARN YOUR PLACE

EMILIA

"Tell me everything," Destiny chimed excitedly as we frolicked down the narrow halls, heading to the dining hall after a two-hour Divination class. "You've been blushing and staring dreamily into space all day! You weren't even listening to Priestess Thea. You and that mysterious mortal got up to some thaaangs last night."

I hugged my notebook to my chest, unable to pry the grin from my lips. My heart had been beating erratically since last night. I couldn't stop going over it all in my head. "Nothing happened," I replied with a long, wistful sigh. "We just stayed up late and...talked."

"Liar!"

"I'm serious, Des," I insisted. "We just talked. We were supposed to go through all these books Adria picked for him, but we didn't get to it. We just talked about nothing, and it was the best night ever."

Destiny searched my face for a moment and then shrugged in defeat. "Fine. I believe you. Only because you have 'virgin' written all over your face."

My cheeks heated but I couldn't argue. She was right. I wondered if it was that obvious to everyone else. To Michael? Did it matter? I realized after a moment of thought that it didn't matter to me. The grin biting at my cheeks didn't wane in the least.

The tides were finally turning in my favor. Tomorrow was my eighteenth birthday.

My Emergence.

Mother hadn't spoken to me since our unfortunate little run-in back in Sacred Temple yesterday, which told me she didn't plan on throwing me a party. Thank the Goddess. I wanted to just Emerge naturally, here, with my friends. I didn't want to make a big thing of it. I wanted to be here, with my sister, the girls, and... Michael.

My sister's life was still an upturned disaster, but I'd woken up this morning feeling ready to let go of worrying so much. Of course, I would always care about my sister, but The Nyx Show wasn't number one on my list anymore.

I had my own stuff going on—my Emergence. Tomorrow! Tomorrow, I'd finally hold the power of one of the elements. The magic in my veins would be awakened and I'd no longer be this powerless little mouse the other girls looked at like something to eat.

Destiny and I arrived in the dining hall. A large, glorious space, brightly lit by the late morning sun which poured in through the ceiling-length windows along the walls. The entire room was lined with a single long glossy oak table that was set to the nines and adorned with every kind of food imaginable. All the girls were in here, the chattering loud and the laughs abundant. We found a free spot in the middle and slid into place along the bench.

Venus St. Claire and her posse of mean girls sat across from us. I kept my eyes down as I stacked food on my plate and got to eating. I could feel their stares at me, but I didn't give them the satisfaction of looking up.

Being Nyx's sister meant I inherited both her admirers and her enemies. Bianca Star and Cassiopeia Black were amongst the latter group. The two popular fifth-years loathed my sister and therefore, loathed me. I could feel the daggers from their eyes as I ate my fruit and French bread. Part of me wanted to flip them off but there was no point. For the next twenty-four hours, I was still unEmerged. I couldn't go picking fights with girls five years ahead of me in magic.

"I can't believe they let the unEmerged into the Academy at all," Cassiopeia was saying. "It's sickening. I can smell their mortal blood from here. No one should be permitted to enroll until they have Emerged."

"Totally," Bianca agreed, flicking a piece of gold hair over her shoulder. She had wide-set blue eyes and a big nose, sort of resembling a young Uma Thurman. Her element was air, and she was a total show off every time she stepped in the Sphere. Rightfully so. I'd been straight mesmerized watching her manifest whirlwinds and tornadoes like nothing.

Cassiopeia was a Japanese beauty with a blunt bob that made her black hair swish like a silken blade every time she moved her head. She had a baby face, skin as smooth as porcelain, and could wield water immaculately with her eyes closed. I'd watched her closely in the Sphere, admittedly taking notes, seeing as how I was almost one hundred percent sure I was going to Emerge as a waterling. She caught me staring at her once and I knew it made her head grow ten sizes.

"Now, now, girls," Venus chided sardonically. "We must do well by the Goddess and offer charity to the magicless."

Bianca and Cassiopeia giggled. "True," they replied together.

"Emilia is Emerging tomorrow," Destiny snapped, her features wry. "All your shit-talking is pointless. You know she's going to be ten times more powerful than you, just like her sister."

My eyes widened as my skin went cold. "Destiny!" I hissed.

Venus's ruby-painted lips stretched into a malicious smirk. "More powerful than us?" she chuckled. "I think we all know by now that that's not true. I won the battle against her, after all. I am the Keeper of the—"

"You won by default because she got taken away by the High Council before you were finished." Destiny deadpanned. "Everyone knows you didn't win fairly."

At that, Venus's haughty demeanor cracked slightly. She stared across the table at us, the vein in her forehead bulging. Her red lips were pressed in a thin line as she regarded us.

Cassiopeia waved her hand, sending a torrent of water across the table, right at Destiny. A scream got caught in my throat as Destiny was knocked backward, off the bench, onto the floor while relentless water poured over her face. She choked and coughed, jerking around on the ground, trying to block the stream to no avail. Cassiopeia leaped up onto the table, her hands out, fingers splayed as she kept willing the water all over Destiny's face.

"Stop!" I cried. "You're drowning her!!"

The dining hall had fallen silent, all eyes on us.

Cassiopeia did not back down. She kept the torrent of water on Destiny. I lunged toward my friend to block the stream of furious water, but an invisible force hit me and sent me flying. My back smashed into the wall behind us, hard. Bianca had her hands out, using her air magic to pin me to the wall. My arms were spread, my feet dangling like Jesus on the freaking cross. Panic took hold of every cell in my body. Destiny was still being drowned by the insane girl standing on the table, whose eyes were lit with excitement.

"STOP!" I screamed. As soon as the word escaped me, Bianca flicked her wrist and suddenly I couldn't breathe. She stole the air from my lungs. Anxiety coursed through the map of my veins while I struggled to break free.

Venus St. Claire just sat pretty and watched.

Cassiopeia finally banished her water magic, only to then grab a plate full of fruit cake, dumping it all over the very drenched Destiny who was coughing and spewing out water.

"Talk shit again and you'll never see another sunrise," Cassiopeia purred, grinning down at my friend who was glaring up through wide, incredulous eyes. Destiny's eyeliner streamed down her cheeks, her entire face red as she fought to catch her breath. She was covered in cake and fruit and water. The dining hall erupted with laughter and there wasn't a damn thing I could do about it.

No one stood up to come to our aid. This was supposed to be a sacred sisterhood, was it not? Yet all our "sisters" just sat there and watched and laughed. A terrible feeling curdled in my stomach as my body began screaming for air. I'd expected to have to earn my place here at Luna, but I feared that they were all going to let this go way too far.

228

CHAPTER 26
POINT OF NO RETURN
NYX

After Jed Compelled some poor innocent mortal on the street to give him his shirt because I'd destroyed his, we made our way to the Sun & Moon Hotel.

We bustled down the busy sidewalk, neither of us speaking a word as we weaved through the pedestrians. I couldn't shake the foreboding feeling weighing down my heart. Natalia's text came out of nowhere, and I couldn't think of a single good reason why she would want to meet us at the Sun & Moon.

Something bad had happened. I could feel it.

My heart pounded as we rounded the street corner, the hotel coming into view. It stood like an obsidian tower, gobbling up the sunlight rather than reflecting it. It had always been an ominous thing, a colossal black crystal jutting toward the sky in the middle of the city, but today it had an even darker aura to it.

Outside, a crowd gathered.

I recognized some guys from Veneficus standing outside on the sidewalk, all of them trying to get a glimpse inside. A light shimmer clung to the air around the hotel, telling me there was a glamour up.

"What the...?" Jed muttered, picking up the pace.

I scurried behind him, trying to keep up. My heart was in my throat as we reached the crowd of Veneficus students. They all looked pale and panicked. When they noticed Jed, their faces fell. One of them even tried blocking Jedidiah from moving through. "Listen, man," the guy said, "you don't wanna see this."

"Get the fuck out of my way, Jasper," Jedidiah growled, grabbing the poor dude by the shoulders, and shoving him aside.

A warm hand wrapped around my wrist, making me jump. I turned to find Natalia standing there, her brown eyes wide and full of tears.

"What's going on?" I demanded. "Natalia, what the hell?"

"I shouldn't have told you guys to come," she croaked. "I'm sorry! I didn't realize... I just had a vision. I didn't know exactly—"

"Move!" Jedidiah's voice went off like a bomb.

Instinctively, I turned away from Natalia and followed Jed through the crowd. They parted for us now, knowing it was pointless to try and keep us out. I trailed behind his huge frame as we made our way to the front door of the hotel. My brows narrowed when I saw the caution tape, the flock of High Council members, and then all the—

Jedidiah froze and I ran into his back, not expecting him to come to a screeching halt. It was like running into a brick wall. "Ow," I mumbled, rubbing my forehead as I moved around his body to see what he was seeing.

My entire being turned to ice.

My heart failed to beat.

No.

"Jed," I grabbed his arm, my fingers digging into his flesh as he trembled.

The world around us faded away, my brain refusing to admit what I just saw in the foyer of the hotel. Bile rose up my throat, but I pushed it down, clinging to Jedidiah. "We shouldn't—you can't—let's—" I swallowed the words I couldn't say. "Just look at me, Jed. Look at me!"

He tore his stormy blue eyes from the horror before us, fixing them on me. I'd never seen a face so corrupted with despair. Where I usually found rugged, stoic, masculine beauty, I now found a pain so sharp, eyes so struck with shock and grief, he suddenly looked like a little boy. His hand moved to grip my arm, hard enough to make me gasp. The other held his staff shakily, the green crystal on top sparking and hissing with magic that longed to be unleashed.

Tears welled over my bottom lashes. I sunk my teeth into my bottom lip to stop it from quivering.

The urge to throw up all over the sidewalk could hardly be contained.

"Come on," I whispered thickly. "We have to get out of here."

I watched as that gut-wrenching grief on Jedidiah's face morphed into a beast more familiar. Rage. His teary eyes narrowed, his trembling lips pressing into a thin line as his jaw hardened.

"What happened?" he ground out, looking at me but speaking in general.

No one answered. The crowd of guys around us had gone stone-still.

Jed sucked in a sharp breath. "I. Said. WHAT. HAPPENED!" He slammed his staff to the ground, the earth shaking in response to his desperation.

Natalia appeared beside us. "They don't know yet. It—"

Jedidiah let go of my arm and stumbled backward. His chest and shoulders heaved, his face going beat red. He shook his head, gripping his staff with white knuckles.

"HE FUCKING DID THIS. I know he did."

My heart combusted in my chest, my blood roaring. "Jed, please. Come here."

I reached for him, and he grabbed me back, his hand squeezing me once, but then he shoved me away.

In a single heartbeat, the bitter truth set in. That was all it ever took, wasn't it? A moment. A single, fleeting moment. The point of no return could hit you out of nowhere. Without warning. In just seconds, a whole person, the strongest person, could be shattered. All life needed was a moment to do this. To cleave a person apart, to fracture them into a million unrecognizable pieces that scattered aimlessly, never to be put back together again.

I watched this happen to Jedidiah. Here, on the sidewalk, in front of dozens of people. In broad daylight. A sunny, normal day.

He breathed hard and ragged, shaking his head, mumbling intelligibly. He slammed his staff to the ground again and the earth shook, this time without relent. People went flying back, crying out to avoid his wrath.

The sidewalk under my feet groaned and trembled, cracks bursting through the pavement, spreading rapidly.

Natalia grabbed me, pulling me away from him. "We have to get out of here! He's going to blow!"

"No!" I screamed, shoving her away. "Why the fuck would you bring us here, Natalia! WHY!"

My friend shook her head, tears streaming down her cheeks. "I'm sorry!"

Jedidiah's earth shake had the whole street quaking, pedestrians screaming and car horns blaring. Fissures spread through the sidewalk, claiming the street too.

He was about to crack open the earth and send us all down to Hell.

"Jed!" I cried, trying to keep my footing.

High Council members started pouring out from the Sun & Moon.

Jed, even through his anguish, managed to notice this.

The world continued to thrash and shake. The High Council moved in on him. He jutted his staff toward them, sending a hit of telekinesis their way, forcing them back. Just to give himself enough time to pull out his portal globe. Our eyes locked once more, my heart officially breaking in my chest. He tossed the crystal and disappeared into the vortex of spinning light.

The world went impossibly still.

The stillness felt wrong.

I stood there, breathing hard, my eyes scanning over every person here, landing finally on Natalia. Rage burned a hole in my chest. Smoke curled from my nostrils as I clenched my fists, doing everything in my power not to incinerate her. In the back of my mind, I knew this wasn't her fault. But I needed an outlet for this horrifying aggression building inside of me.

I turned sharply on a heel, stalking down the sidewalk.

"Nyx!" she shouted after me. "Where are you going?"

White flames crackled over my fingers, my vision going blurry and red. My short fuse only knew one destination that counted. I was out for blood, and I knew exactly who was going to give me my next fix.

CHAPTER 27
TO THE DEATH
EMILIA

My lungs threatened to burst. I could feel the redness of my face as I struggled against the wall. Bianca gazed at me brightly, enjoying my suffering as she kept me pinned in place.

Cassiopeia got down from the table and took her seat next to Bianca and Venus.

"Should I even bother giving her breath back?" Bianca asked Venus. "Might be best to just get rid of her before—"

Bianca Star suddenly shot up from her seat as a literal fire lit under her ass.

Her magic over me released, sending me crashing to the floor, gasping desperately for breath, wondering what just happened.

Bianca started squealing like a stuck pig, her pink shimmery skirt on fire. She didn't even use magic to try and banish the flames—she was too busy running around like a chicken with her head cut off while her butt smoked.

Cassiopeia sent a blast of water and put the fire on her ass out.

For a moment, everyone was stone-still, wondering what in the seven realms just happened.

Nyx.

She stood in the archway of the dining hall with white fire over her palms. Her beautiful face was etched into a mask of fury as she took in the scenario. Her smoky eyes were ringed with shadow, streaks of mascara staining her cheeks. As if she'd been crying. What the hell?

"Picking on the unEmerged? That's low, even for you, Bianca." There was something hard and ragged about her tone, a startling blankness in her gaze as she stepped forward.

My lips popped open. Despite the hell Bianca just put me through, I suddenly felt scared for her.

I'd never seen my sister's face quite like this before.

"You—!" Bianca shot her hands out, a vengeful cry wailing from her lips, but it quickly turned into a scream of fright as she was propelled backward at Nyx's telekinetic command. Nyx had her hand out, fingers splayed, as she slammed Bianca into the wall, shattering glass portraits and turning them into a mess on the floor. Bianca stayed pinned to the wall, her limbs spread like a star, a horrified look on her face as she tried to struggle free. Nyx's telekinetic hold wouldn't budge, and she held her there as she stalked into the room like a predator.

"You always were intolerable bullies," Nyx snarled, flicking her other wrist, and sending Cassiopeia flying backward to join her friend against the wall. The two girls wriggled and swore, but neither could break free.

The dining room had fallen dead silent, all eyes on Nyx.

With one hand held toward the girls against the wall, my sister kept them in place, and with the other, she flicked her wrist and summoned all the knives from the table to rise, floating midair.

Everyone gasped.

Nyx curled her fingers and assembled the knives into position, pointing them toward Cassiopeia and Bianca as they hovered. The girls struggled and cried out, begging my sister to stop. Venus's face showed no reaction.

My heart was in my throat.

Something was definitely wrong with Nyx. More-so than usual. The cruel blankness of her gaze was wrong and unsettling.

With a sharp gesture of her hand, the knives shot at the girls while they shrieked in horror.

Every girl in the room screamed, including me.

"No!" I yelped.

Thunk, thunk, thunk, thunk, thunk, thunk, thunk, thunk....

One after the other, the knives punctured the wall like darts, outlining the girls' limbs and heads perfectly. A hair away from stabbing them dozens of times in horrible, lethal places.

Nyx grinned, lightless. "Shit. I missed."

"You're psychotic!" Bianca wailed, her eyes plastered wide as they darted side to side, ogling at the knives framing her face and shoulders.

Nyx ignored her, turning to Venus. "As for you, Hollywood, you're coming out into the Sphere with me. Unless you'd like to meet the same fate as your minions."

Venus picked a piece of fruit from a bowl, sitting pretty, unfazed by the chaos and the near-death of her supposed friends. "And what business do we have in the Sphere, my darling Nyx?"

"Everyone knows your 'win' against me was shotty. You and I have unfinished business. Come out to the Sphere and face me one on one again."

"Wait," Venus scoffed, disbelief glittering in her honey eyes. "Are you...are you asking me for a rematch?"

Nyx just stood there.

Venus exploded with mocking laughter. "You're joking! The Celestial Society does not do rematches!" She wiped the fake tears from her eyes as she shook with cackles. "Desperation is not a good look on you, Morningstar. You lost. Get the fuck over it."

Nyx made a sound of annoyance. "You scared, St. Claire? Scared to face me one on one and finish this?"

"You're a trainwreck," Venus bit back. "I don't care how you try to bait me. I'm sure it must be hard to fall from grace and lose your spot as queen, but what's done is done. I won and you lost."

Faye showed up then, standing behind Nyx and assessing the situation through glittery lashes. Her emerald eyes widened as they landed on Bianca and Cassiopeia, outlined with steak knives, faces white with horror.

"Picking on the unEmerged," Nyx explained, nodding toward Destiny.

Faye shook her head with disgust. She rushed over to us and

instantly used her air magic to dry off Destiny. The cake batter dried and fell from her skin, and within seconds, she was good as new. I watched in awe. Air magic always surprised me.

Meanwhile, Nyx's temper heated even more, resulting in the summoning of fire creatures that manifested out of thin air. With just one thought from my sister, the whole dining hall came to life with a plethora of different animals made of fire. Like what the Water Priestess had done with water at the Ceremony that night. Except Nyx summoned dangerous, predatory animals only. She made wolves and dragons and birds of prey, sharks and snakes, and spiders of fire. She let them fly around the room and caught everyone's full attention before she directed them strictly at Venus St. Claire.

Bianca and Cassiopeia fell to the floor, released from the telekinetic hold now that my sister had switched to fire magic.

"Wait!" Venus cried, a strange seriousness in her tone. "Even if I did agree to fight you again, it would be pointless! The Luminary took the Sacred Baton! I don't have it anymore."

At that, my sister's face fell. Her army of fire animals fizzled out.

"What?" she hissed disbelievingly.

Venus's jaw was clenched, her eyes hard. "The Luminary came to me last night and informed me that she needed to be the Keeper of the Baton for now. Something about the vampires. She and the Priestesses need it. Which is bullshit if you ask me. I won it. If they need the Baton, they should just include me in their inner circle meetings. I'm pissed already, so don't tempt me, Morningstar. The next time you and I face off, it will be to the death."

Nyx's breath came out hard and ragged as that information settled over her. I couldn't understand why her features were assembled into a look of pure terror. As if this was the worst news she'd ever heard. She started shaking her head and muttering to herself.

"We're done here," Venus snapped. "Come on girls. Get a hold of yourself."

Cassiopeia rose to her feet, a murderous look etched into her dainty features. Bianca's eyes also had the promise of revenge in them, but the girls refrained. For now.

Nyx didn't stop them as the gaggle of females left the dining hall, leaving the four of us in here alone.

"FUCK!" My sister detonated, tendrils of smoke seeping from her nostrils. *Holy shit.* I'd never seen her *smoke* before. Tears lined her dark eyes with silver as she breathed heavily and started pacing back and forth.

"I need that Baton," she muttered to herself, still shaking her head.

"Why, Nyx?" I had to ask.

Of course she just ignored me.

Faye and I helped Destiny to her feet. She still coughed here and there, her eyes red. But she was okay and that was all that mattered.

Natalia appeared in the archway of the dining hall. She looked an absolute wreck. Her eyes were red and puffy, her cheeks stained with tears. Was that blood on her white skirt?

"Nyx," Natalia rasped. "What did you do?"

"What happened to *you*?" Faye asked Natalia urgently.

"It's the twins," Nyx answered, her voice freakishly monotone. "They're dead."

CHAPTER 28
SAFE SPACE
NYX

L A'S CELESTIAL POST
BREAKING NEWS:
*A tragedy has struck our Society. The second-year firelings,
Demitri and Raziel Ember, heirs of the infamous Roxanna and Grayson
Ember, have been found dead this afternoon. The bodies were discovered
in the lobby of the Sun & Moon hotel, in plain sight. The autopsy reveals
the cause of death was a vampire attack.*

*There were no eyewitnesses on scene, and all the security cameras had
been dismantled prior to the attack.*

*The High Council advises all starseeds to take extra precautions at this
time. "Stay in groups—don't go anywhere alone. Stay in your Academies
as much as possible. It has been decades since the city has experienced rogue
vampires. This is no idle threat, but one to take very seriously," says our
High Lord Aries Vanderbilt. "Please do your part to stay safe."*

Roxanna and Grayson have declined to give comments at this time.

*"Demitri and Raziel were astounding starseeds with much promise."
Our High Lord speaks to us with tears in his eyes. "My own son was very
close to them. They have been taken too soon and the Celestial High
Council will find the culprit and justice will be swift and righteous."*

It is with a heavy heart that we write this article. All of us at the Celes-

239

tial Post send our deepest condolences to the family and friends of the wonderful young firelings.

A memorial for Raziel and Demitri will be held in three days. Stay tuned for more information on how to attend and pay your respects.

Stay safe out there.

·   *Brit Dawn @ the Celestial Post*

We read the article in thick, horrible silence.

Goddess.

I had a little over two hours to get the Sacred Baton in my possession, which was highly unlikely, to begin with, but now this.

Demitri and Raziel were fucking dead.

I couldn't get the image out of my mind.

The girls and I stood silently in Faye's room. The ambiance of glitter and gnome statues and colorful fairy lights did not fit the mood. I shut my blackmirror and threw it across the room, never wanting to see the thing again. It smashed to smithereens and I couldn't care less.

The twins had been murdered in cold blood, in broad daylight.

Immediately, I thought of my shadow torturer.

But Solaris Adder had an alibi. He was down in the Vault with Chancellors at the time of the murder. And beyond that...despite everything... This just didn't feel like something he would do. I had this strange intuition that he was innocent.

So what the fuck?

"Jedidiah?" Emilia breathed his name, a single word that packed a thousand different questions.

I shook my head, my vision turning to a watery blur. "He—he left. I've never seen anyone so...destroyed. The ground started shaking and I thought he was about to collapse the entire hotel but he pulled out his portal globe and disappeared. I don't know where he went."

My heart cracked open at the thought of what he must have been going through. Those twins were everything to Jedidiah. They were all he had. That grumpy motherfucker tolerated no one but them. He had this...sweet soft spot for them I'd always secretly admired. They were obnoxious boys, but that's what made them so great. I loved fighting with them and bickering with them and watching the looks on their face every time I bested them. Knowing they were gone struck a thousand blades through my black heart.

Faye hadn't stopped crying.

Emilia and her weird friend had hardly said two words. I'd walked in on them being tormented by Venus, Bianca, and Cassiopeia. They hadn't even processed that before the burden of a violent murder was packed onto their plates.

"What do we do?" Emilia asked, her eyes focused on me. After all this time, after every stupid, shitty thing I'd done, my sister still looked to me for answers. "Nyx, what can we do?"

I thought about it. It felt like the weight of the world landed on my shoulders at that question. "I don't know," I rasped honestly.

"Do you think it really was vampires?" Destiny wondered.

I looked to Natalia who lifted a shoulder, her eyes far away. "Honestly? It could have been. The bodies... Their throats were ripped out. That screams vampire, does it not?"

"But why would vampires attack Celestials?" I voiced. "They've never done that. Sure, they hunt and kill mortals but never Celestials. Wouldn't the twins be able to fight them off?"

No one had an answer for that.

"You wanna tell us why you need that Baton so bad?" Emilia pushed. She had a strange look in those jewel blue eyes like her mind was half somewhere else.

I swallowed.

"She needs the Baton because Solaris wants it," Natalia answered for me, her voice thick with disdain.

I frowned. "I thought you couldn't See anything involving him."

"I can't. But I can still see you sometimes when you're away from him. I saw you initiating a rematch with Venus St. Claire, and I know there's no way in hell you'd risk your reputation like that unless you were forced to."

My shoulders deflated with a heavy sigh. Well, no point in denying it now then. "Natalia is right," I admitted reluctantly. "I know it's fucked up, but I seriously need to get the Baton and give it to him."

"That must be why the Luminary took it," the bald girl suggested.

"Or she took it because they're lying to everyone about what the true threat is," I clapped back. "Venus St. Claire is under Amnesia regarding Solaris and what he's done with his shadows. The Baton detects deceit. Perhaps the Luminary took it because she is being deceptive, and she didn't want the Keeper of the Baton to discover that."

A pregnant silence loomed over the room.

"Either way, I need it. But who knows where she'd be keeping it?"

"What is he threatening you with now?" Natalia demanded.

"It doesn't matter."

"Honestly, Nyx?!"

Faye cleared her throat. "Can we please not turn on each other?" she said through a trembling bottom lip. "Everything is seriously messed up right now and I need this to be a safe space. This little group right here." She gestured around at each of us, a determined look in those shiny green eyes. "The five of us. We aren't under Amnesia. We know what's going on—to some degree. We're in this together. Please. Don't fight." Her sole focus landed on me. "Nyx, just freaking tell us. We are here for you. Let us in. Let us help."

Her words stirred something deep and nameless inside me. Faye was right.

I needed to drop my pride. A lot of this shit could have been avoided if I'd just been honest with my friends earlier. That guilt hung over me like a dark cloud.

I sucked in a sharp breath and exhaled it slowly. "He threatened my mortal friends. From my hometown. He shadow-traveled me to Marvel's place. He made me look at them and told me he'd eat them slowly with shadows if I didn't get the Baton. Also, he'll throw my magic into the darkness where it will be devoured and gone forever. So, yeah. That's my life."

They stared at me like a party of startled owls.

"I thought you had your magic back..." the hairless girl said, her brows narrowing as she stared down at my hands which had been alight with a furious fire earlier.

"I have some of it," I replied bitterly, folding my arms over my chest. "It's not the same. I only have a fraction of my original power and once sunset comes, it will be gone again. Even now—I can feel it draining. I won't get it back—ever—if I don't get the Baton."

"Can't we just try to get this dragonglass medallion from him?" Faye wondered.

"No." I shot her down instantly. "I would have tried already but seriously—Solaris isn't like anything we've ever known. I wouldn't risk my life or your lives to try and steal from him. His shadows—his power —it's unfathomable. I hate to admit that but trust me. He's something else. He can erase the world... You don't understand until it happens to you. One second, you're standing right here, in the real world, in the light... And then you're not. Suddenly, in the blink of an eye, everything's gone. Warmth, sound, wind, light, people, and existence as a whole. Just gone. Nothing but endless black. No ground, no sky, no land. Just darkness."

The atmosphere chilled and thickened.

My breaths came out shaky, but I kept my spine straight and my chin tipped up as I gauged the reactions of the girls. "And I may be a cold, selfish bitch at times, but I wouldn't risk any of you to that fate, no matter how desperate I am to be powerful again."

Emilia gave me a small smile.

"Why were you with Jedidiah at Lucifer's Playground anyways?" Natalia asked me, her brows furrowed.

I swallowed. "Jed wanted to talk. He's got this idea in his head. He believes that because Solaris was originally a waterling, that he must have an outside source for his shadows... Meaning, he thinks he can be cut off from the source of that power."

A thin silence passed, each of us looking at each other thoughtfully.

Natalia's brows jumped. "Could that be true?"

"I don't know," I murmured. "I mean, he's right about him being a waterling. I accused him of it a while back and he didn't deny it, but he also has the element of shadows. Fact. He suggested to me once that Celestials should be able to wield more than one element. He... He told me the darkness is his. Like, he literally said he spent so much time alone in the darkness, that it became his..."

"Became his," Emila repeated, her eyes far away. "*Became* his. So not inherently his."

"Exactly," Natalia nodded. "I think Jedidiah is onto something."

"Either way, we aren't going to find the source of his shadows before sunset. I need to get that Baton, or I'm fucked." I hated the desperation that laced every word I spoke. I focused on Natalia, knowing she had no reason to help me but wishing with every fiber of my being that she would. "Will you help me find it?"

She squared her shoulders at me, looking me over as if for the first time. My heart thudded in anticipation. Our relationship had become rocky ever since that night on the beach. It was all my fault. I'd pushed her away. I'd kept her in the dark. Now here I was with my tail between my legs, my entire fate resting on her psychic abilities and whether she'd use them to help me.

Finally, she glanced at Faye. "Get me something to use as a blindfold and turn the TV on static."

The four of us sat in a circle on the floor around Natalia as she covered her eyes with a thick black scarf Faye gave her. The flatscreen TV on the wall displayed black and white static which produced the white noise Natalia needed to focus. I flicked my wrist, using what little power I had left to shut the curtains and light every candle in the room. We did a few rounds of breathwork together before silence fell and Natalia descended into the spiritual realms.

I kept my eyes closed, and my spine straight. Time moved differently in this meditative state. It could have been seconds or hours that passed before Natalia spoke. "When's the last time you've been to our room?"

I opened my eyes, realizing she was talking to me. She'd taken the blindfold off, and her russet eyes shone.

"Um, I don't know. This morning, I guess. Why?"

She looked at each of us, her features etched with confusion. "I think... I think the Baton is in our room."

I was up and darting out the door before she even finished speaking. With the girls on my heels, I ran to my room, burst through the door, and gasped at what I found.

The Sacred Baton, placed neatly on my bed with all but a fucking bow.

"What the hell?" I breathed, heart hammering.

"Oh my Goddess," Faye whispered behind me.

I did not make a move toward it. I stood in the doorway, staring at it incredulously. "This feels like a trick."

"The Luminary must want you to have it," Destiny suggested quietly.

Natalia pushed past me, Emilia following in her wake. They stood over the bed and looked down at it curiously.

"It's almost sunset," Faye announced, pointing out the window.

I swallowed the bullet in my throat and took a deep, shaky breath. As if in response to that, a small poof of smoky darkness erupted beside me. We all jumped but it was gone as quickly as it came. A small piece of paper floated in the spot where the darkness had been. Black paper with silver writing. Hesitantly, I reached out and grabbed the message that had been delivered by shadows, knowing damn well who it was from.

Penthouse of the Sun & Moon
Come now. Alone.

CHAPTER 29
BLOOD & OATHS
NYX

oddess damn me. Crossing the city in a mortal taxi while carrying an ancient, beloved Celestial object in my shoulder bag was not the vibe. But things got worse when I arrived at the Sun & Moon and had to walk through an actual crime scene to get to the elevator. The lobby was all taped off. Raziel and Demitri's blood still painted the floor. I fought the urge to cry and vomit as that creepy old guy Mort allowed me through, watching me all the way to the elevator.

I should have been turned away but apparently, Solaris Adder was now the king of this hotel, and his highness was expecting me.

A few cloaked Council members lingered around, watching me suspiciously through their golden masks. The situation was abhorrent.

When the elevator doors finally shut me inside, I released a long breath. My cheeks were warm, my eyes stinging with tears I refused to let fall. Shit. Every time I went to face Solaris, I was fighting fucking tears. Pathetic. I ground my teeth together and willed them away. He wouldn't see me cry this time.

I pulled out the Baton, admiring the pale light it emitted. It glowed like the moon given a different form. I briefly considered stopping the elevator and going back down. Fleeing from here. Letting my magic be thrown into the abyss. I mean, it couldn't be a good thing to hand this Celestial object over to Solaris. Plus, I had no idea how it ended up in my room. If the Luminary truly did give it to me... Well, that just confused things more.

But I was much too selfish to turn back now. I wrapped it back up in the lace pashmina and stuffed it into my bag.

I told myself I was doing this for my mortal friends, but Goddess knew deep down, this was all about me. And my magic.

An eternity passed before I was finally spat into the most opulent suite I'd ever seen.

My breath hitched as the magnificent bird's eye view of the city and the ocean swept me off my feet. Three out of four walls were made of glass, showcasing the entire aesthetic of the City of Angels as if I'd reached a throne in the clouds. The sky had turned deep scarlet, and only a tiny sliver of the sun remained. The golden light spilled into the water, creating what I had always perceived as the stairway to heaven. The sun walking on water, the golden road into the portal of the heavens. Right before my eyes, the sun disappeared behind the horizon, and there was something that felt so final about it.

The penthouse was possessed by a heavy silence that made my skin prickle. I dared to step a few feet across the obsidian floor. It was freezing up here. The chill had my heart racing.

I let my eyes wander, taking in the open, immaculate layout. The kitchen was practically a bar, with glossy black countertops and an actual waterfall on the back wall behind the shelves of liquor bottles. Beyond that was a sitting area, adorned with dark leather couches and chairs, adjacent to an unlit fireplace under an ornate mantle. Planted ornamental trees and the single stone wall gave the place a jungle vibe. Ancient-looking artifacts and statues decorated the space too, making me feel like I'd just entered the lair of an immortal collector.

"Solaris?" I called stupidly.

Nothing.

Great.

A blur of motion made me jump. Before I could even react any further, a woman stood in front of me, dressed in leathers. She was petite like me, her raven hair pulled back into a high ponytail, showing off her dainty, elvan face. Her skin was chalk white, which seemed entirely wrong since her features were Middle Eastern—she should have had warm, brown skin.

My eyes narrowed as I took her in, and when I saw her eyes, I froze.

They were blood fucking red with unsettling black veins swimming below her bottom lashes. She looked so impossibly young—childlike. But the look in those crimson eyes was anything but youthful or innocent.

She grinned as she watched me react to her unholy appearance. I grimaced and backed away from her instinctively.

"So, *you're* what all the fuss is about," she said, her voice high-pitched and snooty. Like a spoiled child. "I don't see what the big deal is." She stuck her nose in the air as she regarded me, taking in every detail, the distaste in her red eyes growing with every second. "Though I will admit," she murmured as her nostrils flared, "you do smell amazing."

"Who the hell are you?" I spat, wishing my heart would stop galloping like a bucking bronco trying to kick off its rider. I did not like this creature. Solaris's little plaything? What the fuck was she?

The tiny, wrong-looking girl smiled at me, and my heart plummeted out of my ass.

Behind her messily painted red lips was a set of shiny, lethal fangs.

Goddess damn me. Vampires *had* returned to the city.

Solaris—was he—?

"I am Ra'ah," she informed me, checking her black nails which were long as claws.

My heart rocketed against my ribs while my vision clouded with rage. It could be no coincidence that the twins had just been murdered in an alleged vampire attack in this very hotel, and now there was a she-vamp loitering in Solaris Adder's penthouse like she owned the place.

My chest rose and fell. I should have been able to incinerate this ungodly little creature on the spot. Yet I had not even a spark of power left now that the sun had officially set.

I couldn't go picking a fight with a vampire while powerless.

I tipped up my chin and scowled indignantly. "Where is Solaris?"

Ra'ah stepped closer to me, nearly closing the space between us. She had an eerie, metallic scent, with undertones of something smoky. "He is hunting." She gestured to the floor behind us.

There he was. The man of the bloody hour. Laying on the floor, a blindfold over his eyes, enclosed in a circle of salt with five candles placed at the ends of his limbs and the top of his head.

"Hunting?" I breathed, taking an impulsive step closer to him, assessing the situation. He was Astral traveling.

A torrent of wicked ideas stormed my mind. Solaris Adder, helpless on the floor before me. Was the Goddess handing him over to me on a silver platter? I could test my theory about the Baton being a stake and use it on him right now. Imagine him waking up to witness me standing over him with the spike shoved into his heart...me being the last thing he saw before he—

"Stay away from him!" Ra'ah hissed, bolting in front of him protectively, fangs bared.

"What are you, his guard dog?"

"Oh, you arrogant little minx. I am everything," Ra'ah purred. "I guard his body while he is away. I slay his enemies and I eat their fucking hearts. I train his army. We are of the same soul, Solaris, and me. I waited over a century for him to return. I never gave up, you know. Never lost faith. I prayed to him while he was gone, and you know what? He heard me."

I stared at her, unable to keep the disgust off my features as I did so. "Er, I have no clue what you're talking about, but okay."

Murderous, scarlet fury manifested in those devil eyes as her lips tore back over her teeth, her fangs on full show. She stalked toward me and my breath caught. "He said I can't bite you. But he never said anything about tearing you apart, limb by limb, piece by piece, slowly—"

Something black shot between me and the vampire, the sound of flapping wings sending my mind into befuddlement. I stumbled back as this flying creature cawed chaotically, attacking Ra'ah with fervent indignation. The vampire squealed and attempted to swat the winged creature away but it divebombed her relentlessly.

"Get away from me!! Stupid bird!" she shrieked venomously.

If I weren't so confused, I would have laughed.

A gust of shadows hit the vampire with the force of a sack of bricks, sending her flying across the room where she collided against the wall with a terrifying crunch. She fell to the floor in a motionless heap of leather, knocked out cold.

Solaris stood in the center of the salt ring, brushing off his black shirt before he stepped over the salt and waved a hand to banish the flame over the candles.

The *raven* who had come to my defence soared toward him and landed on his shoulder.

"Pardon my sister," he muttered absently, crossing the floor to the bar. "Drink?"

"Your *sister*?" I heaved dubiously. My eyes darted between the unconscious vampire on the floor and the giant raven perched casually on Solaris's shoulder.

"What the fuck is going on?" I muttered to myself.

"Bourbon or vodka?"

I blinked. My nerves were in shambles. The raven cawed at me, its large black eyes seeming to attempt to offer support. I sighed. "Vodka. Definitely."

Solaris Adder poured me a drink and slid the crystal glass down the polished bar/countertop. I could feel my heartbeat in every inch of my body as I reluctantly moved across the suite over to him. His proximity made the hairs on the back of my neck rise. The frigid temperature made it even worse. "It's fucking freezing in here," I complained, hoping that my bitchiness would disguise the fact that I was terrified.

"So, you have it, then?" Silver eyes found mine and electricity struck my core. He noted the bag over my shoulder. He seemed genuinely surprised that I'd managed to obtain it and I decided he didn't need to know it had been delivered to me by an anonymous source, whose intentions I knew nothing of.

I hopped up casually onto a bar stool and took my drink, slamming it in one go, ignoring his question. The vodka burned my insides just right, loosening my limbs a little. The tension in the room could still be cut with a butter knife but the sinful liquid gave me just the right amount of courage. "Who's your friend?" I had to ask, eyeing the raven suggestively.

"This is Morpheus," Solaris replied, a hint of pride touching his voice. "My familiar."

My brows jumped. "Oh. Well, thanks for saving my ass, Morpheus. I owe you one, bud."

The raven cocked his head at me, cawing softly.

"Leave us, Morpheus," Solaris commanded.

The beautiful black bird launched off his shoulder and flew toward the glass window. My heart fell as I thought he was going to smash into the glass. But instead, the raven dematerialized, reforming on the outside of the window, taking off above the city.

"Whoa," I breathed.

"You have the Baton." It wasn't a question.

I managed to pry my gaze away from the window. I looked into his fathomless eyes as I asked, "Did you kill the twins?"

Nothing about his face changed. He had that same, emotionless expression of stone he always had. I thought I could see beyond it sometimes, but right now the mask was perfectly in place. "No."

Reluctantly, I glanced over at...his sister. "Did she?"

"Firefly, we are here to discuss much more pressing matters than the unfortunate demise of a couple of mid-grade miscreants."

Anger and revulsion shot up my throat like hot, stinging bile. "You—"

"As much as I love your colorful insults and your pretty little death threats," he cut me off nonchalantly but there was a lethal edge to his tone, "save it. You and I are here to take a Celestial Oath." He waved his hand and a scroll appeared over his palm, handed to him by a whirl of shadows. "So long as you hand over the Baton, this Oath will be finalized and sealed by the stars. You will be bound to this contract, as will I."

He handed me the scroll and my heart went wild.

Before I read it, I dared to ask, "Are you a vampire?"

His stone mask was splintered by the ghost of a smile. "No. I am not."

"Oh. Why do you want the Baton?"

"None of your business."

Fuck.

The way he was looking at me threatened to be my doom, so I

251

turned my attention back to the scroll. I tried to keep my breathing even as I unrolled it and read the neat silver script that awaited me on the black paper.

Woven by the Fates and sealed by the stars, tonight, a Celestial Oath we make.

I, Nyx Morningstar, solemnly swear I will not use any form of my magic against Solaris Adder until the night of Hallows Eve when we will engage in the battle of our elements in front of the entire Celestial Society. If Solaris Adder defeats me, I swear to pledge my full loyalty and allegiance to him and any cause he stands for. Bound to him for the rest of my living days.

I, Solaris Adder, solemnly swear that once I am given the Sacred Baton, I will return Nyx Morningstar's magic in full and bring no harm to her loved ones. I will put my quest for war on hold until Hallows Eve. If she defeats me at the Clash of Spirits, I will vanish from the Celestial Society and never use my shadow magic against any people, places, or things for the rest of my living days. No war will be initiated by my hand.
Signed:

_____

_____

"Bound to you for the rest of my living days?!" I squawked, fighting the urge to crumple the paper into a ball and throw it at his face. "You never said—"

"Deal or no deal, Firefly? I don't have all night."

"This is a Celestial Oath," I rasped, shaking my head. "This...this binds us to our word in ways we can't even imagine. All you have to do is swear to not start a war if I win. The price I pay if I lose is continental. This is not fair!"

"It was never MEANT to be FAIR!" Solaris detonated, an explosion of shadows bursting out of him in a shockwave.

I screamed, arms flying up instinctively to protect my face. The shadows evaporated around him, but the wrath across his features remained. His chest rose and fell, that stone mask finally cracking all the way through. His fist clenched over the table, teeth grinding together as he glared at me. And Jesus Christ, *Goddess damn me*, he had tears in his eyes. "You had three days to choose whether or not you wanted your magic back. You were supposed to pledge your allegiance to me or become mortal. It was a swift, clean deal. You managed to swindle me this far. No more. Choose now. Do you swear this? Or not?"

I breathed heavily, still shaking my head, wishing I could go back in time and never drink that witches vodka that night. As if that would make a difference.

"The deal never had anything to do with the Clash of Spirits!" I argued, fear creeping up my spine. "Do you have any idea what the Clash is?!"

"Yes," Solaris retorted. "The entire Celestial Society will be there, or at least watching from their blackmirrors, to bear witness to our affair. You wanted to battle me one on one, in front of an audience, did you not? Did you really think I would participate in some juvenile battle of the elements at your little school? If we're going to do this, it will be done right."

Shit.

I had no more false hopes to cling to. This was it.

Still, I hesitated.

"I can be at your little friend's house with just a flick of my wrist," Solaris taunted, though there was something undeniably inauthentic about his tone. "I will make you watch as I let my demons off their leash."

I scrutinized his expression, that strange glint in the back of his eyes, and a twisted laugh tumbled out of me. "You hate this." That revelation struck through the ambiance like a throwing ax. He was physically startled at the words. "Look at you—threatening my innocent mortal friends. You *hate* it. You hate your fucking self. Your misery just wants company, doesn't it, Solaris? Your creepy sister isn't enough. Veneficus isn't enough. Whatever shadow army you apparently have isn't enough. You want me to join this pretentious festival of self-loathing. Why? Why me?"

"Because!" he answered desperately. My heart sank as his features warped with grief and despair. For a moment, he looked utterly human. Broken and beaten and lost like the rest of them. "You don't understand now but you will. You are the firefly in the dark. Why would you be there in the shadows with me, why would you be my bridge back into the living world, if you weren't meant to be at my side?"

I searched between his eyes, a foreign sense of urgency pumping through my veins. "I don't know what that means," I breathed, wishing I had all the answers. Wishing I knew why despite everything, he felt so familiar. Not of this world, yet entirely familiar to me. In ways I couldn't put my finger on. I could deny it and cover it up with how much I hated him but beneath that, a terrible truth remained. A truth I still didn't understand but longed to fervently.

"Why are you doing this?" I whispered. "The things you say...the way you look at me...it feels like...it feels like you..." My cheeks pooled with heat and my eyes went downcast. "I understand why you lured me into the shadows to release you. But everything else—stealing my magic, trying to force my hand... I don't understand. Why have you treated me this way? Why didn't you just—"

"Just what?" he snapped, his voice as acidic as his teary eyes. "Why didn't I just play the white knight and court you? Come on, Firefly. You must know that's not the way our story goes."

My heart slammed, and my head spun. *Our story.*

He stood just a couple of feet away, his aura a tangible, dark thing against my skin. I opened my mouth, but nothing came out.

"And like I said before..." Solaris continued, his eyes entrancing me as if he were a serpent. "You needed this."

"I needed this?" I rasped. "I needed you to come and steal my fucking magic and ruin my li—"

"Yes."

I shook my head. "You're unbelievable. You know what the scariest part about you is, Solaris? I can tell you truly *believe* all the insane shit you say."

A pause. Then, "Just sign this Oath, Nyx."

My true name on his lips made it hard to breathe. He'd never spoken it until now. His power thrummed in the air, whirling around me, magnetic and haunting. My magic had completely drained now that the sun had set, and yet, I still felt drawn to his.

Perhaps Solaris had been wrong before, about how I must not have perceived the shadows all those times he said he saw me. Maybe I did.

Maybe I had forgotten...

I thought about my childhood. When I'd accidentally unleashed the magic I wasn't supposed to have yet. All the times I'd started fires or caused explosions or made the ground shake... I *did* black out. I'd always wake up to my mother's frightened eyes. Or Aries's cold, malicious stare. Perhaps in those blackouts, Solaris was there. At the edge of my memory, just out of reach...

"Fine," I whispered, and the world tilted off its fucking axis.

For a moment, neither of us spoke or even breathed.

With a flick of his wrist, he had a feather pen materialize in his hand. The way he could manifest objects out of thin air was beyond startling, but I couldn't focus on that right now. He moved so that he was standing right in front of me, caging me against the bar top while I still sat on the stool. My poor, defenseless heart took off in a frenzy as his closeness became my only reality. Something pricked my arm and I gasped, glancing down to see the pen he'd manifested sticking into my arm like a needle, siphoning my blood.

"Hey!" I squealed but he was already done, handing me the pen which now had my blood for ink. My arm stung. "Oh my Goddess," I whimpered. "You are not seriously suggesting I sign my name in blood."

"What do you think seals the magic in place?"

I blinked up into those merciless silver eyes, my tongue going dry, chest heaving. "And you're going to sign with your blood too?"

"Yes."

"Goddess damn us all."

"And you know the price you pay if you fail to fulfill this oath, right?"

I shivered. "Death."

He said nothing back.

My magic. My friends. My entire life hung on the line.

Sign my name in blood, everyone stayed safe...for now. Sign my name in blood, my magic would return to me in full. Sign my name in blood, I had to face this creature one on one—in front of the entire Society. Sign my name in blood, I could stop a war. Sign my name in blood, I could be bound to him forever. Sign my name in blood, my life as I knew it was over.

I hesitated, waiting for the Goddess to smite him down and save the day.

But I knew the truth. The bitter truth. There were no saviors. Life mirrored nature, and nature was a cruel, vicious beast at the core of it all. Perhaps the Goddess was too. My fate had been cursed from the moment I emerged from my mother's hateful womb. My life; just one long, endless war.

I took the Baton out of my bag and placed it on the glossy black bar top, still wrapped in lace.

Solaris's intake of breath made my skin flush with goosebumps.

I hesitated just a little longer, though we both knew what was about to happen.

Finally, I took the pen and signed my name in my blood.

Solaris took the pen, drawing his blood to do the same. Almost mechanically. The atmosphere was so dense, I thought I'd suffocate. Both of us knew what we were doing... The finality of this. No turning back now.

Once it was done, the paper lit on fire and burned away, our fate sealed.

I felt it. Something shifted...or rather, clasped together.

Solaris grabbed me by the arms, pulled me off the stool, and tucked me into his body. He moved so brashly; I had no time to argue. The shadows swallowed us at his silent command, my body igniting with pins and needles as we traveled through the darkness.

The shadows dropped us off in the middle of the fucking desert.

"What—?" I choked off, the expanse of stars overhead stealing my breath away. I spun around, taking in the endless plane of sand and sky.

He wasted zero time. He pulled the glowing crimson medallion from his jacket and offered it to me.

My attention snapped away from our new surroundings.

I snatched the medallion, feeling the thrum of my power inside it, my body lighting up with sensations I never knew possible. I popped off the top and tossed the glorious liquid down my throat without a second thought.

My full power and I crashed back together like a head-on collision of fire.

And then I erupted.

CHAPTER 30

CHOSEN

EMILIA

One hour till midnight. One hour until I was finally eighteen.

Though, to be fair, our Emergence didn't happen until the exact minute we were born, so no magic would happen for me until 5:55 am. But still.

I tossed and turned in bed, listening to the soft sound of Destiny's even breathing. Our window was wide open, the curtains dancing in the cool September breeze, sending shivers across my skin.

My mind wouldn't stop racing. I thought about Nyx. She'd left hours ago to meet Solaris and had yet to return. I wondered how she was managing him. Had they made their wretched deal? Did she get her magic back?

The twins... I thought about them. It physically pained me. Raziel and Demitri—dead. Murdered. In cold blood. My stomach hollowed out every time I thought about it. They were the first starseeds other than Natalia and Faye who ever spoke to me. Despite being a bit pervy and over the top, I liked them. They'd been quick to start shit, but also quick to come to our aid. Now they were gone.

So much was happening. So much was changing. My mind was like a dryer full of clothes, spinning and tumbling endlessly. And as much as there was to think about, my mind seemed to keep flashing back to one thing.

Michael.

I hadn't seen him today. I knew I should just go to sleep. But I kept imagining his face in my mind, picturing him up there in the tower, reading and writing and being chosen by our Goddess. I still couldn't get over it. It both delighted and terrified me. Before I'd been able to tell myself he was just a human boy and I needed to get over my little infatuation. Now... Now I realized our connection had always been Divine. That sounded amazing but the pressure that came from that revelation weighed me down and held me below the water, where surely, I'd drown.

My thoughts drove me crazy, though. My body felt exhausted, but my mind was on red alert, obsessing over the boy in the tower.

I couldn't help myself. I tossed my legs off the side of the bed and grabbed the ornate candle holder, along with my lighter and a few other goodies I couldn't wait to show off. I didn't bother with shoes or slippers. I tiptoed across the room and slithered out the door soundlessly with my mesh bag over my shoulder, padding down the hall in my pale pink nightgown. I lit the candle and let the muted light guide me down the meandering, narrow halls of Luna Academy.

I bit back my fear as I ascended the dark, spiral staircase that led to Michael's room. Going up a dark staircase alone had always scared the shit out of me as a child. It always felt like there was a demon behind me.

The candle may have provided light, but damn, with the light came the shadows.

When I finally reached the top, my brows knitted together in contemplation. The door opened a crack, spilling out muted orange light.

"Michael?" I called quietly, but no one answered.

I swallowed thickly as I dared to peek through the opened door.

Natalia was in here. My heart jolted at that, though I had no reason or right to feel that way. They were on the floor together. Michael was laying with his head in her lap, his eyes closed. Natalia had a blindfold on, her fingers resting over his temples. Candles on the floor and floating in the air cast warm, golden light upon them. Natalia's magic thrummed palpably. Calm, clear, earthy magic.

Natalia didn't speak or remove the blindfold, but she did acknowledge my presence. She pointed with her head for me to sit down. I knew the drill. If she was using her Sight, I needed to be quiet. My pulse beat steadily as I sat down on the floor, being as silent as possible.

I watched Michael's face. After assessing him for a few minutes, I concluded that he was asleep, which I found odd. His long, thick lashes fluttered like he was dreaming, casting spidery shadows down his cheeks. He even seemed to bite his lip ring in his sleep. He wore his famous ripped jeans with the spiky belt and a wife beater that had seen better days. Every so often he'd jolt or say a word. Natalia remained deathly quiet, her lips popped open as she looked into him.

I waited with bated breath.

My candle had burned down significantly by the time she removed her fingers from his temples and pulled the blindfold off her tired eyes.

I perked up instantly. I expected Michael to arouse as well, but he remained asleep, his head unmoving in her lap.

For a moment, Natalia only stared at me. The look on her face... I couldn't think of a word for it. Moved? Conflicted? Enlightened? At a crossroads?

"What did you See?" I breathed, so quietly she could barely hear me.

Her hands instinctively moved to touch his temples again. She feathered her fingers through his tousled hair and my stomach tightened defensively. The fondness shining in her eyes struck insidious emotions inside me. Foreign, despicable emotions. I hardly recognized myself.

Natalia's warm brown eyes welled with tears. "This mortal... He is precious. A precious treasure, handpicked by the Goddess. One soul plucked out of a sea of billions... He is to be protected at all costs. Do you understand?"

A wave of prickly energy crashed over my flesh, her words swarming like angered hornets in the core of my being. I had to choke down the urge to snap at her. If anyone knew Michael was special, it was me. To hear her say it like it was brand-new information made my heart swell and ache. Also, a murderous rage screamed from the back of my mind, but I hushed it. What had come over me?

"I know that," I replied evenly, though my throat worked and my teeth ground together.

She was still touching his temples and his hair. Lovingly. He looked so peaceful, sleeping there in her lap. Natalia was doting and soft and wonderful. She looked angelic in the candlelight. Her energy radiated purely and here I was, a jealous brat who had the nerve to let my judgment be clouded by my own confused emotions.

Natalia began humming a beautiful tune. It made Michael's eyelids flutter open. His gaze landed immediately—instinctively—on me. As if he sensed me here while he was dreaming.

A lazy smile slid across his lips, striking lightning through my heart. "Emilia."

He sat up and Natalia shuffled backward, rising to her feet, stretching her limbs, and groaning in pleasure as she did so. "I'll leave you two." She grinned at me before moving toward the door.

"Wait," Michael said to her. "What did you see? Did you find what you were looking for? Er, what were you looking for again?"

"Mortal boy, you are the Eighth Wonder," Natalia told him softly, a playful smirk on her lips which made it difficult to decipher if she was kidding or serious. "I must sleep now. I will see you tomorrow night."

She'd been coming here every night since he arrived. It made me feel some type of way. Knowing he was up here alone every night with this lovely, enchanting, magical woman who was seeing so deeply into him. What I just walked in on was nothing less than intimate. Sitting in the candlelight together on the floor...

I swallowed down the bitter jealousy and smiled at Natalia before she vanished down the stairs.

When I turned back to Michael, he was already looking at me. His eyes were hooded and tired, his mouth still toying with a lazy smile. "What are you doing here so late?"

Good question. What was I doing here so late?

"I brought you something," I said. I grabbed my mesh bag and reached inside. Michael's eyes lit up like a kid on Christmas as I pulled out the little tin full of weed and a quartz wizard's pipe Destiny had let me borrow.

"Fuckin' eh!" he chimed, the shit-eating grin taking over his features and making my pulse hasten.

I giggled as I handed it all over to him, not knowing the first thing about weed. I never tried it before. I'd been around people who were smoking it, like Nyx and Michael and all the rest of our friends, but I'd always been too nervous. I had enough anxiety as it was. Nyx used to smoke it like a chimney and my mother couldn't stand it. She'd walk around all glassy-eyed and it would trigger every demon Esmeralda had. I steered clear of all that noise, but it didn't seem so terrible now.

"I was dreaming about you," he told me nonchalantly as he packed the bud into the pipe. "Kind of fucking weird having that girl spying on my dreams, but apparently, they're prophetic." He laughed absently at that. "Who would have thunk it, huh?"

For some reason, my eyes welled with tears as I watched him. One soul plucked out of billions... This wonderful, chaotic, mischievous delinquent from my hometown. The boy with ripped jeans and piercings and too many tattoos for his age. The kind of boy society disregarded. The kind my mother disregarded. A little heathen, chosen by our Goddess, to be protected and cherished, for his dreams were filled with prophecy.

It made sense. It made so much freaking sense. Michael was always telling me about his dreams. His dreams of shadows and fire and superpowers. I'd always listened loosely... Michael loved his dark comic books and was always reading horror novels. I thought that was where his dreams were coming from. But now...

"What was the dream?" I asked lightly, wondering if I was visibly trembling or if that was just my body's new heightened vibration.

"You were ice skating," he said, still focused on what he was doing with the weed. I regarded him intently. He bit his lip ring, and his brows narrowed. His brown eyes flashed up to me, catching me staring. "Yeah. Everything was ice and you loved it. Your sister was there, too. She was mad. She had this great big shadow following her around. It seemed like... It kind of seemed like she was dangerous. Ha. I don't know."

I let out an uneasy laugh. "Sounds about right."

"Lighter?" He glanced pointedly at my bag.

"Oh, right." I handed it to him, and he lit up, hauling the smoke through the Gandalf pipe, looking all sorts of beautiful.

He exhaled through his nose like a dragon and then offered the pipe to me.

I stared at it, unmoving. "I don't smoke."

"I know." He laughed, his eyes instantly slanting and turning red, making him look even cuter somehow. "Wanna try?" His spine stiffened then, so suddenly I thought something happened. He looked around the room in paranoid concern. "Wait, do you think your Goddess will mind if I smoke in here? Is that, like, against your religion?"

"We're not religious!" I exclaimed with a giggle. I shrugged. "I don't think she'll mind. Weed is a plant. Plants are of the earth. Our Goddess is of the earth."

"Perfect," he sighed, taking another toke, and blowing smoke rings at me. "I thought your Goddess was of the stars?"

I broke the rings with my finger, smiling as I did so. "As above, so below."

"Oh," Michael murmured, pretending he understood. "Hey, it's almost your birthday. That's a big deal for you angels, right? Natalia was saying, er, something."

"We're not angels," I argued, skin prickling at the thought of him seeing us that way.

He frowned at me. "What? Of course you are. I mean. Right?"

I smirked, reaching out to shove him lightly. The contact instantly ignited electricity up my arm. I swear he felt it too, the way he bristled. I cleared my throat as my eyes went downcast. "You can call us angels if you want."

"You are angels. Well, you are, anyway." He scoffed as if I were being ridiculous. He offered me the pipe again, brows raised playfully, a challenge lit in his eyes.

I bit my lip and he noticed. I glanced at the pipe, considering. He shuffled closer to me on the floor, so our knees were nearly touching. "I'll pack a fresh bowl," he declared and did exactly that. I watched with my heart in my throat as he piled the dank, green bud into the wizard pipe. He held it out to me. I didn't take it.

"Fine," he sighed dramatically, grinning impishly at me. Our gazes locked as he brought the pipe to his lips and lit the end. My heart hammered as he shifted even closer to me, bringing his face mere inches from mine. He finished his toke, but he didn't exhale the smoke. "Come here," he murmured, only letting a tiny bit seep out between those tempting lips.

My eyes widened but I was intuitively leaning in, head spinning. He leaned in too, our lips so close it physically ached not to erase the space between us. His face glowed in the candlelight; every single feature carved with divine perfection. Not because he was perfect, but because he was perfectly Michael.

With only a tiny sliver of air between our lips, Michael blew out his smoke into my waiting, slightly open mouth. I inhaled fervently, taking his breath, his smoke, and his life force into me. The map of my veins burst to life, and I swore my blood began to glow and sizzle. His lips nearly brushed mine, his tousled hair feathering against my forehead. He'd been looking at me the entire time but now his eyelids fluttered shut.

My stomach erupted with delirious butterflies that swarmed my insides in a riot of beating wings.

The instinct to run ambushed me.

My arms and legs seized up with the impulse to dash away from him. I was a coward and a hypocrite. I judged my sister for the way she self-sabotaged and shut others out, but I was no better. The boy I wanted with every fiber of my being sat not even a breath away from me, his lips so close to mine, I could already taste them. And I wanted to run.

I needed to run.

Hastily, I made the incline to shuffle away but a warm, firm hand gripped my wrist and locked me in place. Michael opened his eyes, a heavy-hearted gleam shining over them. "Are you really going to run from me again, Emilia?" he whispered, his lip ring brushing my bottom lip as he spoke. I tasted his bittersweet words on my tongue. That dark, boundless gaze had so much sorrow hidden within it. Sorrow he kept tucked away behind his rebellious, carefree mask.

I let my focus drop to his lips, my heart pumping blood furiously through my veins. The silver ring through his bottom lip caught the light of the candles, tempting me nearer. Maybe it was the weed, but suddenly I couldn't imagine ever leaving this spot on the floor.

My flight instinct screeched to a halt and shifted into reverse. I needed to be closer.

I dared to close the space between us by taking his lip ring between my teeth, shocking us both.

I wasn't sure what came over me, but I rolled with it.

My pulse thrashed like a thunderstorm. The way he stiffened against me melted the butterflies in my stomach, turning them into molten liquid. His arms were instantly around me. I flung mine around his neck, tangling my fingers in the back of his hair as he gasped into me, his lip still caught between my teeth. Goddess, he tasted amazing. He felt amazing. My core tingled in a way that made my thighs clench, anticipation writhing up my spine like a serpent in a tree.

His mouth moved to close over mine, but a stampede of elephants started charging up the stairs and we shot apart as if we'd been electrocuted.

I could hardly breathe as my attention flew to the door, confusion knitting my brows together. Who in the seven realms would come up—

Nyx burst through the door, practically making it fly off the hinges as she stumbled into the circular room, stinking of alcohol and smoke and regret. Her heavy black makeup smudged down her cheeks, her silver hair a wild mess around her drunk face. She held a bottle of vodka in one hand while the other hand waved around, alit with white flame.

I guess my sister got her power back.

Her glassy, half-open eyes landed on us, and a shit-eating grin took possession of her lips. "Ohhhhh, look at this," she sang, wobbling toward us, hiccupping as she banished her fire magic. "How cuuuteee." Her nostrils flared then, realization lighting behind her eyes. "Wait—are you guys smoking pot? EMILIA?! WOOO! Light me up! Is that a fucking Gandalf pipe! Omagoddess!!"

"Nyx." I hissed. "What the hell have you gotten into?"

"Ahhh, little sister, the night I've had!" She lost her footing as she spoke. No wonder. The heels on those black boots she wore would be the death of me. She went tumbling town, managing to angle herself to land on the mattress behind us. She fell upon the books and journals, grumbling in annoyance as she pushed them out of her way and sat cross-legged on Michael's bed like it was hers.

"I signed my soul to the devil and then got drunk with him and his vampire sister." She hiccupped and laughed humorlessly as she popped the top off her liquor bottle and slammed some of it with a grimace.

I blinked. Michael and I shared a loaded glance.

"Nyx..." I breathed, chills blowing across my skin.

"My life is over." She cheersed the sky. "At least I managed to destroy that stupid fucking medallion. Good riddance. Thooooough, I did keep a tiny piece of it. Ha! Suck it, Solaris." She grabbed a small shard of red glass out of her bra and held it up to the light of the candles. "Can you believe I was bested by a piece of glass? Life is a mockery of the soul."

I got up and crossed the small space to sit next to her on the bed. I had no clue what to do—Nyx Morningstar was not the type to be coddled or consoled. So I just sat there and offered my listening ear. Michael stayed on the floor, hugging his knees, watching us through an expression I couldn't quite read.

She tucked the piece of glass back into her bra, which I couldn't imagine felt good. Though I was beginning to understand that for my sister, pleasure and pain were the same entity.

"I have to battle Solaris Adder on Hallows Eve. At the Clash of Spirits. You know that Hallows Eve is the one night in a year when the veil between our world and the spirit world is the thinnest. Magic is heightened. Which meeeeeans: our magic is the strongest that night. His shadows will be even more powerful! I can't even lie to you, Emilia—I think I'm going to fucking lose. Haaa. What a joke." She choked an unsettling laugh and hiccupped. "I am powerful as shit. But Solaris? He —" She cut herself off with another hiccup which turned into a sob. "I'm done for, little sis."

My heart thudded slowly behind my ribs. "Well, doesn't that mean your magic will be amplified too? You're already the most powerful starseed in—"

"Yeah, the most powerful *starseed*," Nyx spat bitterly, wiping the tears away. "I'm still fairly new to being Emerged. Solaris is like, above and beyond the Embodied and the Exalted... He's a century older than me and has this fathomless power that I stand no chance against. Just like when he lured me into the shadows that night on the beach. He bested me then. He will do it again."

I scrutinized the miserable, defeated look that swathed my sister's features. My heart cracked and spilled empathy up my throat, making me swallow hard. I'd never seen her this way before. I'd never seen her doubt herself—doubt her own power. She'd always walked with her head high and her eyes on fire, looking at everyone and everything like it was all hers to conquer.

"You are not like the others," I told her softly. "You are Nyx Morningstar. Named for both the night and the dawn. You could do magic before you Emerged. Mother always acted like that was such a bad thing, but how could it be? Remember what Jedidiah said? Your fire is different. Celestial fire. Sun fire! What are shadows to the fire of the sun itself?"

Nyx stared at me through bloodshot eyes, considering.

"The light shines in the darkness, and the darkness does not overcome it," Michael said, making my sister's head snap in his direction.

Her lips curled back in disgust. "Did you just quote *the Bible* to me?"

Michael shrugged lazily, picking up the Gandalf pipe and packing it with fresh weed. "It's prophetic," he explained casually.

"He's right," I voiced. "The light always wins."

"Ha!" Nyx snorted indignantly. "Well, maybe I'm not light. You ever think of that, hmm? Maybe I'm just a raging fucking wildfire that does nothing but destroy. That's the thing, right? When has my power ever done anything good? I am just as terrible and corrupt as the rest of them. For all of this to land on me is a cosmic mockery. You know, sometimes I think the Goddess is quite insidious."

Michael handed her the wizard's pipe and her depressive aura went up in smoke, a childlike grin lighting up her face.

I opened my mouth to protest since she did not look like she needed any more substances in her system but screw it.

"Did...did you say you got drunk with Solaris and his vampire sister?" I wondered incredulously as I suddenly remembered what she'd said before.

Nyx hauled on the pipe and then tilted her head back, exhaling the smoke slowly, watching it rise to the ceiling. "Yeah, I did. I wasn't thinking straight. Drunk on my own power n' shit. Solaris shadow traveled me to the desert to give me my magic back and I exploded like a bloody volcano. It was epic and I'm pissed he didn't get it on video. He took me back to his suite at the Sun & Moon and the next thing I knew we were all drinking together."

"Fuck me." She collapsed down against the sheets, her smudged eyes falling shut. Those long dark lashes fluttered restlessly but her breathing evened out almost immediately.

I peered down upon her face as she passed out. She started snoring obnoxiously which made me laugh. Michael had a fondness in his tired eyes as well. I offered him a smile. "Sorry about your bed."

"It's okay," he replied genuinely. "It's big enough for the three of us." He moved over and laid down beside Nyx, tucking one arm behind his head. He looked pointedly at the spot on the other side of her. "Stay."

I swallowed thickly, goosebumps rising over my arms. Nyx sprawled out in the middle of the bed, snoring like a banshee, and yet nothing had ever appealed to me more. I tucked myself in beside her, peering over her face to meet eyes with Michael. He grinned lazily, his heavy eyelids threatening to close. "Goodnight, Emilia. Oh, and happy birthday."

Right. It had to be well past midnight now. My chest heated as I thought about it. My eighteenth birthday.

"Goodnight," I whispered.

I let my eyes close. To my surprise, sleep found me right away, like it was in a hurry to claim me. I fell into a series of peculiar dreams. Dreams of ice and shadows, fire, and dragons. Every image was fleeting, leaving me breathless in the dream state. I tried to grasp each one of them, but they were little more than swirling visuals in a tornado, passing my mind's eye before I could comprehend what I was seeing. One thing stayed the same: In every dream, Michael was there.

I WOKE UP WITH A JOLT, WHISPERS FADING IN MY EARS AS I opened my eyes and took in the impossible world around me.

The ceiling above was adorned with dazzling, textured patterns of blue and white, which glimmered as the morning light spilled through the small stained-glass window. The pattern continued down the walls, over the floor, covering everything in this room. I blinked, sitting up, completely miffed. Confusion swamped my brain as my breath puffed out in thick, white clouds. Why was it so freezing up here?

I reached out to touch the strange, beautiful pattern on the floor. I gasped as my fingers brushed along the cold, smooth yet gritty surface.

It was ice.

Everything had completely iced over.

Nyx and Michael remained fast asleep, oblivious to the frozen phenomena.

I shook them awake frantically. "Guys! Wake up!"

They both groaned their complaints, reluctantly opening their eyes. Nyx's hand immediately flew to her forehead, a grimace tearing across her lips. "Fuck my life," she whined, clearly suffering from the hangover from hell.

"Look!" I wheezed in panic.

They sat up together and looked around, their faces falling.

Michael's eyes lit up.

Nyx looked like someone had pissed on her in her sleep.

"What's happening?" I demanded breathily, looking to my sister for answers.

I couldn't understand why her expression darkened and bittered. Her obsidian eyes swept over the room before landing on me, almost accusingly.

We left Michael to go downstairs and investigate.

The entire Academy had turned to ice as if Jack Frost visited us overnight. Every wall, statue, painting, piece of furniture—all were covered in a beautiful sheet of twinkling, blue-white ice.

In the common room, girls in their nightgowns were giggling in wonder, skating across the iced-over floor, which looked like a frozen lake.

The Priestesses were here too, exchanging peculiar looks. The Luminary's eyes fell on me.

Nyx was staring at me too. More specifically, her eyes had fallen to my hands. I followed her gaze, gasping as I realized my fingers were covered in the same frosty pattern as everything else.

"Well, well, well," my sister drawled, something dark hidden within her tone. "Happy Emergence, little sister. Thank the Goddess you're not a fireling."

CHAPTER 31

ALONE

NYX

I slammed my flaming fists into the punching bag, grunting while beads of sweat drenched my face and clothes. I'd been beating the shit out of this thing for the past hour, listening to my angriest playlist on full blast through my headphones, dying for release. Yet the mind-bending rage that coiled within me had not relented, not even a little.

I only stopped because I could no longer see straight.

I gave the punching bag a final kick before falling back onto the mat, my breath leaving me in chaotic, heavy heaves. I stared up at the twinkling moon-shaped roof of the Sphere while I waited for my heart rate to slow down.

The Sphere was packed today, almost every girl from Luna occupying the space at different stations. My minions had been loitering around me this whole time, looking a little marvelled, but mostly terrified. Other girls watched me too, but not with the same admiration I was used to from them.

I had my magic back. Fully. My power coursed through my veins, lighting up my flesh with a golden glow, my tattoos back on full show. After all this time, after all that insufferable push and pull with Solaris, I finally got what I'd been wanting so badly.

But what did it even matter?

Nothing changed.

I wasn't exactly sure what I had expected to happen after getting my power back, but it wasn't this. I figured the girls would all come back and follow me once more, but Venus St. Claire's posse of minions only grew.

Perhaps it would just take a while for things to go back to the way they were.

But it had already been two weeks. How much longer would it take for them to remember who I was?

I yanked out my headphones and sat up, my attention snagging to the entrance of the Sphere just as Emilia stepped through.

Girls instantly flocked to her, greeting her with beaming faces and incessant chatter. Her cheeks flushed with heat as she awkwardly yet charmingly received their affection. I watched, feeling like I was witnessing something from outside a glass window, looking into a home I'd never belonged to.

They love her.

This realization crystallized a little more every day. My sister had Emerged not just as a waterling, but as a waterling with the power of ice. This was rare—it took most starseeds eons to learn how to wield ice, if ever. Not only that, but her Emergence had gone viral on Celestial media.

The entire Celestial Society was obsessed with her.

And for what? What had she done to prove herself? She'd won no battles; she'd climbed no ladders of success. She possessed a rare power, sure, but what had she done with it? Nothing.

Her blue eyes met mine from across the Sphere and she had the audacity to *smile* at me.

I scowled back, grabbing my things as I rose to my feet and strutted out of there.

She called after me. I ignored her.

Back in my room, I texted Jedidiah again. I'd texted him an embarrassing number of times at this point, but I hadn't heard from him since he portalled himself away from the Sun & Moon hotel. I gnawed on my lip as I sent him more messages, trying all sorts of different approaches. From heartfelt paragraphs, to sassy jokes, to selfies.

He never responded, not once.

I couldn't blame him, nor could I imagine what he was going through. I just wished he would talk to me.

Natalia showed up a little while later, her black ringlets sweaty from her session in the Sphere. She gave me nothing but a side eye before she locked herself in the bathroom and took a forty-five-minute shower.

She was pissed at me. What else was new?

She had accused me the other night of treating my little sister like shit. She wasn't wrong but she also didn't understand. I was sick and tired of girls parading into Luna Academy and being treated like royalty without doing anything to earn it. I had *worked my ass off* to secure my position as queen and look how fast that had been taken from me. Now Venus was living the life I had risen from nothing to claim, and it looked as though Emilia was coming for it too. How could this be possible? Because their magic was sparkly? Because their doe eyes captivated the hearts of admirers everywhere? I didn't fucking get it.

When Natalia finally emerged from the bathroom, I sat up on my bed and tossed my blackmirror aside. "Hey."

She moved to the closet without looking at me. "Hi."

I sighed. "Listen, Natalia—"

"I don't want to hear it, Nyx. After everything you've done, after all the shit you let happen because you were too proud to tell anyone what happened to you... I just—I don't understand you at all! You have your power back, and yet you are crueller than ever. You won't give your sister the time of day! How do you think that makes her feel? Are you seriously that insecure and jealous that you can't be happy for your own sister now that she's truly one of us?"

I blinked. "Wow. Tell me how you really feel."

She gave me a flat look. "Look, I love you. I always will. But I cannot condone your behavior. To be brutally honest with you, you suck lately. I hope you can look inside yourself and face whatever is eating at you so badly. Or else you're going to end up just like your mother. Bitter and alone."

My eyes widened, my jaw going slack. I fumbled for a comeback, but

I had nothing. My heart hammered in my chest as her words loomed over me like a dark cloud.

The worst fucking part was that she was right.

I swallowed the lump in my throat, blinking away the hot tears that pricked the back of my eyes. I cleared my throat. "Have you had any visions about Jedidiah?"

Natalia pulled a sweater over her head, her eyes softening a little as they met mine. "You're worried about him."

"Well, yeah," I replied, tossing my hands in the air. "Why wouldn't I be?"

"You guys aren't exactly friends."

"No one deserves to go through what he's going through, though. Even assholes like him."

She sighed, moving to come and sit at the end of my bed. "I actually took it upon myself to look for him the other night. He's in the Rocky Mountains."

My brows jumped. "Why would he be there?"

"Well, when I saw him, he was raging against the earth. Causing all sorts of earthquakes and avalanches. If it wasn't so sad, it would have been epic."

"I need to see him," I muttered aloud, shocking us both a little. That should have been a private thought. "I mean, you know... He shouldn't be alone right now. I just—whatever. It's not important."

Natalia's gaze roved over me in a way that made me feel naked. "You don't have to hide your heart all the time, Nyx. Vulnerability is not a weakness."

I scoffed.

Speak for yourself.

CHAPTER 32
DEBAUCHERY & DESIRE
EMILIA

Nyx left the Sphere as soon as I showed up. I was right in the middle of offering her a smile and a wave before she dropped everything and stalked out of the yoni-shaped entrance like she was getting away from a dumpster fire.

She'd been like this ever since I Emerged.

She was more miserable than ever. Getting her power back didn't immediately solve all her problems. Imagine that!

A cold, biting sorrow wafted across my skin. Tears threatened to spill over onto my cheeks, but I bit them back with determination. I couldn't let her get to me like this. Why was she so bitter toward me? Because I had Emerged as a waterling? Was that it?

I had to banish my miserable curiosity. The Nyx Show had hit a downward spiral, even after getting her magic back. She wasn't going to suck me down with her.

I focused on Priestess Adria who led us through the racks of physical weapons and training females, leading the way to the elemental ring.

At least I had Destiny. She'd Emerged a week after me—as a fireling! Her big, boisterous family had showed up at the Academy and whisked her away for a week of partying and celebrating in the Dominican. My mother hadn't even shown up to give me a gift, let alone party. I was relieved—the way I felt about my mother was confusing. After what I saw in the Sacred Temple, I was glad she stayed away.

I was beyond glad and relieved to have Destiny back now. We stuck together as we slipped into the ring behind the Water Priestess.

Around twenty-five girls occupied the Sphere, most of them in the combat area, focused on physical training rather than element wielding. That didn't stop them from pausing what they were doing to watch us in the ring. Everyone loved gawking at me these days.

"Okay, girls," Adria chimed. "Stand a few feet apart. Feet planted firmly on the ground. Shoulders squared. Chin up, spine straight. Good, good. Now, hold your hands out in front of you, palms up. Focus on your breath. Six seconds in, six seconds out. Yes, wonderful. Keep that up for a few minutes." Our Priestess circled us, assessing our stances, nodding in approval.

"Wielding the elements is not just magic," she informed us. "It is art. An ancient art, an art that is your birthright. Now, hold your hands out and focus on the power inside you. Summon your element in a neat, clean, contained manner."

Destiny and I were more than thrilled to obey. Within seconds, she had a healthy orange flame writhing over her two palms. I grinned, my heart racing wildly as I shut my eyes and focused a moment on my breath. A soft, tinkling sound filled my ears and I opened my eyes to find a perfect flurry of sparkling ice over my skin. It stayed contained over my palms, keeping together in a whirling spiral pattern. The ice itself shone like blue crystals. I couldn't believe this was *me*.

Fire and water were supposed to be inherent rivals, but I never felt that way with Destiny. Her magic inspired me, it didn't trigger me or make me feel like I needed to challenge it. My sister, though... I sort of felt that way about Nyx. I couldn't explain it. Something about her power made me want to fight her. She must have felt the same way and that was why she was pushing me away. Though her doing that only made me want to strike against her more.

More girls joined us in the ring, eleven of us standing in a circle around the Water Priestess. She walked us through exercises of growing and shrinking the size of our expressed element. It was a bit difficult to shrink my ice back down once I'd made it grow, but by the end of it, I caught on. If I breathed in deep and slow, my element naturally waned.

When we were dismissed for lunch, I was straight giddy. My power was growing rapidly and gaining control of it was working out easier than I expected.

I couldn't wait to tell Michael about all of this. I hadn't been to his room in a few nights. Classes had me exhausted and I knew he was busy most evenings with Natalia. I had to fight against the urge to be murderously jealous about that. After Nyx interrupted our kiss, we hadn't come close to having another moment. Was that because he was falling for Natalia? Spending all that time alone together...

Ugh.

I banished those thoughts from my mind as Destiny and I entered the dining hall for lunch. My friend had changed since Emerging—she'd gotten bolder, wittier, and more skeptical. Reminded me of my sister. I guessed firelings had a certain nature to them. So when she led us straight to the center of the long, gothic dining table to sit directly across from Bianca, Cassiopeia, and Venus St. Claire, I felt like I was living in The Nyx Show 2.0. What was it with firelings and starting drama?! If it were up to me, we'd sit on the far end by our freaking selves.

They didn't even look at us.

Destiny shot me a dark, mischievous smirk as we sat down on the bench. I swallowed and looked away quickly. *Please don't start anything.*

The lunch spread smelt like heaven. I couldn't wait to dig in. Practicing magic always left me ravenous. I kept my mouth shut as I piled my plate with fancy cheese, cured meat, and fresh fruit. Destiny, on the other hand, picked at grapes and stared across the table at the three girls who had assaulted us two weeks ago.

They still wouldn't look at us.

It didn't feel like being ignored, either. It felt like being feared.

That couldn't be right, though. Could it?

I kicked her foot under the table, trying to urge her to stop glaring over there like she was trying to burn them down with her golden-brown eyes. Which had gotten even more gold since she Emerged. Destiny's irises were swimming with shimmery, molten gold that hinted at the smoldering power coursing in her veins. She got living tattoos, too. All in silver. Serpents and foxes swirled on her arms, her fingers decorated with lines and circles and moon shapes. She had gemstones placed throughout the light dusting of dark hair atop her head. She was truly embracing her Celestial nature.

Fortunately, Venus and her followers didn't take her bait, and so we managed to get through lunch without a showdown.

We spent the rest of the day in the Athena Library, studying old myths on how to merge fire and water to create Aether. Destiny was right into it, but admittedly, my mind was far away.

On our way out of the library, we passed a plethora of pictures on the wall that made me stop and stare. An intuitive pull had me spotting one single face out of hundreds.

My mother.

There she was, young and radiant and...happy looking. Nothing like the cold, callous woman I knew today. She stood in the common room of Luna Academy, when both the school and the city were brand new, with a group of other girls, smiling and looking uncharacteristically happy. The old class photos had charm. I skimmed my eyes over each face. "Wow," I murmured.

Destiny grinned, enjoying the old photo as much as me. She reached out and pointed to a beautiful woman standing beside my mother. She had dark blonde hair and big blue eyes and looked oddly familiar. "That's Nymeria Stone," my friend informed me. "Jedidiah's mother."

"Oh wow," I breathed. "She's gorgeous."

"She was powerful, too."

"Was?" I retorted, curious.

"Yeah. Rumor has it, a few years ago, she gave up her magic and left the Society to live out her mortal life in Maine or something."

My brows jumped. "What? Why?"

Destiny shrugged. "It's just a rumor, but I think it's true. I guess being married to the High Lord isn't all it's cracked up to be."

For some reason, that gave me a chill up my spine.

"That's Natalia's mother, Samantha Ambrose," Destiny continued, pointing to a dark-skinned woman who resembled our friend uncannily. "She was... Well, don't ever repeat this to Natalia, but her mother was into making dark objects. Her father too. They got in trouble a few years back and were banned from using any kind of magic outside of wielding the elements. Natalia doesn't even speak to them. She lived with one of her aunts before she came to Luna. I've heard that her parents have been slowly declining into insanity after all their usage of dark objects."

I stared at my friend with my brows lowered. "How do you know all of this?"

"I told you! I've been reading Celestial media since I was thirteen." She gave me a mischievous smirk followed by kissy lips. "X-o-x-o, gossip girl."

"Shut up," I laughed, shoving her playfully.

"But you know the one thing I don't know?"

"What's that?"

"Who your father is."

I nearly choked on my saliva.

"No one knows and it's killing me, Emilia!"

My body felt ice cold and fire hot at the same time. "Including me." I snapped. "My mother never told me or Nyx who he was. Morningstar women only bed men to get pregnant. The father never stays. We don't talk about it. Ever. If Nyx heard you ask me this, she'd murder you!"

"Whoa," Destiny put her hands up in mock surrender. "Okay, the Morningstar girls have severe daddy issues. That explains a lot. Noted."

"Destiny!" I cried, and she laughed.

WE WENT BACK TO OUR ROOM AND BY THE TIME WE GOT there, I was beat. I slid into my comfiest PJs and opened my latest romantasy book. Nothing like a little fae romance to end a long day.

I thought about Michael, about going up to his room in the tower, but my body refused to move from this position. I knew I could count on seeing him in my dreams, anyway. He was there every single night, so vividly.

"Girl," Destiny cawed from her bed where she lay on her stomach, feet in the air behind her. Her face was lit up by the blue light of her blackmirror. "You'll never guess what Celestial Tea just posted."

My brows jumped, intrigue gripping my heart. "What?"

"The Society's Hottest New Couple: The Darkbringer and his Red Queen." She read the headline with an animated, mock-news anchor tone, turning her blackmirror so I could see the screen.

A photo of Solaris Adder with Venus St. Claire nestled cozily at his side awaited me. They were at some low-lit club, looking intimate.

"Oh my Goddess," I murmured, bewildered. That visual was not right. The two of them were a true match made in Hell.

"I feel like your sister is going to lose her shit."

"My sister always loses her shit," I grumbled.

Destiny laughed and went back to scrolling on her blackmirror. "It says they've been spotted in several different Celestial Sites around the city. Fucking weird, man."

"My sister's two adversaries pairing up," I mused aloud. "Poetic, in a dark, ironic way. It seems like the universe is always moving against her."

"My granny always said that if the Divine carves a difficult path for someone, it's because they have a great purpose. People with easy lives never do anything significant." Destiny offered.

I scoffed. "Your granny sounds lit."

"Oh, dude. She is! I hope you can meet her one day. She rolls the best fairy blunts and serves the strongest martin—"

Our dorm room door burst open, making us both jump. Nyx stood there, dressed like she was going clubbing. Tall black boots, a short black dress bedazzled with gems, her living tattoos whirling with adrenaline. Her hair was blown out, and her makeup dark and smoky. "Get up. We're going out."

Destiny sat up, intrigued. "Where?"

I clutched my book to my chest, narrowing my eyes at my sister. "I'm tired."

"Oh, shut up. Wear something black and hurry up. You've been Emerged for two weeks and haven't even stepped foot on Moonrise Blvd."

"Moonrise Blvd!" Destiny chirped excitedly, throwing her feet off the bed to stand up and move over to the closet. "Hell yeah. I'm down."

"See, little sis?" Nyx taunted. "Your friend is cooler than you. Get up. Cab will be here in fifteen."

)) ● ((

I SAW THE RED FLAG WAVING BOLDLY IN THE WIND WHEN IT was just the three of us who piled into the cab. Natalia and Faye weren't coming, which meant, my sister was up to something. There was no way she just wanted to hang out with me and Destiny for fun. I mean, she had hardly even looked at me in the last two weeks. She avoided me like the plague. Now she wanted my company? Yeah right. But here I was, going along with her shenanigans, as always.

When we were dropped off on Sunset and Vine, Nyx grabbed the street sign and the world changed, all protests inside me fizzled out.

Moonrise Blvd was a freaking dream.

I'd never seen anything like it. It was like an enchanted carnival in street form. Everywhere I looked there was color and magic and wonders beyond anything I could have ever imagined. The Hollywood strip had always dazzled me, but this was next level. The crystal towers here were three times taller and brighter than the ones at Luna Academy. Fire dancers were performing on the street. Jungle trees and vines were growing amongst the concrete buildings, with glowing neon butterflies and dragonflies darting about. We passed a grand theater, a plethora of interesting little trinket shops, bars, diners, record shops, a roller rink— shit, there was even a floating Ferris wheel.

Destiny was in the same boat. We exchanged an excited look, both giggling as we followed my sister down the lit-up sidewalk.

When Nyx led us to a place with bright neon letters reading Lucifer's Playground, though, my giggles died.

The music from inside boomed and practically shook the ground under our feet. A long line of colorful, decked-out Celestials lined the sidewalk, waiting to get in. A ginormous bouncer stood at the door, dressed in all black, including dark glasses which kept us from seeing his eyes. His arms were folded over his broad chest, his expression flat and fixed.

"Nyx!" I hissed. "What the hell is this place?"

"The lightbringer's lair," she quipped back without looking at me. "A place of debauchery and desire. Be quiet. Let me handle this." She

281

strode right up to the grumpy bouncer, flicking her long pale hair over her shoulder. "Hey, Damien," my sister cooed. "Been a while."

He stared at her for a moment, unmoving. Then he stepped out of the way, allowing her to go inside.

"I brought my little sister and her friend along," Nyx explained, gesturing toward me and Destiny.

The bouncer, Damien, grunted but didn't argue. He let the three of us inside, ignoring the complaints of the people standing in line.

I couldn't imagine that any good could come from entering a club called Lucifer's freaking Playground.

My heart was in my throat as we stepped onto the scene, my eyes wide as I took it all in. The ground level was scattered with lounge tables and leather sofas which encircled the lit-up dance floor that was packed with sweaty, glittery bodies. Loud trance music harassed my eardrums. The bar at the far end was worked by women with colorful hair and barely any clothes. A wrap-around balcony lined the second floor, and it was just as busy up there as down here. Floating neon lights gave the ambiance an ethereal glow. There was a stage on the right side where the DJ was set up, his blue hair spiked out in every direction. Floating platforms hovered over a few feet off the ground, with fire and air dancers performing scandalously on top of them.

I'd never seen so much skin in my life. Some women didn't even wear tops. Oh, Goddess—the more I looked around, the more sin I saw. Naked women with painted skin gave lap dances to men on the leather sofas. My cheeks were fire hot. I felt like I needed to stare at my feet.

"Holy shit," Destiny yell-whispered to me.

All I could do was give her a wide-eyed look in response.

"Come on, younglings," Nyx barked, grabbing my wrist, and towing me through the crowd.

People stared. Not just at my sister, but at me. Some of them pointed right at me, talking amongst each other. About me.

It appeared that my fifteen minutes of fame was not up yet.

CHAPTER 33
LITTLE POISON

NYX

As soon as we got to Lucifer's Playground, I ditched the girls. Emilia needed to learn how to fend for herself in situations like these. She was so damn timid, like a little fawn hiding under its mother. I slipped through the crowd as her and her friend ogled at all the sin occurring around us, disappearing amongst the glittery bodies.

He was here. I could feel him.

I prowled through the low-lit club, my senses on high alert while my eyes scanned the faces of everyone here. Though I knew looking for him out on the main floor would be pointless. Surely, he was off somewhere private and secluded.

My heart pounded as I pushed through the heavy black curtain into the back of the club. The same place Jed and I had met up not too long ago. The morning his world ended.

I pushed the images from that horrible morning out of my mind. I had to focus. I was here for a reason. Letting my mind wander would not serve that purpose.

I found the back area empty, save for one small group.

Sitting in a moon-shaped booth was the Darkbringer and his Red Queen. My mouth went dry at the sight of them. Unholy yet magnificent. A cold, slithering sense of dread coiled in my belly, and for a split second, I considered turning around and leaving. What the fuck was I doing here again?

Their booth was full of Venus's Hollywood friends—some of them world-famous. Not intimidating at all. I noted each face, swallowing hard as I strutted forward and dared to approach the man who'd turned my world upside down without lifting a damn finger.

Venus saw me first.

Our gazes locked and my stomach swooped. Instantly, her features went from a smile to a scowl. I didn't want to acknowledge, not even to myself, how stunning she looked. Her long red hair fell loose around her shoulders, her neck drenched with crystal necklaces. Her tight, crimson outfit was encrusted with crystals as well, catching the light without her even having to move. She muttered something in Solaris's ear and then silver eyes collided with mine.

A slow, malicious smirk slid across his lips.

My cheeks heated but I kept my chin up, my heeled combat boots cracking against the floor. Everyone turned to face me, though I paid them no mind. I crossed my arms over my chest and looked Solaris dead in the eye.

"Can I talk to you?"

He didn't reply. He just stared at me, seeming to notice how my blush deepened at every passing heartbeat. Venus glared at me, though she said nothing, which was unlike her. The rest of the celebrities at the table ogled at me like I were some exotic animal on display at the zoo. I wanted to incinerate them.

"Solaris," I snapped. "It's important."

He released a long-suffering sigh, as if I were such an inconvenience. Then he said something that I missed to Venus, and her stare went eerily blank. She ordered her friends to move, all of them shuffling out of the booth at the same time. She didn't look at me as she passed, stalking away through the heavy black curtain, leaving me alone with Solaris.

My brows lowered as I tried to figure out what the hell just happened.

Why would she be so obedient to him? Venus St. Claire did not strike me as the submissive type. She didn't even give me a single dirty look or utter one of her famous passive-aggressive insults as she left. Fucking weird.

"Sit," Solaris said, gesturing to the now empty booth.

"What, are you Compelling yourself friends now?" I scoffed, sliding into the spot the furthest from him.

He said nothing, staring at me evenly.

My heart dropped. "Wait! Are you actually Compelling them?" I shot another look to the black curtain they just passed through.

"Don't be ridiculous," Solaris drawled. "Celestials cannot Compel other Celestials."

I scowled at him. "Sometimes I don't even think you *are* a Celestial."

He grinned, amused. "What is it you need, Firefly?"

Now that we were alone, there was nothing to distract myself away from the way he was looking at me. From the way he *looked*. The floating chandelier above us favored him with the muted red lighting, making all his striking features even more bewitching. I had to wet my lips and fold my hands to stop them from fidgeting.

"Cat got your tongue?" he teased, cocking a brow.

"We need to talk about Hallows Eve."

This confused him. "There is nothing to discuss."

"Oh, but there is. It's October now. You have yet to challenge me in public. If you don't start something between us, there's no guarantee we will be placed with each other at the Clash of Spirits. At this point, they're going to pair me with Venus St. Claire. Everyone's already comparing us, dying to see us fight again. No one has given any thought to me versus you."

"You think I don't have ways of pulling the strings and making sure we end up together in that arena? Please."

"You don't realize how things work around here. Hype is everything. We need to have beef in public before we face off in front of the entire Society."

"Have *beef*?" he scoffed indignantly. "Could you be any more juvenile? When they see us ignite in the arena, it won't matter that they never thought of us together before. They will see us, and it will be known. Our battle will be glorious. We will make history, mark my words."

My breathing was heavy. I hated how nervous I was, even though I was no longer powerless. His presence sent my nerves through the ringer, and yet I had walked into this willingly. I should have known better.

"You're here for something else," he accused, raking that relentless, metallic glare over my face. Reading me, like an open book. "What is it you truly want?"

I couldn't deny it. I opened my mouth to do just that, but no words came out. My pulse roared in my ears, the red lights above suddenly feeling hot on my skin. It was stupid—I was so beyond stupid for coming here. For coming to *him*.

"I should go." I went to slide out of the booth, but his hand caught my wrist, tugging me back. His skin on mine sent ice and fire up my arm, goosebumps rising instantly. I reefed my arm out of his grasp and shot him a dirty look.

"What is it you truly want?" he asked again.

The sincerity in his tone made it hard to breathe.

The words tumbled out like vomit. "I want you to take me to Jedidiah. He's been gone for over two weeks. Shadow-travel me. Natalia says he's—"

"In the Rocky Mountains," he finished for me. An undeniable strike of rage flashed behind his eyes. He schooled his features quickly, but I saw it. The shock. The envy. "He's busy. He will be back when he's ready."

"How do you...?" I trailed off, thinking back to that evening at the penthouse. Him and his salt circles! "You've been Astral-spying on *Jedidiah*?" His interest in Jed wasn't just unsettling, but confusing. "I swear to the Goddess, if you spy on me like that, I'll curse you!"

"I have been cursed all my life, Firefly."

We stared at each other, the atmosphere thickening. His jaw clenched, his fingers curled into fists on the table. "Did you really think I would take you to him?"

I had to look down. His eyes were burning a hole through me. Suppressed fury rose up my throat like bile while my heart crashed behind the cage of my ribs. "I don't know what I thought. I just know that those twins were brutally murdered in the foyer of the hotel you're *living* in with your psychotic vampire *sister*. I know it was her, Solaris. You can deflect all you want like the first time I accused her, but I know. And once Jedidiah gets his shit together, he will kill her. And you can wipe up her guts from the floor when he's finished!"

"You know nothing!" Solaris hissed.

My gaze lifted to his, something electric snapping between us. "Take me to him. It's the least you could do. He shouldn't be alone right now."

A tense pause. Then, "And what comfort would *you* be to him, Firefly?" His tone was acidic, matching his glare. "You, the little poisonous girl who did nothing but torment him and those twins? The night I Astral Snatched you from the beach, what had you just been doing, hmm? You are out of your mind for coming here, not only to ask a favor from *me*, but thinking that it would bring the Groundshaker any solace to see *you*."

Each word hit like a bullet. The truth of them.

The backs of my eyes burned. I slid out of the booth swiftly, and this time he did nothing to stop me. I stalked out of there with my heart in my throat and tears threatening to spill down my cheeks.

CHAPTER 34
REVENGE ENTHUSIAST
EMILIA

Nyx ditched us, and without her, I had no idea what to do with myself.

I felt so out of place.

Destiny had let me borrow one of her little black dresses, and it was cute enough, but everyone here was dressed like we'd crossed over into some futuristic-slash-medieval timeline. Which made no sense, really, but it was just the way it was. Ancient Rome met a techno-cosmic future.

"Where the hell did she go?!" I whined. This was just like her! Force us to come out with her and then take off the second we arrived at this blasphemous hellhole. "We should just leave."

Destiny shrugged, her eyes sparkling with a curiosity I did not share with her. "I don't know, dude. This place is kinda lit."

When a group of cute guys approached us, I wanted to bolt. Destiny, on the other hand, turned into a sultry-eyed minx, giggling, and standing with her chest not so subtly pushed out. Her silver tattoos whirled and pulsed, her eyes bright with gold flecks under the neon lights.

She was a natural in this world. Unlike me. I stood back awkwardly, wishing the ground would open and swallow me whole.

"You girls must be newly Emerged," one of the guys said, and I couldn't help but think he looked like his name should be Chad. His gold hair fell over his brows, his tanned arms full of living tattoos that pulsed a little too quickly for my liking. "I haven't seen you around here before."

His friends nodded in agreement, one of them raking his eyes up and down my entire body. He had dark hair and a stocky build, dressed like a male model. He licked his lips and smiled, moving closer to me. "I'm Hendrix. You're Nyx Morningstar's little sister, aren't you?"

"Uh-huh," I replied absently, my eyes scanning the club, hoping to see my sister.

"Are you a stuck-up bitch like her?" Hendrix asked, laughing.

My neck practically snapped, the way I turned back to look at him. My features crumpled into a scowl. "Excuse me?"

Destiny suddenly looked entirely uncomfortable.

Hendrix shrugged, his arrogance oozing off him in waves. "Your sister's got a reputation. But not you. You're fresh, aren't you?" He stepped even closer to me. I backed away on instinct, his pungent cologne making me gag.

When Hendrix shrieked like a little girl, everyone within earshot looked our way. At first, I didn't understand, but half a second later, the guy went up in white flames. He screamed and flailed around, trying to put out the fire that claimed his entire body. It went out within seconds, leaving him standing there naked, covered in ash and a few smouldering remnants of his pretentious clothes.

His face was struck with horror, his hands immediately flying downward to hide his newly exposed junk.

"You have a reputation too, Hendrix," that familiar, smoky voice purred from behind us. "For being an arrogant pig with a small dick. Looks like both of our reputations are true."

Nyx emerged through the crowd, her face smug as she admired her work. My sister, forever the revenge enthusiast.

"You bitch!" Hendrix wailed.

His friends dispersed, clearly dying from second-hand embarrassment.

I choked on a laugh. Destiny looked like a red balloon ready to pop, unable to hold in her snickers.

"Come on, you two," Nyx snapped, grabbing my arm, and leading us away.

All eyes were on us.

I followed my sister through the club, my heart hammering in my throat. "Nyx!" I hissed. "Where the hell did you go?"

"I leave you alone for ten minutes and you manage to attract the worst group of guys on the planet. Whatever am I to do with you, little sister?"

"You brought me to a place called *Lucifer's Playground*. What did you expect? That I would find my knight in shining armor?!"

She ignored that. Nyx led us to the bar and ordered shots. The way her eyes kept sweeping over the entire place was not lost on me.

"Nyx Morningstar," a smooth, masculine voice said from behind us.

I turned, instantly recognizing the guy who approached. I'd seen him all over Celestial media. His name was Maverick. He was famous in both the Celestial Society, and the mortal realm. He was an airling, and a basketball star. If I remembered correctly, he went to an academy in New York City.

Great.

I made a mental note to *never* return to this place.

He moved right in on my sister with heady confidence. Maverick was gorgeous, all tall and dark-skinned with a dazzling white smile that gleamed like a toothpaste commercial. His hair was buzzed short, his muscular arms alive with silver tattoos that moved fluidly along his flesh.

I fought the urge to roll my eyes into another dimension. This was the last thing my sister needed right now.

"Maverick Madriu," Nyx greeted, a sly grin tugging at her lips. "What are you doing on the west coast?"

"Oh, you know," Maverick winked as if they shared a secret. He moved over to the bar and paid for our shots, hardly taking his eyes off Nyx. "Actually, I'm transferring to Veneficus. I just signed on with the Lakers."

"No way!" Nyx chimed, reaching out to shove him playfully, though I could tell her interest was fake. "That's dope."

"Right?" Maverick grinned and ordered us another round of shots.

Destiny and I shared a loaded glance.

"This is my sister, Emilia. And her friend, uhhh..."

"Destiny," I piped up, unable to hide the annoyance in my tone.

"Oh yeah!" Maverick said, his eyes lighting up at me. "You're the iceling girl everyone keeps talking about on Celestial Tea. No shit, eh? Fire and ice sisters? Haven't heard of anything like that ever happening before. Nice to meet you, I'm Maverick." He held his hand out to both of us and we shook it.

"Er, yeah." Nyx's face crumpled with a grimace. "Anyway, when did you get to LA?"

"Just portalled in last night," Maverick replied. "How're things at Luna? I heard Venus St. Claire goes there now. That must be...interesting."

Nyx rolled her eyes. "Yeah, she's a real peach. Shit's good. Same old, same old."

Destiny and I shared another wide-eyed glance. My sister, the professional bullshitter.

Maverick started talking about basketball, but Nyx's attention gravitated upwards, to the second-floor balcony. I watched her spine stiffen, her eyes widening for a brief second before she schooled her features. I followed where her eyes went, and my stomach fell out of my ass when my gaze landed on Solaris Adder.

He stood behind the balcony railing in the low red light, staring down at my sister with an expression that made my insides go cold. Venus St. Claire stood at his side, though she wasn't looking down here, she was busy chatting with another girl who I didn't recognize.

Damn. Solaris was more bewitching and unsettling than I imagined. I'd seen photos of him, yeah, but seeing him in the flesh was an entirely different experience. Whenever my sister spoke of him, I'd pictured a monster. But the creature looking down on us now was more like some greater being peering in on our world from beyond the veil—a god, perhaps. A cruel, vengeful god who had his sights set on my sister.

"Oh, fuck," Destiny whispered in my ear. "That's him!"

I swallowed hard. "I think we need to leave."

"Come on, Maverick," Nyx growled, grabbing him by the arm and towing him forward. "Let's dance."

"Nyx!" I called, but she ignored me and disappeared through the crowd with Maverick.

So this was why she brought us here tonight. To play some ludicrous game of cat and mouse with Solaris Adder and Venus St. Claire.

I turned back to the bar and took the shot of brown liquor that stung my throat and gave me the urge to throw up.

"Should we dance?" Destiny asked me, the neon lights overhead changing from red to purple.

I shrugged, aghast. The music blared, making my head pound as the alcohol settled in my stomach. "I don't even want to be here!"

"Well, we're here," my friend said. "And everyone is staring at you, girl. Let's dance. What could it hurt?"

I could think of a thousand ways it could hurt, but when Destiny gave me puppy dog eyes, I caved. She lured me out onto the dance floor, into the center of all the shimmery bodies. We were surrounded by bright eyes and living tattoos and colorful hair. She grabbed my hands and held them as she began to sway her hips to the music. Her shit-eating grin loosened me up a little. I tossed my head back and laughed, knowing this was crazy but screw it. I copied the way she moved, hoping I didn't look as ridiculous as I felt.

Something about the energy in this club had my anxiety going up in smoke. Perhaps it was the combination of all the different Celestial magic packed into one place, but the more I danced, the less I gave a shit about anything.

I let my inhibitions fly out the window, my hands in the air as I moved my hips to the bumping music. My eyes fell shut, the world fading away as dancing became my only reality.

When I opened my eyes, I caught sight of Nyx through the crowd, grinding on Maverick. Normally, this would disgust me, but I couldn't help but giggle. My sister was freaking hot, and Maverick Madriu was just as attractive. The two of them put on quite the show. People were filming and taking pictures, and neither of them seemed to care.

Solaris Adder watched from above with a smoldering expression that sobered me.

Nyx noticed him at the same moment. Well, something told me she'd been extremely aware of him the whole time. Even from where I stood, I felt the tension that coursed between them.

A devilish look took over my sister's dark eyes and then she whispered something into Maverick's ear. I watched as Maverick laughed and then summoned his air magic to lift Nyx onto one of the floating platforms which lacked a dancer. The entire club erupted with cheers for her. She grinned darkly, calling upon her fire magic. White flames ignited over her palms and traveled up her arms. The crowd cheered her on and her head grew ten sizes at the praise. She flicked her wrist and the music changed, confusing the DJ but he went along with it. A filthy beat played for her, and she danced with her fire in a way that made me feel like I was seeing something private, seeing something I shouldn't.

"Oh, my Goddess!" Destiny cawed in my ear. "Holy shit, dude. Your sister is fire. Literally. Ha!"

I once read that firelings were natural performers, and that theory proved true now. My sister knew exactly how to make people go crazy for her. She danced like a true seductress. She tossed her fire and caught it, whirled it in a tornado, and made it do all kinds of tricks. It circled her arms and legs like a serpent of flame, and her eyes were siren-like as she swept them over the crowd.

I watched her in awe.

She dropped it low, grinding her hips while she swished her flaming hands. All eyes on The Nyx Show.

An urgent protective instinct rose inside of me. I wanted to go up there and cover her up, bring her down, and take her out of here. But that was moot—she would never listen to me. Screw this! After everything she'd been through—she finally got her magic back, at such a high price, and this was how she chose to spend her time? Making a spectacle of herself? In front of Solaris Adder, no less.

That was what this was all about. This was about him. He stood on the balcony in his long, outdated jacket and stared at my sister as if she were a house fire. They had something weird going on. Beyond all this blackmail bullshit. The way he looked at her... I couldn't think of a word for it.

Suddenly I wasn't in the mood to party.

As if I'd ever been in the mood.

"I'm leaving," I told Destiny. I pried my eyes off my sister and turned sharply on my heel.

"What? But—"

I ignored her, stalking through the sweaty, kaleidoscopic crowd. I swallowed the lump in the back of my throat, my eyes burning.

The ground under my feet turned to ice as I left.

CHAPTER 35
DARK BUT JUST A GAME
NYX

Fate had finally shifted in my favor.

After my little show at the club, I was back on the Celestial Society's radar. People were talking about me again—in a good way. Well, I mean, of course, there were some hating ass bitches but that only made it better. Being seen with Maverick Madriu gave me big points, taking the attention off 'the Darkbringer and his Red Queen'.

I was coming back for my place on top.

Emilia was pissed at me, but she'd get over it. I had to do what I had to do.

I hadn't heard a word or seen a shadow of Solaris in days, so that was another win. The look on his face as I danced—ha.

I spent the next few days teaching the first-year firelings how to make animated, 3D shapes out of flames. I needed to make nice with the Fire Priestess again and being immersed in lessons was the way to do that. Bridget hung back and watched me take the lead, seemingly impressed by my recent change in attitude. I was impressed, too. But not with myself. With Emilia's little friend Destiny.

She caught on the quickest out of all the girls. Most girls had a hard time creating a basic sphere or a cube, whereas Destiny mastered it right away. She excelled rapidly just as I had, learning how to cast fire in the shape of animals almost immediately. She couldn't control her fire creatures yet, though. Bridget had to banish them before they burnt down the Sphere. Still, I realized I had underestimated her.

"Good job today," I told her when we were wrapping up. She gasped as if I'd slapped her, her spine straightening like a bunny on high alert. An incredulous smile broke out across her face while she stammered her thanks. Was praise from me really so shocking? Okay, yeah.

After today's session, I was dog-tired. I didn't bother with dinner—I had some snacks stored in my room. I hustled up the spiral stairs, excited to have the room all to myself. After dinner, Natalia would head straight up to the mortal boy's tower to spy on his dreams or some shit. Meaning, I'd have the place to myself for a good couple of hours and that was glorious.

I burst into my room, gearing up to get a running start to my bed like a small child but came to a screeching halt when I discovered what was waiting for me there.

Jedidiah.

Sitting on the edge of my bed, heavy leather boots planted on the floor. His head stayed down, even when the door clipped shut behind me.

My chest tightened. He looked wrecked. He'd lost weight. Had he eaten a single thing in the three weeks he'd been gone?

"Jed," I breathed, hand flying over my thundering heart.

He looked up. The hollow, vacant, destroyed look in his eyes hit me like a pole through the chest. He had cheekbones sharp enough to cut glass. Every detail of his face was etched with despair.

The great and terrible Jedidiah Stone, broken. The fractured remains after the fall of his ginger pillars.

He wore all black, looking unlike his usual flashy self. He held his staff at his side, the crystal at the top pulsing with emerald light. For a moment, with the new sharpness of his features, the stormy glint in his eyes, and the all-black attire, he resembled Solaris.

I swallowed thickly, feeling as if all the oxygen had been sucked from the room. I had the urge to move over to him, but something kept me rooted in place.

"How did you get in here?" I asked quietly, looking around as if the answer would appear in smoke letters in the air. The wards... How could he get past the wards?

"I learned a thing or two about dismantling wards from my father," he rasped, looking me dead in the eye. "And I hate to break it to you, but I don't think your Luminary intends to keep anyone out. The wards were weak as shit."

What the fuck?

I attempted to steel myself. "What are you doing here?"

"You seem nervous," he pointed out. His eyes roved over me slowly and suddenly I felt naked, standing here in my leather tights and sports bra, still sweaty from my session in the Sphere.

I opened my mouth but said nothing. His words were true. Anxiety spiked in my blood, coursing through my veins like a raging river. I'd wanted to talk to Jedidiah from the second he'd taken off from the hotel. Looking at him now, I wasn't so sure that was a good idea. His unstable energy matched with the cruel blankness of his gaze made my heart race.

"You got your power back, I heard," he went on. "I guess congratulations are in order. What did you have to give up in return? Your soul?"

"Something like that."

He made a noise that suggested he figured as much. "That was quite the show you put on the other night. I knew you were all types of crazy. I didn't realize you were also a—"

"A what?" I snapped, shaking my head incredulously at him.

He scoffed but didn't finish that thought. He moved on to something worse. "So, you and Maverick Madriu, hey?"

I rolled my eyes and crossed my arms. "Please. Guy's a fucking idiot. I mean, what Celestial gives a shit about something like basketball? But you're not here to chat about my recent social affairs, are you, Jedidiah?"

He rose to his feet, towering over me in my room which now seemed way too small. He may have been leaner than he once was, but the guy was still a fucking skyscraper.

Those stormy eyes raked over me leisurely. "I think you know who killed them."

Lightning struck my chest. I had the sudden urge to run out of the room.

I *suspected* Ra'ah killed the twins. I had no concrete proof, but my intuition told me it was her.

Jedidiah had always been a grumpy motherfucker but the anger on his face now was different. Dangerous rage, laced with immeasurable grief.

Grief and fury—a deadly combination.

"I don't," I half lied, wishing my voice had more conviction.

"Don't bullshit me," he warned, his tone hard and scathing. "It was him."

"I don't know, Jed. I swear. If I'm being honest, I don't think it was. Not directly, anyway. I asked him point blank. He told me he didn't do it."

"You little liar—"

"We can't talk about this here!" I wheezed.

He slammed his staff into the ground. The floor shook, the walls rattled, and pictures fell from their places. His ability to summon instant earthquakes had always been both alluring and unsettling. Now, I couldn't think of a worse power for someone in his condition to have. I fought to keep my balance, trying to stay calm and call his bluff. He wouldn't bring any harm to Luna Academy. Or me. Would he?

"If I willed the Earth to open up and swallow us whole, do you know what we'd find down there?"

I stared at him through an open mouth while the room and everything inside it continued to tremble violently.

"Answer me," he demanded.

I nearly lost my footing to his wrath. "I don't know!"

"We'd find your Goddess," he snarled and lunged at me. I screamed involuntarily, raising my arms to block the blow I was expecting. Instead, his big, strong arms wrapped around me and pulled me into him. Surprise wove into every cell of my body. He tossed something into the air, summoning a swirling vortex of golden light.

"No!" I cried pointlessly as he heaved us both through the portal.

Traveling by Jedidiah's portal globe last time had been rocky, but it was nothing compared to the turbulence now. I howled into the void as we tumbled through the ether. I saw nothing but frantic patterns of light and dark. Pins and needles as murderous as an angered hornet's nest possessed my senses. We were sucked into the most vicious undertow of the cosmos before it spat us out in the middle of a warzone.

We landed together on the hard floor of what had to be a demolition site.

I panted, desperate to catch my breath as I looked around, trying to figure out where we were. It was dark as hell in here. A weak fire crackled and smoked under a shattered mantle, casting only a hint of orange light throughout the space. At one time, this must have been a house. Or maybe a cabin? A nice one, judging by the few things that remained intact. But now, the walls had been knocked down, and rubble and dust scattered all over the floor from its violent end. More stars than I'd ever seen in my entire life twinkled down on us through the missing roof. Broken furniture scattered around like dismembered body parts. Whatever happened here, no one got out alive.

"What do you think you're doing? Kidnapping me!" I yelled furiously as he rose to his feet and dusted himself off. "What is this place? Take me back at once, you psycho!"

He casually strode through the pathway that had been paved through the rubble and chaos, leaving me as if he didn't even know I was there.

I released a disgruntled noise and chased after him. He led me out onto a stone terrace where the freezing wind hit me in the face. I gasped at the unexpected temperature, my wild eyes taking in the broken railing. I moved forward to look over the edge. My stomach hollowed out, the sense of freefall possessing me as reality settled in. Beyond this terrace was nothing but infinite darkness. I smelled snow. I squinted, making out the shape of white-tipped treetops and nothing else.

My heart thrashed, the stars overhead seeming to giggle at my befuddlement.

We were on top of the fucking world.

"Where are we?" I breathed.

Jedidiah stared into the dark, unmoving. "My father's hideout in the Rockies."

"Oh, shit," I replied instinctively, taking another look around. The place had been built right into the top of the mountainside. By the standing remains, the house must have been immaculate in its day. Built for a king. "What happened to it?"

"I happened."

"Oh." Of course. The ground shaker. I should have known. It had Jedidiah's wrath written all over it. "Why did you bring me here?"

"To get the truth out of you."

A chill rushed up my spine as he pried his eyes from the dark to fix them on me. He looked devastating in the starlight, both beautiful and terrifying. His hair fell over his brows, but he raked it back, a habit of his.

The look in his eyes shot a bullet into my nerves, making them scatter desperately.

We'd been playing our little back-and-forth game for over a year now, but I'd never truly feared him. Not even when he buried me six feet under. He knew that if anyone could crawl their way up from Hell, it was me.

I took it as the utmost challenge.

The bonfire party had been wild that night. High, high energy. I'd burned off his shirt and half of his hair after he challenged me, knowing damn well I was about to wake his worst monster. He'd made the ground open under me, filling the hole in over me, sealing me in my grave.

When I'd clawed my way to the surface with flaming hands, when I'd burst through the dirt with a victorious scream on my lips, he knelt there waiting. Knowing I could do it. The anticipation mixed with fascination I'd found on his face as I emerged from my early grave was ingrained in my memory forever. He wasn't angry. He didn't care that the crowd roared and cheered for me and not him. He was fucking proud. Proud of me. What kind of foe was that?

Back then, things were different. We were ruthless to each other, yes. It was dark but still only just a game. I didn't truly fear him. If I hadn't risen from the earth he would have brought me up himself. It was all about the thrill of the fight, the testing of character. The pushing of limits. We weren't out to literally kill each other.

Now, up here on top of the world, in the middle of nowhere, all alone, the only people he loved murdered and him believing I was protecting who had done it... Perhaps those old rules didn't apply anymore. Maybe this time he was out for blood.

"I swear," I told him, voice strained. "I swear I don't know. I wouldn't lie to you, Jed. Not about this."

"Maybe I'm the liar," he jeered, to my confusion.

I shivered in the cold wind, wondering what he meant by that. I was too afraid to ask.

"Jedidiah," I whispered, making his breath hitch. His eyes shone as he looked at me, though his jaw remained hard. His grief was palpable. The air around him was dense and corrupted with pain I could feel on my skin. "I'm so sor—"

"Don't!" he snarled, stepping forward rapidly to close the space between us. His hand found my throat before I could even process his change of demeanor. He shoved me closer to the edge, making my heart fall out of my ass. He pressed the crystal of his staff to my temple, his lips tearing back over his teeth. "Don't you *dare* fucking look at me like that. Don't you dare say that shit to me. You don't *pity* me, Nyx!"

The back of my tall black combat boots teased the edge beyond the broken railing, the expanse of blackness ready to claim me.

My veins coursed with chronic adrenaline, my eyes rolling back as I rode the wave. I clung to his arms, clinging to life. It was intoxicating, though, knowing death and I were dancing this close right now. His iron hold on me was unbreakable. I could feel his breath on my face, so I opened my eyes, finding him a whisper away. He held me beside the edge, his bruising fingers around my throat as he looked deep into my eyes, searching for something.

I laid myself bare—I had nothing to hide.

The wind fought to take me with it into the abyss. It howled in my ears, promising me a wild ride.

I could have *easily* fought him off with magic. I could have reduced him to a pile of ash at my feet if I saw fit. The unhinged, hungry look in his eyes now—it seemed like that was exactly what he *wanted* me to try and do. But fuck satisfying his violent delight. That was what he expected of me. What everyone expected of me. I'd always been so easily set off, like a human land mine. Not anymore. I was done being baited into conflict. The next time I unleashed myself, it would be on my terms.

He was looking for a fight, and if this were happening a month ago, I would have been the right girl for the job.

I smirked while I struggled to breathe, letting the truth shine in the depths of my dark eyes. He would not get what he wanted from me. Perhaps that would piss him off even more.

But I could handle him. Shit, I understood him. I understood the need to crush others beneath your feet just to keep yourself standing.

We were similar, terrible creatures, him and I.

The truth rung in his eyes, in the air around us. The truth of the loss he suffered. How irrevocably his life was changed forever. He was utterly alone in this world now.

He *needed* it to be a fight. Just like I did when I was in pain. Anger was so much easier than sadness.

"Go ahead," I wheezed, relishing in the heat of his hand as it wrapped around my tender throat. I enjoyed the pain as much as he enjoyed causing it. But the fact that he wasn't squeezing hard enough to stop my breathing was a sign of his inauthentic threat. I held my arms out like wings then, leaning back instead of clinging to him as if I planned to fly off the mountaintop myself. "Toss me over the edge. That would solve a hell of a lot of problems, honestly."

"Fuck you," he spat. "Fuck your overconfident act. You're terrified of me right now. You might be sick enough to be enjoying this a little bit but beneath that you're scared. You're afraid I'm going to go too far. Do you think I can't see that? Do you think I can't *see you*, Nyx? Do you think I don't know the real reason you lit my feet on fire that night at the club instead of just dancing with me? Because you were afraid of me then, too. For a completely different reason. I know you feel this thing between us. You cover it up with your fury and your games, but I see it in your eyes every time we're together."

I was robbed of speech, and not just because he had his hand around my throat.

My heart thundered out of control. I half expected it to explode from my chest and hit him before it fell to the ground in a wet lump of dead flesh.

He searched between my eyes, his expression a war of emotions fighting for first place. He held me at the edge, waiting for me to do something. Anything.

"You are a coward!" he shouted, gripping me harder. "You got your magic back but what does it even matter? You're still just as useless and powerless as before!"

I snapped a harsh laugh. What a strange life this was. On one side, I had a man who made it his life's mission to steal and control my power to be assured that I wouldn't use it against him. On the other side, I had a man who desperately *wanted* me to unleash my power onto him as his own personal brand of punishment.

Duality rules all.

"I can't stand that look in your eye," Jedidiah hissed, pressing his staff harder into my skin, the pain sharp and exhilarating. "You feel sorry for me. You pity me. We don't do that shit, Nyx! I don't need you to *pity* me, I need you to *fight* me!"

An earth-shattering revelation hit me as I stared into the depths of those dark ocean eyes.

Jedidiah didn't want me to fight him.

He wanted me to kill him.

He brought me up here in the middle of nowhere to ensure I would be afraid. He held me at the cliff's edge to make it seem like I needed to fight for my life. So I would react, so I would lash out. He planned on taking this way too far. His anguish was in control.

He was looking for a way out, through me.

"No," I growled, heart hammering. "My magic is mine to use as I please. It is not yours to summon. So, either let me go or push me off this fucking mountain, Jedidiah."

He held me there, still waiting. Waiting for me to erupt.

I refused.

He took me by surprise when he pulled me away from the hungry edge. He released his hand from around my throat, stepping back, as if in shame. He tossed his staff to the ground, the emerald pulsing frantically with magic he refused to unleash. Defeated way too soon, by words alone.

I rubbed the burning skin where his hand had been, my chest rising and falling while the wind played in my hair. Some sick, twisted part of me was bummed the game was over. Perhaps it wasn't a game tonight.

There was no reason for my heart to feel so soft, but it did. The raw pain in his eyes stripped me of my usual furious nature. Turned me into someone I didn't even recognize.

"I'm not going to hurt you, Jedidiah," I vowed, pushing my wild dancing hair out of my face. "You think I don't *see you*? Do you think I don't know exactly what all of this is? You are hurting and you want—"

"Why not?" He cut me off. "Remember the way I knelt in front of you while you were tied helplessly to that chair? Remember the way I fucked with you and got the truth out of you using Compulsion in front of everyone? How weak you were, at my mercy, unable to fight me off? I even made you admit how much you like it when I choke you. Your face was so red, and I devoured your humiliation like candy."

Fury rose up my spine like a fiery serpent. I clenched my fists and squared my shoulders. "Yeah, you were a real prick."

"And you do like it, don't you, Nyx? Every time I unleash my demons around you, you like it. You liked it when I buried you six feet under the fucking earth. You like that I'm always grabbing you, unafraid to touch you, unlike every other man in this world. You even liked it when I just held you over the edge of a goddamn mountain. You are just as fucked up as me. But now that it's just us, no big show, no party, no cameras, no audience—you're just a coward! You won't fight me!"

The burning in my chest could no longer be detained. White fire ignited over my clenched fists, licking up my arms to fan out behind my elbows in the wind like flaming wings.

His eyes lit up, reflecting the bright blaze. His lips parted in awe. "There she is."

I bared my teeth at him. "Fuck you. I'm not just going to fight you because you bait me. I'm over that shit."

Something on his face darkened. "Ah. But what if I were *him*, Nyx?"

My heart dropped; cheeks went ice cold.

The stars in the sky seemed to take in a wistful breath as they watched us.

"Would you fight *him* off? Would you burn *him* down? After every terrible thing he's done, I'm sure all it's done is pique your interest. I'm right, aren't I?" Jedidiah accused me, his expression darker than words could express. "You *like* him. Finally, someone deranged enough for you."

I couldn't muster up a coherent sentence. I stared up at him, shaking my head.

"That weak, pathetic shadow creature who must suppress your true nature to face you? He needs you powerless. Not me. *Never* me. I want you like this. With all that fire in your veins and the outrage on your lips. I want that. I brought you here knowing we both need this fucking release. I brought you here knowing you could be the end of me. You could burn me at your stake right now. I would go happily. You should, Nyx. Why aren't you? I deserve it! I fucking deserve it!"

Every single word settled like warm honey in my stomach, sweetening me to my core.

I banished my flames.

His chest rose and fell as he watched me, confused.

I stepped closer to him, making him stiffen. His eyes narrowed as I drew nearer, unsure about my unusually gentle demeanor. I backed him into the wall. He retreated. As if he feared me. It made my blood rush faster in my veins, his reaction to me. The vulnerable shine in his eyes, the way his throat worked nervously. I placed my palm over his chest and his heart rocketed against it.

"Jed—" I began softly, but he cut me off.

"Don't, Nyx," he breathed warily. He grabbed my wrist and shoved my hand away.

His rejection triggered a wall of ice to go up around me.

"Fine," I muttered, backing away from him.

Something came over me then, something deadly. The revelation hit me like a freight train, head-on. Jedidiah had the right idea.

The frequency in the air changed, a high-pitched ringing going off in my ears as the truth settled in. My breath caught as a strange, posses-sive instinct took over me.

I let my feet carry me backward, back toward the edge of the terrace.

"Nyx, what are you—?"

I held my arms out like wings again, my hair flying in the wind and a smile breaking across my lips, as I leaned back and let myself fall over the edge.

CHAPTER 36
AWAKE IN THE DREAM
EMILIA

I grabbed the front of my pale lilac dress and ascended the spiral stairs to Michael's room, one hand gripping the gold ornate candle holder, holding it out in front of me so the small flame illuminated the stairwell.

Every time I came up here, my heart raced. I knew I would find him on the floor with Natalia while she sifted through his dreams. He'd wake up as soon as I arrived. We would smile at each other, so many unsaid words passing between us in the thick air.

Tonight was something different, though. Natalia had pulled me aside at dinner and said we needed to go beyond the fairy door in the Serpent's Wood. She didn't say why, and my mind had been whirling with anticipation all night. I hadn't been beyond the fairy door since the Luminary gave us a tour of the academy grounds.

Michael's door was open a crack, spilling warm light onto the stairs. I steeled myself and then knocked softly.

"Come in," his voice answered.

My brows furrowed. My knock was a courtesy. No one ever replied. Natalia was always too busy Seeing into Michael's dreams, and Michael was too busy dreaming.

I stepped through the door and found him waiting awake and alone.

He sat at the wooden writing desk, a journal open in front of him, a floating lantern over his head for light. He wore a Pink Floyd t-shirt and faded jeans. His eyes were tired, but he grinned like he was happy to see me. He folded the journal shut, setting down the feather pen. "Are we off to the magic door now?"

"Where's Natalia?" was what I replied. In a harsh tone, too. *Nice.*

"She's already in the forest. We finished our session early tonight because... Well, I don't really know why, exactly. She was distracted the whole time. She Saw something and then bolted off, saying she'd meet us there."

"Okay. Come on then."

"Emilia." His lazy, accented voice wrapped around my name like a caress. A caress I felt down my spine, gentle yet suggestive. I shivered.

"Yes?"

"Are you angry with me?"

"W-what?" I stammered, my pulse jackhammering in my temples. "Why would you think that?"

"You look at me as if you can't stand me."

His words shattered over me like glass because they were true. I *couldn't stand* looking at him. The beautiful boy in the tower would be the death of me. He turned me into a creature I did not understand.

And my ice magic made me cold. Literally and figuratively. I remained in the doorway, unmoving, unmoved. My internal world was ruled by chaos but on the outside, I was a frozen sculpture whose expression would never change from neutral.

I wanted him to see through it. Which only made me worse, I thought.

A light dusting of frost manifested on the walls around me, spreading the artistic pattern throughout the room, tinkling like distant Christmas bells. My ice caught the firelight and glittered like a thousand tiny diamonds.

His lips popped open in awe.

It spread and spread, across the walls and the ceiling, and the floor, threatening to cover his entire room. I squeezed my eyes shut and inhaled a long, steady breath. Calling my power back home. Heavy heartbeats roared in my ears. When I opened my eyes, the frost was gone.

"Michael," I murmured, voice surprisingly even. "I just have a lot going on. Emerging into this frozen thing... It's been a lot. Don't take me personally. Come on."

Sorrow gleamed in his eyes, but he offered me a nod as if he understood.

"Shit," I muttered suddenly. "I don't know how to cloak you, though. You can't be seen."

Michael grinned, hopping up from his seat. "So we'll be extra stealthy. It will be like that night we trespassed on old man John's property to go swimming in that river spot. Do you remember?"

My heart thudded dully, an aching lump of flesh inside me. "Of course, I remember."

It was the most exhilarating night ever. I'd never done anything like that before. Sneaking through someone's yard...fence hopping...setting off sensor lights and darting into the shadows. Back when the highest stakes I knew were the risk of being caught running through a yard by an old man. Simpler times.

"Okay," I decided. "Let's go."

We descended the spiral stairs into the glow of candlelight. Michael was so close, his chest brushing my back as we made our way down. I could hardly breathe, my mind a swirling vortex of outrageous thoughts. Magic made my brain work differently. I couldn't rein my consciousness in. I had zero control of my internal self, but at least I mastered outward composure. A perk of being governed by something as still as ice.

We tiptoed through the hallways, going unseen.

Music and voices came from different rooms, but the hallways were empty, save for the portraits of Goddesses and statues of dragons and owls.

Michael and I said not two words to each other.

We were in the clear, passing through the doors of the Academy silently. The Elemental Sphere lit up the courtyard as if the moon had fallen to the ground. Crickets sang, fireflies darting through the air while we made our way to the Serpent's Wood.

He couldn't take his beautiful eyes off the Sphere. "What is that?" he asked wistfully.

"It's where we do our elemental magic," I explained. "Firebending, waterbending, all that. There's a ring which is kind of like a boxing ring and that's where we compete. We exercise and learn combat there as well. It's way bigger inside than it looks on the outside."

"Brilliant," Michael whispered.

"Come on," I urged, grabbing his arm, and towing him along. His skin was warm and touching it sent electricity up my arm. I went to let go of him, but he snatched my hand and laced his fingers with mine. My eyes widened and I didn't know how to react, so I simply didn't react at all. I let him hold my hand as we made our way to the mouth of the trees.

We didn't have time to marvel over the magical fairy door hidden in the Serpent's Wood. Once we passed through the portal, we moved quickly through the path of floating tealight candles until we reached the moonlit clearing.

Natalia, Destiny, and Faye sat in a circle in the grass, waiting for us.

Michael and I joined them in the grass, the music of crickets playing from the edge of the clearing.

"You made it," Faye beamed.

"Yeah, hey," we breathed in unison. My stomach dropped at the synchronicity. I didn't allow myself a glance at him, though I wondered if he felt it too.

Natalia swallowed, her dark eyes sweeping over each of our faces. "Okay, so, I'm just going to get right into it." She took a deep breath. "After spending all these nights sifting through his dreams, both old and new, I've Seen that his dreams are entirely prophetic. But...they're more than that. Yes, he dreams of things that often happen later in real life, but the phenomenon does not stop there."

Natalia's attention was fixed on Michael, who sat next to me in the grass, chewing his lip ring. His expression was deep and unreadable. My heart fluttered painfully at the way they looked at each other.

"When Michael dreams, he isn't just at the mercy of his own

subconscious or the collective unconscious like the rest of us. He...has *power* there. Authority over the unconscious. He seems to be able to cross over into the dreams of others...and into the memories of others."

Michael stiffened, his brows lowering as if this were brand-new information.

Natalia gave him a soft, encouraging look. "You had no idea that's what you were doing, did you?"

He didn't reply.

"Still...there's more. He can bring things from his dreams into the physical world. It's like...it's like he's this bridge. A bridge between worlds, merging them together... What he does in the Dream Realm has the power to manifest into reality, instantly. I've been reading a lot in the Athena Library, trying to find information on Michael's dreaming abilities. Trying to find similar cases to his. Turns out, there pretty much are none. Not in our library, anyway."

Natalia's focus traveled over each of us before she fixed it on Michael. "Tell them about the museum."

He paled.

"It's okay," Natalia cooed. "You didn't do anything wrong."

His eyes went downcast. Countless heartbeats tolled by before he spoke.

"My family and I left London when I was eight. We landed in New York City and lived there for a couple years before we moved across America to the west coast. My mother and I have always shared a love of art. She used to take me to The Met a lot. I loved it there. I would dream of it all the time, of being in the museum. One night, in my dream, I decided to take one of my favorite pieces. One of the unicorn tapestries... I took it down off the wall and walked out with it. When I woke up, the unicorn tapestry was hanging on my wall, right above my bed."

No one said a word.

Destiny and I shared a wide-eyed look.

"You...you stole something from The Met...in your dreams?!" Faye gasped.

Michael seemed entirely uncomfortable. He raised his arms, exasperated. "No. That's impossible."

"Tell them what happened next," Natalia urged.

He stared at the ground. "These people in cloaks showed up at our door." His voice was quiet, strained. "They wore golden masks, hiding their faces. Right away—somehow, they knew what I'd done. They barged into our home and interrogated my entire family. They were able to hypnotize my parents and my sister, but it didn't work for me. I pretended it did, though. They asked me a million questions and I just played dumb. After they finished interrogating us, they took the tapestry. They erased my family's memory and tried to do the same to me. Again, I pretended it worked. Then they left. All this time—I've been telling myself it was just a dream. There's no way any of that was actually real, right?"

None of us were breathing.

We each stared at him through wide unblinking eyes and open mouths.

He cleared his throat, his cheeks reddening. "It's crazy. It wasn't real. I'm a vivid dreamer, that's all."

"It was real," Natalia deadpanned. "I Saw it myself. It was real, Michael."

He breathed in through his nose, denial etching his features.

"Tell them about your mother," Natalia urged. "About her sickness."

Michael's brows narrowed and he shook his head. His eyes welled with tears and my heart shattered. "There's nothing to tell."

"Of course there is!" Natalia insisted. "You don't have to be afraid or ashamed about any of this, Michael."

"You tell them then!" he snapped. "You seem to know more about my dreams than I do."

She handled his aggression with grace, remaining poised. She let off a little, craning her head to look up at the stars and moon. The trees around us swayed in the wind, seeming to listen to our conversation. Crickets sang from the tall grass. All around us was nature's music, filling in the blanks when no one spoke.

"It's not my story to tell," Natalia sighed. "I understand it makes you uncomfortable, Michael. But they must know what you are capable of."

He didn't say a word. He kept his eyes down, relentlessly chewing on his lip ring. "You tell them, Natalia."

She didn't protest again. "When Michael was twelve, his mother fell ill. Lung cancer. By the time they found it, she was in stage four. She refused chemo and was given two months to live. Michael spent every minute at her bedside. One night, he had a dream.... I will spare the details. As I said, it's not my story to tell. But Michael healed his mother. In a dream. What he did...I've never heard of anything like it being possible. He healed her in the Dream Realm and when he woke up, she was...luminous. Healed, in real life. The doctors didn't understand. It was a miracle."

Michael was shaking his head, in denial.

"Okay, okay," Destiny cawed, holding her hands out. "Wait a minute. You are really saying he healed his mother's cancer in his dreams?"

"Yes," Natalia answered, her tone as firm as her face. "That's exactly what I'm saying."

I stared at Michael, but he wouldn't look at me.

All. This. Time.

All this time I'd been so worried about him and magic. Before I came to Luna, I trained myself to let go of him, thinking he'd fall under Amnesia once I Emerged. And even though that had been proved untrue, I still felt guilty about him being dragged from his life and immersed into the Celestial realm of magic. But he'd been experiencing the supernatural all along.

And he never said anything to me about it.

We'd been alone up in that tower for hours. Yet he never breathed a word of it.

My heart ached with a sense of betrayal. Perhaps I had no reason to be upset but I couldn't help the way it hurt.

It explained a lot. Why he was always so calm and unfazed by everything.

"Jesus," Faye breathed. "So not only is he Marked and protected by the Goddess, but he has an ability that no one in the Society possesses? His dreams literally come true?"

"I think that is *why* he's Marked and protected by the Goddess. To keep him safe while he sleeps." Natalia suggested, making my heart tighten. "His dreams have the power to manifest into reality. He sees things long before they happen, in a way much different from what I See. He also consistently crosses over into the dreams of others. Dreams and nightmares."

"Somehow I feel like we haven't even reached the main point you're trying to make yet," Destiny muttered, cocking a brow at Natalia.

"I think the Goddess sent Nyx to find Michael for a very specific reason," Natalia said. "His dreams are a major key. Like I said before, I've been in the library studying dreams. There's a Grimoire of Dreams that I'm unable to read because it's in the Old World elemental tongue. Perhaps there's something in there... Anyway, while I haven't found any similar cases to Michael specifically, I have found other things."

She sucked in a deep breath before she continued. "I think we can use Michael's dreams to find out more about Solaris. I think I might know a way to link our minds so we can project ourselves into Michael's dreams. It's called Dreamwalking, where our consciousnesses merge and we dream together. If we get a piece of Solaris's clothing, or hair, or something to link us to him, Michael can find him in the Dream Realm, and his subconscious will be laid bare for us to pick through. And perhaps we could find the source of his shadows and cut him off from that source. If not that, we might at least be able to discover a weakness of his."

Destiny's jaw dropped. "Okay, whoa—"

"Seriously?" Faye quipped, her emerald eyes wide.

"It sounds complicated, I know," Natalia admitted. "But Michael's abilities are profound. If he can bring things back from the Dream Realm, if he can heal the sick, he should be able to do this. He told us that day in the hotel that he had dreamt of the shadow before. We must find something physical that will link us to Solaris, and from there, anything is possible."

We all exchanged peculiar looks. Michael's eyes remained down.

"It's too dangerous to go against Solaris any other way... We stand no chance against him in the physical. We don't even stand a chance against him in the Astral Realm because he has constant access to it through the shadows. But in the Dream Realm... We will have the upper hand." Natalia's eyes gleamed as she spoke. "The Goddess wanted us to figure this out. I just know it."

I swallowed thickly and looked at Michael. He gave me a sad, unsure shrug.

"So how do we do it?" I asked.

Natalia grinned. "I'm still figuring that all out." She reached into her dress pocket and pulled out a pouch of dried herbs. "For now, you guys need to start sleeping with mugwort under your pillows. It's time to start training our minds to be awake in the dream."

CHAPTER 37
THE THIN LINE BETWEEN PLEASURE & PAIN

NYX

Freefall was an exquisitely horrifying sensation.

Wind clawed at me and howled like ravenous wolves in my ears. Somewhere in the distance, I could hear Jedidiah screaming.

I surrendered to the black endlessness. I could smell snow and pine as air rushed violently against my face. This was a pretty damn good place to die. The creatures of the forest would pick clean my flesh, and my bones would become one with the mountain. It was better than anything I could have asked for. Honorable. Swift.

My freefall felt like seconds and centuries wrapped into one paradoxical impossibility. I'd never felt so free—so powerful yet powerless. At least this fate was one of my choosing. No one forced me into this. No one blackmailed me or coerced me or demanded this of me. I stepped off the ledge of my own free will, and that was enough.

I let my hands erupt with flames that trailed after me as if I were a falling star.

A low roaring sound hit my ears and traveled across my flesh as I plummeted into the blackness. It was a voice—Jedidiah's voice. Impossibly close. My eyes had been closed but I opened them now, just in time to see his body plunging toward mine. In the same instant, a burst of swirling light ignited below me, just before we hit the treeline. I fell into it, the portal devouring me like the hungry jaws of a Celestial beast.

The glorious freefall turned into a tumultuous ride through the angry ether.

The portal spat me out onto the terrace, back up on top of the world, with Jedidiah's limbs tangled with mine.

"What the FUCK was THAT!" he exploded, grabbing me by the shoulders as he heaved me up onto my feet. My brain could hardly process what just happened. My feet were planted on the stone platform of the terrace, safely on the ground. Yet my stomach was still alive with the sensation of freefall. He gripped my shoulders, eyes wild and his face contorted with fear and rage. "You are MAD!!" he screamed at me. "Fucking MAD!"

My heart thrashed like war drums, and all I could do was tilt my head back and laugh.

"Now you're laughing!! You're fucking laughing!"

"You started this! Sorry that *your* little suicide mission didn't go as planned! At least I had the guts to do it myself!"

"Nyx!" he cried, his voice breaking. "You are insane! What is the matter with you? What is *the matter* with you?!"

The tears welling in his eyes snuffed out my delirium.

"I don't know," I answered honestly. "I don't know."

He wrapped me in his arms and held me so tightly I couldn't breathe. "You're mad," he kept saying, over and over. "Mad. Don't you ever—*ever* do anything like that again. I'm sorry, Nyx. I shouldn't have brought you here. I'm sorry. I'm sorry. Jesus Christ, I'm so sorry." He kept saying it until his lips trembled too hard for words to escape through. He clutched me desperately, refusing to let go, his hand caressing the back of my hair.

Whoa.

I couldn't recall a time anyone ever held me in such a way. No one ever...consoled me.

I leaned back to look upon his face. His expression gutted me.

We stared at each other while the wind howled. We were so close I could see his pulse hammering in his throat. His tragic loveliness intoxicated me. He searched between my eyes as the emotion burned in his.

Then his hand was on the back of my neck, pulling me into him as he leaned down and crushed my lips with his. I gasped when we collided. He swallowed the sound like a starving man at a feast.

We detonated.

It was less like a kiss and more like an attack. We were all heat and gasps and frantic pawing. His hands were everywhere as if he were trying to figure out how to claw his way inside me. His mouth was bruising and intense, making my head spin and my thighs shake. He hoisted me up, wrapping my legs around him as he carried me inside through the carnage.

I kissed him as if my life depended on it, my fingers knotted in the back of his hair. He tasted like whiskey and rock candy. My core sizzled with fervent heat, pressure already building up between my legs.

He nearly tripped over the chaotic mess while he carried me inside, scoffing against my lips as he caught himself. We passed through another space which I didn't bother to look at since I was too busy devouring him. Suddenly he dropped me. My back hit a soft bed.

Bewildered, I took in the bedroom that was only half destroyed. The jagged, yawning hole in the roof overhead let the pale moonlight spill upon us, giving me just enough light to see.

"Wow," I muttered breathlessly. "You really did a number on this place."

"I thought you'd like it," he said, voice grated. He stood over me, his eyes spitting fire while he took in every single detail as I lay below him. "The destruction."

"I do," I told him honestly, my tone laced with longing.

He grabbed the neck of his shirt, pulling it over his head. My breath caught as he bore himself to me. All this time, I'd never seen Jedidiah shirtless. Which was odd now that I thought of it, considering how fit he was and all the beach parties I'd seen him at. The tanned planes of his stomach and the lean, muscular shape of his shoulders made my insides tingle, but something else snagged my attention even more. Dozens of lightning-shaped burn scars peppered his torso and shoulders. Phantom pain erupted over my flesh.

I knew those scars. Those were the handy work of his father. I'd felt that pain many times in my life.

The vulnerability in his eyes rocked me. Shame swathed his features, triggering my most protective nature.

He could have healed himself. Celestials only bore the scars they wished to keep. These were a statement. Or a reminder.

I let him see the smoldering promise in my eyes. I let him see I understood.

He was so beautiful it hurt.

I sat up, moving to my knees on the edge of the bed. I brushed my fingers over his heart, trailing a delicate line to the first visible scar. He caught my wrist abruptly, his grip hard enough to make me flinch.

He grabbed me by my shoulders and pushed me down onto the bed, leaving me breathless. My core throbbed agonizingly just looking at him. He was right, before. I loved the way he handled me. He hesitated before he made another move. He seemed nervous and looked guilty. As if he thought he was doing something wrong. "Are you sure?" he murmured, the glint in his eye telling me he expected me to run.

Perhaps I should have. *Morningstar women don't ride men, we ride dragons.* Fuck that, though. Until the dragons return, why keep myself bound to this vow? Perhaps that was why my mother was so hostile. She didn't allow herself pleasure.

"I did just hold you over a cliff..." he went on darkly, an anxious edge to his tone.

I shrugged, heart racing. "It's what we do," I sighed. "And you chickened out."

He leaned down over me and grabbed my face in his big hand, rather brashly. He searched my eyes. "Did you know I would catch you? Was it part of the game?"

I peered up at him through my lashes, giving him my best sultry eyes. "Baby, you will never know." *Because I don't even know.*

I took his bottom lip between my teeth, biting and sucking to coax a throaty sound from him. He kissed me roughly, and deeply, turning my limbs to jelly.

I pulled back, my heart hammering. I reached for the zipper in the middle of my sports bra, my fingers shaking as I unzipped it and let it come apart, exposing myself.

Heat sprung to his eyes and his jaw went slack, a feral sound escaping him.

My stomach knotted something fierce.

"You're fucking crazy," he rasped. Visible desire that made my toes curl consumed him as he admired my breasts. In truth, I couldn't think of a moment when I felt more powerful. "And so beautiful. Everything you are is gold. I can't get enough of it."

"So, take me, then," I whispered. A challenge.

Soon, my clothes were a mess on the floor. He took in every detail of my naked skin, my swirling tattoos, and the rune under my heart that matched his.

He stared down at me as if he were trying to discern if this was real.

My own vulnerability at that moment had me squeezing my eyes shut. Sex was too intimate, even in its most carnal form. Besides a few thoughtless nights as a teenager, I mostly avoided it. At all costs. Clearly, it was the Morningstar nature. I could hardly handle being seen in such a way. Open, wanton, at his mercy. I thought about taking him up on his earlier offer and fighting him instead.

"Open your eyes," Jed whispered. His lips trailed a path of kisses from my throat to my navel. "Don't hide from me."

My breath came out shaky as I kept my eyes shut. "I can't."

"Look at me, Nyx."

My pulse thrashed. Gingerly, I obeyed.

His gaze snared mine, hooking me indefinitely. My breathing labored as he went down on his knees on the floor, grabbing my hips and guiding my body to the edge of the bed. He pushed my thighs apart, bearing me to the open air, making me gasp. The pressure between my legs was becoming unbearable. I needed release and my heart was beating so fast in anticipation. His expression had my stomach in a constant state of flip-flop.

"Look at you," he rasped from between my thighs. "A fucking painting."

When his tongue met my clit, I cried out, ecstasy exploding from the base of his touch, bursting through the map of my veins. A primal groan rumbled from his throat as he worshiped at my altar, the sound stirring nameless sensations in the pit of my stomach. He didn't bother to be gentle as he feasted on me, showing me just how much he'd been craving me all this time. I gripped the sheets for dear life, my heels struggling for purchase. Everything felt so good—I could hardly stand it. He kept his fingers wrapped around my thighs, pushing them apart. My back arched, eyes rolling as his tongue worked its wicked magic.

The orgasm blew me apart like the death of a star. Bright, psychedelic patterns burst behind my eyes as I rode the wave of euphoria, my entire body trembling. Faintly, I heard him unbuckle his pants. I felt his weight on the bed, his arms sliding under my back to pull me up and lay me down on the pillow.

Jedidiah looked at me like I was both his doom and his salvation. He climbed on top of me, his head disappearing to kiss and suck my throat. I sighed wantonly, his hot skin brushing mine. I let my fingers trail from his shoulders to his chest, down his abdomen, and beyond. I gasped as I wrapped my fingers around his impressive—and honestly intimidating —arousal. *Goddess damn me.* My cheeks flooded with heat, and my stomach clenched with both tension and desire.

He released a rough sound of pleasure or maybe agony as I pumped him. He brought his lips to mine and kissed me hard. Our tongues battled and danced. He bit my bottom lip, hard enough to draw blood for him to taste. I cried out, bewitched by the thin line between pleasure and pain.

The primal needs inside me turned me into a feral creature. I guided the crown of his cock to the wetness between my thighs and the way he fucking gasped in response to the feel of me ensnared my soul. I bit my lip, tasting blood, reveling in the way his face looked right now. Possessive. So, so possessive.

"Jed," I moaned, wrapping my arms around his neck, painfully gripping his hair. "I want you now."

His shiny eyes met mine. Electricity zapped between us, our magic rising to the surface upon eye contact. My stomach did a somersault as a wave of his power washed over me. *Earth. A fortress. Indestructible. Infinite. Vast and fecund. Vivid. Enigmatic. Protective. Prosperous. Calming. Lonely. Temperamental. A steadfast, unwavering energy of fathomless strength. The power of life, stillness, and expansion.*

In turn, he experienced the raw energy of my fire. I even saw flames

321

reflecting in his dilated pupils, fire lighting up his veins under his tanned skin.

We stayed locked in each other's eyes as magic, desire, pain, pleasure, grief, rage, confusion, and passion merged between us like the gods were sewing us together. My brain couldn't grasp how profound the moment was.

My body surged with a sense of urgency. He felt it too. He brought himself to pulsing arousal between my legs, trepidation battling with his insatiable need to be inside me. "I'll go slow," he promised hoarsely, looking down as he prepared himself.

"Fuck that," I breathed. "I can take it."

He scoffed nervously, eyes sparkling. "Nyx, you're so—"

I shut him up with a harsh kiss, pulling him into me, wrapping my legs around his waist. I sealed the deal, giving him no choice but to thrust inside me. I cried out as our bodies clasped together, the burning rapture turning my limbs into molten liquid. He roared like a whipped lion, one hand gripping my hip, the other nested in the back of my hair.

He held back at first, barely moving as I adjusted to how much he stretched me, filled me. Torment and ecstasy wove together and overtook me, my skin burning in a way I'd never felt before. His face was raw and unguarded while he watched me take him.

"*God*, you feel so good," he breathed, his voice fractured. "Are you sure you're okay?"

"Yes," I vowed breathlessly, tightening my legs around his waist, urging him on.

He fucked me and it felt like falling off the mountain all over again. All that pent-up aimless aggression we both carried was released tenfold. He didn't go easy on me. His hand found my throat and I moaned, murmuring inaudible pleas as he kissed and nipped my lips and squeezed my throat. He knew exactly what I wanted, and he delivered.

I completely lost myself in the way he felt and didn't care to ever find that bitch again.

I shattered. Combusted. Ashes to ashes. Dust to dust.

The sounds he made, the flex of his muscles, the sight of our bodies moving together. I was a goner. I came again, hard and fast, and he met me there. He thrust into me punishingly, pressing his forehead to mine as he groaned my name and found explosive release.

And *as if* I was done. I allowed him a minute to catch his breath before I pinned him to the bed and rode him under the pale light of the waxing moon. He held my hips and watched me like I was a supernova.

We went all night long. He took me every way he could imagine, maneuvering my body this way and that, and I surrendered to him. Just for tonight. Just until the stars were kissed goodbye by the pink glow of dawn.

AFTERWARD, WE LAY BREATHLESSLY, NAKED AND TANGLED IN the sheets, looking up at the sky as it changed colors through the demolished roof.

My heart would not slow. My body would not stop shivering with all sorts of exciting aftershocks.

Somewhere during the throws of passion, Jedidiah's magic went on a rampage. All around us were beautiful, vibrant manifestations of the earth element. Viny plants growing up and down the walls, alive with neon flowers. Brightly colored dragonflies and butterflies darted about, this way and that, going from flower to flower, plant to plant. I was absolutely marveled! He'd turned the room into a jungle. I'd hardly ever seen him do anything besides make the ground shake and combust. When I said something about it, he waved me off and rolled his eyes as if the occurrence bothered him. I asked what his problem was and all he said was, "Real masculine, flowers and fucking butterflies."

He lifted onto one elbow, reaching into the drawer of the night table beside the bed. It was the first piece of untouched furniture I'd seen besides the bed. He grinned as he pulled out a pack of cigarettes. He plucked one out, and placed it between his lips, looking like a movie scene. His messy sex hair fell over his brows, his face boyish as he offered the pack to me. "Want one?"

My brows jumped. "A cigarette? You? Really?"

He shrugged. "Cigarettes after sex. A tradition I learned from mortals."

I laughed softly. "You hate mortals."

"I don't." The affirmation in his words surprised me. "And I know you don't. So have a cigarette."

Fuck it. I picked one and put it between my lips, summoning a flame over the end of both his and mine. My inhale felt good. Tight, restricting, a little painful, yes.

Pale smoke swirled up to the sky while dragonflies buzzed about, and for a while, neither of us said anything.

The silence was bliss. Nothing uncomfortable about it.

When the sky morphed into blood orange, I gasped a little. I couldn't remember the last time I'd seen the sky at sunrise.

My cheek tingled with energy, making me turn my head on the pillow to catch Jedidiah staring at me. We were far enough apart that our bodies weren't touching, though his hand wandered close to mine.

The way he was looking at me summoned a wave of insecurity over me. "What?" I demanded harshly. "Why are you looking at me like that?"

He cracked a small smile. His face was lighter now, with not as much grief and rage etched into his features as before. It was still there, his pain. But now there was light too. That warmed me.

"Solaris Adder is a fucking idiot," he said, and my heart flipped.

I couldn't keep my brows from jumping. I didn't know what to say back. I was shocked he would bring up Solaris right now.

"He doesn't know how to fight you in the way you like. He's done everything wrong. Stealing your magic and forcing you to do shit against your will to get it back." He gave one bark of a laugh. "Fucking idiot. Making you feel small. Every time you and I faced off, I made you look like a queen. You always came out on top, and everyone loved you for it."

I watched his face as he spoke. "Are you saying you've been *letting* me win?"

He scoffed. "Nah. I just know you."

"Solaris thinks he knows me," I murmured, letting my eyes wander as I stared up at the brightening sky. I reached up with my hand, my finger pointed, smiling slightly as a silver butterfly landed on the tip of it for a second. "But like...he isn't playing a game with me, Jed. He... Solaris isn't even a real person."

"What do you mean?"

"I mean... His entire life has been nothing but isolation and confinement. People like you and me can't even imagine what that would be like. Our families may have been shit and our relationships questionable, but we had people. We've been free to do as we please. Solaris has never even experienced the world or been around people. Half the time, I think he's playing a character. He doesn't know who he is, so he just takes on the embodiment he thinks fits best... He's being what he thinks he should be, considering."

I could feel Jedidiah's eyes on the side of my face. "Hm," he grunted. "Sounds like you've put a lot of thought into this...like you really care."

I turned my head on the pillow to face him, my brows knitting together. "Of course, I care. I have no choice but to! The guy emerged from his prison realm and hooked his claws into *me* right away. Stole my magic—blackmailed me with it. He shows up out of the blue, like a ghost. In and out of my life. Whenever he wants. And I may have my magic back but I'm nowhere close to free. I signed a Celestial Oath and am bound by fate to battle him on Hallows Eve. He's everywhere, even in *pillow talk* with you! I can't escape him."

"You're battling him on Hallows Eve?"

"Yeah. Sold my soul, remember? At the Clash of Spirits. It was the deal I made to get my magic back. If I win, he must leave and never use his shadow magic against anyone ever again. If he wins, though... He gets what he wants from me."

Jedidiah stared at me wordlessly, his wheels turning.

"You shouldn't have caught me with the portal globe, Jed," I said, my voice barely more than a whisper. "I was doing everyone a favor by stepping off that ledge. If I died, Solaris would never face me on Hallows Eve and his Oath would be broken. He would die. Our fates are bound. I die, he dies." I gave a humorless laugh, knowing damn well my eyes were misty and sad. "You shouldn't have come after me."

"I will always come after you." Jedidiah shot back right away, a grave sincerity in his tone.

I swallowed thickly, blinking away hot tears.

For a while, neither of us said anything. The atmosphere was dense enough to slice with a spoon.

He was the first one to break. "I have something for you. If you won't be an idiot about it."

I scoffed, my face scrunching into a grimace. "Okay? What is it?"

"Seriously, though. You can't just go waving it around, showing the world you have it. Promise?"

I rolled my eyes, curiosity mixed with anticipation jittering across my skin. The idea of a gift had my mood brightening considerably. "I promise! Now, what's my present?"

He snorted, leaning back toward that night table drawer. I checked out the flex of his back and shoulder muscles as he did so. Delicious. His scars somehow made him even more appealing. I had the mind to lean over and lick each one.

"Damn, Jedidiah. You got a lot stored away in there." I teased. "How come everything in this place is destroyed except the bed, huh? Is this where you bring all your conquests? Do you impress all the girls with your fabulous destruction?"

He pulled something rather large and covered in silver cloth out of the drawer, sitting up against the pillows and headboard. I shuffled up to match him, my eyes on the cloth. I clutched the sheets to my chest, feeling giddy like a kid on Christmas.

"I destroyed this place by accident. Instead of fixing the damage, my father just abandoned it. And no, I've never brought a girl here. I come here alone. The kitchen is somewhat intact, and the shower is too. It's quiet."

He peeled back the folded cloth, revealing a sheath, from which he drew a glorious blade.

My breath caught.

It was the most magnificent dagger I'd ever seen.

The shiny silver blade caught the light as he picked it up and angled it around. Sapphires and rubies were encrusted in the hilt, thrumming with magic. It may have been in perfect condition, but I could tell it was ancient. Celestially forged, not for the possession of mortals.

"This," Jedidiah began, "is a flaming dagger. I stole it from my father a while ago. He has a habit of taking trophies from the people he... Anyways. This dagger is ancient and it has a sentience, Nyx. Kind of like that Sacred Baton. This dagger bonds with whoever has it, but it's also a moody thing, and if it doesn't like your energy, it won't work for you."

"A flaming dagger?" I peeped, both excitement and nervousness sweeping through my veins.

"Yeah. I saw you with that pathetic little switchblade that night we went to see your mortal friends. I thought you should have something like this instead."

"I have my power back now, though. What need do I have for a blade?"

"Come on, Nyx. Everyone needs a good blade. This dagger will only work for a fire bearer. Your flames will activate it, but here's the thing: it has its own eternal flame inside." He grinned darkly. "It's a magical object, but it's not *your* magic. I thought... I thought you should have it. You might not be able to use your magic against Solaris Adder, but you might be able to use this. Just take it. Just in case. I can't stand the idea of you being defenseless around him."

My heart thumped slowly in my chest. I swallowed the lump in my throat. "Jed," I whispered.

"Just have it, Nyx," he insisted, placing it on the sheets of my lap.

I stared down at the dazzling blade.

Then my brows furrowed as I registered what he said. "I'm not *helpless* around him. I head-butted him and punched him in the face twice."

Jedidiah stared at me for a moment before a snappy, incredulous laugh tumbled out of him. The admiration that lit up his eyes made my stomach tighten. "Brilliant."

Guilt melted over me like hot wax. "Jed... You know... What happened tonight... It doesn't change anything."

His brows lowered, all humor and light vanishing from his expression.

"I mean—we—I can't be, like, your girlfriend or—"

"Shut up," he spat, his lovely face contorted with offense as he waved me off. "Don't be such a sketch. I'm giving you this, so you have the chance to slit Solaris's throat. Nothing more."

I felt like he was lying but I didn't pursue the argument.

"Also... There's something you should know. The vampire threat is real. It's not just a story the Council invented to cover up the truth about Solaris. A vampire den was found in the city. They fled, but they were there and there were almost a hundred of them. Rogue, uncivilized vampires."

My brows jumped. "Seriously?"

He nodded with his eyes downcast.

Admittedly, I pretended to be a lot more shocked than I really was. I mean, after meeting Solaris's sister, I kind of figured there was some truth to the vampire story.

I gripped the cool, silver hilt of the blade and gasped as it spontaneously doubled in size. I gave him a wide-eyed look, but he only nodded, assuring me that was supposed to happen. *Amazing*. It was small enough to conceal on myself easily but could lengthen long enough to swipe a head clean off. I could feel its magic nudging mine, trying to get me to tango. I took a deep breath and allowed my magic to spark the blades. It ignited with a rich orange flame at my telepathic command.

"Oh, my Goddess," I whispered, angling it around. He was right. This fire was not white and insanely bright like mine. This was a true orange flame, belonging to the blade.

I beamed like a jubilant child.

CHAPTER 38
SIREN SONG
NYX

The next few days, I was on cloud fucking nine.

I went to all my classes. I taught Firebending in the Sphere with Bridget. I was back to my vibrant, powerful, superior self and everyone noticed.

I'd posted all over social media that I'd be competing in the second half of Clash of Spirits. People went nuts.

I was the number one trending topic on Celestial Tea.

Fuck yes.

If I had to face this shadow bitch, I may as well make a show of it.

The Clash of Spirits was a riveting yet unusual tradition. The event was only held every thirty-three years, so I'd never been alive for one, but I'd read all about it. It was, in one way or another, a Hallows Eve show put on for the dead. Or rather, those beyond the veil. Everyone in the spiritual realms would be watching. Celestials from all over the world portalled in to attend. Anyone who was anyone would be there.

I'd recently learned it was being held in a mortal sports stadium, which I found odd. Of course, the entire thing would be glamoured, but still. The days leading up to the Clash would consist of giving sacred offerings to the Goddess and other deities, fasting, honoring nature, and living slowly and thoughtfully.

The day of Hallows Eve, though—things would pop off.

Despite being a performance for spirits, the affair was purely carnal. For us, anyway. It began with enchanted party favors and live music. Mirroring a music festival of sorts, but that was only to build up the energy and set the stage for the real thrills.

After the music and dancing, came a different kind of entertainment. The ruthless kind that mortals outlawed a long time ago.

The Battle of Elements was like a gladiator fight, but with magic. Two warriors would face off in the arena. Sometimes only one would walk away. Killing was discouraged, but not forbidden.

With the stakes being so high, only the fiercest and most notorious Celestials dared to sign up to compete. This year, I was on that list.

It was rare for people my age to compete in the Clash. Starseeds weren't always permitted to participate, not unless they had a certain ranking of power. Again, I was on that list.

The other starseeds on that list were Venus St. Claire and Maverick Madriu. Celebrities—imagine that. The two of them would be an interesting battle, I had to admit. But the main attraction would be me vs. Solaris Adder. The Society had never seen anything like us before.

I wasn't scared. I was fucking electrified. Determined. Ready.

The future of our Society rested on the fate of this battle. I could stop a war.

The Luminary and I had only spoken a couple of brief times since I'd made my Celestial Oath. Delphyne was impossible to read, though. I still had no idea if she was the one who gifted me with the Sacred Baton or not. Who else would? I couldn't decipher how she felt about everything or what her role in all of this was. It was strange how withdrawn she'd become, too. She'd been busy the last couple of weeks, busy in the Sacred Temple praying to the Goddess. Hopefully whatever she was doing would help me triumph against the insufferable Darkbringer.

After a long, glorious day of being back to my amazing, queenly self, I took a hot shower and got ready for dinner. It had been a while since I'd gone downstairs and attended a meal with the rest of the girls at Luna. Tonight, my hiatus was officially over. I needed to choose the right outfit, to remind everyone who I was. Venus's little reign of terror was coming to an end.

I left my hair long, wavy, and natural, though I packed on the charcoal eyeliner and painted my lips with my favorite shade of Wrath. My shimmering gold tattoos were swirling wildly, evidence of my spiked adrenaline. I decided tonight was a night to wear red. I slid into my most daring crimson dress, knowing its Roman Goddess style would make a statement. It had gold and quartz encrusted at the shoulders before the silky material fanned out into a cape behind me. A golden belt coiled around my waist to show off my figure. I placed a crown of thorns and roses above my forehead as the final touch, but the look still didn't feel quite complete.

I knew what was missing.

I strapped the flaming dagger to the outside of my thigh, concealed under the skirt of my dress. Perfect.

My reflection in the mirror was intense.

I looked like a warrior queen ready to watch my enemies' heads roll.

A whirlwind of shadows erupted behind me in the glass. My entire body turned to stone, but I didn't outwardly react. I had grown accustomed to these intrusive entrances.

Solaris appeared in the reflection of the mirror. My heart failed to beat.

What had I ever done to give men the impression they were free to magically show up in my room unannounced?! I needed to put a perimeter of salt around the room. This was getting out of control.

"Hello, Firefly," he said, his tone rich and smooth like honey dripping from the comb. My flesh ignited with traitorous goosebumps at the sound of his voice. He wore his long black warlock jacket, his luscious hair framing that unfair, ethereal face. Damn the Goddess for crafting him this way.

His silver gaze slid leisurely over my body before our eyes met in the mirror. My heart dropped when I saw the coldness in them. A quiet fury that was more frightening than any loud outburst smoldered at me through the glass. Was he pissed that I'd jumped the gun on announcing our face off at the Clash?

Then it hit me, by the possessive undercurrent to the way he was looking at me—he *knew*.

He knew about me and Jedidiah.

Somehow, some fucking way, he knew. Solaris and his salt circles and Astral "hunting." He saw us. I could feel it. It was a palpable truth in the room.

I clenched my fists and took a deep breath, determined to remain poised.

I wouldn't humor him.

"What do you want?" I asked icily.

"I'm afraid I must steal you away," he sighed, waving his silver-ringed fingers in the air casually. "Though I would prefer you if you followed along on your own merit."

"Follow you? Perhaps you've taken a tumble and hit your head because if you seriously thought I'd follow *you* anywhere, you're brain dead."

"Skip the theatrics. You will want to see what I have to show you."

I cocked a brow. "Is that so?"

"Yes. Come with me."

"And just where do you think you might lure me?"

"Somewhere you will loathe," he said. "You will loathe it with your entire being and therefore it will feel glorious when I allow you to destroy it."

My tattoos jumped, reversing their direction, and spinning wildly, giving away my peaked interest.

I had yet to turn around. Solaris and I remained looking at each other in the mirror. Me in my Goddess dress, a crown of roses and thorns settled above my brow. Him in his long jacket, looking like a King of Nightmares. Tangible rage smoldered in both of our eyes. We did make a striking pair, I couldn't deny. It was a despicable revelation to have, considering everything. But the truth didn't give a shit about my personal bias.

That wasn't the only truth laying itself bare, either. Being in my small dorm room alone with him did all sorts of strange things to my body. His dark power thrummed in the air, coiling around me, beckoning my fire like a siren song. We'd been in close proximity before, of course, but never with me at my full power. Now, his magic felt like a magnet for mine. It made me dizzy with the wanton instinct to unleash myself upon him. My hands trembled with need, the need to release my flames to dance with his darkness. *Not yet. Soon.*

"You should know," I began smoothly, a wicked glint in my eye, "I'm seeing someone. And although these little sadistic rendezvous between you and I are anything but romantic, this does feel unwarrantedly intimate. And violating. You have no right to show up here. I signed your Oath and played your game. There is no reason for you to be here, still crossing my boundaries."

"You're seeing someone," he breathed back, no emotion flashing across his voice or showing up in his words. "Is Hell also frozen over? If I look outside, will pigs be flying?"

I rolled my eyes.

"Come with me, Firefly. I promise you want to see what I have to show you."

I inhaled a steady breath, my fingers brushing the dagger at my thigh. If anything went wrong, I could slit his throat. I wondered if that would be enough to kill him. Probably not. It might, however, grant me enough time to escape whatever hell he sought to drag me into.

"You want to bring me somewhere I will loathe so I can destroy it?" I scoffed. "Unfortunately, I have other commitments tonight. Maybe another time."

"It must be tonight," he insisted, reaching into his long jacket. He pulled out the Sacred Baton and my stomach hollowed out. He grinned at the change on my face. "Let me show you what this *really* is."

CHAPTER 39
BY THE HEART
NYX

"You're joking."

Solaris chuckled.

Bright morning sunlight stung my eyes. I held my hand out to block the unexpected rays, blinking rapidly as my brain refused to acknowledge where he'd taken me.

"Welcome to the Vatican City, Firefly."

My eyes swept along the massive stone walls of St. Peter's Square. Humans bustled around like worker ants, completely oblivious to the truth of the land on which they stood. My heart knocked dangerously behind my ribs as reality settled over me. Solaris really brought me halfway across the world, to one of the most notoriously corrupt cities in existence.

I side-eyed him. He continued to stare forward, a small smile on his lips as he set his gaze on the incredible Basilica.

St. Peter's Square was packed with tourists who stopped to stare if they caught sight of us. I became horribly aware of my appearance—my whirling tattoos, my crown of thorns and living roses, and the other-worldly details of my dress. Not to mention Solaris, the silver-eyed creature, dressed like a fucking death eater. We looked not of this world. And unlike LA, the people here noticed.

"Shouldn't we have glamoured ourselves?" I whispered harshly, crossing my arms over my chest in an attempt to hide my moving tattoos.

"No," he answered simply. "Let them know we're here."

He linked his arm with mine and started forward.

My skin prickled with electricity, the instinct to reef out of his grasp rising up my spine like a furious snake. I kept my composure, though, because something unspoken urged me forward. I calmly unlinked my arm with his, shooting him a scowl that said *as if, asshole*, but refusing to put up a fight as I kept my steps aligned with his.

I willed the golden tattoos on my arms to stop moving for the time being.

My pulse hammered in my temples as we strode through the mass of bodies scattered through the Square. We turned heads and made people stop to marvel. Solaris seemed to enjoy it. It made me entirely uncomfortable. I was used to going unseen.

Mortals never noticed me like this in Los Angeles. I always strutted those city streets looking like my best, Celestial self, and yet hardly anyone batted an eye. Here, the humans reacted as they should. They sensed we were different. Some of them looked fearful over this. Others seemed intrigued. Some skeptical, thoughtful.

We approached the entrance of St Peter's Basilica and my entire body erupted with goosebumps, the hairs on the back of my neck standing on end. The architecture took my breath away. It was so— huge. Built at a time when giants still walked among us. I'd never felt so small before, not even when standing under the stars. Sculptures of angels, gods, and men gazed down on me, judging silently as I passed beneath them on the polished floor. This church was something else, built for a different time, a time when magic and mayhem ran wild. When gods and mortals walked the Earth together.

"Solaris," I breathed. "What are we doing here?"

"Your family descends from this land, does it not?"

I narrowed my eyes. "My true family descends from Venus and Draco."

"You are the blood of the dragon riders of Old Italy, are you not?"

"My family lived and ruled in many different places over the millennia. I would say our time in Old Italy was the most insignificant. Stop avoiding the question. What are we doing here?"

He smirked, an infuriating sight. I had to look away.

"In this case, I'm afraid it's better if I show, not tell."

"Of course," I grumbled, letting my eyes wander along the high pillared walls, determined to focus on the ethereal detail of the Basilica rather than the heart-stopping smile of the man who sought to ruin my life at every turn. Carved angels watched over me knowingly, seeming to giggle at my predicament.

Solaris led me through the wondrous and daunting Basilica, muttering facts and pointers about the art and altars we passed. I wondered how he knew so much. For someone who was said to have grown up underground and been sentenced to a century of shadows, he knew an impressive amount of history. Perhaps he was granted access to books at some point? I listened half-heartedly, though, more concerned with all the wide-eyed looks we were getting from the mortals.

"Wait," I muttered, coming to a halt. "You expect me to *destroy* this place?!"

A few heads within earshot turned our way, giving me abhorrent looks.

I swallowed, ignoring the way Solaris chuckled as we kept moving. "Not today, Firefly. Not today."

I glared at the side of his face, but he pretended he didn't know. "So you were lying then?"

"No. I told you the truth too soon. Though often, that does more damage than a lie."

"Oh," I said stupidly.

We passed the Altar of Transfiguration, which literally had the preserved body of a Pope under it on display. I grimaced and commented on how gross it was, successfully offending every worshiping human within hearing distance of us.

"You dare come here," a low, raspy voice spoke harshly from behind us.

I turned to see an old man dressed in black, carrying a Bible in one hand, and a cross on a chain in the other. A priest? He glared at us as if we were rats who'd just crawled up from the sewer. "I know what you are," the man growled. "Your kind is not welcome in this holy place." He held the cross out toward us. "Leave, demons!"

Every person within a hundred-foot radius turned to watch the blooming conflict.

Solaris grinned, amused.

The old man's face reddened with fervent indignation. His beady eyes focused on *me*. "I know what you are, witch! You are a daughter of the serpent whores! I know those golden marks on your flesh are the mark of the devil! For you to even step foot in this House of God is an act of war."

My cheeks heated but I had no words. Everyone was staring as this man held out his cross as if I were some demon who needed to be exorcized. But more than that, he looked at me as if he knew me.

No mortal had ever spoken this way to me before. Not even before I Emerged. They always had this subliminal respect for me, like they knew what I was, somewhere deep down. But this man...he knew what I was, and he vehemently hated me for it. I found myself opening and closing my mouth, trying to think of something to say.

My lack of response, apparently, served as an invite for him to continue insulting me. "Are you hard of hearing, witch? Leave, at once!" He pointed the cross at me as if he expected it to repel me. In a way, it did. My fire flared in my belly, my fingertips sizzling, longing to unleash my magic.

Solaris stepped forward, closer to the old man. "That's quite enough." He spoke calmly, but I was keen enough to sense the sleeping threat hiding in those words.

"You take her out of here!" the man went on. I couldn't understand why he was seemingly okay with Solaris but not me. "If you were wise, you'd take this filthy whore and burn her at the st—"

The man's words cut off as a wet, fleshy sound made my stomach fall. For a moment, my brain didn't process what was happening.

Solaris had punched his fist *into* the man's chest.

The old man's eyes were wide and darting, mouth opening and closing like a fish out of water because Solaris had him by the heart.

"NO!" I cried. "Stop!"

But the Darkbringer ignored me. He stared coldly at the old man whose life was in his hand, literally. Nausea took over my being. The sight of Solaris wrist-deep in this man's chest cavity horrified me. I was used to magical violence, yes, but this...this was nothing like the chaos of elements. My jaw hung open, a thousand words flying up my throat but none of them made it off my tongue.

He looked into the man's eyes as he reefed his arm back, tearing his heart out. The awful ripping sounds mixed with the terror across the man's face rendered me immobilized.

There were dozens of witnesses!

The screams and cries of horror erupting around me sounded as if they were coming from far away, perhaps from the outside of a thick glass window.

Solaris held the bloody heart in his hand. My brain wouldn't process that this was real. I felt like I was looking at some dark, twisted painting.

The man blinked and choked, standing there for a few seconds before he collapsed to his knees, his life flashing before his bulging eyes. He fell to the marble floor and twitched before settling motionlessly as a pool of blood expanded around him.

Solaris stared down at what he'd done for a moment before he nonchalantly dropped the human organ to the ground, where it landed with a wet thud. Then he turned to me, grabbed me by the elbow, and led me away. He swung his other arm in a swift motion and sent a gust of shadows throughout the room, touching each person. I watched their expressions go blank for a moment, and I knew what he'd done—he wiped their memory.

Mayhem ensued behind us as we left the room. The people may not have known who was responsible for what just happened, but the body remained. The screams and cries behind us as we fled the scene echoed through my mind, imprinting in my brain.

My heart was a heavy stone rattling in my chest, weighing me down.

"What the fuck was that!" I hissed when we were far enough away.

"I didn't care for the way he spoke to you," Solaris replied nonchalantly. "And here I thought getting the blood of a Scribe was going to be a chore."

"You can't just kill any mortal that disrespects us!"

"Oh, but I can," he replied with an infuriating grin.

"He was a priest!"

Solaris's face crumpled in disgust. "Please. He was a Scribe. If you're still angry at me for killing him an hour from now, we'll talk."

My skin was ice cold, and my hands were clammy and shaky. It felt wrong to just walk away after what just happened, but I found myself doing it anyway.

Solaris led me into another section of the Basilica. A smaller, quieter space.

His silver eyes swept the room, making sure no one was looking. He hooked my elbow with his fingers and led me to the wall where we stood in front of two carved cherubs that eyed us, freakishly sentient looking. In the space between the cherubs, their hands were extended out in such a way that looked like they should have been holding something. As if a beam or a wand had been removed from their chubby marble fingers. Solaris seemed to be waiting for me to catch onto something, but I only stared at the strange wall in confusion.

"Something's missing," Solaris mused. "What do you think that might be?" he pressed, reaching out with a silver ringed hand, brushing his long fingers between the baby angels.

After what had just happened, how could he assume I could focus on anything but—

A bolt of lightning struck through my chest as the revelation hit me. "The Sacred Baton."

He made a sound of disgust. "Please, don't call it that. You are much too intelligent to be so fooled."

Solaris reached into his jacket and pulled out the glowing Baton. My heart raced. I glanced around, afraid we were being watched.

"This, my dear Firefly, is the Moonbeam."

My breath hitched.

"It is made of moon rock and infused with moonlight. It has many purposes. It is a weapon, a token, or a key. Your Luminary is quite crafty, calling it a baton. Hiding it in plain sight. While it does have a habit of sensing deception, that is merely a side effect of being made of moonlight. You must have realized at some point that it is not what she says it is."

"Solaris." My blood roared in my ears. "What are you saying?"

He offered the 'Moonbeam' to me.

I stared at it.

"Go on," he urged softly. "Take it. Slide it into place, in the hands of the cherubs. They are waiting."

"You're insane."

"You're afraid."

I swallowed thickly and steeled myself. I snatched the Baton—er, the Moonbeam—and let its magic flow through my veins upon contact. Yes, I had always known there was something more to this curious object. I always knew it looked like the fucking moon.

"Trust me," he whispered. "You want to see what it does. Where it will lead you."

"I would never trust you." I spat. "Maybe you're right. Maybe this isn't a baton. You know what I've always thought it was? A stake. Perhaps I should test that theory now. Have you ever been impaled through the heart, Darkbringer?"

He laughed a musical sound. "You are brilliant."

"Fuck you," I muttered, unable to look into those metallic eyes as they shone upon me.

"Place it between the cherubs."

"How will we get it back?"

"We won't."

"What?" I gasped.

"Stop stalling."

My heart was going wild like a stampede of horses trying to break through my ribs. My mouth dried as I tilted my head up to take in the dome-shaped ceiling above us. Angels watched over me, and this time, they seemed to encourage me. I must have been going mad, but every fiber of my being desired to do as Solaris instructed. I didn't want to obey him, but something bigger than him urged me on.

So I slid the Celestial object into the waiting hands of the sentient-looking cherubs. It locked in place as if it were made to be there. Shit— it looked like their fingers tightened around it. Seconds later, a door manifested in the wall and crept open for us, leading down a staircase into a pit of darkness.

"Light the way, Firefly."

CHAPTER 40
DRACONIAN STARSEED
SOLARIS

For eons, I'd roamed the darkness of my self-made prison realm, seeing nothing. One could not imagine what it is like to endlessly search through a sea of black, with nothing but a tiny glimmer of hope gripping your soul, hope that maybe one day you would once again see light. It was a sick sense of hope that you didn't actually believe in, but you clung to it anyway, because, without it, you would be undone. You could not imagine it, if it never happened to you.

You also could not imagine the feeling that struck your heart when one day, that light you'd been hoping for, appeared.

The light you didn't even believe in anymore.

The first time I saw it, I thought it was a figment of my imagination. My own inner delusions manifested outside of me. I didn't trust the light. In truth, at first, I resented it.

This tiny, flickering white light, way off in the distance, looked like a firefly.

I thought it was a trick.

But the light kept appearing and disappearing. Ebbing in and out of my perception over a fathomless amount of time.

Finally, I decided to go after it.

I followed the firefly through the ravenous dark, though I never seemed to get closer.

It would be impossible to determine how long I trailed that tiny, fluttering light.

I was about to give up, you see. It had to be a depraved joke by the divine, making me trail a hopeless light. More punishment.

As I was about to abandon my quest of following the firefly, well, that was when I finally drew nearer. The light grew bigger as I approached it. I came close enough to see the light was *a girl*.

It was impossible. A white flame in the form of a young, dainty girl. Like a fire sprite, but I knew she was not a sprite. She couldn't see me, that much was true. I stood right in front of her, this small human child, her aura as bright as the sun. It warmed my face. It thawed my heart.

I could see the world surrounding her—she illuminated it for me.

The sun, the trees, the grass. I could see it all.

She was in the human world. But part of her flaming spirit existed in the shadows. With me. How could that be?

The first time I saw her, she was just a child. I watched her erupt in the middle of a room full of children sitting at their desks. I watched her mother lose the battle of trying to control her. But time moved differently from where I stood, and she grew fast. The girl became a young woman. Restless and chaotic, a magnet for trouble. I could see her bedroom with all the strange pictures on the wall. I could even hear the racket of music she listened to. I could feel her rage and her restlessness. I watched her mature and pack up her life and move to the City of Angels.

During all this time, I began to see other things. The world beyond my Firefly. She became a bridge back into the material world.

She brought Morpheus to me. He'd been near her one time while I was observing her, and sensed me there, beyond the veil. He flew between realms and found me in the shadows, offering to be my familiar. Of course, I accepted. He became my eyes and ears of the living world, and he too was a bridge.

I just didn't know how to cross that bridge.

Not until the night I managed to anchor Nyx Morningstar's astral body in my prison realm and forced her to erupt with her exquisite, catastrophic power.

She was a mythic fireborn creature, created in the image of fury.

I physically *heard* the wards crackling, going up in her Celestial flames. She burned me free like nothing. A hundred years trapped in those shadows before her, and she had us out within minutes of her arrival. It was the single most terrifying and glorious thing I'd ever borne witness to.

Now, I followed the firefly through the dark once more.

She led the way, unafraid.

I followed her down, down, down the tightly coiled spiral stairs to the crypt.

Despite everything, we went together seamlessly. The truth of that set my dead heart on fire. Because if it was this easy to have her at my side after everything I'd done, I could only imagine how natural we would have been together if I'd dazzled and courted her.

She was right, about what she said that night. I'd spent way too much time alone in the dark. It showed.

"How far down are we going?" she breathed. The bright flame over her extended hand flickered wildly, casting performative shadows of us on the stone walls.

"To the bottom," I answered.

"Great," she muttered sardonically, shooting me a dark look that lingered longer than she meant for it to. When she glared at me, her eyes were teeming with fire and passion, intense enough to burn me to the ground. And though her passion may have been fuelled by the murderous desire to see me dead, I couldn't help but appreciate the fact that she felt so strongly about me at all. Most never got a second glance from her. But when our eyes met, they locked. Every time.

She was meant to be mine. Why else would she have been in the shadows? Why else would she be here with me now?

Slithers of doubt and regret coiled up my spine. Perhaps everything I'd done had only pushed her into the arms of another.

Morpheus saw her and the Groundshaker. Their little episode at the top of the mountain. He'd *put his hands on her*. Threatened to throw her off a mountain. Instead, she hurled herself off the cliff. And to close the act, they slept together.

I had almost murdered him, but the Fates put their hand on my shoulder and whispered, *No*.

She was even more unhinged than I'd ever imagined, and that was saying something.

I hated it. To my core, I hated it. Still, though—strategically, I could use this to my advantage. I wanted the Groundshaker. His power and his rage, standing behind me. Pursuing him hadn't seemed plausible before. He struck me as the kind that would not bend nor break. But perhaps he could be *lured*... Something told me I could get to him through Nyx Morningstar. He would follow her anywhere. Even into my wolf den. If she were to stand at my side, he'd be there by default.

Perhaps he saw himself as a better man, more worthy of her than me. But what I did to her was necessary.

She *needed* an ego death. She possessed great power, yes, but she was too reckless and idiotic with it. She was completely asleep. She needed my rude awakening to inspire her to reassess her approach to magic. She paraded around her academy, playing queen, focused on meaningless, trivial things, even though she had an otherworldly power that was given to her for a divine purpose. She didn't even realize that. She'd needed to be set straight.

And while she may have been the personification of fire and light, that did not make her inherently benevolent. She could hate me all she wanted for what I did to her, but she had it coming. She couldn't stand being bent to the will of another, yet she tyrannically ruled her school, and more specifically, her three chosen soldiers. No, not soliders. Minions, she called them. She ordered them around and they obeyed her loyally, without question. Despite the fact that she wiped out their true identities and remolded them in her own image. Minion One, Two, and Three. I couldn't tell if I was impressed or disgusted. Was that what kind of ruler she wanted to be?

Not even I could tell if it was an act or not. Did she even know their true names? Did she lower them to this 'minion' title to keep them below her and in line? To strike fear in others? To flex her influential power? Was she really that ruthless and careless in dealing with others?

Or did she present herself this way as a defense mechanism? Was the cold, callous demeanor her armor? Or was it her true form?

Every fiber of my being longed to dominate her. I couldn't help it. The need existed within me on a soul level. This tiny, defiant creature. With her chin always tipped up, managing to look down the bridge of her nose at me even though she was about two feet tall. She was rude and selfish. She was a destroyer and a cynic. Everything she touched turned to ash.

She was a wildfire incarnate.

The exact opposite of me. My most primal, instinctive nature fervently longed to quell her flames. I needed to impose myself upon her. It was an instinct that went way beyond me, way beyond her. The cosmos were created to be this way. The tension and magnetism between opposite forces ruled everything.

One could not just let a wildfire forever run rampant. The flames needed to be contained. At the very least, they needed to be wielded with purpose. To destroy with purpose.

Every time I tried to conquer her, she chewed up my efforts and spat them back at me with a sneer on her blood-red lips.

Sometimes I thought maybe she liked it. Our twisted dynamic. Her heart always raced around me. She eyed me with disgust and disdain, but sometimes I'd catch a glint of desire. A desire that brought her great shame. I wanted more. I wanted her to realize how perfect we were for each other. The embodiments of light and dark. Fire and shadow.

She may have hated me now, but that would change.

In the shadows, I used to hear a voice. Phantom-like, genderless. It would speak to me sometimes, while I was observing her. *She must be yours*, it would whisper. *Without you, she will veer off her path. Unleash yourself on her. Wake her. Claim her.*

The voice filled my head with all these visions, showing me what could be.

So when I broke free of the shadows and was given a second chance at life, I did what the voice told me to do. I snared her, and though my methods may have been mad, I had her.

Much like a caged lion, she lashed out. Each time she pushed back, each time she defied me, all it did was make me want to dominate her more. She needed it. She needed me. She was powerful and glorious but without my counsel, she would burn out before she could hit the apex of her power. She needed me by her side.

She just needed to realize that.

You'll show her, the voice promised.

Today was my chance for redemption. To show her what I could truly offer her.

After what I gifted her on this day, I could never be perceived as purely evil. If all went wrong, though, we would be dead.

But I was a gambler by nature. *May the odds be in our favor.*

"We are, like, ten stories below the Vatican," she voiced, sounding like she was talking to herself. I could hear her heart pounding. She had charmed her fire to hover over our heads rather than having to hold her fist out like a torch. "Why did you say we won't be getting the Sacred Ba —er, I mean, the Moonbeam back? Isn't it unwise to leave it here?"

"Once it has been used as a key, its magic is null and void. It's still moonrock, but it holds no light or magic now that it's been used to open a passage into the crypt. There are countless passages leading down here, all hidden, all requiring their own unique object to open a door. Once a passage is opened and used, it closes forever. The object used as a key becomes dormant."

"How do you know all of this?"

"Banish your fire," I told her, dodging her question.

She stopped her descent and turned to glare at me, those obsidian eyes sparkling with defiance. The crown of roses and sharp thorns gave her a fascinating shadow on the curved wall around her. The shadow of a dark, powerful queen. "We won't be able to see anything!"

"The light will give us away. It will see us."

Her face paled. "It?"

I grinned slyly. "You need not worry. I have a feeling it will take a liking to you. That's why I brought you, after all."

Her lips tore back into a snarl. "Where the fuck are we going? I won't take another step until you tell me."

"We are going to the entrance of the Secret Library."

Her black eyebrows knitted together. "Elaborate. Now."

346

"Under the Vatican, there is an ancient, hidden library, abundant with all true history records and occult texts."

Her eyes flicked to the side, considering. "Okay. I knew that. Well, I heard rumors anyway. But what is the 'it' you are—"

"The door of the library is guarded by a great beast."

Her intake of breath sounded painful. Her black eyes bulged.

My grin broadened. "And you, a Morningstar born under the sun of Ophiuchus, a Draconian starseed, have the best chance of getting past this beast."

Her heart thundered behind that silken red dress, hammering like the drums of war as she looked up at me through wide eyes and parted lips. Her beauty was crippling. Her gaze went downcast, her expression deepening as she fell into a train of thought I wished I could hear.

"We are almost at the door," I said. "You will need to banish your flame when we reach it."

Her stare flicked back up to me as if she had forgotten I was there.

"Fine," she huffed, continuing down the stone steps.

"There is no door!" she wailed when we reached the bottom. A dead end. She trailed her hands along the wall, her face crazed with betrayal. We stood at the bottom of the stairs, in a small, suffocating round space that seemed to lead nowhere.

She lifted the skirt of her red dress, shocking my abdomen with heat as she exposed her bronze thigh, and pulled out—

—a silver dagger that met my throat.

Her eyes sparked with an honest threat, and her lips pulled back over her teeth. She backed me into the wall, holding the blade to my throat, pushing hard enough into my flesh to draw blood. Her warm body and smoky scent intoxicated me, her death threat driving me wild. She pressed herself against me and I had to suppress a groan as she conjured an aching heat to pool in my groin.

She was crazy. I couldn't get enough of it.

"Take me back to Luna Academy right now or I swear to the Goddess and all her creations that I will slit your throat. Right here, right now."

I grinned down at her, wishing I could freeze this moment in time.

She was utterly bewitching. All fury and beauty and angst. I wanted this image blown up.

"Get that stupid smile off your face!" she shrieked, pushing the blade deeper into my flesh, making me hiss. Blood dripped over the dagger, onto her hand. This was, what, the third time my blood had spilled for her? How did she always manage to catch me off guard? Perhaps I just enjoyed her vicious little attacks.

"You kill me, Firefly, and you die too."

She didn't miss a beat. "I don't care. The world will be better off without both of us."

"That's debatable."

She was on her tiptoes, caging me into the wall, the promise of death dancing over her features as she glared up at me. My heart pounded furiously against her. I knew she could feel it. And despite her goal being to intimidate me, all she was really doing was turning me on. She felt that, too. Her eyes widened with indignation as she felt the swell of my cock against her stomach.

"You're sick." Her cheeks heated and I could hear her pulse thundering, but she didn't back down.

"The door is under your feet, Firefly."

For a moment, the words didn't register. Then she looked down. The granite floor had an ominous face carved into it, the mouth yawning under her absurdly heeled combat boots. Realization washed over her features, and she stepped back, releasing me.

The slice on my throat healed all too soon.

Her chest rose and fell. The bloody dagger shook in her trembling hand.

"Go ahead," I murmured, not ready to stop playing. "Kill me."

Her face crumpled into a grimace. "Would slitting your throat even be enough to kill you?"

I chuckled. "Find out."

She stared at me, breathing hard. Considering.

She tucked the blade away, strapping it against her tanned thigh once more. "I'm surprised you don't bleed black." Her voice was low and laced with disdain so feverous you'd think her tongue would catch fire.

My veins were alive with shocks and tingles. Her breathing echoed off the stone. I had all these rash ideas swarming through my mind, ideas that took all my strength to douse out.

"Only the blood of the Scribes can open this door," I said as I held out my bloody hand. It was still warm and wet and fresh.

"What is a Scribe?"

I held in the dark scoff that almost escaped my lips at that. "A record keeper of sorts."

"But he looked like a priest."

"Yes. Well. You should know by now; things are hardly ever as they appear."

I heard her swallow.

I knelt and placed my palm down on the face on the floor. "Banish your flame," I demanded. After a few seconds of defiance, she listened, and the world went dark. "And don't scream," I added before I muttered the opening charm.

The trap door slid open under our feet, and we plummeted into the dark.

I caught her in my arms before we hit the unforgiving stone floor of the crypt. She managed to hold in her cries, but I could feel her pulse thrashing wildly in every inch of her body. For a moment, a moment so brief I thought I imagined it, she clung to me. An instinct, of course, provoked by the sudden freefall. But my entire body ignited as her fingers clutched the back of my neck, squeezing for dear life.

As soon as my feet were planted on the floor, she tore away from me, muttering profanities.

The crypt was just as I'd seen it from the shadows. A large square space, half the size of a sports field, smelling of mildew, damp stone, and feral animals. I had Astral Traveled here before but could never make it through the door. The wards were literally impenetrable. Not even Morpheus could get through, and the raven could fly between realms. The only way in was to be blessed by the guardian who dwelled here.

"Take my hand," I whispered.

"Eat shit." Firefly shot back, dusting herself off as she looked around, completely blinded by the dark.

"I can see," I told her. "If you take my hand, I can share my power and allow you to see as well."

She glared in the wrong direction, giving the finger to a nonexistent person in front of her. I bit back a chuckle, refusing to give up. "You want to see this, Firefly."

"I hate that stupid fucking nickname, you know that? I wish you would just—"

A rustling of chains in the distance made her shut up and freeze.

I dared to lace my fingers with hers. She needed to see. She pulled away at first, but I sent my power up her arm and she gasped, her eyes widening as she inherited my night vision. She blinked rapidly a few times, her dark eyes sweeping the entire space around us. Her attention landed indefinitely on the beast coiled up in the center of the room.

Her breath caught in her throat.

I felt time stop for her.

And then she moved forward.

Her legs carried her without her mind's consent, it seemed. Where most people would scream and run the other way, this fireborn girl approached the sleeping beast, her black eyes sparkling with awe and desire.

I stayed rooted in place, tugging her back. "Wait."

"Solaris," she breathed, her chest rising and falling, her fingers grasping mine so hard her knuckles had gone white. She looked around, taking in every inch of the dreary space. The walls of the crypt had wept many tears for this fallen beast. The entire place was wet with them, streaming down the stone walls, and pooling on the hard floor. She noticed this, her breathing getting faster by the second.

The ginormous gray reptile lay coiled up in the center of the crypt, chained and bound to forever guard the trap door into the Secret Library. Its tattered, ripped wings were tucked behind its back. Both its horns were cut off. Many spikes from around its face and down its spine were missing as well. I scanned over the rest of the body, noticing that countless scales and claws had been removed. They'd taken everything from this creature, leaving it as nothing but a shell of what it once was. Left it alone in the dark, just as they did me. It was barely recognizable. I wondered if Firefly would know what it was.

She started shaking her head, her lips trembling, eyes watering. My brows narrowed. Her reaction confused me. She took in the truth in front of us, so many emotions passing over her expressive face, the energy wafting off her enough to make me dizzy. "What have they done to her?"

Her?

Tears spilled over those long bottom lashes, streaming down her cheeks. Sorrow billowed out of her, overtaking the crypt, powerful enough to devour me. I'd never felt anything so...so raw, so passionate... My throat bobbed, the atmosphere thickening as I fought to neutralize her potent radiation. I hadn't expected her reaction to be this emotional. That was a mortal trait, was it not?

But there was nothing mortal about her at that moment. The look on her face was primordial, her elemental instincts rising to the surface in the presence of the beast of old. Even her sorrow was made of fire. Most sadness felt like water, but hers was a slow-burning flame, almost molten, spreading slowly and thoroughly. She wept the way a volcano wept, smoke seeping from her nose and tears as hot as magma flowing with the promise of devastation for all who dwelled nearby.

"We need to get it to move," I said quietly, unsure of how to deal with her current condition. "It's laying on the—"

"*She*," Nyx Morningstar snarled, turning to me with a blaze behind those teary, nightshade eyes. Her lips tore back over her teeth, fury alchemizing the grief on her face. The despair became rage, lava turning to a wildfire. She gave me a silent warning before she took her hand out of mine. Her flesh erupted with Celestial Fire, bright and hot and writhing fiercely. It started over her hands, licking up her tattooed arms and fanning out behind her like a cape in the wind.

She woke the beast.

Its head jerked up at the audible burst of fire and light, and that was the moment I learned that it did not have eyes. They'd been harvested. It was blind, sniffing with its large, spiked snout as a primordial growl rumbled from the back of its throat.

A furious sob ripped out of her. "A dragon," she wept. "A dragon. A *dragon*. Solaris!"

The dragon snarled, the sound rasped but clear. The ancient beast sniffed the air, lifting one front leg to move closer.

"I'm here!" Firefly called, her tone firm and self-assured. The dragon's head snapped in her direction. In *our* direction. "Tell me how to free you."

CHAPTER 41

NIAXUS

NYX

The dragon roared in response, a shockwave of sound bursting through me, rattling the entire stone crypt. I didn't move, did not waver. My chest heaved and my eyes spilled countless tears, but I kept my spine straight, feet rooted in place, refusing to show fear.

Whoever did this to you will pay.

With blood and fire and screaming, they would pay for this. This promise and threat hatched inside me like a newborn creature, ready to grow and reign hell upon its enemies.

Nothing mattered anymore. Nothing. Not Venus. Not Solaris, or his war, or what he'd done to me. Not the Clash of Spirits and the impending fate of my Celestial Oath. Not the future of our Society or the world itself. None of it fucking mattered, not anymore.

I was looking at *a dragon*.

A dragon that had been harvested and mutilated beyond recognition. This wondrous, powerful, fathomless creature—our oldest guardian—was sentenced to an existence of withering down in this pit, guarding a Secret Library.

I could hardly see through the filter of blind rage that filmed over my eyes.

The dragon rose shakily up on her front legs. She sniffed the air, tendrils of smoke escaping her nostrils when she breathed out. Her ragged wings fanned out behind her, too weak to extend fully. She whined and snarled, trying to pinpoint exactly where I stood. My heart pounded a hole through my chest.

"Firefly," Solaris whispered. I half forgot he was even here. "Once she sniffs you out and realizes you are not one of the Scribes, she will—"

"Shh!" I hissed, turning to give him a cold look.

I came from a long line of ancient dragon riders. I would not fear this dragon. Even if she did turn on me, I would not blame her. How could I? Looking at what they'd done to her, I was surprised she didn't roast us on the spot.

She struggled closer, her long snout inhaling the air in front of me. She paused, sensing us here. Her lips tore back as she growled, revealing her decayed, pointed teeth. Many were missing. My fire burned hotter as fury overflowed in my veins. She seemed to sense my flames, blowing smoke from her nose as she tried to figure me out.

"I am Nyx Morningstar," I declared. The dragon stilled, listening. "Descendant of Alexandria Morningstar, queen, and dragon rider from the Old World. I hold the power of Celestial fire." I bowed low, knowing she couldn't see me, but dragons felt energy. She would feel my respect. "I am abhorred by the condition in which I have found you. I will—"

"We are here to get into the library!" Solaris hissed, interrupting me.

"Back off," I warned, turning to him with fire in my eyes.

A furious roar shook the crypt. Dust and stone rained over us from above. The chains around the dragon's neck and feet rattled. My heart plummeted to the pits of my guts as she reared her head back, her throat glowing orange as she opened her mouth and spat fire.

Strong arms wrapped around me and heaved me out of the way just in time. My own fire was banished upon contact with Solaris. The dragon fire lit up the dungeon for a few seconds before it burnt out, leaving me blind in the dark.

The chains kept rattling and dragging across the stone floor, a warning that the dragon was on the move. She roared again, the sound penetrating my soul. Solaris yelled something I didn't quite catch before he grabbed my hand. Then we were running—running senselessly through the dark. He gave me his night vision, but it didn't matter. My fight-or-flight kicked in a beat too late. Panic exploded through my limbs. A *dragon* was coming after me.

The crypt lit up with orange light as she breathed fire again, this time angling around the entire space, determined to destroy us.

I could feel the infernal wave at my back as we fought to outrun her blaze. The dragon cried out in despair, heaving another furious breath of fire. We kept running. I couldn't tell what way was right or left or up or down. I just kept moving, one foot in front of the other as fast as I could go.

"We have to leave," Solaris declared. "Abort. We can come back. She's going to—"

"We're not leaving her down here!" I exclaimed.

My chest rose and fell rapidly. I stopped running. Solaris's fingers ripped from mine as I halted.

I knew what I had to do.

I turned just in time to find the ginormous beast at my back, standing right over me with an open mouth glowing with the promise of fire.

"Firefly—MOVE!"

I did no such thing.

She unleashed her wrath upon me, bathing me in dragon fire.

I winced away uselessly, a scream tearing from my throat as the ravenous downpour engulfed me. Way off in the distance, as if in another world, I could hear Solaris shouting. But the dragon fire became my only reality. It burnt away my crown, my clothes, my jewels. The scorching heat felt glorious on my skin. I could see creatures in the flames. A whole world of fire, a world uncorrupted by mortals or Celestials. I saw snakes and owls and dragons, turtles and lizards and foxes. *Yes*, I thought wistfully. *Yes, I know you. Take me home. Return me to the fires from which I came.*

When her inferno finally relented, I was still standing, unscathed. Embers burned at my feet, giving me just enough muted light to see.

My naked flesh was painted black, my hair full of the ashes of my crown.

Only one thing remained. My fingers brushed along it incredulously.

The dagger on my thigh. Like me, it survived the trial of dragon fire.

Your companion may pass, a voice in my head said. An otherworldly echoing female voice that reminded me of rushing water.

I looked around, confused. I blinked blindly into the endless expanse of darkness. My heart hammered behind my ribs as I realized the only possible source of the voice was the—

Tell him to go now, the dragon commanded.

My lips popped open, but no words came out.

She Who is Named for the Night and the Dawn. I have waited lifetimes for you. I do not desire to wait any longer. Tell your companion he may pass through the door into the Secret Library. He has thirteen minutes.

"Solaris," I breathed, and then he was right there. His fingers laced with mine and he shared his night vision with me. I looked up into those metallic eyes and found them staring down at me with a look so intense my knees almost gave out. He said nothing. He held my stare, his gaze refusing to wander over my newly exposed body. "She says you may pass through the door. You have thirteen minutes in the Library."

He went to tug me along with him, but I held my ground, letting go of his hand. "I am staying right here. I will see you when you get out. Hurry now. Thirteen minutes."

"Nyx," he said, startling me with the usage of my true name. "I'm not—"

The dragon roared in warning.

"Go," I insisted. "I'll be fine."

I felt him hesitate for a moment in the dark. And then I felt him leave. I heard the sliding of stone over stone, knowing he'd found the door.

I was alone with the dragon.

Girl who does not burn, you have finally come.

I cleared my throat, seeing nothing through my misty eyes. "Yes. I am here."

I willed fire to my hands, holding them out as two torches to illuminate the space. The great dragon loomed over me, her neck craned down to be closer to my face. She looked gray, but now that we were so close, I could tell she used to be a beast of blue. At one time, her scales must have shone like sapphires.

Phantom pains erupted in my body as I took in the sight of her. All her wounds, her missing scales, missing eyes, horns—they'd taken everything. Yet she remained.

"Tell me how to free you," I begged. "I'll do anything."

Good, she answered. *I am Niaxus, the last living dragon from the Old World. Many, many moons ago, I was bonded to your bloodline. An ancestor of yours once mounted me.*

I blinked rapidly, which did nothing to stop the tears from flowing down my ash-stained cheeks. "You are Sophia's dragon," I professed, my words tasting like tears. "But you're supposed to be dead..."

You will find much of the history you are told is a lie.

To that, I had no objections, nor any words at all. I just stared up at her in a heart-wrenching kind of wonder.

She lowered her snout even closer to me, the hot air from her nose blowing gently against my skin, smelling of smoke. She seemed to be encouraging me to touch her. I banished the flame over my left hand, my arm shaking as I held out my palm and gently placed it against her dull gray scales while my eyes instinctively fluttered closed.

I gasped fiercely as the vision exploded over the back of my eyelids.

My belly swooped with the sensation of freefall, my hands gripping the reins as the magnificent blue dragon dipped down, leaving the clouds behind as we plummeted toward the earth. A whoop of excitement tore through my lips as my dragon straightened out, her great shadow darkening the world below. The profound sensation of two heartbeats pumped in my chest, mine, and hers. Beating as one. We flew over the dense, neverending forest. Niaxus let out a screech, her leathery wings cracking like thunder as they beat the air. My thighs tightened around her neck, the insatiable heat of her body warming me to my core. I urged her in the direction I wished to go, smiling as the wind played roughly with my hair. These joy rides were everything to me. I wished they could last forever. But much like the sweltering summer, which was meeting its inevitable end, this too would pass.

I blinked rapidly as the vision faded, leaving me breathless and yearning.

I'd been gifted a glimpse of the world through the eyes of Sophia Morningstar. I just knew, deep in my bones, that was her.

"Niaxus," I breathed, unable to come up with the right words. "That was..." My voice broke, my tears finishing the thought for me.

You will free me today.

"Yes," I vowed.

Take the blade from your thigh.

My brows knitted together but I would not question the dragon. I banished the flames over my flesh and reached to slide the dagger free from its fireproof holster. I willed the blade to ignite, illuminating the crypt with flickering orange light.

Over the millennia, man has wondered how a dragon breathes fire. There are many theories, some close to the truth, some not. They have said it is because of venom in our throats. Or crystals that manifested in our lungs. Today, I will tell you a secret, child. Our fire comes from a spark up our spine that ignites in our hearts.

She lifted one of her huge hands to point to the center of her chest, just under her long throat. Her heart. *This space has many purposes. It is a Celestial Forge, capable of both Creation and Destruction. It is also a soft spot. If I am struck there with a magic-forged weapon, I am dead.*

My mouth dried. Where was she going with this? I didn't like this secret. A doomed feeling settled over me as I waited for her to continue.

You must strike hard and true.

"Wait," I muttered, shaking my head. "I'm here to free you, not kill you!"

Death is freedom, Niaxus supplied, her ethereal voice firm and reassuring. *You would be giving me the greatest gift of all. And in return, I have a gift for you. I have been hiding it for centuries, but I cannot contain it any longer—it is ready. You must act fast. Strike me in my soft spot. Once I have fallen, reach into the wound and retrieve what I have been keeping hidden. Take it back with you. Bury it in the earth and release it with fire.*

"But," I was still shaking my head, refusing to process what she was asking of me. "Dragons are supposed to be gone. But you're here, in the flesh. I can't—I'm not going to just—I can't *kill* you!"

You don't see the full picture, but you will. Trust me, girl. I am a dragon of old. I do not wish to see your kind without the guidance of mine any longer. The world has suffered enough. You are part of something bigger. The prophecy is already unfolding.

"Come back with me," I pleaded. "Solaris can shadow-travel us somewhere—we can get you out of here."

I am at the last verse of my scripture. My final words are for you.

"Wait—"

Niaxus roared and I froze, mouth hanging open.

The Lightbringer faces the shadow and the scorpion ascends. The dreamer awakens to merge two worlds. Darkness holds up a mirror and demands eyes or a tamer. The summoner of ancient ones proves true. Redemption lies in the power of three. Free the silver rainbow trapped by ravenous false arteries. The sun bleeds a new path, a stolen world remembered.

Each word oozed over me like hot wax, both warming me and hardening me.

I gaped up at the dragon, unable to grasp that this was real.

Niaxus moved closer to me, exposing her long, scaled throat. *Now take the blade and strike true.*

I shook my head. "I can't. Please, Niaxus. *No.*"

You must. Do it now.

I held the flaming dagger in a trembling hand, tears turning my vision into a watery mirage.

Fear is a monster that must always be vanquished, she urged. *All eyes beyond the veil are watching you.*

Something about those words triggered me into action.

I released a furious cry and lunged forward, gripping the dagger with white knuckles as it doubled in size at my telepathic command. I put every ounce of my strength into the blow. I slashed the flaming silver blade across the dragon's soft spot, disbelief electrifying my veins as it cut through her steeled flesh so smoothly.

Hot, smoking blood splattered across my face and chest. Niaxus shrieked, shaking the crypt, and blowing out my eardrums. I didn't know what came over me, but I howled and struck her again. Two times, then three. Creating three slashes, the shape of an X with a line through it. With one final strike, I stabbed the dagger into the middle of the X.

I flung myself backward, moving out of the way of the falling dragon.

She hit the stone floor hard. I lost my footing, my ass hitting the unforgiving floor with a thud. Dust and rubble rained upon me. I thought the entire crypt was going to cave in at the impact.

I watched through a filter of horror as she bled out, dying instantly.

A terrifying, dreadful silence possessed the crypt.

I stared at what I had done but I couldn't believe it. I didn't want to. This had to be some trick—an illusion, a nightmare. I kept shaking my head, muttering intelligibly.

I shuffled forward, sobs tearing out of me. I collapsed beside the dragon and wept over her body.

Her wound began to *glow*.

Radiant golden light broke through the angered flesh at the base of her throat, calling me. The light seemed to be burning a path out of her skin, opening the wound until it was a gaping cavity.

Once I have fallen, reach into the wound and retrieve what I have been keeping hidden.

It seemed barbaric. But I had come too far to turn away now.

I heaved in a few breaths, trying and failing to steel myself. I crawled over to Niaxus's bleeding wound and pulled out my blade. Her blood was thick and warm, coating my ash-kissed skin. I continued to weep as I prepared myself for what I was about to do.

I plunged my hand into the dragon's throat with a shuddering breath. I rooted around through her hot blood and flesh until my fingers brushed something impossibly hard and smooth, like stone, hot enough to have been sitting on smoldering coals.

I gritted my teeth and grunted as I forced myself to reach in as far as I could, my entire arm inside the dragon until my hand wrapped around the object she'd been hiding in here. I pulled it out, shouting wordlessly as I did so.

I tore myself free and fell backward, struggling to balance the heavy thing in my hand.

Incredulity blossomed in every cell of my body as I gawked at the stone. Over half a foot tall and wide, it had the undeniable shape of an egg. I used my fire magic to burn away the thick layer of blood, astonished to find that the stone beamed bright gold, gilded with a pattern of scales. I blinked rapidly but my brain wouldn't process the truth of what I held in my blood and ash-stained hands.

Solaris found me like that. Crouched on the floor next to the fallen dragon, covered in the remnants of death, clutching the impossible stone. He stared down at me in a way that seemed like he was ready to fall to his knees before me. Like I was a goddess. A vengeful goddess, rising from the depths of the Underworld to lay waste.

In turn, I assessed him. Under one arm, he held a red leather book. In the other, he held a strange triangular glass vial.

"Take me back," I whispered, desperate. "Please. Get me out of here."

He shoved the items into his jacket and swept me into his arms without a second thought. I didn't fight him off. I held the hot stone to my chest and buried my face in the crook of his neck, feeling his thrashing pulse. "Not to the Academy," I added quietly. "I can't go there right now."

I told him where I needed to go, my voice broken but absolute.

"Yes," he replied hoarsely. "Yes. Anything."

For the first time, I welcomed the whirlwind of shadows that swallowed us.

CHAPTER 42
VIAL OF SHADOWS
SOLARIS

After she'd buried the golden dragonstone, she demanded I bring her back to the penthouse. She showered in my shower, and then she slept for three days straight. In the guest room, tangled up in the sheets and hugging a body pillow against herself as if she owned the place.

So many times, I found myself in her doorway. I couldn't help but study her, endless questions running wild in my mind. Her pale hair sprawled around her like a tangle of silk, her breathing deep and steady. She even frowned in her sleep.

I had anticipated she would somehow bond with the dragon. But I did not expect...whatever the hell that was. I couldn't shake it—the vision of her, crouched there in a pool of dragon's blood...

I would have stayed in her doorway forever, but unfortunately, I had other obligations. Like putting myself through absolute hell—mingling with the students of Veneficus.

I sat, bored, listening to Aro spout off about ancient magic he clearly knew nothing about. I needed to keep up appearances and convince the Society I was one of them. So I suffered through his lecture, sitting amongst all the young male Celestials that seriously needed to wake up and realize everything they were being taught was a joke. All they did was focus on elemental magic and absurd myths. These Academies didn't teach any important spell work or true history.

The second the pathetic excuse for a lecture was over, I shadow-traveled myself back up to the penthouse to check on my guest.

My insides turned to granite when I found Ra'ah there, lingering in Firefly's doorway.

"What do you think you are doing?" I growled, making her jump out of her ghostly skin.

"Can't you just shadow-travel her back to her stupid school?" my sister whined, trying to feign innocence. She strutted away from the guest room, hopping up on a bar stool. "We have business to attend to."

I glared at my sister for a long moment before I went and stood by the wall of glass overlooking the city, my brows pinched together.

"You're just going to ignore me now?"

"Are you dense?" I snapped without looking her way. "I signed a Celestial Oath. Even if the girl wasn't here, I wouldn't be able to work on anything anyways. We must wait until after I beat her at the Clash of Spirits."

I reached into my jacket and pulled out the dark object I'd been keeping on my person possessively. I held the Vial of Shadows in my hand, twirling it restlessly. I'd forged it, down in that hellhole they'd kept me in all those years. Part of me was surprised they had put it in the Secret Library, but then again, I was sure this thing had caused them more problems than not.

It was made of smoky quartz, shaped like an upside-down pyramid, hollow inside. Runes were etched into the sides, thrumming with power. It was the last remaining dark object capable of doing what I needed to do. Hard to even believe I'd managed to possess it. No one had been able to get into the Secret Library in nearly a century, not even the Scribes. The dragon had turned against everyone. Everyone but her.

"Want to play a game?"

I shot her a wry look. "A game?"

"Chess?" She smiled wider, an unsettling sight. "Remember how much you used to love to play?"

I winced. She and I would spend what little time we had together playing that game. In that cold, steel room with eyes watching from outside the two-way mirror. For me, they weren't fond memories.

"I'm busy, Ra'ah."

"You're staring out a window, brother."

"I am thinking."

She scoffed. "You had a century to think alone in the shadows, did you not? Come on, play a game of chess with me. I have something to show you."

I sat across from her at the bar. She had already set up the board, and she won the game of rock, paper, scissors and made the first move. Juvenile strategy, sure, but it worked, nonetheless. As always, my sister moved one of her white knights first.

I moved a black pawn. "What is it you have to show me?"

Her red eyes were fixed on the chessboard. She contemplated for a few moments before she decided to copy me and brought a pawn out. Then she reached into her long jacket and showed me something that made my heart fall.

"Where did you get that?" I hissed, instinctively reaching out to snatch it from her.

"Ah, ah, ah." She shook her head at me. "This is my creation, and you cannot steal it. Make your move."

I stared at her, hating that she was right. With a grunt, I slid another pawn two spaces forward.

She grinned, pleased. "I have had it since our great escape," she explained, placing the red wooden music box on the bar top. It was small enough to fit in the palm of her hand, but the power it possessed was staggering. She moved her knight again, making her way across the chessboard. "I still possess many of the objects I forged down there."

"And what do you plan to do with that one, sister?" I asked as I slid my bishop across the tiles and took out her knight.

She hissed with disdain. "It only has one use, Solaris. I think you know what I mean to do with it."

"You may not use it without my permission."

"You are not my master!"

"Perhaps not," I replied smoothly, watching as she chose to bring out her second knight. My sister never learned from her mistakes. "But you are unable to think clearly, so you must come to me before you make any rash decisions. Understand?"

She folded her arms across her chest and glared at me. I slid a pawn out onto the board, making way for my queen.

"You used your medallion to steal your little girlfriend's magic—and in the process, she destroyed it." Ra'ah moved her knight and took out the pawn I just moved, as I anticipated. "Who are you to tell me what I can and cannot do with my own dark object? You used one of yours and got it destroyed. I forged this, down in that godforsaken pit. It's mine. I can do with it what I please."

"You are not the same person you were when you forged it, Ra'ah," I muttered as my queen took out her knight.

Her red eyes lit with indignation. "Fuck you, Solaris. You don't even know me."

"I know enough."

She chose to slide her bishop across the board to take out one of my knights which hadn't even left its original space. "You're stalling. Why? Because you have a little crush on the witch? Just fuck her and be done with it already. We have glorious revenge to act out, brother. Don't lose the plot."

A low sound rumbled from the back of my throat. With rapid speed, I reached out to grab the music box, despite knowing it would burn anyone who dared to steal it from its maker. My sister hissed like a venomous snake, snatching the dark object. "You cannot steal it!"

"No, but I can send it to the shadows where it belongs," I threatened honestly.

"Why would you do that? I thought you would be happy I still possess this trinket! Do you know what we could do with this? We could use this and—"

"*Enough*, Ra'ah!" I snapped, shadows seeping out of me as a warning.

She gave a long-suffering sigh, then moved onto the next pain in the ass subject. "Fine. But about what you said before—I made no Oath. Give *me* the Vial of Shadows and the grimoire. I have eager and willing test subjects waiting for me back at the warehouse."

I turned to give her a sour look. "You? You are not capable of—"

She hissed like a wild animal, cutting me off. "You have forgotten. I may be a vampire now, but I was once just like you, brother. A waterling. Remember? I know my way with the elements. One does not have to be a pure-blooded Celestial to be a successful alchemist. Let me do this. We don't have time to wait around."

I stared at her, considering.

"Put some of your shadows into the vial. I'll follow the steps in the grimoire and try it on a couple of my newbie vampires. You know I've been scouring the city for lost souls, Turning them when they fit our requirements. I have a whole mob of willing test subjects, just waiting... If it doesn't work, no harm done. We will wait until after Hallows Eve. If it does work, though..." Her dark red lips split into a maniacal smile. "Revenge will be sweet, brother."

My brows lowered. "You have been Turning mortals? How many?"

"Why does your face look like that? This is what we wanted, Solaris. I mean, really. I get that you're a guy who was locked up for a hundred years and probably reeeaaaallly needs to get off, but can't you just fuck Venus and get it out of your system? Your obsession with the silver-haired fire witch is clouding your judgment! We had a plan, Solaris. Remember? And originally it never involved her. We were supposed to make an army! And now you have the Vial of Shadows and we can do just that. Stop with this pussy whipped shit. I want blood to flow and heads to roll."

I blinked down at her, abhorred, and slightly confused. My mouth opened to berate her, but she went on before I could get a word in.

"You successfully got into the Secret Library, and we have what we need now. This is our chance, Solaris. You said we would make them pay. I waited a hundred years for you. I'm done waiting."

I shook my head, but it meant nothing.

Perhaps my priorities were in disarray.

But for her to pursue her own plan without my consent had my chest filling with tangible disdain. Who did she think she was? My teeth clenched as I regarded her, standing before me with a thousand dirty secrets dwelling in her crimson eyes.

"No."

Her face fell. "What?"

"I said NO, Ra'ah. You went behind my back, Turning mortals without my permission. Do you understand how idiotically reckless that is?"

"They're in a warehouse outside of the city! I have everything under con—"

"Save it. I said no." I flicked my eyes to the window, away from her. "We can proceed with our plans after Hallows Eve, at my command. And you will terminate every single vampire you have made behind my back. Could you be any more thoughtless? To think I would inflict my shadows upon vampires? I did not take you for a dimwitted imbecile, sister!"

"If you inflict them with your shadows, they will be sired to you! They will obey you!"

"I said no, Ra'ah. I never intended on using vampires. Deal with what you have done. And report back to me when you are finished."

The silence that followed densified the room.

My sister glared at the side of my face.

"You will regret this, brother. I have other ways of getting what I want. You may have lost the plot, but I'm still marching onward." She darted out onto the terrace and leaped over the edge before I could utter a response. She would survive the thirty-story drop. I was glad to be rid of her. I had no interest in playing this ridiculous board game.

I knocked her king piece over and returned to stand by the window, overlooking my city.

Morpheus glided into view as soon as she was gone, as if he were waiting for her to leave. I wouldn't put it past him. He came soaring through the darkening sky until he reached the glass window. He dematerialized, reforming on the other side of the glass, taking his place on my shoulder.

"Morpheus. Any news?"

Yes. I was watching the High Council, just as you asked. They are planning something that may come as a shock. May I show you instead of telling you?

"Of course."

Our telepathic connection kicked in, but before I could see what he had to show me, we were interrupted.

"Not only do you have a raven, but you *talk* to it?" Nyx Morningstar stood in the doorway of the spare bedroom, her silver hair a chaotic mess and her voice extra raspy. The shirt I'd given her to sleep in nearly reached her knees, but she didn't seem to care how she looked, she still deemed herself fit to judge me. Rightfully so, I supposed. She did look effortlessly magnificent, draped in my shirt, eyes struck with sleep. Her black brows were high on her forehead as she took in the sight of my raven.

"We'll continue this conversation in a moment, Morpheus."

My familiar cawed once before he launched himself off my shoulder to go take his rightful spot on his perch above the fireplace.

Her eyes followed him incredulously.

I offered her a sly smile. "Sleep well?"

She glared at me and crossed her arms over her chest. "Actually, yes, I did. Turns out, wicked shadowlings have the comfiest beds. I had the most vivid dreams too. But alas, my time as a stowaway on this ship of misery is over. Your shadows can take me home now."

She walked over to me, never taking her eyes off me. Not until she reached the window, and then the view of the city stole her attention from me. I couldn't take my eyes off her. Right now, she looked, dare I say, half normal. Like a human girl, groggy from sleep in an oversized t-shirt. Nothing like the warrior goddess I'd found crouched in a pool of dragon's blood, clutching a golden egg.

She was a wonder of this world.

"Solaris," she said, her voice husky and low, "I have to ask you something."

I would tear down the sky if she desired it. "Yes?"

"Did you know?" Her black eyes met mine. "Did you know about the dragon? I mean, not just that she was there, but what they'd done to her?"

I swallowed, mesmerized by the depth of emotion on her face. "No. I'd only seen it there, vaguely, in the dark. I knew it—she, I mean—I knew she was down there, guarding the door. I did not know the condition she was in."

She nodded and looked away. "Do you know who is responsible?"

A pause gave room for the tension between us to densify. "Some things, even I do not know."

"But what about the Scribes? You said..." She trailed off, her eyes wide and hopeful and slightly murderous.

"They are record keepers, and while they do act as guardians of the Vatican, they have no control over what happens in the crypt."

"So, who—?"

The elevator dinged, startling us both.

Venus St. Claire strode into the suite, wearing a long red trench coat, her fiery hair cascading behind her like a flag in the wind. She stopped dead when she saw the two of us standing here together.

It only took her a moment to collect herself. "Well, well, well," she chimed, though her tone was inauthentic, and I could see the jealousy lighting behind her eyes like a firecracker. "What, pray tell, is going on here?" Her gaze snagged on Nyx Morningstar's bare legs under my shirt. Her rumpled hair and makeup-free face.

Venus and Nyx were women of twin natures, both incredibly formidable and dead set on being on top, so naturally, they couldn't stand each other. Nobody likes a mirror that reflects too honestly.

"I was just leaving." My Firefly in the dark looked at me while she spoke, a grin playing at the edges of her full lips. She had a devilish glimmer in her eye, one that shone like trouble. She turned on a heel and strutted back to the spare room, opening the door wide to reveal the messily slept in bed. She grabbed her dagger and then came to stand by me once more. She reached out and touched my arm. *Touched my arm.* Affectionately. Clearly just to mess with Venus, but still, my veins came alive with electricity, unlike anything I'd ever felt. "Thanks for everything, Solaris," she purred, and I felt her voice in my goddamn stomach.

She strutted to the elevator in nothing but my shirt, her feet still bare. She grinned deviously as the doors slid closed.

Venus glared at me. "You're sleeping with Nyx Morningstar?"

"No."

She cocked an orange brow. "You can tell me. It's okay, I'm not a jealous girl."

"That's a lie," I said, smoothly. Then I locked eyes with her intensely, instantly gripping her with my Compulsion. *"I have a job for you,"* I told her.

Her eyes were blank, her spine straight as she listened to me.

"You are going to throw a party and you will not be inviting Nyx Morningstar."

CHAPTER 43
FIRE, ICE, & EVERYTHING NICE

EMILIA

"This is going to be legendary, honestly," Faye chimed, a mischievous grin tugging at her shimmery pink lips. Rays of sunlight spilled through the long, stained-glass windows of the Athena Library, drenching her in gold. The old leather book open on her lap was written in a language the rest of us couldn't understand, but she could read it just fine. "We'll need copper wire and some silver. Natalia, you'll have to make an elixir of mugwort, witches cauldron, blue lotus, and lavender, but other than that, it seems straightforward."

Natalia had a contemplative expression. I could tell she was chomping at the bit because she couldn't read the Grimoire of Dreams. It was written in a forgotten, elemental language from the Old World. Faye's family descended from the fae, hence her namesake, so she'd grown up learning this outdated tongue.

We sat in an aisle of books, hidden deep in the library. We'd been here all day. Tonight was the night.

Michael sat next to me, his back leaned against the bookshelf. He fidgeted with the rip in his jeans. He'd been lightyears away for the past three days.

Destiny paced, restless. She was nervous about tonight.

I didn't know how to feel.

"We'll need an anchor," Faye went on. "AKA someone who stays on the outside, keeping watch, making sure we can be pulled from the Dream Realm if something goes wrong."

"Someone who stays out?" Destiny perked up. "I'll do it."

Faye smirked. "I figured."

"Well, I don't think four of us need to be going in anyways." Natalia voiced. "I think two of us should stay out and be anchors. Destiny and Emilia."

My spine stiffened. "No. I'm coming in."

Natalia sighed, reading my face, and deciding not to argue. "Four of us cramming into Michael's dream might be a bit much. From what I've read, from the books I could read, it's easy to get distracted in the Dream Realm, even when lucid. Your own subconscious fears and desires can lure you off. If there are four of us, that's four times more outside influence. I think there should only be two or three of us going in."

"Well, I get to go in," Faye insisted. "I'm the one who's actually read the Grimoire of Dreams." She patted the old leather book.

Natalia looked at Michael expectantly. "Who do you think should go in?"

He flinched under the sudden 'all eyes on him' situation. He chewed his lip ring for a moment, scanning each of our faces. Finally, he shrugged. "Why not four? Four seems good. Four elements. Four seasons. Four dreamwalkers."

I smiled.

"Technically there are five elements, but okay," Natalia grumbled, though her protesting stopped there. Her dark eyes fixed on me. "Have you heard from your sister?"

A bitter laugh tumbled through my lips before I could stop it. "No."

Three days. Three days she'd been gone, without so much as a word. She'd left her blackmirror here and judging by all the messages on her front screen from Jedidiah, she wasn't with him. Leaving only one viable option. She was with Solaris Adder.

I should have been more alarmed, right? Worried? But I wasn't. For reasons unknown to me, I wasn't concerned. Mostly just annoyed.

"I can't See where she is. So obviously she's with him." Natalia murmured. "But I do know she is okay. I keep getting distorted images of the High Council, though. They're going to do something today—maybe even come here? I can't See why..."

"If the Council is coming, should we wait to do this?" Faye wondered, picking absently at the corner of the page her grimoire was open to.

Natalia bit her lip, considering. "Well, tonight is the first quarter moon. Half light, half dark. This is the ideal moon phase for Dreamwalking."

Heels click-clacking on the floor stole our attention. My heart fluttered. I knew those fast, furious stomps.

Low and behold, she-who-must-not-be-named rounded the corner and stopped short when she saw us. My sister wore a simple pale dress, adorned with silver jewels. The dramatic, heeled combat boots on her feet should have clashed with it but somehow, they worked because Nyx Morningstar could pull off anything. Her hair was piled on her head in a messy top knot, her face free of makeup. She had a couple of books clutched to her chest. The one I could see was about dragons.

"What in the seven realms are you guys doing?" she demanded.

"Where in the *seven hells* have you been?" Natalia shot back, rising to her feet.

Something was different about my sister. I couldn't quite pinpoint it, but I did pick up on it right away. She seemed...harder, somehow. "Solaris kidnapped me," Nyx answered vaguely. "Good to see you've all been worried sick."

"We know you can hold your own," Natalia said.

Nyx snorted. "Yeah? Well, don't let me interrupt whatever it is you guys are cooking up. Looks important." Her black eyes settled on me bitterly before she whirled on a chunky heel and made to leave.

Natalia shot a burst of earth magic at my sister, a vine manifesting out of thin air to wrap around the books she held, snatching them away from her and gifting them to Natalia's waiting hands.

"Hey!" Nyx shouted indignantly.

Natalia studied the covers of the aged books and skimmed through the pages. "Reading about the dragons of old, are you?" The Seer seemed surprised over this. "Finally taking some interest in your lineage, or what?"

"Should I interrogate you on what you are doing, dearest Natalia?" Nyx's eyes were cold as she glared at her friend. "Give me back the books."

Natalia sighed and handed them over. "Are you okay, Nyx?"

"I'm fine," my sister snapped.

"Shouldn't you be training for the Clash of Spirits?" her friend pushed.

Nyx's expression darkened, and the scent of conflict permeated the air.

A bluster of frantic footfalls saved her from having to answer that question. Her minions appeared, all three of them. It unsettled me each time I saw them. My sister's little bleach-blonde doppelgangers freaked me out.

"There you are," one of them said. "What do you want us to do about the saints and sinners situation?"

Nyx stared at them blankly while they gave her their big-eyed looks.

"What are you talking about?"

"Venus and Solaris's saints and sinners party!! They just announced it but it's already all the rage." The minions glanced at each of us suggestively while one of them held up her blackmirror to show us the poster for the party.

"When is it?" Nyx ground out, her jaw clenched, eyes hard.

"I-it's tonight. In the Sphere. Also, it's super exclusive, invite only, and, uh...y-you're kind of not invited."

"For the love of the Goddess, Minion Two! What did I tell you about stammering like an idiot? I can't stand it when you do that! I don't want to hear another *word* of this party. For you to think that *this* was important enough to come to interrupt me when I told you I needed to spend the day alone studying!" My sister stomped her boot on the floor and conjured a line of fire toward her minions. The girls squealed and thrust themselves backward, away from my sister's wrath. "Get out of my sight!"

With bugged eyes, they ran, white fire chasing after them.

Once they were gone, my sister banished her flames. But the fact that she'd just conjured fire in the middle of a *library* was outrageous.

"What the hell is your problem, Nyx!" Natalia cried.

Nyx shot daggers from her eyes at no one in particular, not speaking a single word before she turned and left us high and dry.

We dispersed after that, the mood spoiled.

DESTINY AND I HAD SPENT THE REST OF THE DAY challenging each other in the Sphere.

By the end, we'd had quite the audience.

We were a dazzling clash of ice and fire. The music of hissing steam filled the luminous Sphere around as we tangoed, taunting each other. Destiny shot fireballs at me, and I'd blocked them with shields of twinkling ice. I sent torrents of ice-laced snow her way, and she had dismantled my efforts with hearty streams of orange flames. It was an even fight. We kept falling into fits of laughter every time our elements canceled each other out to make dramatic steam. Girls hooted and hollered, cheering us on, filming us for the rest of the Society to see later on social media.

Priestesses Bridget and Adria had watched from the sidelines, their faces etched into prideful grins as they spoke amongst each other.

Then we'd been kicked out early because Venus needed to set up for her party.

After that, I was freaking starving, so we went back to our room and showered and changed for dinner.

Destiny finished getting ready first. She flopped onto her bed while I stood in the mirror, fixing my hair.

She picked up her blackmirror and checked Magigram and Celestial Tea, and sure enough, there we were. Videos of our little session in the Sphere had already gone viral.

"The new generation of ice and fire has reminded us why these are the superior elements," Destiny read the blast from Celestial Tea aloud for me. "It has been centuries since two Celestials of these opposing

375

powers have managed to tango so playfully. The tension between water and fire is often lethal, but these younglings make light of the ancient conflict and turn a battle of elements into a dance of fondness and trust. Is this a match made in heaven? Fire, ice, and everything nice? Or are these two destined to fall prey to old instincts? We're all dying to find out!"

My hand flew to my heart as I turned away from my own reflection. "Does it really say that?"

Destiny's lips twitched into a grin. "Yup. We're just casually making history n' shit. And we look damn good doing it if I do say so myself."

I laughed warmly. "I didn't even realize all of that. Our magic doesn't feel...it doesn't feel like conflict. It feels like..."

"Like it wants to be together?"

I swallowed, emotion rising up my neck in the form of heat. "Yeah. Like that..."

Destiny smirked and tossed her blackmirror aside. "You nervous to project yourself into your boyfriend's subconscious tonight?"

I started at her words, steeling myself a beat too late. "He's not my boyfriend."

She snorted. "Does he know that? I swear that boy looks at you like you carry the sun and moon on your shoulders."

My heart pounded achingly. I couldn't think of a reply.

She rose to her feet, her long charcoal dress with the fanned-out skirt rustling at her knees. The bodice was fitted tight around her bust and waist, showing off her figure. A plethora of silver chains and gemstone pendants hung from her throat. Her makeup was dark and smoky, with bright graphic eyeliner making her whole face a bold statement. Silver tattoos whirled on her arms and the side of her neck, crawling up through her buzz cut. She looked epic.

I looked down at my own pale blue dress, the bare skin of my arms. It was clear I wasn't adapting to my Celestial nature as quickly as her. I sighed, dismissing the thought.

Two quick knocks informed us of someone's arrival, but they didn't bother to wait for an answer. Faye helped herself inside our room, dressed in all white with two feathered angel wings strapped to her back.

"So, uh..." She grinned mischievously. "Change in plans, girls. We're going to that saints and sinners party."

"What!" I yelped. "Why?"

"Because. Natalia thinks her visions of the High Council she had earlier have something to do with the party. She says we should be there."

Destiny was all too willing to drop everything to crash the party, so I swallowed my protests, trying to ignore the nagging sensation inside me telling me things were about to go horribly wrong.

CHAPTER 44
SAINTS & SINNERS
NYX

A party. Really?

After everything we just went through, he was throwing a party with Venus St. Claire. At *my* fucking school, no less! In *my* Elemental Sphere!

And *I* was not invited!

What in the seven hells was his problem!

As if I wasn't going to go.

Oh, I'd be there alright. Even though it was complete bullshit. I *begged* the Luminary last year to let me throw a party in the Sphere for Summer Solstice and she had said no. She'd said the Sphere was a sacred space that was only to be used for training and magic. Apparently, those rules didn't apply for Hollywood starlets and psychotic shadow terrorists.

Something about the whole thing was off. It almost felt like bait but —screw it, I was taking it. What was he trying to pull here? Solaris did not strike me as the party throwing type.

Would my gut instinct keep me from going? Absolutely not.

Sure, the smart, responsible thing to do would have been to stay in my room or in the library, studying shadow magic, preparing to beat him at the Clash of Spirits, but it could wait just one night, though, right?

Probably not, but I found myself texting my minions, telling them we were going to that damned party. I also ordered them to stop by Faye's room and grab me a pair of wings to borrow.

Now, I'd never been one to choose shock value over substance, but tonight, I wanted to do the unexpected. Since crashing the hot party I wasn't invited to probably wouldn't shock anyone, I decided to dress as an angel while I did it. No one would expect Nyx Morningstar to choose saint over sinner. I found a thin, white nightdress at the back of my closet. It barely covered my ass, and was a blink away from being see-through, meaning it was perfect. I slipped it over my matching pink bra and panties, and then slid some pale stockings up my thighs.

I didn't have any white shoes. I didn't let that stop me. I glamoured my favorite pair of heeled combat boots to be white. I left my hair loose, falling over my back and shoulders in waves of voluminous silver.

As a final touch, I cast a flaming gold halo over my head.

I grinned wickedly at my reflection in the mirror. It may have been a total lie, but I looked hella good as a saint.

Where in the seven realms was Natalia? I checked the time on my black-mirror. It was well past dinner now. Was she spending another evening with my sister's mortal boy? For some reason, that irked me. Emilia needed to step up and lay claim. It was beyond obvious she was in love with him.

My minions arrived at the perfect time, flooding into the room, gushing with compliments. Minion One brought me a pair of white feathered wings, sliding the straps over my shoulders for me.

Perfect.

Last but not least, I decided to strap the flaming dagger to my thigh. If the Archangels wielded flaming swords, so would I.

"Wow, Nyx," Minion Two breathed. "You look incredible!"

My minions were dressed as sinners, and that was okay with me. Nothing like an angel leading a pack of devils into the belly of the beast.

Perhaps I'd been a tiny bit harsh to them in the library earlier. I'd nearly reduced them to ash. Oops. In retrospect, though, it was a wise move. I'd been without my magic for so long, and they were starting to get suspicious. They were now reminded of the power I held and the danger I could inflict.

We spent the next hour pre-drinking in my room because I needed to douse this weird anxiety and arrive fashionably late. I hardly ever hung out with my minions like this, but it was a necessary distraction tonight. My brain was a fucking mess. One intrusive thought after the other. I kept replaying what had happened in the crypt. Over and over. From being bathed in dragon fire, to slaying that dragon, to the way Solaris had looked when he found me. All of it, it haunted me.

But it didn't feel real. It was more like I'd awoken from a crazy dream.

My mind wouldn't stop reeling. So I drank about it. Even pulled out the forbidden bottle of fae-bubbly I had hidden under my bed. This shit was like ecstasy. The last time I drank enchanted liquor, things didn't turn out so well. But how could things get any worse?

Fuck it. Just for tonight, I wanted to forget all the heavy stuff.

My minions squealed as I popped the cork and flicked my wrist, so the music turned up.

The pink, fizzy liquid burned its way down my throat, warming my insides immediately.

I HATED TO ADMIT IT, BUT THE SPHERE WAS INSPIRED.

Venus St. Claire had gone all out with this party, her Hollywood nature coming through. The interior of the Sphere took on the appearance of a ballroom rather than our magical training gym. My lips popped open as I took it all in. The dome overhead had been glamoured to appear as the night sky in its most cosmic glory. An entire galaxy of stars splayed out above us with pink and purple hues bleeding through the velvet darkness. It took my breath away.

At ground level, the devil was in the details, with all the red and black decorations in between the heavenly whites and golds. Everyone here had gone all out, each costume unique and eye-catching. A sea of horns and halos. There were more sinners than saints, so I appreciated my look that much more.

That fae-bubbly had me feeling *good*.

"Um, excuse me!" a shrill voice harassed my ear to the left. "You weren't invited, Morningstar."

Bianca stood with her arms crossed, wearing red lingerie and devil horns, her face assembled in a scowl. Cassiopeia Black came up from behind her and eyed me the way a cat might eye the mouse it's about to pounce on.

"What in the seven hells are you doing here?" she hissed. She was dressed scantily in black and red, giving me the stink eye from hell. She was a cutie, though. I'd always thought so, despite her vehement hatred of me. Perhaps it made her even cuter. She crossed her arms over her chest, waiting for my response.

"Hey, Cassi," I said sweetly.

"You weren't invited, Morningstar."

"Oh, please." I waved her off. "The best parties are the ones you crash. Now run along before I turn your polyester knickers into ash."

My minions giggled.

Cassi glared at me but didn't bite back.

"No. Venus strictly said you are not allowed here! Leave before things get ugly." Bianca stepped closer to me as if anything about her presence was threatening to me.

I blinked at her. Then laughed. Howled, really. "You're not serious?"

She held her hands out, summoning cyclones of wind over her palms. Her blonde hair whipped around, her eyes hard.

People were watching our little interaction. Giving me the perfect opportunity to tip the scales back in my favor. When Solaris stole my magic and rendered me powerless, I'd been seen as weak in public too many times. Like the time Venus confronted me in the common room in front of all the firelings and I did nothing to fight back. Girls had filmed that and posted it on Celestial media, tarnishing my name and reputation.

Now people were watching Bianca challenge me, and fuck if I wasn't going to put her on her ass.

All I had to do was glare at her and curl my fingers inward and the tiny amount of clothing she had on her body burst into flame.

Her squeals overpowered the music. She jumped around desperately trying to pat the fire out. As expected, Cassi came to her rescue, throwing out her hands and shooting water over her flaming friend. I cackled as the fire was doused, leaving Bianca as an ash-stained, smoking mess, some of her lovely blonde hair burnt off.

Bianca screamed with fury, hurling a gust of wind at me, which I easily shielded and returned to sender. Her own magic had her flying backward. The girl was a crispy-fried drowned rat on the ground, and I hadn't even lifted a finger.

I smirked, a bitch queen triumphant.

My eyes flicked to Cassi, wondering if she wanted to tango. She glared at me, her chest rising and falling before she turned sharply and went after Bianca.

"Hm," I muttered. "Too bad. I love sparring with Cassi."

I strutted into the party, tickled pink with my grand entrance.

People whispered, stared, and snapped pictures of me. No one spoke to me.

My eyes swept the room, in search of one face. I scanned the dance floor and the walls. My heart sped up as I thought of him, but before I finished scathing the place, I knew he wasn't here. Jedidiah was giant enough to stand out without having to look too hard for him. My shoulders slumped with disappointment when I concluded he definitely wasn't here. Instinctively, I checked my blackmirror, but he hadn't texted me back. Not fucking once.

What was his problem? During my little episode with Solaris and the Vatican, when I hadn't had my blackmirror, he'd texted me a hundred times. As soon as I returned and messaged him back, he ghosted me.

Mind games had never been a thing before with us. But I guess now that we'd added sex to the mix, things were different.

Whatever. I banished him from my mind.

"Venus is going to freak when she sees you," Minion One squealed.

I smirked. "Can't wait." I plucked a champagne flute off the tray of a passing waiter and assessed the faces of everyone here. The dance floor was packed with Veneficus and Luna's finest. Perfect.

"I don't see Solaris or Venus," I muttered, trying not to show too much interest, although their absence was tangible.

"They haven't come out yet," Minion Two said.

I made a sound of annoyance and sipped my champagne.

"Maverick Madriu is looking at you!" Minion Three informed me.

I couldn't fight off the eye roll if I tried. I didn't have the energy to fake interest in his basketball affairs. "Come on," I demanded, crossing through the party with my minions on my heels.

"*Of course* you came," Natalia's voice tittered in my ear. She rolled up on me with Faye, Destiny, and Emilia on her heels, all of them dressed as sinners, except Faye, who looked saintly in white, of course.

"Why wouldn't I?" I rallied back, quirking a brow.

"There you are!" Emilia said. My sister's gaze raked me up and down in disbelief. "I can't believe you came as a saint!"

I offered her a smirk and struck a pose. "That's the point."

"You look amazing!" Destiny cried, her eyes wide as she admired my halo of fire. "Honestly, white is your color! Your eyes POP!"

Her sincere enthusiasm made my cheeks warm. "Er, thanks. I didn't really expect to see you guys here."

I found myself unable to stop my eyes from roving up and down my little sister. She wore a tight black crop top, a leather mini-skirt with fishnets and boots. A pair of red horns made of quartz sat atop her hair. Clearly, someone else did her makeup. Smoky black. She looked...She looked like me.

I didn't say anything, but still, she blushed and looked away.

My heart burned for some reason. The fae-bubbly must have been messing with me. I had the urge to reach out and hug Emilia. I wanted to cover her up and take her out of here and tuck her into bed where I knew she would be safe.

"Are those *my* angel wings?" Faye wondered, her brows narrowed.

"I borrowed them," I replied sweetly, moving in on her. I wrapped my arm around her neck and kissed her on the cheek. "You don't mind, do you, beautiful?"

"Oh, Goddess," Natalia muttered, rolling her eyes. "What have you gotten into tonight?"

I grinned maniacally. "I maaaay have had a couple flutes of fae-bubbly. Want some?"

My roommate's shoulders slumped in relief. "Well, fae-bubbly is better than witches vodka."

"Nyx." Emilia's voice was laced with a seriousness I had no interest in. "What happened with Solaris? Where were you? Are you okay?"

A sinking feeling swamped my stomach, threatening to kill my buzz. "Do I look like I'm not okay?"

Her lips popped open. "No. You look beautiful. I just meant—"

An audible crash stole our attention, a storm of shadows erupting in the center of the Sphere, right in the middle of the crowd. Solaris emerged with Venus St. Claire at his side.

Everyone noticed them at the same time, and I practically heard all the hearts fall. They were devastating, both dressed as sinners. No ordinary sinners, either. The two Celestials made their debut as the King and Queen of the Underworld itself.

Venus wore scarlet lingerie underneath a long lace robe with crimson fur trim that trailed behind her. Her hair was blown out and wild, and two thick red horns ascended from the top, with a crown placed in the middle.

Solaris...Solaris was hard to look at.

He didn't wear any red. He stayed true to his all-black attire, rocking a new jacket I'd never seen him in before. It stayed open, not buttoned up like his other one, long enough to flood the glossy floor behind him. Underneath he wore a sea of black fabric, silver chains glistening around his throat. He too had horns, though his were long, slender, and curved, like that of a gazelle. His silver eyes were shadowed as if he'd applied charcoal under his bottom lashes.

There went my heart, crashing and burning something fierce in my chest.

His eyes met mine at the same moment. Instinctively, as if he sensed me here, which I knew he did.

Suddenly I felt stone cold sober.

"Oh my Goddess," one of my stupid minions breathed. "They look...."

"Shut up," I snapped, stalking away to find a waiter who had something stronger than champagne.

The party tolled on, and Venus St. Claire didn't even get upset that I was here. Not even one dirty look was sent my way. I thought she would single me out as she always did, giving me an opening to spar with her and Solaris. No such thing happened, which made me realize how pathetic I was. After everything, I was really here, *hoping* for drama?

This night turned out to be way lamer than I'd imagined. Venus giving me no reaction made me feel stupid. She clung to Solaris's arm as they buzzed about, socializing, and being admired by everyone who'd quickly forgotten about me.

"Why don't you dance with Maverick?" Minion Three suggested. "Last time, you guys—"

"I don't want *Maverick*," I hissed, checking my blackmirror again. Still nothing from Jedidiah. I'd sent him a picture of me in my angel costume, looking all innocent yet sexy, and he still didn't bother to say anything back. Asshole.

"Wow, that is a hot picture. Now I wish I didn't throw my blackmirror off the mountain." The deep, masculine voice purred in my ear from behind, turning my stomach to knots right away.

I gasped a little, turning to find Jedidiah standing behind me, so close our chests touched. He wore a long dark jacket with the hood up, hiding most of his beautiful face.

"Jed," I breathed, my body lighting up with a sense of relief that felt unnatural for me. My heart rocketed as I threw my arms around him and let myself sink. The fae-bubbly had me acting all sorts of strange ways, but I didn't care. Apparently, neither did he. He pulled me into his huge, infernal body, holding me up.

"I've missed you," he whispered in my ear. The music blasted, but my senses were hyper focused on him. "Where the fuck have you been?"

"It's a long story," I said into his chest. Goddess, he smelt heavenly.

I tilted my head up to look at him. The party continued around us, but I saw nothing but him. The dazzling, scantily dressed bodies dancing around us turned to a backdrop of glitz and glamour.

"A halo. Really?" His voice was light, playful.

His pupils reflected the ring of fire over my head. "Yeah. Just trying something new. What are you? A sinner or saint? I can't tell."

"Neither, baby. I'm just a ghost."

My brows jumped.

"Er, can you please tell your clones to leave? They creep me out."

"Leave us!" I hissed to my minions, and they scattered like startled bunnies.

He chuckled, the sound warming my chest like a shot of vodka.

"This party is pretentious as hell." We pulled apart, only slightly. He held me at arm's length, assessing me. "But you look... Well, you look stunning, Nyx. You always do."

I beamed. Then registered what he said before. "Wait, did you say you threw your blackmirror off the mountain?"

He scoffed. "Yeah. You ghosted me. I got a little pissed off."

"A little?" I quipped, raising a brow.

He shrugged, feigning innocence. "I may have raged. Are you okay? Where were you?"

"If you threw away your blackmirror, how did you hear about the party?"

He rolled his eyes. "Do you always have to answer a question with another question? I came back into the city today. Heard about it through the grapevine. I only came to check if you were here. Which you are. And you look like you're in one piece, but something's different about you." His stormy eyes narrowed, becoming quizzical. He brushed his thumb over my lip, searching between my eyes as if he'd find answers written within them. "What happened, Nyx?"

"Well..." I swallowed. "Solaris, he—"

"Speak of the devil and he doth appear."

My heart plummeted, goosebumps igniting over my exposed flesh at the sound of that smooth, tantalizing voice.

Jed's arms around me locked, pulling me tighter as he instinctively stepped in front of me. Solaris grinned, standing there with his hands folded behind his back.

"Easy," Solaris mused, his tone casual. "I only came to see how you are enjoying the party. So glad you could make it, Groundshaker."

"Right." Jed's voice was hard.

He pulled his long staff out from the inside of his floor-length jacket. Slammed the bottom of it to the ground and summoned an earth shake that had the party squealing and gasping.

The warning hung in the air like smoke after fireworks.

Solaris raised his hands in mock surrender. "Relax, I'm not here to mess with our girl. Though, I would like to ask her to dance." His metallic eyes flicked to me, and I felt them on my skin, like he was touching me.

Our girl.

He held out one of his silver-ringed hands, waiting for me to take it.

Jed grunted, staying planted like a tree in front of me, keeping me from him. "You touch her and I'll crack open the earth and send you down to the Ninth Circle of Hell."

My stomach knotted, heat sizzling in my abdomen. Goddess, why was that so hot?

Solaris beamed. "Oh, how wonderful. Your death threats are almost as exciting as hers."

My heart thundered. I should not have been enjoying this.

But when Solaris nodded downward, my breath caught, all delusions of pleasure going up in smoke. Shadows rose around Jedidiah's feet, hissing as they formed into snake-like creatures that threatened to devour him.

"I'm not scared of your stupid little shadows," Jed growled, unfazed. "You want to fight? We'll fucking fight—"

"Jed," I cut him off. Solaris's eyes brightened, his grin widening.

"No, Nyx," Jed snapped, his focus still on the Darkbringer. He took a threatening step forward, getting up in Solaris's face. Dozens of eyes were on us now. "Why don't you stop with the parlor tricks and fight me like a man? You look pretty scrawny under all those drapes you wear. You want to threaten me, man? Let's do this. No magic, no gimmicks—just brute strength. What would you be then if you couldn't hide behind your shadows?"

People got their blackmirrors out, waiting for chaos.

Solaris appeared absolutely *enthralled*. He rubbed his palms together, his silver rings gleaming as he stared deep into Jed's stormy eyes. "Why would we fight like men, when we can fight like gods?"

My heart tripped over itself.

I could tell by the seething look on his face, Jed was not going to let this go. "Stop," I begged, grabbing his arm.

Jedidiah was powerful. Probably the most powerful starseed in the Celestial Society, next to me. But I knew the true length Solaris's power could go. I wasn't going to lose him to some pissing contest at a fucking saints and sinners party.

Jed turned to me slowly, his eyes full fire and fury. "Why?"

"It's fine," I murmured, hating that I had to do this. "I'll dance with him. I'll come find you after, okay?"

If looks could kill, I'd be dead. Blue eyes burned at me, betrayal bleeding over his features. "The last few days... You were with him, yeah?"

I swallowed. "Jed, I—"

He turned without another word, stalking across the glossy floor. People parted for him, murmuring as he past. I watched him go with a stone in my throat and an ache in my heart.

I should have gone after him.

I didn't.

Solaris moved in on me, his expression pure arrogance. I scowled up at him as he slid one arm around my waist, the other taking my hand as he led me into a dance I didn't know. When had the music turned into a slow song? I hadn't even noticed.

"You're an asshole, you know that? What the fuck is all this about, anyway?" I demanded, looking around suggestively at the party.

He offered me one of his famous psychopathic grins. The smug prick. "You look ravishing, Firefly."

"Well, you look terrifying," I spilled, my attention caught on his horns while the words slipped out before I even knew what I was saying. It made him smile.

The light of my halo illuminated his face, the glow accenting the sharpness of his bone structure. He cocked a brow at the halo curiously, though he said nothing of it.

My heart thundered erratically, the party around us fading into nothing. His hand held mine, the other on my waist, sending traitorous shocks through my body. I should have been reefing myself out of his grasp, yet I made no move to leave him. His metallic, unplaceable scent disarmed me. Like he just stepped out of a realm made of all silver and citrus trees. The magnetic pull of his shadows sang to my fire, and at that moment, I couldn't imagine anywhere I'd rather be. Which was a horrifying revelation I'd take with me to the grave.

"Venus wants me to ask you to leave," he mused, paying close attention to my face as he spoke.

A smile tore across my lips at that. "She does!"

"This pleases you?"

"It does, very much," I quipped. So she'd been playing a poker face earlier. My presence here *was* getting under her skin. Wonderful!

"You're a wicked little thing, Firefly."

I pursed my lips. "So, are you asking me to leave?"

"I would never be opposed to your presence."

"I'm sure your girlfriend doesn't appreciate that."

Either it was just me, or the party had gone quiet. Vaguely, I was aware that all eyes were on us. I could feel the scorch of Venus's envy and the judgment wafting off my friends.

He laughed. A snappy yet musical sound. "Regardless of my personal delights, what in the *seven hells* are you doing here?" Suddenly his grip on me tightened, hard enough to send shocks of pain up my arm, making me gasp. With just a thought, he made the halo above my hair burn out and disappear. His lips touched my ear, a tumble of chills rushing across my skin upon contact. "After everything, you still can't resist your scheming and social climbing. I knew throwing a party with your rival and not inviting you would draw out your most despicable, outdated nature. Perhaps you'll never change, Firefly."

What the...? I went to pull away from him, but his iron grasp only pulled me closer, in a threatening way. Our bodies pressed together, my face against his chest. My heart thrashed but I refused to show fear or discomfort.

"What are you doing?" I breathed.

"What are *you* doing?" He tightened his grip, making me whimper. He leaned down, his nose grazing my throat as he planted a single, aggressive kiss over my thundering pulse. A damp, sinking heat flooded my being, weighing me down. I was wanton and limber, my skin tingling with fear and desire. "You reek of enchanted liquor. You should be past this."

Solaris had exploded through my life, leaving nothing but chaos and destruction in his wake. He interrupted me at every turn and ripped the rug from under my feet every chance he got. He made me powerless and small. Before him, I'd always been the hunter, never the prey.

Everything he'd done had seemed so unforgivable and out of line before.

Until he whisked me halfway across the world and brought me to a dragon. Until he proved the glory of my bloodline was not lost.

Until he proved that his presence in my life held purpose. Real, paradigm-shattering purpose.

No Solaris? I would have never found Niaxus.

The truth had me sinking.

He was starting to feel like my own shadow made manifest. Like a dark mirror, reflecting my own truth back at me.

Like right now. He was *right*.

What *was* I doing here? A horrible heat crept up the back of my neck, a lump so big forming in the back of my throat, it choked me.

Just days ago, I had faced off with a *dragon*. She told me I was part of something bigger. She gave me her last words and her most precious possession.

I'd been reeling about it nonstop, hardly able to grasp the profundity of it all.

Deep down, I... I felt like I wasn't worthy.

Here I was, proving myself right. Letting Niaxus's trust in me be in vain.

I let go of his hand and shoved out of his grasp. He let me go, and watched me curiously.

I felt beyond ridiculous. Standing here in my skimpy little night dress and stockings, trying to cause trouble and mess with Venus St. Claire. My cheeks heated as my own absurdity made itself known. I wished the floor would open and swallow me whole.

The world around me felt like it was going by in slow motion. I glanced from side to side, to all the people watching me. I realized something in that moment.

These people had never worshipped me. They'd probably never even feared me. They just...didn't like me.

And why would they?

"Enjoy your party," I rasped to Solaris, my eyes burning.

I turned to leave. My heart pounded in my throat as I kept my eyes down, refusing to look at anyone as I began my walk of shame.

I am such a fool. My mother was right about me.

I was halfway to the exit when the music cut off abruptly.

"Nyx Morningstar," a deep, authoritative voice boomed. I snapped my attention up toward the voice, my stomach plummeting when I found three High Council members standing in the entrance of the Sphere. Their golden masks glimmered in the low light, all three of them moving toward me.

The party went dead silent.

"You are under arrest for glamoured impersonation of your Luminary, the theft of the Sacred Baton, and the usage of black magic."

"No!" someone—Emilia—cried.

Panic raged through my veins, and the ground under my feet began to tremble violently, mimicking my bones. Indistinct chatter and exclamations harassed my ears. I stumbled backward, my fight-or-flight instincts making me clumsy. But there was nowhere to go.

A set of iron chains clasped around my wrists before my brain could process a single thing. A scream got stuck in my throat as the three cloaked figures closed in on me and I was swallowed by a portal of vicious light.

CHAPTER 45
MORNINGSTAR WRATH

EMILIA

They took her.

In front of the whole party. While everyone just watched. Including me.

I ascended the steps of the Sacred Temple with my heart raging and my head spinning.

"LUMINARY!" I cried, my eyes sweeping the temple and landing on her indefinitely.

Delphyne stood there, still as stone, watching the Eternal Flame while the triple goddess loomed behind her.

I trudged over to her, nearly losing my footing. The girls were at my back, following diligently, though no one had said a single word since we left the Sphere.

"Nyx has been arrested!" I howled, eyes welling with hot, stinging tears. "The High Council—they showed up, they took her! They said she impersonated you! They said she stole the Sacred Baton and practices black magic! Quick, we have to make this right! You must tell them she's innocent!"

When the Luminary made no sign of being startled by this news, my heart stopped beating.

Slowly, her turquoise eyes lifted from the fire to look at me.

Her cool stare was like a gunshot to the chest.

"I'm sorry, Emilia," Delphyne murmured.

"Luminary, what do you mean?" Natalia demanded, stepping forward. "The accusations against Nyx are lies! She didn't steal the Baton and nor did she impersonate you. I know this to be true!"

"Girls," Delphyne looked pained. "This is out of my hands. I know you cannot understand. I know you will deeply resent me for this. But I cannot intervene. This is the Divine Unfolding, and it must go this way."

I stumbled back a little, shaking my head. "You can't just add the word Divine to a situation to justify it!" I hissed, tears spilling over my bottom lashes.

"You have to tell them there's been a mistake!" Faye said. "Surely you have the power to sway the High Council!"

"I have far less power than I care to admit," our Luminary replied. Her bright eyes lined with silver, but her posture remained straight, and her energy absolute.

"So that's it?" Destiny cried. "You won't do anything?"

"There is nothing I can do."

This couldn't be happening.

An immeasurable swell of despair washed over me, dulling my senses, and pulling me deep into the abyss. The light of the Eternal Flame waned, my world going dark.

I sank.

They took her.

The accusations against her were staggering. Impersonation of an Exalted Celestial was a felony. Theft of a goddess-forged object was too. I had no idea what the punishment for using black magic was, but added to the other two accusations, I could only imagine the worst.

And our Luminary wasn't going to do a damn thing about it.

Reality closed in on me, a howling vicious beast that snuffed the warmth from my veins and turned my world into a hostile prison of ice.

"Emilia!" Destiny shouted. I couldn't figure out why she sounded so far away.

"EMILIA, BREATHE!" Natalia's voice was like a sonic boom that woke me from a deep slumber.

My eyes snapped open. I found myself in the eye of a blizzard. The triple goddess statue had three heads but no faces, yet she still managed to watch over me as I turned her Sacred Temple into a deadly winter storm. Ice and snow blustered in cyclones, harassing the Eternal Flame and the other women in here with me.

"That Morningstar wrath," I heard the Luminary say. "*In somnos!*"

The Mother had mercy on me, a warm dark hand landing on my shoulder while a whispered lullaby led me into a deep, dreamless sleep.

CHAPTER 46
MUSIC OF RAVENS
JEDIDIAH

I stood at the edge of the terrace, staring off into the expanse of snowy forest splayed out below, remembering the sensation of freefall as I launched myself over the edge to save Nyx.

The air up here was freezing, but I'd adapted. I hauled on a cigarette and watched the ravens fly in and out of their treetops, chattering with each other while stars blinked down at me.

I would probably never return to LA now. Fuck that city, and everyone in it. This half-standing cabin in the Rockies was starting to lose its appeal, sure, but I had nowhere else to go yet.

An audible crash sounded from inside. I stiffened, knowing that dreadful sound. A portal. Someone was here.

Sickening desire and anticipation swamped my insides. Despite my better judgment, I hoped with every fiber of my being that it was Nyx. What happened between us was supposed to be a hormonal one-time thing, but I was having serious withdrawals and I didn't know how long I'd make it without another hit of her.

In my gut, though, I knew it wouldn't be her. I'd walked away from her tonight. Left her there with *him*. She wasn't one to chase.

As expected, those weren't the heavy footfalls of Nyx Morningstar strolling casually toward the terrace. My blood froze in my veins. I instinctively tossed the smoke over the edge and rubbed my palms on my pants. Fuck. He found me.

"You always were a sentimental fool," Aries chided. His enormous frame took up the entire gaping doorway, his horns angled ominously toward me. His staff buzzed at his side, just dying to be used. He looked around, a mocking expression on his face. I hadn't spoken to my father in months. Hadn't seen him in over a year. Ever since my mother left, we'd become like strangers. I was his biggest regret, the son who took his mother's name and had no interest in being his heir.

"So this is where you've been hiding. You did enjoy this place as a child, didn't you? Some of the few times you were ever happy."

I cleared my throat. "Father."

"You remember that time we came up here as a family for the Winter Solstice? Just me, you, and your mother?"

His words caught me off guard. I released an incredulous sound, my cheeks pooling with heat. "I guess. Yeah."

"You were happy then."

"I was five."

"Actually, you were seven. You showed such promise. Your mother and I tried for two centuries to have a baby, you know. We tried everything. Every incantation, potion, or ritual imaginable. Nothing worked. We gave up. And as soon as we gave up, well, that's when the gods gave us you. When you were young, you were my pride and joy. You loved listening to all my stories. You were excited about being my heir—about being the next High Lord. You looked up to me."

"That was before you took me under your wing and showed me the ropes."

"Ah, yes. The truth has always been hard for you."

"No," I retorted, my voice like ice. "I have no problem with the truth. I have a problem with tyrants who abuse their power in every way possible."

He made a sound of disgust. "You're weak, Jedidiah."

"What are you doing here, Father?"

He looked me up and down, slowly. "You left the party early. I take it you haven't heard."

"Heard what?"

He smirked and my guts fell out of my ass. I knew that smirk. That was the smirk of cruelty and death. Who was on the other end of that terrible smile this time?

He pulled out his blackmirror and offered it to me. "See for yourself."

I hesitated. He grunted in a warning.

I released a breath before I reluctantly snatched the device from his massive hand. I tapped the screen awake. My entire body turned to stone as I read the words waiting for me.

LA'S CELESTIAL POST
The Fall of the Society's Favorite Fireling
Nyx Morningstar, Arrested for Theft, Identity Fraud, and Black Magic

The notorious second-year fireling from Luna Academy was caught stealing an ancient, Celestial object that was forged by a goddess of old.

Every third moon cycle, with the blessing of the High Council, Luna Academy allows its students the chance to win possession of the Sacred Baton, an object that carries fathomless power. Earlier this year, Nyx lost claim of the baton fair and square to fellow Luna student, and Hollywood starlet, Venus St. Claire. The fireling proved to be a sore loser, and later glamoured herself to appear as the Luminary before she stole the Sacred Baton from its rightful Keeper. The Baton is currently missing.

Using magic to impersonate an Exalted Celestial is a felony.

The crime trail doesn't stop there. Nyx Morningstar has allegedly been practicing black magic. Countless students at Luna Academy have attested to this. It has been revealed that she Compelled a group of young girls to be her slaves. Sources say she even made them change their appearance to look like her. Her "minions", she called them. The girls have since been released of the dark magic, returning to their original, unique identities.

The fireling was set to compete in the Clash of Spirits, but thanks to Divine intervention, the Society will dodge this bullet.

May this be a lesson and warning to everyone. Be careful who you trust.

The accused is now being detained until the trial. If found guilty, she is facing a century of imprisonment. The trial starts tomorrow at sunrise where she will be judged by the High Council.

· *Brit Dawn @ LA's Celestial Post.*

My hand shook.

My heart had never pounded so fast.

Aries gave a deep, unsettling chuckle. "Look at you. What, are you going to cry, boy?"

"This is bullshit," I ground out, unable to process what I just fucking read.

"Is it?" my father taunted.

"You allow Solaris Adder free rein, but you arrest Nyx? You allow the media to spew these fucking lies about her?"

"I think it's the cold hard truth. Your little girlfriend is a disease that must be eradicated quickly. Do you know what's the most interesting part? When we brought her into the Institution and I strip-searched her, you know what I found? Aside from her silky naked flesh, that is?"

My heartbeat crashed in my temples, my vision turning red. He strip-searched her? He saw her? Touched her?

The ground beneath my feet shook.

"Easy," Aries warned.

I didn't even have my staff on me. I tried not to let my confusion show. After a moment, the earth relented.

He reached into his long cloak and pulled out the key to my demise. "I found the flaming dagger."

My heart crashed and burned, dropping out of my body completely.

He took a threatening step forward, pointing the silver blade at me. "I wonder...where oh where could she have gotten this from?"

His steeled expression contorted with rage, his horns sizzling with an electric charge. I opened my mouth but the ability to speak was robbed from me as my father unleashed the insidious power of his staff on me.

He wrapped me in tethers of electricity, shouting at me all the while, though I couldn't make out a single word. The searing, burning, wrong wrong wrong pain became my only reality. I couldn't even scream, couldn't move. Electric shock burned my flesh and my spirit, turning my vision white and scattered.

I ebbed in and out of consciousness...trying my hardest to cling to coherence despite the staggering pain.

When I gained control of my senses, my father stood right in front of me, his eyes dark and vacant.

My stomach swooped.

"Wait—" I managed to say before the electricity condemned my tongue.

"You've always been nothing but a disappointing, embarrassing burden. Just like your mother. You might as well have just left with her when she gave you the choice, boy. I thought perhaps you stayed because you would grow out of this disgusting nature, but I was wrong. And now you have assisted our enemy. I will not have it anymore. I gave you chance after chance to prove yourself. At least you managed to be consistent—consistent in your failures. Goodbye, Jedidiah."

He plunged the dagger into my stomach, an explosion of agony going off inside me as he shoved me over the edge of the mountain. I was too shocked to cry out. All I heard as I fell to my death was the music of ravens.

CHAPTER 47
DRAGON SLAYER
NYX

I began to fucking pity Solaris. That was how low I sunk.

Alone in the endless, unforgiving dark, I imagined his life, and how this was all he'd known. No wonder he was the way he was. I understood. Fuck him, though. He watched them arrest me and did nothing. He'd misfired his wrath. Emerging from his shadow prison and targeting me? Rather than the true enemy? Yeah, fuck him. He may have spent too much time alone in the dark. Me? I'd get out of here somehow, and when I did, every single person responsible would burn.

Time didn't exist in the dungeons. I was sure of it. I was also convinced the people of the Society had no clue this place existed. I never did, not until they brought me here.

The Celestial Society was supposed to be a free society. Ha.

There were others here. Down in the dark, presumably underground, with not even a single candle lit for us. Tunnels and tunnels of cells. Some people moaned in agony, in despair. Others talked to themselves. Some cried. I stayed dead silent, tuning them out with my own blustery thoughts.

I refused to acknowledge the disgusting mattress in my tiny cell. I remained curled up in the corner on the cold, damp, uneven stone floor.

My ass was painfully numb. The heavy, magic-blocking chains on my wrists left bruises and lesions. My arms ached. Powerless, again. Chained, again.

With my knees hugged to my chest, I stared off into nothing, imagining my revenge.

I quaked with fury. And a chill.

I couldn't decide who was first on my kill list. Aries? Solaris?

What about our reigning Luminary?

She led me into this like a lamb to slaughter. She was the one who insisted I challenge Solaris Adder. It was she who suggested I take the Celestial Oath. She took back the Sacred Baton from Venus St. Claire and gave it to me, didn't she? So why did she allow them to arrest me for something I did not do?

She knew. She knew I was bound by a Celestial Oath.

If I was trapped down here and missed the Clash of Spirits—I would be breaking my Oath. That meant death.

I bit back sobs as revelations washed over me like acid rain. This was her plan all along. Not only would I be breaking my Oath, but Solaris would be too. If he didn't face me one on one at the Clash, his word was just as broken as mine.

He would die.

That was her plan. I was a sacrifice. Brilliant, really.

She made me bind my fate to him so my death would ensure his.

There was only one thing I could do for now. I had to make sure I didn't die. He had to come for me. My stomach leaped as silver eyes harassed my mind. He would come for me—he had to. His life depended on it.

ALONE IN THE DARK, I DREAMED. A LOT.

I dreamt a fire sprite visited me in my cell. Her tiny body, made of pure flame, her black eyes and wry smile—it was all so real. Like she was really there, right in front of me. She promised me this was part of the

Divine plan. When I woke up, I swore I could smell smoke, but it was clearly just my mind playing tricks on me.

I also dreamt of Solaris—more than I could ever care to admit. I dreamt of the night he and I got drunk together, with his freaky sister. The memory played over and over in my mind's eye. The way he looked at me, the nervous way he laughed when I told a bad joke or the way he rolled his eyes when his sister and I shared the same taste in music.

All the dreams felt so real. But each time I woke up to find that they were not.

THE SCREECHING OF STONE AGAINST STONE MADE MY SPINE stiffen. Someone entered the tunnels.

Prisoners roared and cried for help and mercy as the faint orange light of a lantern lit up the long pathway. Heavy footfalls echoed off the walls. I held my breath.

A guard appeared in front of my cell. He was faceless, of course. No one involved with the High Council showed their face. But apparently, guards weren't important enough to have golden masks. His face was merely shrouded by a black veil. His long, dark green cloak was wet and brown at the edges from trailing back and forth through the gross tunnels. He held the dim lantern up, saying nothing while his keys jingled, and he inserted one into the magical lock on the barred gate trapping me in here.

"I'm getting out?" I breathed, adrenaline spiking in my blood.

The guard scoffed. "Your trial starts now."

"Trial!" I exclaimed. "Oh, bloody hell. Just tell Aries to slit my throat and be done with it."

"You will address him as High Lord!" the guard snapped, lunging at me. I gasped as his big, hard hand wrapped around my arm and jerked me upright. My body screamed with pain, but I bit my lip to stifle the groan that longed to escape my throat. My entire lower half was numb. I fought to keep my footing as he put a sack over my head and pulled me out of there.

My poor, bare feet were bruised and bloody by the time we reached our destination. The guard removed the sack from my head and shoved me forward.

I took in my surroundings and a bitter laugh tumbled through my lips.

It looked like a scene out of *Eyes Wide Shut*. Dozens of white candles lined the floors and floated in the air, illuminating the black space with cool light. Not a window in sight, telling me we were still underground. Weeping stone walls stood high, yet the space still managed to feel suffocating. I stood in the center of an obsidian floor, enclosed in a protection circle carved into the floor and gilded with gold, shaped like a pentagram. Dozens of cloaked figures in golden-horned masks loomed outside the pentagram in a perfect circle.

Our reigning High Lord, Aries Vanderbilt, was the only one with his face on display. He sat in a chair that was more like a throne, marking the top of the circle like the head of the snake in the Ouroboros symbol. His horns sizzled with sparks as he glared at me, his staff at his side. My skin instantly erupted with derisive shivers at the memory of those eyes raking hungrily over my naked flesh. The bastard had strip-searched me. Took my flaming dagger. Locked me in a dungeon to rot until he was bored and needed something new to play with.

"Wow," I chided, eyes sweeping the ominous room. "Am I being initiated into the Illuminati, or—?"

I barely even saw the lightning bolt before it struck me in the chest, turning my words into a howl of agony as I crashed to my knees. Aries snarled, his staff pointed at me in a warning. "You will speak only when spoken to, Miss Morningstar."

I swallowed the bullet in my throat and refused to cry.

"You stand before your High Council, on trial for the crimes of theft, impersonation, and black magic," Aries said. "We will give you a chance to come clean, and perhaps we can come to an agreement that is mutually beneficial."

Mutually beneficial?

I fought the urge to snort. Of course, he wanted something from me.

I rose back to my feet, my spine stiff as I held his cold eyes. "This hardly looks like a trial." I rasped. "Shouldn't there be witnesses? A jury? Shouldn't I have someone to defend me?"

He boomed an insidious laugh in my face. "We are not mortals. You will be judged by your High Council, and you will be grateful we are even doing this much."

I bit my lip to refrain from lipping off.

"Speak the truth today, Miss Morningstar, and you will be able to return to your life. It won't be as it once was, but it will be better than the alternative."

Death.

"What do you want to know, High Lord?"

"We know of your little trip to the Vatican." Aries deadpanned. My insides turned to ice. That was not what I expected him to say.

"We found out the good old-fashioned way, too," he went on. "Your magical signature was cloaked, however, we did find evidence of your presence in the crypt. We found a single hair of yours. Yes, one of your long silver hairs, lying neatly in a pool of dragon's blood."

My heart was trying to carve a hole out of my chest. Sweat dripped down my back, and my breathing fast. I couldn't believe my ears. Was he actually saying these words or was I having a psychotic breakdown?

"You slayed the dragon of old," Aries remarked, seeming unfazed over the dragon's life. But there was a spark in his eye. A knowing. A curiosity. "I do not believe you did this on your own merit. You come from a long line of ancient dragon riders, after all. I wouldn't expect you to slay one if you found one. I believe the dragon asked you to do it. And I believe it paid you in fathomless riches for your service."

I couldn't speak if I wanted to. Thank Goddess he wasn't asking questions.

My breathing echoed off the stone walls.

"Amongst all the blood, we found something else, something other than your hair. We found a residue... A residue that only comes from one source. A dragonstone."

I would be sick if he kept going down this road.

"A dragonstone, of course, is a dragon egg. A magical, dragon-forged gemstone that when tended to properly, hatches the greatest creature in all of Creation. And now you, Miss Morningstar, are in possession of one, aren't you?"

A low chorus of murmurs rumbled through the circle of cloaked figures.

My tongue was bone dry. My brain couldn't process what was happening. This wasn't about the Sacred Baton—I mean, the Moonbeam—at all.

"AREN'T YOU!" Aries detonated, jerking the tip of his staff in my direction. A threat of pain and torment. One I knew all too well.

"I don't know what you're talking ab—"

A furious blue stream of electric power shot at me, exploding my stomach, and sending me down to my knees once more. I ground my teeth hard enough to shatter them in my skull. I would not scream.

"I will offer you a deal, Miss Morningstar." Aries's voice was low, cold. He rose from his chair and took a step closer to the pentagram that trapped me. "Tell me where you have hidden the dragonstone. Tell me, and I will release you. You can compete in the Clash of Spirits and fulfill your Celestial Oath."

Of course, he knew about that. My eyes instinctively flew around the room, over each cloaked figure, every gilded mask. *Luminary, which one are you?*

He might as well have asked me to stand here and try and squeeze blood out of a stone for him.

I would never tell him where I buried the dragonstone.

That truth seemed to shine in my eyes, reflecting back at me through his.

A staggering fury slithered up my spine like a poisonous snake, filling my mouth with acid. Did Aries have anything to do with what had been done to the dragon? Had it been him who harvested her? Her scales, claws, horns, teeth, her fucking eyes? My heart picked up as these thoughts curdled in my mind. I had to swallow the burning desire to lash at him with my poisonous tongue. Now was not the time. Not here, with chains around my wrists.

"The Darkbringer brought you there," Aries whispered. Clearly, he was fishing. He didn't know for sure, but it only made sense. "What did he take from the Secret Library?"

I stared up at Aries, our High Lord, the massive brute. His curling ram horns gave him such a god complex. He didn't deserve them. Part of me didn't even believe they were natural. His name wasn't really Aries, perhaps his horns were a sham too. He was a liar and a tyrant and an abuser. I hated him with every fiber of my being, but I also hated Solaris, and owed him no loyalty. "A book," I answered.

"What book?"

"I have no idea." Truth.

He believed me. "What else?"

I shrugged. "A weird glass thing."

"Elaborate."

I waved my hands in exasperation, my chains rattling angrily as I did so. "I don't know. I didn't get a good look at it. I was all fucked up."

"Where is the dragonstone?"

My tongue manifested a mind of its own. "You know I'll never tell you, Aries. You can shock me, torture me, keep me locked in the dungeons as long as you want. But my fate is sealed. If I don't face Solaris on Hallows Eve, I will die. And shit, even if I do face him, I'll probably lose. Either way, the path for me is cursed. You'll get nothing from me. You will never find the dragonstone."

"You are making a mistake," Aries warned, looking like a bull that wanted to charge me.

"Look at you. Look at all of you. This—" I gestured at the figures around the room, "—this is the noble High Council of the Celestial Society? This is who people trust to govern them and keep order? A bunch of faceless, dark figures looming in some musty underground chamber of a secret jail?" A snarl tore at my lips, all fear vanishing like a candle flame in the wind as I turned back to Aries. "You told everyone you were arresting me over the Sacred Baton—which I know isn't its true name, by the way—but you don't give a shit about that. You want the dragonstone." I laughed. "You want what you'll never have, Aries. True power. Not this blasphemous lie you have somehow created—"

He released a feral roar before a surge of malevolent power erupted at me. Stinging hornets stormed inside my chest, my nerves frying beyond comprehension. My vision turned to a burst of violent blue and white before unconsciousness took mercy on me and the world slipped away.

CHAPTER 48

DREAMWALKERS

EMILIA

Three days passed and I was unconscious for most of them because my Luminary spelled me to sleep.

Life went on. The Celestial Society stopped for no one.

Jedidiah Stone had been declared a missing person.

My sister's trial was apparently put on hold.

And life just went on.

Venus St. Claire was the new reigning Queen of Luna Academy. She was all over Celestial media, boasting about her position, and her upcoming battle at the Clash of Spirits. I never thought myself to be a murderous person. But I guess you discover new things about yourself, given new circumstances.

I now had a list of people I wanted dead. Including the three traitorous little bitches who had turned on my sister and spewed abhorrent lies about her. Her 'minions'. Nyx may have been overly cruel and bossy to them, but I knew for a fact she hadn't used dark magic to make them follow her. They chose to. After testifying against her to the Council, they left Luna Academy, which only made things worse for my sister. I vowed to myself and the Goddess that if I ever saw them, their deaths would be a glorious, frozen affair.

I stood alone in my room, watching from the window as the sun slid lazily behind the horizon. Another starry night would soon rise to greet the world.

Destiny didn't spend much time in our room. Right now, she was down in the dining hall for dinner. I couldn't blame her for staying away. The room was in a constant state of being frozen over.

I couldn't help it. My energy naturally turned this place into a glacial cave. Every single thing had a shiny coat of frost and ice over it. I didn't bother trying to rein it in because honestly, I liked it. I liked being able to see my breath. I liked being surrounded by my frozen magic. I was like an ice dragon, hiding away in my cave.

A soft knock on the door made me jump. I narrowed my eyes. Destiny wouldn't knock. And I knew Natalia's knock—it was just a quick two raps. Reluctantly, I crossed the room and opened the door.

Michael stood outside my door. I gasped, wondering why in the seven hells he was risking being seen. I grabbed him by the front of his gray t-shirt and pulled him inside, shutting the door behind him. He gave me a sheepish smile before his eyes swept over the place and widened. "Wow," he muttered. "Natalia wasn't joking."

"What are you doing here?" I asked, my tone as frigid as the room around us.

His face was vulnerable with emotion as he stared at me. He chewed his lip ring for a moment, stirring nameless sensations in my stomach. "I came to see you. I know you are not doing well. But I wanted to tell you... There is hope."

I swallowed, hard. "I wish that could be true."

Michael's voice was low, hushed. "We have a plan, Emilia."

I sniffed, hot tears burning the back of my eyes as I tried to choke them down. "What can we do? Nyx is in prison, and we—"

"I can't say too much," he interrupted me gently. Big surprise. Apparently, there was a lot Michael kept from me. "The more of us who know, the higher the chances of being caught. But I promise you, Emilia, we have a plan. The Clash is in a few days. Your sister will be there."

I shook my head, nearly insulted. "How do you figure that?"

He shrugged lightly. "You never took my dreams seriously. I would always tell you about them, and I could tell you didn't really care."

My chest tightened. "Michael, I—"

"No, it's okay. I understand, trust me. But do you remember that dream I used to tell you about? It was recurring. The one where we fought demons for sport? It was always the same. Always in a big sports field, with a huge audience, and monsters everywhere. There was a team of us fighting them. Your sister was always there. And you, too. Doesn't that sound like the Clash?"

"Maybe," I answered slowly, my heart knocking achingly against my ribs. "But there is only one monster to fight, and it doesn't even matter anymore because he will be dead in two days."

Michael moved closer to me. We stood side by side at the window. My heart instantly picked up at his closeness, my body's natural reaction to him. I swallowed thickly, letting my eyes go downcast.

"Come with me. Beyond the fairy door. We are going to Dreamwalk. We have everything we need to find Solaris and—"

"You know what?" I cut him off harshly. "I don't even think Solaris is still the problem here. I mean, everything he's done is so screwed up... But then there's the High Lord... The media... The Luminary... It feels like our own Society is the malevolent force. All the lies they are allowing to spread! It just makes everything so confusing. We made all these plans to disempower Solaris...and in focusing on that, look at what happened. My sister was betrayed by the very people who are supposed to look out for her. Solaris's vendetta against the Society is starting to make sense. So I just don't understand why he went after Nyx..."

Warmth wrapped around my unsuspecting hand, making me gasp. Michael laced his fingers with mine and shuffled closer, his breath making the hairs on the back of my neck rise. "I hate to break it to you, Emilia, but your Society reminds me of the Capitol in the Hunger Games."

For reasons unknown, his words lured an unhinged laugh out of me.

"You know what you need?" Michael went on. "Faith."

"Faith?" I choked, shaking my head incredulously. "Faith in what?"

He shrugged. "Your Goddess? The mystery of it all? I can't explain it, but I think everyone is exactly where they need to be. Come with me tonight. I don't want to Dreamwalk without you."

"Michael, I'm sorry to say, but that plan is moot. None of that matters anymore."

"Really?" He challenged me. "When the sky was falling on your sister, what did she do? She came back home and found me. She didn't know why or how, but your own Goddess led her to that shitty old warehouse back home to find me. She brought me back with her, here to LA. I am here because of her. Don't you think there's a reason for that? Do you really think I don't play a part in all of this?"

I stared up at him through parted lips, my heart thrashing. "Why didn't you ever tell me? About your dreams? About the tapestry and the High Council visiting you? Even after you arrived at Luna and learned the truth about me, you never told me you had experienced the supernatural before. Why?"

He searched between my eyes. "I don't know. My whole life, I've felt crazy. Like I'm just some insane person who can't tell the difference between reality and a dream. You have no idea what it's been like. Not knowing what's real and what's not."

I swallowed hard.

"Come with me, Emilia. What do you have to lose? Natalia believes Nyx will be at the Clash of Spirits and she will face Solaris. We need to make sure she wins. The shadow man may not be the only problem, but we have to make sure your sister isn't trapped in an eternity of allegiance to him."

"How will Dreamwalking help her win?! I'm sorry, I just don't see it."

"Have faith in me," he breathed, putting his hands on my arms. Those big brown eyes burned a hole in my soul. His closeness became my only reality, the warmth wafting off him in heady waves. Our lips could be touching if I leaned up just a little...

My chest rose and fell.

"Fine."

411

Beyond the fairy door, no floating tea lights were set up to guide our way. Michael and I trudged through the dense forest as the twilight hour blanketed the world in a soft blue.

We found the girls waiting in the clearing, but it looked a lot different than it had the first time.

Natalia had used her magic to get rid of a patch of grass in the center of the clearing, creating a perfect circle of fresh dirt. All around the perimeter of the circle were tall white candles, aglow with yellow flame. The girls stood outside of the circle, in the grass, murmuring amongst themselves as Natalia continued to create the space. There was a pile of leather books in the grass, and on top of them were six potion vials, along with one pouch of dried herbs.

As we drew nearer, I noticed a shape in the dirt. A pentacle, the five-pointed star. Not only was it engraved in the dirt, but a thick copper wire overlined the dirt, manipulated to fit the shape of the star.

Destiny rushed over to me, gathering me into a suffocating hug. "You came!"

"I knew it," Natalia breathed. She wore a brown tasseled dress, looking all forest-witch chic. Her throat was drenched in silver and copper chains, her wrists too.

Destiny released me. Michael and I took in the setup through wide eyes and silent lips.

"I know it looks like a lot," Natalia began.

"It looks like we're summoning a demon," Destiny quipped, her silver tattoos whirling along her brown flesh. Faye giggled nervously.

"Oh, come on," Natalia reprimanded. "You've seen too many movies." She came over to me and Michael right away. She took off one of her long, silver chains and put it over his head. He looked puzzled but didn't stop her. She did the same with a copper chain, then turned to me, and gave me one of each as well. "The silver protects us. The copper aligns us."

Michael and I shared a loaded glance. "Okay," we spoke together.

"I have created a potion that will instantly put us in a deep sleep. I have also created the antidote in case we need to be woken up before sunrise—or if we fail to awaken at sunrise ourselves. We will lay in the circle together, and when we fall asleep, we will all be together in the

Dreamstate." Natalia reached into the pocket of her loose dress and pulled out a photograph. A photograph of Solaris. "Hopefully this will be enough."

I noticed she had only given Michael and me the necklaces, not Faye. "Is it going to be just the three of us?"

"This time, yeah," Faye answered, looking a little put-off.

"This time?" I quipped. I didn't know we had plans to do this again.

"Never mind that," Natalia insisted. "We must begin. We start at the appearance of the first star and will be finished the moment the sun comes up."

"Okay," I agreed, though my heart hammered nervously.

"But before we start—there are a few crucial things you need to know. The Dream Realm is an unpredictable place, ruled by the unconscious. We have no idea what we will see. You must stay focused—don't look around too much, for your own subconscious fears and desires can manifest there and lure you away. We have to stick together and stay lucid. Destiny and Faye will be here keeping watch. They will use the antidote and wake us up if anything goes wrong. Like if we start convulsing or get a bleeding nose or something like that, they can—"

"Whoa, whoa," I said, appalled. "What do you mean if we start convulsing?"

"It's just a precaution," Natalia insisted. "If you don't feel comfortable with this, I'm sure Faye will swap places with you."

"No. No, I'm fine."

"Okay. Good." Natalia handed the photograph of Solaris to Michael, who stared down at it with a peculiar expression.

"I have something else that might help link us to him." He reached into his jean pocket and pulled out something small and red. My brows jumped when I realized it was a piece of the dragonglass medallion. "I found this in my bed after you and Nyx slept over. It belonged to Solaris, so I thought maybe..."

"Perfect!" Natalia cried. "Amazing, Michael!"

My pulse spiked, but I had no words to share.

With her guidance, Michael and I stepped into the circle, which I noted was also outlined with salt. She instructed Michael to lay perfectly over the five-pointed star, with his head at the top, and limbs splayed to match the shape. Then she told me to lay slightly curved beside him on one side, while she took her place on the other.

"The potions, Faye," Natalia demanded.

Faye uncrossed her arms and sighed. I knew she didn't want to stay out of the dream and keep watch. She was the one who'd translated the Grimoire of Dreams for Natalia. Unfortunately, I wasn't selfless enough to give her my spot.

She grabbed the three glass vials and handed them to Natalia, who handed one to me and Michael. The three of us sat up but no one made a move to take the potion.

Natalia craned her neck to look up at the deep blue sky.

For a moment, nothing happened.

Then the first star twinkled into view.

"Okay, now," Natalia declared.

Michael and I shared a quick look, sitting there in the dirt, inside this magic circle. We each chuckled nervously before popping the corks and downing the purplish liquid inside. I winced at the bitter, earthy taste but it went down smoothly enough.

"Now lay back down," Natalia instructed.

The heavy sleepiness rushed at me like a charging bull. I hardly had time to rest my head before the hungry darkness claimed me.

CHAPTER 49
BY DESIGN

NYX

Eternity.

Eternity was the curse that possessed me in the dark. Time remained fathomless, even when I made a point of counting the seconds. The minutes. The hours. I counted, and yet I could still not grasp how aimlessly the wheel of time kept spinning. It all just blurred together into one eternal moment of darkness, starvation, and loneliness.

No one brought me food. No one brought me water.

My tongue, teeth, throat, nose—all dried up. Air barely made it out of my lungs. When it did, it made an awful wheezing sound.

I couldn't feel my body, but that was a mercy. Agony had been my only companion until finally, my senses gave out. I'd been curled up against nothing but stone, and the hardness drained me of all sensations. The only thing that proved I was alive was my ability to dream. I would dream of being back in the world, in the light. Then I would wake up down here and be reminded that death had yet to claim me.

It would come soon, though. I could sense it. The Clash of Spirits would commence anytime, and that would be it for me.

I'd been clinging to this false sense of disgusting hope. Hope that he would come for me. Surely his shadows could penetrate the wards of this prison and set me free. I believed he would come—if not for me, for himself. But he didn't, the fucking bastard. Solaris left me down here to rot, despite it sealing the fate of his own demise.

Death began to feel like a gift. A gift I couldn't wait to receive.

This darkness, this loneliness—it drove me mad. It made me see myself so clearly, and what I saw was terrifying. The truth of who I was mocked me. I had never been queen. I was not resurrecting the royalty of my bloodline. Ha. My life had been a lie. Even before Solaris siphoned my power, I was nothing. Nothing but an explosive, arrogant show-off who lacked any real depth. I'd been too afraid of my own shadow, I focused on nothing but my fire. My fire and the way people perceived me. I wanted my classmates to worship me. I wanted them to fear me. I wanted the Society to see me as the most powerful starseed of our generation, even if it wasn't true. And as long as they saw me how I wanted them to, that was all that mattered.

None of it was real.

Look where it got me. Locked away in the secret dungeons, praying for death. This was all by my own design. As much as it killed me, I had no one to blame. I had manifested this. This was a prison of my own making, finally materialized fully. It started with having my power stolen, being chained by vines and shadows... The Goddess had slowly waded me into this self-fulfilled prophecy.

In the outside world, my image was shattered. I'd been arrested in my knickers in front of everyone. Obviously, the story had blown up and everyone knew about my lowest moment. I didn't even get to go out with a blaze of glory. I was a joke.

Maybe in the next life, I'd get it right.

But I was on death row, and these were nothing but the pathetic musings of a dead woman. Perhaps I only came to terms with these truths because I hoped it would lessen my karmic load upon my passing. Such dreams were a farce.

Stone grinding against stone made me jump. Prisoners erupted with moans and cries as someone entered the tunnels. My chains rattled while I sat up straight, my back screaming with stiffness. Heavy footfalls came this way. My heart did a backflip in my chest. I wanted to die in peace—I had no interest in being Aries's plaything any longer. *Please don't let them come for me.*

Orange light approached my cell, along with the stomping footsteps. A massive cloaked figure appeared outside the bars, peering in at me.

I hissed and flinched away from the light. Even though it was warm and muted, it still stung my eyes.

Jingling keys sounded like nails down a chalkboard as they unlocked the gate and pushed it open. I opened my mouth to protest—no, leave me alone, go away, please—but no sound came out. My throat was too dry, and my spirit too fractured.

The enormous figure invaded my cold, damp cell. He knelt down in front of me and I winced away, a raspy sound escaping between my cracked lips.

I tried to scream as the guard scooped me up in his arms and hauled me out of there. He stalked toward the exit without putting a sack over my head, which made my stomach clench with dread. If it didn't matter that I'd be seeing the way around here, it was because I wouldn't be coming back. He was carrying me to my death.

"No," I managed, though the sound was dusty and embarrassing. *Let me die on my own. Please don't take me to him.*

Prisoners hollered and yowled, begging for mercy and food and water. Each and every one of their voices stabbed me like a dagger through the ribs. I couldn't look at them as we passed their cells.

The guard carried me through a large stone door. We ascended up a set of stairs lit with floating candles before finding another hallway. There were candles here too. I squinted against the harassing light, though curiosity willed my eyes to adjust.

The hairs on the back of my neck rose as the scent of burnt flesh and fresh blood assaulted my nostrils. I knew the smell of death. I instantly started to writhe out of the guard's arms.

No no no no no please no

This hallway was scattered with bodies.

Thick blood pooled on the floor, but the guard walked through it with casual ease. The wet thud of his feet ignited the most primal level of fear in my chest. I jerked around in his arms, desperate for release but his hold on me was like iron. Horror clutched my heart as we continued to pass over a plethora of slain bodies. They were maimed and burnt beyond recognition. The smell gagged me.

My brows narrowed in confusion when I realized the bodies were draped in thick, green cloaks.

Guards.

Someone had murdered the guards!

But that made no sense.

My brain wouldn't compute as the guard who held me led us up another stairwell. He kicked open the heavy door at the top and grunted as we trudged through. I wriggled against him, to no avail. A thousand questions stormed up my throat like wild horses but none made it off my tongue because I was interrupted by an audible burst of swirling light.

We launched through the portal while a scream shot out of my dry, cracked throat.

We tumbled recklessly through the ether before being spat out in a place that was way, way, way too fucking bright.

I hissed like a vampire and threw my hands over my eyes. My heart thundered, my blood rushing loudly in my ears.

"Nyx," someone kept saying. "Nyx, it's me! You're okay. You're safe now. I'm here."

Time stopped.

I lowered my hands, my cracked lips popping open. One soft whisper of a word escaped me. "Jedidiah."

CHAPTER 50
SNAKE DIVINER
EMILIA

The Dream Realm was blue.

Yes, the whole world had this ethereal, muted blue filter over it. Like being inside a sapphire.

I gazed in wonder. The environment around me was unstable and changing. First, I saw an expanse of dark trees, which then became a town or developing city, but before my brain could register, it morphed and reassembled into one singular house.

I looked down at my own hands, letting out a wistful sigh as I took in the appearance of my skin. I had soft, translucent whitish-blue flesh, with a slight dusting of sparkles shining under the flickering streetlight.

"Emilia," said the most beautiful voice in the world.

I turned to see Michael grinning down at me. My heart exploded as our eyes met. The Dreamstate made him even more devastating than he already was. His skin shimmered, his lip ring catching a twinkle. "It worked," he beamed.

On the other side of him, Natalia stood, her skin less translucent but equally shimmery. She stared straight forward at the house before us.

I glanced around, trying to make out where we were. It was hard to see far away—everything got gobbled up by the dark blue realm. All I could make out was the tall, Victorian house, and a few trees around it.

We stood on the sidewalk outside of the fenced yard. A single streetlight lit the ambiance for us, leaving no room to wander.

"Anyone know where we are?" I peeped. My voice sounded the same, but perhaps a little more musical.

Both of them shook their heads.

"Should we go inside?" Michael asked.

"Just wait," Natalia's eyes were far away, and she held up her hand. Listening for something or waiting for something, I couldn't quite tell.

Someone came at us from down the sidewalk, appearing like a phantom through the blue fog. His enormous stature and unmistakable features had my stomach hollowing out. Those ram horns cast an ominous shadow against the sidewalk as Aries Vanderbilt stalked toward the house.

The High Lord? The three of us instinctively backed away from him as he pushed through the gate into the yard. Of course, he couldn't see us —this was a dream. We shared a quick three-way glance before watching him approach the front door with a duffle bag over his shoulder.

Movement in the grass distracted him and he stopped halfway. He made a sound of disgust as he stepped onto the grass and lifted his foot, stomping down hard on something. "Filthy vermin," he spat, glaring at the ground for a moment before turning back to ascend the front steps. He knocked once but opened the door himself and walked inside.

Natalia moved first, leading the way to check what he had stomped on.

I gasped. A garter snake. Squished and dead.

"What kind of omen is that?!" I breathed, anxiety rushing up my spine. We hadn't even been here for two minutes, and we were already coming across dead animals. Symbolically, that was a red flag, right? "Aren't we supposed to be looking for Solaris? It seems like we're in the High Lord's dreams!"

"Relax," Natalia said. "I told you; the Dream Realm is an unreliable place. We have no idea what we're going to see. Come on, you two."

She led the way up the front steps, not even hesitating for a second before she pushed through the front door. Warm light spilled out, soft music playing in the background. Natalia went right on in, zero fucks given. I swallowed the lump in the back of my throat and followed as Michael went inside too.

We moved through a hallway, and when I went to examine the pictures hanging on the walls, I found them blurry and hard to make out. Or distorted like a Picasso painting. I narrowed my eyes, moving from picture to picture, each one less intelligible than the last. Right before we made it to the next room, a photo in a black frame grabbed my attention. This one was clear as day. It was a picture of my mother, mid-slap. My sister's face was pushed to the side, her expression of horror and pain as my mother laid one on her.

My heart dropped.

What was *this* doing here!

I gaped at the horrible photo and then suddenly my mother's eyes became sentient. They turned to me, and her face twisted with disgust. "What, are you just going to stand there and watch!" my mother hissed. "Useless daughter!"

I sucked in a sharp breath, horrified as I stumbled backward. My mother continued to glare at me, her hand locked in an eternal slap of my sister's face.

Something warm tugged on my wrist. I jumped, turning to face Natalia. She led me away from the photo, her expression grave. "What did I tell you, Emilia? You can't get distracted by your own subconscious fears. Stay focused."

"Okay," I breathed, trying not to panic. "Okay."

Michael grabbed my hand, squeezing lightly. I met his eyes, trying not to focus on the details of the space around us. The look on his face made my stomach fall, and suddenly my back hit the wall. He caged me in, burning desire scorching in his gaze. I released a soft sound of surprise and then his lips were on mine.

The kiss consumed me. One of his hands knotted in the back of my hair, the other on my hip. He groaned into my mouth and the sound filled me with a sensation that had my toes curling. His body pressed into mine, his warmth lighting me up like a firecracker. He tasted like summer. I wanted to drown in it. I clung to him, desperate for more, desperate to feel every single inch of—

"Jesus Christ, you two!" Natalia's intrusive voice made us freeze. "My Goddess! What did I *just* say!"

Michael and I pulled apart, his lips shiny and swollen with evidence of our kiss.

My dream heart thrashed. I wanted to shove Natalia away and attack him with my lips all over again.

"Bloody hell," she groaned. "You two need to get it on in the real world if you're going to Dreamwalk together. Let's go!"

Our eyes stayed locked for a moment. Our heavy breathing was synced. I wanted him more than I'd ever wanted anything, but somehow, we managed to put our desire aside and follow Natalia through the house.

We got closer and closer to the music and voices, and finally, we came to the mouth of the great room.

A fire roared on the far wall with a pot of simmering stew hanging over it. Candles lined every surface. A lush, furry throw rug took up the floor. A small child sat on it, no older than three, playing with a wooden toy horse. A beautiful woman sat on the sofa, a violin on her shoulder as she played a soothing, enchanting tune. She had dark hair with glossy red undertones and wore a long forest-green gown. She played the violin with a smile on her face as she watched the child play.

Aries stood like a dark cloud over by the fire. The duffle bag he brought had been dropped to the floor. He held his staff by his side, his eyes boring into the flames. "You cannot stay here any longer," he said.

She acted as if she didn't hear him.

"Would you quit playing that thing for a minute, woman! I came here to speak to you!"

She sighed and set down the instrument. That was when I noticed she wore the red dragonglass medallion around her neck. "It has been months since you have come to see us."

The child looked up at Aries. The color of his eyes! Bright blue like frosted water. Nearly silver.

"You are lucky I have even allowed you to stay here as long as I have. Lucky that I even visit at all! I diligently bring you money and fabric to weave your clothes, as you wished of me, and you show me no gratitude."

"Oh, Lord Vanderbilt, I am grateful," the woman chuckled. There was a mischievous glint in her eye. "Has your lovely wife bore you a son yet?"

"You will not speak of Nymeria," Aries growled. "She is highborn, unlike yourself. If you had better breeding, maybe you could have been my wife."

"A highborn Celestial who can't have children," the woman scoffed. "You are High Lord, and you need an heir." She gestured to the child on the floor. "You have one, right here. He is your blood. He is your son. And you want to know something, Aries? The Emergence spell doesn't work on him. If you would only give him a chance—"

"He's a bastard! Even if he was powerful, his existence will never be anything but shame!" Aries shouted, his face etched with disdain. "I've had enough of your tricks, Allegra. I know you can do fancy performative woo-woos to make it seem like the child can do magic. I know better. Celestial children cannot do magic! You just want your scurvy little half-breed to be the ladder you use to social climb. I shan't be fooled. You are lucky I didn't make you kill the babe in the womb."

"Your ignorance is astounding." The woman, Allegra, rose to her feet. She moved over and knelt beside the child on the rug. She ran her fingers through his thick hair, which was the same reddish-black shade as hers. "He is special," she murmured, gazing upon the child with fervent love in her eyes.

"What is happening right now?" I had to ask. This seemed freakishly...real.

"I think we're in a memory," Natalia breathed.

"Who's?" Michael wondered, seeming equally as miffed as me.

"Shh," Natalia urged.

"I have come to tell you it's time for you to move on." Aries deadpanned, his eyes cold. "I will give you enough riches to last a lifetime. But you must leave. Take the child and leave this place, and never return."

Allegra laughed. "I shall do no such thing. If you do not wish to claim the child, that is your mistake. I have no doubt he will grow up to be one of the most powerful Celestials the Society has ever seen. He can be your heir, or he can be your undoing. I am okay with either of these outcomes, dearest Aries."

Aries's face went the shade of beetroot. His fury was palpable. "Your entitlement, Allegra! You think because you had a drunken affair with the High Lord that it gives you the right to make such threats—"

"Why do you deny him!" she shouted, cutting him off. "You know he is your son! And despite everything, I know you love me, Aries. You have been showing up on my doorstep on your own merit for years. You may cover it up and deny it, but I know how you feel about me. It disgusts you because of what I am, but that doesn't stop it from being true. The child is your blood, he holds great power! Why do you deny him so aggressively? He—"

I'd never seen a face more venomous than Aries's at that moment. Something about her words turned him visibly homicidal.

He shook with quiet fury, his temperature rising. "Because he was born to a lowborn whore! He was a mistake! You are desperate to make sense of something senseless. I should have never stuck my cock in you. Look what it's done to you. You're mad. Creating all these theories and ideas in your head, trying to keep me! The child is nothing special. He will Emerge once he comes of age, and his power will be subpar. He may be half me but he's also half you. And what have you got, huh? You can talk to snakes? You can make them do your bidding? Where I'm from, Allegra, that's known as black magic. You'd be burned at the stake for it. Do not test me again. Take the child and leave or I will take matters into my own hands."

"Goddess, Aries..." Allegra breathed, the firelight reflecting in her eyes. "Look at what you've become. You don't even see what they're doing to you! You're losing yourself! Soon there will be no traces left of you at all."

For the briefest, most fleeting second, vulnerability flashed behind his black eyes. He rejected it, however, and remained hard. "Shut up, woman. You are deflecting because I'm right and you cannot stand to be wrong."

Allegra stood up, her eyes darkening with offense. "You dare stand there, a man reliant upon a staff to perform magic, and tell me my powers are subpar?" She snapped a bitter laugh.

Aries's staff crackled with lightning bolts. "I have infused this staff with my own magic. It is a powerful amplification tool."

"Sure," Allegra quipped. "Or maybe you were just never that good at summoning magic on your own."

"I won the Divine Rite! I earned my place as High Lord! I am the most powerful Magician in the Celestial Society! I triumphed over Sophia Morningstar and her dragon! You dare stand there and accuse me of lesser power!"

"Your version of the story, sure."

Aries's lips tore back over his teeth. He took a threatening step forward, with the staff pointed at Allegra. "Leave, witch! Take the child and leave! If you are not gone by the time I return tomorrow, I shall do away with both of you my own way!"

"We will not go!" she declared. "This is our home!"

"Fine," Aries said, his voice dark and his eyes menacing. "Then you leave me no choice but to—"

The child on the floor began to cry, upset with conflict.

An explosion of ice erupted from under the boy, spreading across the floor like leaking bright blue light. Angry frost traveled throughout the entire room, crackling like frozen flames, claiming the furniture, and climbing up the walls.

Allegra leaned down and grabbed the child, bouncing him in her arms and cooing softly in his ear. She patted his back and consoled him with so much love and admiration in her eyes.

Aries's jaw fell open as he looked all around, incredulous. "How are you doing that!"

While Allegra consoled the child, the ice stopped growing. "I told you," she said harshly. "He can do magic. How could I fake this magic, Aries? I am an earthling, and not a very powerful one, as you always remind me."

Aries blinked, staring at the bright-eyed child in a whole new light.

"So it's true, then," he murmured. "He can do magic."

Allegra rolled her eyes. "Yes, you ignorant brute. I have been telling you this since his first birthday. He does magic regularly. His element is, as you can see, water. In its highest, crystalized form. He is born with his sun, moon, and rising in Scorpio. Ever since his birth, ravens flock to the house at all times. He is special, I told you."

In the arms of his mother, the child looked around the room, as if he heard a noise. Those bright eyes wandered and eventually landed on me. On us—the three of us standing in the doorway. He stared right at us as if he could see us.

My stomach swooped.

At that moment, I knew exactly who the child was. Perhaps I'd known this whole time.

Solaris.

The revelation was like getting kicked in the gut. My eyes widened and I turned to gauge the reactions of my friends.

If this child was Solaris Adder, that meant—

"Give him to me," Aries said coldly, interrupting my thought. The absolution in his tone chilled the room.

Allegra backed away, gripping the child tighter. "Absolutely not."

"You wanted me to claim him. Give him to me, Allegra."

She shook her head, her spine stiffening. "You do not get to change your mind at the drop of a dime because you now know he is powerful. If you wish to claim him as your son, as your heir, you can start by—"

"I will NOT be commanded by a lowborn snake diviner!" Aries exploded, trudging toward her. "Give me the child, Allegra!"

"*Serpentis praesidium*!" Allegra howled, stumbling away from Aries as he threatened to close in on her.

Snakes slithered out of the fireplace, out from under the furniture, manifesting out of thin air it seemed, hissing as they came to the defense of the woman and the child. Large, thick snakes of all different colors snapped and lashed at Aries, whose face was white with terror as he went shuffling backward.

Allegra turned to run out of the room with the child in her arms.

Aries growled in annoyance as he held out his staff and willed it to demolish the snakes with a shockwave of electric power. The snakes screamed and writhed in agony before they sizzled into piles of bones and ash, and then he was after Allegra who was attempting to run upstairs.

Aries jerked his staff at the fleeing woman. "Vita furtiva!" he snarled, sending a bolt of blue power at Allegra. It pelted her in the side of the head with a sickening sound. She went down right away, and Aries was there to catch the child before he could hit the ground with his mother.

She tumbled down the stairs and settled at the bottom in a motionless, unnatural heap. I knew by the cold, pale stillness of her that she was dead.

Oh, my Goddess.

Aries stared down at her for a moment, a wailing child in his arms. Ice exploded from under Aries's feet, just like before in the great room. But this time the ice was laced with darkness. Shadows rose from the ground where the angry frost was growing, licking up the High Lord's legs as if to claim him. Aries stared down at the phenomenon, quickly putting it together that this was the child's magic.

He muttered a spell that rendered the child unconscious before he turned and left the house.

The three of us shared a heavy glance before we dared to follow him.

But when we pushed through the front door, we didn't find the quiet night waiting for us outside. Instead, we were led into another room, a room that had nothing to do with the house we were just in. The landscape of the dream—or memory—changed completely. Now we were inside a bright white room sealed shut with a steel door. Not a home, but some sort of facility.

"Oh my gosh," I murmured, turning to share the moment with my friends but—

They weren't there!

I gasped, whirling around, realizing I was alone here.

Panic scorched through my veins but before I could fall into hysterics over losing Natalia and Michael, the scene before me snatched my attention indefinitely.

The child, older than the last one we saw, sat chained to a metal table. His red-black hair had been shaved off completely, those striking eyes still bright, but not blue. They were now pure silver, too bright for this world. There were wires strapped to his head and hands, hooking him up to a machine behind him. He had aged maybe five or six years, his face gaunt and shadowed. He avoided his reflection in the large mirror on the wall. Instead, he focused on what sat atop the metal table. A cage with a nervous white rabbit inside.

"Solaris," a soothing male voice coming from nowhere yet everywhere said. I didn't recognize it. "How are you feeling?"

He winced. His eyes were bloodshot and squinted as if the lights on the ceiling burned them. He didn't answer the question.

"Do you think that maybe today you could finish the exercise? Can you show us what you did to Dr. Jones?"

I realized now that the voice was coming from speakers on the wall. The source must have been behind the mirror—the two-way mirror. This was an interrogation room...

The child, Solaris, didn't take his eyes off the white rabbit. He trembled but said nothing.

"Do you remember what you did to Dr. Jones, Solaris?"

He gave them nothing.

"We'll get you more books. You love books, don't you? We have a hundred more we could give to you if you'd just do what we ask."

He remained immutable.

"If you show us what you can do, maybe we can talk about going up to the surface for a walk. Wouldn't that be nice?"

Solaris's brows lowered. "I don't believe you."

A pause.

"I want this to go smoothly, Solaris. If you do not cooperate, I am obligated to stimulate you. Your power seems to come with emotion, and if you do not do as I asked, I will be forced to trigger those emotions."

The child chained to the metal table swallowed but said nothing more.

A handful of heartbeats went by.

"You've been asking about the world. We can give you maps to look at, Solaris. Maps and books on all the great cities. We'll even throw in some newspapers for you to see what's going on out there. You can learn about it all. Later today! What do you say?"

The machine behind Solaris began beeping and lighting up, which must have meant his heart rate was increasing.

Still, he did not oblige.

"Solaris," a new, deeper voice came through the speakers. My spine turned to steel. That voice, I knew. Lord Aries Vanderbilt.

Solaris knew it as well. He bristled in his seat, straightening slightly. The machine behind him beeped faster.

"Do you remember how I promised I would let you see your mother if you cooperate with us?"

The child's eyes burned with tears. His stoic front was crumbling now that Aries had entered the situation. "I don't believe you."

Aries chuckled darkly. "You are a sharp boy, I will give you that. Though you are intolerably stubborn and moronic. You should know that I killed your mother the night I found you."

Solaris sucked in a sharp breath, tears spilling over his cheeks. He clenched his jaw and his fists, attempting to rein them in. The machine going off gave him away.

"You believe that, don't you, boy? I was doing you a favor. If you were to grow up under her, you would be nothing. Here, in this special facility I created just for you, you will ascend to greatness beyond your wildest dreams."

He squeezed his eyes shut, shaking his head. His chest rose and fell, and his temples beaded with sweat. He tried with all his might to stay composed, but his magic burst out of him violently. The last thing I saw before I was banished from the memory was an explosion of darkness that swallowed the world whole.

I SHOT UPRIGHT, AWAKENING WITH A HARSH GASP.

The material world bubbled into view, my head spinning.

The dirt under me felt rough and cruel, the coolness of the night making it impossible to breathe.

"There you are!" Destiny cawed from outside the circle.

"Jesus Christ," Natalia wheezed, her hand over her heart.

"Emilia," Michael was right by my side, his hand on my shoulder. His warm brown eyes were the only thing that brought me back down to earth. The memory of his lips ravenously on mine made my cheeks warm, and my lips tingle.

They came out of the dream before me, that was clear. Four sets of worried eyes stuck to me as I fought to catch my breath.

"How long have you guys been awake?" I managed to ask.

"Only a few minutes," Michael assured me. "Are you alright?"

"I think so. How could I remain in the Dream Realm without you?"

"Somehow, you must have branched off on your own." Natalia offered, though she sounded unsure. "What we saw—that wasn't just a dream. That was a memory. A repressed memory that's become a nightmare."

"That child, was that—?" Michael started but he couldn't finish.

"Solaris," I breathed. "The child was Solaris." And he started out with the power of ice.

"You guys saw Solaris as a child?" Faye asked with raised brows.

"What we just saw—that means—" Natalia couldn't finish. Her deep brown eyes met mine from across the circle and an unspoken understanding passed between us.

"What?" Destiny desperately wanted to know. "What did you see?"

I swallowed hard.

"We saw your High Lord," Michael answered, his tone thick with disdain.

"The High Lord?" Destiny and Faye retorted in unison. "I thought we were looking for Solaris?"

"We were," Natalia answered. "And we found him. Aries Vanderbilt is his father."

The clearing went dead silent. Not even a cricket chirped.

My chest rose and fell. Destiny looked to me, as if for an explanation. "It's true," I rasped. "It's true."

"So what does that mean?" Faye whispered.

"It means Solaris and Jedidiah are fucking brothers," Destiny declared, her eyes wide and bulging.

"Half-brothers," I supplied. "Different mothers."

"It makes things a lot more complex," Natalia said. "He killed Solaris's mother and then took him."

Faye and Destiny shared a horrified look.

"What did you see when you were alone, Emilia?" Destiny asked.

I swallowed, my pulse still thundering. "I... I don't know. I think it was another memory. Solaris—he was older. He was in some interrogation room or something with all these wires strapped to his head. They were trying to provoke him to use magic. I think I saw into the Star-Cross project... Aries was there, and it was just..." I trailed off, my chest rising and falling. Words evaded me, and my friends decided to let me off for now.

"*Aries?*" Destiny hissed, her eyes wide with shock. "As in, the High Lord? Involved with the Star-Cross project?"

I nodded.

The clearing went eerily silent.

"Should we really be surprised?" Natalia grumbled, shaking her head, eyes hard. "After what we saw him do to Solaris and his mother, I wouldn't put anything past that demon."

"Did any of this lead you to the source of Solaris's shadows?" Faye had to ask.

"I think so," Natalia replied, to my surprise.

I narrowed my eyes. I'd witnessed Solaris wield both ice and shadow. Meaning he naturally possessed those two elements, right?

"What is it?" Faye asked.

"Grief," Natalia said. "I believe the source of his shadows is grief."

CHAPTER 51
THE UNFORGIVEN

NYX

J ed wouldn't explain anything to me until after I bathed and ate. It
was infuriating.

He wouldn't even tell me where we were. It was a house, a nice
one. I could smell the ocean and hear the crash of the waves
outside. He carried me into the bathroom and filled the clawfoot tub
with hot water and fragrant oils. I could hardly speak, my voice lost and
broken, but that didn't stop me from popping off with endless, frantic
questions. Questions he didn't bother to answer. He stripped off my
prison cloak, ignoring my wails for him to close his eyes even though
he'd already seen me extremely naked. All protests died on my lips as he
lifted me up and lowered me into the hot water.

He left me alone in the bath, with a heavy glass of water that I drank
obnoxiously.

I was *free*.

Jedidiah broke me out of prison. I hadn't seen that one coming.

I washed myself and soaked for as long as I could, but I needed these
blasphemous, magic-blocking chains removed. That was the only reason
I ascended out of the bathtub, regretfully leaving the soothing water
behind.

My eyes swept around the candlelit bathroom, trying to find a clue to where we were. Everything in here was glossy cream or gold. Undeniably mortal. A trio of beach pictures staggered down the pale wall. There was a toothbrush holder on the marble counter with two toothbrushes, one pink, and one blue. A curling iron sat beside the sink next to a plethora of different fancy facial care products. This was clearly someone's house. A woman's house.

After I wrapped myself in a white plush towel, I dared to venture into the next room. An attached bedroom—the master bedroom, by the look of it. It was dark in here, unlike before, with only a few white candles to provide light. I moved across the soft carpet, over to the California king bed. On the night table, there was a picture frame. I picked it up and took a look. A couple. A gorgeous, opulent-looking, middle-aged mortal couple.

"What the...?"

"Yeah." Jedidiah's voice made me jump and whirl around. He stood in the doorway, leaning against the frame, arms crossed over his chest. His lovely face was hard and cold as stone. He wore *mortal* clothes—a gray t-shirt and black jeans. I'd never seen him dressed so casually. "I borrowed their house."

"You *borrowed* their house?"

"Yeah. They're just some rich mortals who spend half the year in New Zealand anyways. I may have Compelled them to head back early and leave everything to me for the next six months."

A few heartbeats tolled by.

"But why?" I breathed.

"Come on," he coaxed, gesturing out the door. "I made you some food."

"I want these chains off, Jedidiah."

"I know. You'll have to wait. We have some things to discuss first."

I scoffed indignantly. "So what? Am I *your* prisoner now?"

"No. But before I take those off, you need to understand some things. Come on. I made your favorite."

He led me through the hallway into the extravagant kitchen that overlooked the dark, moody ocean. The house had an open, modern layout. The kitchen, dining room, and great room all merged into one giant space. A piano sat next to the sliding glass door leading out onto the terrace.

"Where are we?" I asked.

"Malibu," he replied.

My will to argue fell flat when the scent of seasoned red meat hit my nostrils. Jedidiah gestured to the kitchen island where he had a spot set for me. A steaming plate of hot food robbed me of the ability to give a shit about anything else. I hopped up onto the bar stool and couldn't even give a fuck about my chains as I gawked down at the food. Prime rib, garlic mashed potatoes, a kabob of smoked cheese and olives, and not a single green vegetable in sight because apparently—he knew me.

"How did you know this is my favorite?" I peeped.

He scoffed. "I listen when you talk, believe it or not. You mentioned it one night at a party when you were drunk. You wanted a hot meal. You listed it off exactly. And then you fell off the table you were dancing on and burnt off the dude's eyebrows who tried to help you up."

My throat tightened. "You remember that?"

"Just eat, Morningstar."

I actually cried when I took the first bite. Every mouth full after was orgasmic, even laced with my tears.

Jedidiah sat down at the piano and played a song while I cried and ate.

I didn't even know he could play.

The slow, haunting melody of a song I knew all too well possessed the room with its beautiful melancholy. The Unforgiven. The music—it flowed out of him so naturally, so brutally. He poured his own essence into the resonance which already carried so much pain. Like a primordial tune of oppression and betrayal, one that had been traveling the cosmos for eons, just searching for a soul to express itself through. More thickness gathered at the back of my throat. The music penetrated me right into the depths of my darkest truths while the lyrics played along in my head.

Never free, never me. So I dub the unforgiven...

When he finished playing, my plate was empty.

The bath, the food, the music, and the much-needed cry—I felt alive again. I was ready to hear the truth.

I slid off the barstool, still in my towel, still in chains. I moved across the hardwood floor and took a seat next to him on the piano bench. He didn't look at me. His head was hung, his fingers still resting over the keys, like he wasn't quite done playing.

"Jed," I whispered. "Tell me what's going on. How did you break into the prison? How did you kill those guards? They were *burned*."

Dark, stormy eyes collided with mine and for a moment it felt like I was falling. "I know my way around the Institution."

His words impaled me. *Of course. Of fucking course.* The dungeons were underneath the Institution.

I cleared my throat, letting that one roll over me. "You killed those guards."

"I did." Zero remorse showed up in his voice or his face.

"How?"

An unsettling smirk played with his lips. "I learned something new."

My brows jumped. I waited for him to go on.

He held his hand up then, above the piano, in between us. He stared at me intently as he summoned orange fire over his palm.

I gasped.

"Oh, my Goddess!"

Jedidiah Stone, the notorious, ground-shaking earthling, was bearing *flame*. Over his own flesh.

I blinked incredulously, the undeniable heat of his blaze warming my face. He banished the fire all too soon, gauging my reaction.

"No staff..." I breathed, mystified.

"No staff," he agreed. "Can you believe it?"

Like Solaris, I almost said, but refrained. I couldn't believe this.

"I felt different after you and I...after what we did. And there was that moment, that moment right before we... Didn't you feel it? Our magic came to the surface, and it felt like it intertwined or something..."

My heart was beating so fast.

"Did you feel different? After? Like your magic...enhanced?"

"I–I don't know. I—" My mind whirled as memories from the night I was arrested played in my mind's eye. There was a split second, right before they chained me... I'd been overthrown by panic, and the ground began to shake. Could it have been...was that Jedidiah's power being expressed through me?

He watched my eyes light up with the revelation of this.

"We Power Shared," I breathed, incredulous.

"No one has been able to do that for centuries—if not longer."

"What does this mean?" Adrenaline coursed through my veins, my arms rising with goosebumps.

His dark blue eyes teemed with vigorous emotion. "I can't say too much, Nyx. In case we are being watched. But I've communicated with Natalia, and she has a plan. A plan to ensure you win your battle against Solaris. The Clash of Spirits is tomorrow. You've been weak and starved and tortured. You need to nourish yourself and prepare. Tomorrow, you will take down Solaris, and get him and his plight out of the way. And then the real war will begin."

Rapid breaths surfed between my parted lips as I processed this. "How am I supposed to just show up and face him? I am supposed to be in prison, remember?"

He smirked. "All anyone cares about is a good show. We will glamour ourselves so no one will recognize us. We can hide in plain sight. It's Hallows Eve, after all. Everyone will be in costume. We can be whoever we want. *Whatever* we want. And when it comes time for Solaris to stand on the field, you'll be there. And it will be fucking epic. They won't be able to deny you."

My brows had narrowed long before he finished speaking. "Why do *you* need to hide behind a glamour?"

He smirked, but there was no humor to it. "Because my father thinks I'm dead."

I blanched. "What?! Why would he think that?"

Jedidiah turned to look out the window. The moon hung over the ocean, casting a path of silver light across the roaring waves. His throat worked. "Because he tried to kill me and he doesn't know he failed."

His words were like a vacuum shoved down my throat, ripping the breath from my lungs. I gaped at his profile while he refused to look at me. Shock quickly morphed into rage.

Aries tried to kill Jedidiah. His own fucking son.

"What did he do to you?" My voice shook.

"He stabbed me in the gut and shoved me off a mountain. And I deserved it. I fucking deserved it, Nyx. I told you that night, what I deserved. I threatened to push you off the very same edge. And instead of punishing me, you slept with me, bypassed my demons, and treated me like I was worthy of something other than revulsion. I didn't deserve any of it, Nyx, not after how I've acted. I'm no better than my father."

"You are," I insisted fervently. "You are a better man."

"Oh yeah? Really? Exactly when have I ever been a better man? The night I buried you underground? The time I nearly seduced your sister in front of a hundred people in the Sphere just to mess with you both? Or maybe that time I kidnapped you and brought you into the middle of nowhere and—"

"Okay, I get it!" I cut him off. Reality felt like a noose around my neck. "Whatever. We're both fucked up. At least you *want* to be better. That's more than can be said for most people in this wicked world."

He stared at me and said nothing.

"Tell me how you're alive," I whispered.

Those words made his face tighten. He ran his fingers through his hair and looked away as he spoke. "I...was falling. Panicked, dying. Fire shot out of my hands, just like you when you fell. It... Something inside me snapped. I...I remembered my portal globe and used it to catch myself. The stab wound...that was a bitch to heal." He looked entirely disturbed as he relived the memory.

His shakiness had my brows narrowing, but he dismissed the subject before I could question him.

He shifted on the bench and rose to his feet, offering me a hand. I stood with him, my heart doing backflips behind the cage of my ribs. He moved us away from the piano before he took the chains binding my wrists into his hands. He wrapped those talented fingers around the iron and willed fire out of his flesh. I watched in awe as he summoned a violent blaze that turned the iron bright white before it melted and crumbled to nothing.

I gasped as freedom reigned.

My magic rose to the surface of my flesh, the glorious, heady feeling making me sway. My skin tone changed, my senses heightened, and my mind refined into the weapon it was created to be. The bruises and lesions from where those insidious cuffs began to heal. White fire sparked off of my fingertips as a vicious smile took its place on my lips.

"Thank you," I said, my voice thick.

His face was a mixture of pride and sorrow. "Come," he insisted, lacing his fingers with mine and tugging me down the hallway, back to the master bedroom. My pulse quickened at the ideas that came into my head as to why he was bringing me in here. But instead of coaxing me to the bed, he brought me to the luxurious walk-in closet and turned on the light.

"Holy shit," I muttered, looking around. This woman had more clothes than Natalia and I combined. It was more like a boutique than a closet. I gawked at the shelves of shoes and racks of dresses, but Jedidiah pointed to the back. To an outfit displayed on an actual mannequin. A dark green gown made of sleek silk hugged the artificial body tightly. No encrusted jewels or accented golds. The dress was serious, not flashy. A daring slit up each thigh matched with the flowing cape at the back gave it a seductive, villainous vibe.

Beside the mannequin were a floor-length mirror and a plush stool with a large gift box on top. Jedidiah nodded toward it. "Open it."

"What is all this?" I wondered, both nervous and excited.

"Just look in the box."

I approached it like it might have a ticking time bomb inside. A dark green bow adorned the top of the white box. I lifted the lid slowly, my heart thumping in anticipation. For a moment, my brain didn't register what awaited me inside. I stared down, confused at why I was looking at a nest of viscous golden snakes, frozen and gilded in time. Then the reality settled in.

A Medusa headpiece.

It was gorgeous, ornate, and ominous.

I turned to Jedidiah, at a loss for words. He smirked proudly, crossing his toned arms over his chest. "It's Hallows Eve, after all. I know how much you love to dress up."

I smiled, glancing back down at the heap of golden snakes. It was perfect.

"Why are you being so nice to me?"

He scoffed, his cheeks flushing at that. Jedidiah Stone—blushing. Never thought I'd see the day.

"I'm not," he insisted stubbornly. "You and I are birds of a feather, Nyx Morningstar. Outcasted renegades. The Society discarded us both like trash. And when I take down my father, which *I will,* I need you by my side, lighting up these motherfuckers with your Celestial fire. I want you on my team. Fairly. Not forced. Not manipulated. By your own furious free will, I want you with me on this."

I looked up into those stormy eyes and felt the sincerity of his words in every cell of my being. I didn't even have to think about it. "Yes."

The shock on his face made me giggle. He'd expected a fight. But my fight was not with Jedidiah, not anymore.

"You better sleep, woman," he murmured. "Tomorrow is Armageddon."

I stepped closer to him and placed my palm on his chest. His heart slammed against my hand, evidence of my effect on him. I loved the way his heart was always racing around me.

"All I did in that hellhole of a prison cell was sleep. I'm not so tired."

He swallowed, hard. I'd never seen him look so...nervous. "Well." He cleared his throat, his eyes falling downcast. "Want to watch a movie?"

I almost scoffed. *No, that is not what I had in mind.*

"Sure," I replied half-heartedly.

"Okay. I'll go put something on. Help yourself to this lady's clothes."

He left me in the closet. I heard him flick on the bedroom TV. My heart began to beat unsteadily at the thought of casually watching a movie with Jedidiah Stone while we passed the time until our world imploded.

I slipped into a pair of silk sleep shorts and a tank top. The clothes fit perfectly, which was odd. I found a brush and ran it through my hair, attempting to tame these long, silver locks that had been neglected for far too long. When I looked half-ass human again, I emerged from the walk-in closet to find Jedidiah staring at the static TV, looking puzzled. He held the remote in his hand, pressing buttons that weren't doing anything.

"I don't know how to work this mortal shit," he mumbled. "Been a while since I watched TV."

He sat on the edge of the bed, looking worn. I approached him slowly. He glanced up from the remote, his attention snagging on my bare legs. He stiffened slightly and my stomach tightened.

I came and stood in front of where he sat. He dropped the remote and instinctively put his hands on the back of my thighs, opening his knees and pulling me closer. The static on the TV lit the room with pale, flickering light. He looked up into my eyes, pain swimming through his blue irises. "Who would have thought," he murmured, "that it would be you and me against the world?"

I made a soft sound and reached out to put my hands around his neck. Jedidiah was good at putting on a strong front, but I could feel the sorrow coming off him in waves. His best friends were murdered in cold blood, and his own father nearly made him join them in the afterlife. I don't know what we ever did, him and I. To deserve these cruel, twisted fates.

I pulled him into me, and he allowed it, resting his head against my chest, his hands on the back of my thighs still. I ran my fingers through his hair and held him. We stayed like that for some time.

I could see the truth so clearly now, in the honesty of the moonlight that shone through the open drapes. The truth he worked tirelessly at keeping hidden. The truth that shamed him. Jedidiah was *good*. He'd kill me if I ever spoke those words out loud. Perhaps I had to be mad to believe such a thing, considering everything. But in my bones, I knew it was the truth. Perhaps I'd always known. Hidden beneath all that anger and trauma and arrogance, was a boy who didn't know how to love or be loved. A boy who'd been raised by Lord Aries Vanderbilt, who'd never been given a proper example of a good man. He carried his father's hand-me-down cruelty because that was all he knew. I could relate, wholly.

I wondered what we could have been like if the people who brought us into this world hadn't royally fucked us up.

"The last thing I ever said to the twins..." His voice was rough, fractured. My heart ached before he even finished the thought. He kept his face buried in my skin. "I was an asshole. Just a fucking asshole. They

440

were the only people to ever treat me like I was worth something, and I was nothing but awful in return."

"Jed... They loved you for who you are. They knew—"

"I don't want to be shit like my father. I don't know why I am the way I am when I fucking know better. Me and you... Nyx, we have to be better than our parents. We can't carry on their legacy of lies and cruelty. We have to be better. The gods let us Power Share. We have to be better."

I held him against my heart, his words settling in my stomach. I didn't even have it in me to be offended that he'd said 'the gods' rather than the Goddess.

"Okay," I rasped.

When he pulled back slightly, his azure eyes were shining with emotion. Raw, vulnerable, alluring. I cupped his face in my hands and leaned down to softly press my lips to his.

The first time we'd kissed, it was explosive. Manic. But not this time. Our lips moved slowly, experimentally, as if we were both made of glass. My stomach swooped, heat pooling in my abdomen. It may not have been as frantic as last time, but this kiss was deeper and wholly possessive.

He pulled me down onto his lap and I gasped into his mouth. I straddled him, feeling his hard length beneath me, making my head spin. He groaned as I swiveled my hips, moving fluidly over him, driving us both wild. I hooked my fingers on the bottom of his shirt and pulled it over his head. His tanned, muscular shoulders and chest had me releasing a soft sigh. My eyes traveled over his beautiful, scarred body.

There should have been a scar on his stomach from where his father stabbed him, but I found none. Curious, that he would heal one, but not the rest.

"Is it bad that I like these?" I whispered, trailing my finger along one of the pale lightning bolts on his chest.

"Shut up," he growled, his lips claiming mine once more. His hands gripped my hips, and he guided my body to grind over him, filling us both with need.

I leaned back to pull the tank top over my head, tossing it across the room. He made a throaty sound before he took my nipple into his mouth. I moaned, arching my back, knotting my fingers in his hair. His lips were everywhere. My breasts, my throat, my lips. One thing was for sure; this man knew how to worship me. The damp heat between my thighs had me pushing down against him, then rolling, electricity shooting up through my whole body.

"I knew it was pointless to get dressed." I giggled breathlessly.

"Yeah." He scoffed. "You have no idea how hard it was not to rip that towel off of you and fuck you on the piano."

A firework went off in my belly. Goddess, that would have been hot. "Why didn't you?"

"Because you're you," he murmured, kissing my throat.

"What does that mean?"

He pulled back to look into my eyes. My heart tumbled at the look he gave me. Severe, toe-curling desire lit his blue eyes with flames. Literally. I could see fire magic dancing in his irises—the ocean on fire. "You're Nyx Morningstar. You're...you're a fucking goddess."

He grabbed my hand and pressed it to the centre of his chest, over his thrashing pulse. He was hot to the touch. "I know you've felt this. What my heart does every time I'm with you. The first time I ever saw you, I shattered. And I knew—I fucking knew you would be my undoing. You proved me right seconds later. I've been yours from the minute you lit me on fire."

My chest filled with an emotion I'd never felt before. Some kind of embarassing whimper-slash-laugh tumbled through my lips. His words had me frozen. I searched between his eyes while I breathed rapidly, unsure of how to receive such a testament.

Say something. Say something.

"Kiss me more," I rasped after a moment.

And he did. He kissed me like it was his religion. I rolled my hips, moving on him in a way that had every single nerve ending in my body sizzling like a live wire. This was exactly what I needed. My last night alive, I just needed—

"Wait," he said hoarsely, and there was something dire in his tone that made me freeze.

I didn't expect him to appear so...pained.

"What?" I breathed.

His throat worked. He pushed my pale hair out of my face, behind my ears. The gesture was uncharacteristically gentle. "If we do this..." His voice cracked and he cleared his throat before he continued. "If we do this, it stops being just a heat of the moment one night stand between us."

I gazed down at him, my lips parted. I should have said something but the ability to speak had escaped me.

I wasn't used to this side of him.

I wasn't used to to this, *period*.

"You know I could love you, Nyx." My heart did a clumsy backflip in my chest. "I know you don't want that. I know you. But if we do this, if we cross the line from one night stand to...whatever this makes us... I don't know if I'll be able to stop myself. From loving you. Gods know I've fucking tried. You disarm me. I don't know if—"

I crashed my lips to his because he needed to shut up. He was over-thinking this. Tears burned the back of my eyes, and I needed him not to do this. I needed him to just take me. Take me as I was. Without needing to lay claim. Without expectations.

"Jed," I whispered against his lips. I cupped his face in my hands as he pulled back slightly to look at me. "You were right about that first night, okay? You were right. I *was* afraid of you, that night at the club. I knew what we could have been, and it terrified me. So I attacked you. You were right. But don't do this now—we can't go there. Please, Jed. Please, just—"

And then his mouth was on mine. Fierce, possessive, passionate. I felt him toss his feelings to the side for now. Perhaps it was selfish, but I knew he was mine in the way I needed him to be.

I pulled away to stand up and slip the sleep shorts off. A glorious, strangled sound left his throat as I stood naked before him. My heart thrashed against my ribs as he unbuckled his belt and jeans, letting his arousal spring free. My eyes popped, and even though I'd seen it before, it seemed more startling this time. Instinctively, I sank to my knees before him, hungry and ready to take him in my mouth.

"*No*," he snarled, reaching out with one of those long, strong arms. He grabbed me by the elbow and jerked me up, pulling me onto his lap. I gasped at the unexpected gesture and the rage pooling over his face.

"You *never* get on your knees. Not even for this. Not for me, not for anyone. You fucking understand me, Nyx?"

I gaped at him, my belly a mess of knots. "You don't want—?"

"*Never* get on your knees." His face was an inch from mine, his eyes severe. Jed was full of fire now, I could see it, feel it. He gripped my face with one hand, his palm hot against my cheek. "Never, Nyx. You kneel for no one. Promise me?"

I searched between his eyes. I didn't understand the severity, but I liked it. Fuck, I loved it. "Promise."

He stared at me for a moment longer until he was satisfied. Then his mouth devoured mine.

I swiveled my hips so that my slick, throbbing pussy slid across the length of his cock. His eyes rolled back, his hands gripping my ass. His jaw was slack, his face possessed with euphoria. I kissed him forcefully, biting his bottom lip until I tasted blood. Sweet, yet earthy. A breathy moan escaped me, my fingernails digging into his shoulders while his tongue invaded my mouth, the friction between us nearly making me pass out.

We kissed like the world was ending and this was the only thing that might save it.

I put my hands on his shoulders and brought my hips up. He knew exactly what I wanted. He reached between us and lined himself up with my entrance. I sank down onto him, crying out as the sting of ecstasy ignited between my thighs.

Jed watched my face as I adjusted to him inside me, his eyes hooded. I moved on him, slowly at first. The look on his face, it was everything. He was entirely bewitched by me.

"Fuck," he hissed. "Nyx, *my god.*"

"Yes," I breathed, leaning my head back. His mouth closed over my nipple as his hands gripped my hips. I knotted my fingers in his hair as all civility left my being. I turned feral, riding him until I couldn't feel my legs.

Goddess have mercy.

I saw stars as I came. It didn't take long, but I didn't have it in me to feel embarrassed. He was just...*so good.* I became a writhing ball of pleasure, collapsing into him. In a whirl of unexpected motion, he grabbed

444

me and flipped us over. My face hit the pillows, and he crawled over me, trailing kisses up my spine. His hard chest pressed against my back, his skin as hot as a furnace. My heart was already a racing, fluttery mess, but now it was just unhinged. I panted, desperate for him to be back inside me. His breath tickled my ear as he kissed the side of my face.

I shrieked and bucked my hips when he smacked my ass, playful but hard. He chuckled darkly. "You know how long I've wanted to do that? This *ass*," he groaned, squeezing it before his fingers slid into me from behind. I mewled, burying my face into the pillow, cocking my backside up to grind against him. "Fuck, look at you. You look so pretty when you come undone," he whispered huskily, sliding his fingers out to circle them over my clit.

"Jed," I whimpered, writhing under him with need. "*Please.*"

I didn't have to see his face to know he was grinning smugly. "Do you want me to be gentle, princess?"

Princess?

"No," I whined into the pillow. "Fuck no."

"Good girl," he growled before he grabbed a fistful of my hair and reefed my head back. I cried out, and his body fully pressed into me from behind so he could angle his head around to kiss my open mouth. It was a punishing kiss, one that I felt in the depths of my stomach. Then he thrust inside me, claiming me in the most primal, masculine way, and I did exactly what he said. I came undone.

CHAPTER 52
BLOOD IN THE WATER
NYX

It was dawn by the time Jedidiah fell asleep with one long, heavy arm draped over me.

You know I could love you, Nyx.

You disarm me.

Fuck.

For a while, I just stared at him. I was in dangerous territory, that much was true. I was crossing so many lines with this man, doing and saying things I could never come back from. He was once my adversary —and now he was my ally, my lover. The way he looked at me...the way he touched me, tasted me, worshipped me...

My stomach was knotted with guilt as I gazed upon his peaceful, sleeping face.

He deserved better. Which was a comical, horribly ironic fate. Jedidiah Stone deserved better than *me*.

There were moments last night, moments when he was buried inside of me, that silver eyes flashed in my mind. Wicked, abhorrent, disgusting—the way my body exploded and reacted to such thoughts and visions. In the midst of pleasure, I should not have been thinking of Solaris Adder. Yet he kept invading my mind. His mythic face, his shadows, his hands with all the silver rings, his fathomless eyes. What it would feel like if he were in Jedidiah's place...

As I said. Jedidiah deserved better. And I needed to seek immediate psychiatric help.

We didn't just have sex. We held each other. We talked for hours. He caught me up on everything the media had been saying about me.

In turn, I told him the truth about Solaris. The entire, nitty-gritty truth. I told him about how Solaris claimed he could see me in the shadows for years. How I was his bridge back into this realm.

And then I told Jedidiah about the dragon in the crypt—and the real reason why his father had imprisoned me.

We were on the same page, me and Jedidiah. Solaris's plot needed to be vanquished. And then we would move on to Aries and his Council of lying, psychopathic imposters.

The Clash of Spirits was only hours away.

I hadn't been training. Hadn't been fuelling myself properly. All I had was my power and my will. It had to be enough.

I snuck out of bed, grabbed a knife from the kitchen, and went out into the backyard, which was a beach.

Gentle waves lapped at the sand, ebbing, and flowing in perfect rhythm. The sky was a deep, vengeful orange. A sliver of the sun appeared from behind the horizon, the promise of a new day.

I stood at the shoreline and I watched the sun rise over the ocean. Birds chirped and seagulls cried out.

I stepped into the ocean, wading in up to my knees.

On the morning of Hallows Eve—the veil between worlds was as thin as it could be. The closeness of the ethereal realms was palpable. Visible in the bright orange-red dawn. I could feel eyes from the beyond watching me.

The entire Society would be making their offerings today. The girls at Luna would all be gathered in the Sacred Temple, making altars, and giving their thoughtful, unique offerings.

I had nothing to give.

"Goddess," I began to pray, but my voice rasped and wavered.

Hot tears burned my eyes. I had no words. What could I possibly say? The salty truth streamed down my cheeks, dripping off my skin, into the ocean. An offering. A prayer made manifest.

My energy would have to speak for me. My tongue was on strike.

I squared my shoulders and drew in a steady breath, letting the last of my tears fall. Once my vision cleared, I held my hands out, gripping the knife in one, holding the other palm up. I gritted my teeth and made no sound as I slid the blade over my flesh, drawing a stream of crimson that poured generously off my skin, into the ocean.

I stared down at my blood in the water. Watched it disperse. *May it be enough.*

CHAPTER 53
MIRAGE
EMILIA

I made no offerings.

I did not leave my room all day. Destiny begged me to come down into the Sacred Temple to make an offering. She said it was bad juju if I didn't. I didn't give a shit. When she realized I wasn't going to budge, she switched her approach. She started gushing to me how magical everything was—the Priestesses had enchanted jack-o-lanterns to come to life and make whimsical jokes! How fun! I refused. I remained in our room and watched the hours roll by.

I would not indulge this cursed day. I had no interest in trivial magic tricks and some pimped-out, hyperactive version of Halloween.

But that didn't mean I wasn't going to dress up. As the last whispers of daylight paraded outside, I got to work on myself.

Though, my look was not a costume. It was my true embodiment.

I became the personification of ice. I used nothing but my own magic.

A skin-tight, strapless silver dress hugged my slim frame flatteringly. It hit the floor in a sweep of liquid silk, but the slit all the way up the right thigh had my legs on full show. I covered the dress in a layer of frost which sparkled when it caught the light. I took inspiration from my sister's golden tattoos when I created my own, using ice. I willed a crown of jagged ice that looked like glass to manifest atop my head. My untamed hair had crystals throughout it, all the way to the tips. I left my face free of makeup, though I froze my eyelashes white.

I looked frightening. Otherworldly. Dangerous.

One might not perceive ice as a threat until it comes for them.

I took a long, hard look at myself in the mirror, coming to terms with who I was becoming. With who I had always been, deep down.

A figment of darkness erupted behind me in the glass. I gasped and whirled around, my hand flying to my throat in surprise. Following the gust of swirling shadows, Solaris Adder appeared.

Here. In my room.

The sight of him hit me like a fist down the throat, ripping the breath from my lungs. At first, I thought he was beautiful. Devastatingly so. But as the silent seconds ticked by and I allowed my gaze to rove over him intensely, I realized that was a lie. Or a mirage. His bright eyes were unnatural—demonic. His cheeks and jaw were too sharp, like he had knives for bones. He cocked his head and glared at me expectantly and instantly I thought of a serpent hypnotizing its prey. I felt entirely unsafe, every single cell of my body blooming with defense.

I blinked, half expecting him to disappear. He didn't. Silver eyes pierced me like a dagger and pinned me in place. It was at that moment, that Goddess-forsaken moment, that I realized how screwed my sister was.

His presence was dense and all-encompassing, tangible in every breath I struggled to draw.

Visions of what I'd seen in the Dream Realm danced across my mind's eye, reminding me of the child Solaris had once been, the child with the same power as me.

He grinned as he regarded me and my reaction to him. He wore a long black jacket with ornate silver buttons. His hands were folded behind his back. His dark reddish-black hair looked like it would feel like silk, all lustrous and windblown.

"I didn't think you would embrace your true nature so quickly," he mused, his tone velvety and casual as if we were close familiars. "Yet here you are." He gestured at me, my dress, my crown. "Marvelous."

"What are you doing here?" A miracle—a bloody miracle that I could speak.

"Don't play dumb," he said, and something about his voice made my spine stiffen. A sleeping threat lingered within those words. "Where is she?"

Confusion had my brows knitting together. "Who?"

Solaris stepped closer.

His metallic eyes raked me up and down, contemplating me. "You really don't know."

"Don't know what?" My voice was too breathy.

"Your sister escaped."

His words were a bucket of hot water pouring over my head. My heart raced and the room around me wouldn't stay still. I had no clue—I hadn't heard anything. Did she? Could it be true?

"I had no intention of letting her miss the Clash of Spirits," Solaris went on dutifully. "But when I showed up to free her, she was already gone. Wherever she is, she is cloaked with magic, not even I can penetrate." He spoke quietly as if he were mostly talking to himself.

I swallowed, eyes darting back and forth as I considered this possibility. Who would have freed her? Who could have?

"Be prepared to lose her to me." Solaris deadpanned, snapping my attention up to him. "I will beat her tonight, in front of the entire Celestial Society. It will go down in history, mark my words. And when I defeat her, she will kneel to me—she will be mine. She will do as I will. Prepare for the monsters I unleash in her. And for the ones she unleashes in you." A violent smile slashed across his lips, revealing his perfect white teeth.

He was baiting me. Looking upon his face, feeling his magic in the room, it was hard not to believe that he would beat her. But my stubborn Morningstar nature had me keeping my chin up. Natalia had a plan. Nyx had escaped prison. We still stood a chance.

I looked into his eyes, trying to find remnants of the child I'd seen in the dream. Did he know who he was? Did he know Aries was his father? Why had he been targeting my sister all along, rather than those who actually wronged him?

I remained poised. Cold, and indifferent. I tipped my head up to level him with a stare. "Bold of you to presume she is mine to lose. My sister belongs to no one, Darkbringer. You are no exception. No matter what cruel twist of fate befalls us, you can assure yourself, she will never be yours."

His jaw fell open slightly, his eyes lighting up with amusement. He opened his mouth to spar with me, but the door handle twisted and jiggled. Solaris vanished in a storm of shadows just before Destiny burst into the room.

"WHOA!" she shrieked. "Emilia, you look fucking amazing!"

I just stood there, frozen and mute. My cheeks were cold, my heart thudding, dull, and aching in my chest.

"Dude...you okay?"

"I'm fine," I whispered, staring at the spot on the floor where Solaris had just been. "I'm ready to go."

CHAPTER 54

BEWITCHED

EMILIA

I f I had an image in my head of what Hallows Eve in the Celestial
Society would look like, even my wildest dreams, I couldn't have
come up with this.

In a sea of colorful, scandalous horror, we flooded into the Los
Angeles Memorial Coliseum, surrounded by outlandish characters and
mythical creatures. Since tonight was the night when the veil between
worlds was thinnest, magic was at an all-time high. Meaning the people
around me weren't just dressed up in costume, they were done in full-
blown glamour, taking on the appearance of anything and everything.

I spotted neon mermaids and glittering faeries mixed in with famous
fictional characters. Angels and demons could be found in pairs. Heads
were adorned with horns or antlers, crowns, or extravagant headpieces.
Wings and tails and claws drew my attention from nearly every angle. I
met cat eyes and snake eyes and the squared pupils of a goat man who'd
transformed his bottom half into a furry brown rump with hoofed feet.
Everywhere my eyes touched, I found a colorful supernatural freak who
took the concept of Halloween to the next level.

I was bewitched, hardly able to grasp the magic of this.

The inside of the coliseum had been magically altered. Crystal
towers jutted up from the ground above the stands, lit with energy,

powering all this fathomless magic. Instead of thousands of red, plastic seats crammed close together in the stands, it had been transformed into an ancient amphitheater made of all stone. It was like stepping back in time to watch gladiators fight to the death.

The ancient ambiance, though, was invaded by the future. Floating spotlights orbited above to light the center, as well as huge hovering screens to give everyone a close-up look at the action. The football field had been painted black, with a huge blue ring in the middle where the battles would take place.

The Celestial Society; forever an impossible paradox of the past and future.

Natalia and Faye led the way as we threaded through the crowd, looking for a spot.

Natalia was dressed as a classic witch with a black pointed hat. Faye, of course, was a faerie, with glamoured wings that fluttered behind her back. Destiny was all done up as Maleficent, and damn—she looked incredible. Not to mention unsettling.

And Michael... He was a dark version of Peter Pan. Faye's idea. She dressed him up in an olive-green tunic and curling elf boots, a dagger strapped to his hip. She glamoured his ears to be pointed. Instead of a hat, he wore a sharp crown of wiry copper, resting on his forehead, just above his brows. She gave him a mask of shadows around his eyes, to portray him as a thief. "Peter Pan is a villain, after all," Faye had explained. The dark mask made his brown eyes pop with flecks of amber and gold. He looked so...ethereal. Like one of us.

Natalia chose our spot for us. We were four rows from the field, close enough to see everything clearly without needing to rely too much on the help of the big screens.

Once we sat down, a mortal servant appeared with a tray of champagne flutes. The champagne was pink and glittery—clearly enchanted.

"We're good," Natalia told him firmly.

Faye pouted as he nodded and left.

"We need to keep clear heads," Natalia said. Her tone was sharp, leaving no room for bullshit.

"This is wild," Destiny mused, her eyes sweeping over the entire coliseum. "Look at this place."

"Look at the people," Michael added wistfully. "It's like something out of a movie."

My chest felt tight. I swallowed, not having anything to add to the conversation.

Natalia still hadn't disclosed the plan. Apparently, she was waiting until the very, very, very last minute. That wasn't nerve-wracking at all.

I watched silently as more and more decked-out Celestials filed in. The coliseum could have easily held twenty thousand people, but only about half of that was here tonight.

An event for the Celestial elite. Which apparently included me.

The fire dancers continued their extravagant performances. Halfway through, a mob of water and air benders came out, clad in silver and white, adding their magic to the show. Fire met water in the sky and turned to colorful steam, which the airlings then transformed into fireworks. The fireworks dissolved into creatures of pale steam that charged around the stands, right in front of us. The crowd went crazy. I was unmoved.

"Doja Cat is performing, I heard," Destiny gushed.

"Yeah, I heard that too!" Faye supplied a bright smile on her pink shimmering lips. The two of them giggled together, chatting excitedly about the show.

Maybe I shouldn't have been pissed off that they were enjoying themselves, but I was. Actually, screw that. I had every right to be pissed. This night could be the end of my sister's life, and here they were, chatting and being merry.

But this was the Celestial Society, after all. I was no longer in the mortal world. Cursed fates and cruel, hopeless odds were the social norms here. What did Nyx say to me that night? *This is how our universe works, Emilia! Do you want to grow? You want to level up? You want a purpose? Then you gotta walk through your own personal hell and come out the queen of it. Otherwise, you might as well just be a clueless mortal, living in stagnant comfort.*

It was like she manifested this all by herself.

My palms were clammy as I thought about my sister incessantly. I kept looking for her. Which was stupid and pointless, obviously. She wouldn't just show up and join the crowd, would she?

455

Solaris said she broke out of prison, yet nothing had been mentioned in the Celestial media about it. Our High Lord was most likely too proud to admit they lost her.

A girl dressed up as Medusa caught my eye as she ascended the stairs beside us. She wore a nest of hissing gold snakes upon her head. Under the striking headpiece, her long blood red hair fell straight down her back like a ruby blade. Her eyes were glamoured to be bright green reptilian slits. Her cheekbones were enchanted as well—appearing inhumanly sharp as if she had blades under her skin. Her long, dark green dress with the attached cape trailed behind her, though her legs were exposed through the slits up to her bronze thighs. She was gorgeous and strangely familiar. I couldn't take my eyes off her.

At her side was an enormous man dressed as Death. He wore a black cloak that drowned him, leaving a train of darkness in his wake. His face was hidden under the draping hood. At his side, he clutched a giant scythe, and it wasn't just a costume prop. The thing was a deadly weapon.

The girl's snake eyes met mine. As if she sensed me staring while she passed. My heart sank as our gazes collided. Did I know her? She looked so...

Her dark green lips curved into a hint of a smile. She gave me a sly, knowing look. Like we shared a secret. Then she tossed up the rock n' roll sign at me and my stomach fell out of my ass.

Nyx.

She looked away as the revelation hit me. I watched her ascend the stairs, finding a spot higher up in the stands.

It was *her*. No doubt about it. She'd glamoured her hair, eyes, and cheeks to disguise her identity but I knew my sister and that was her. Her huge, unsettling companion had to be Jedidiah.

My mouth had dried. No one else noticed her but me. My lips popped open. I shut them instinctively. I needed to keep this to myself. To keep her safe and hidden.

Nyx is here.

My pulse would not relent.

I tried to focus on the field. The elemental performers finished their routine and the crowd cheered wildly.

The coliseum darkened, the spotlights zeroing in on the black field as Aries Vanderbilt appeared out of a portal of spinning light. His curling ram horns sizzled with blue, electric power. The Society erupted in praise for their High Lord. I felt sick to my freaking stomach.

"Thank you, thank you," he chided smugly. The applause eventually waned, though he didn't seem to mind in the least that it dragged on a beat too long. "Welcome to the thirty-third Clash of Spirits!"

More cheers.

Holy crap. I had no clue there had been so many. I'd never even heard of this event until I joined Luna Academy.

"Tonight, the veil is thin, and magic is at its all-time high." Aries's voice boomed through the arena. "Eyes from many different worlds will be watching the show tonight. Therefore, only the most powerful and notorious Celestials get the honor to perform and compete. Tonight, you will see the best of the best!"

The large floating screens started showing off all the famous people in the audience. Some of them were Hollywood stars, well known in the mortal realm as well as our Society. It became clear to me—the truth. The mortal realm and the Celestial Society weren't entirely separated. The elite from both worlds was one entity.

I grimaced as three small flying eyeballs appeared in front of me, hovering before me like bees. I nearly keeled over and died when I realized they were cameras.

Cameras focused on me.

It was as if someone shoved my head underwater, the way I heard the audience erupt from far away as my own face hit the big screens. Time moved impossibly slow, my limbs going numb. I hardly recognized myself. Frozen. Stoic. Perhaps even beautiful. I stayed non-reactive, even though my insides were in complete turmoil and duress. I looked like I'd rather be anywhere but here. Good.

They knew who I was. They were cheering for me.

It felt like an eternity passed when the cameras finally moved on and showcased others, leaving me breathless.

"Now!" Aries declared. "I present to you, the champions of tonight's show!"

A gate at the far end of the area opened, and a parade of chariots being pulled by black horses flooded onto the scene. Just when I thought the audience couldn't get any wilder, somehow, they managed.

There were seven medieval-style chariots doing circles on the midnight grass, two Celestials in each one. I noticed Maverick Madriu, dressed as a basketball player. (Original). Venus St. Claire, dressed as the Scarlet Witch, stood in a chariot next to Solaris Adder. Solaris was dressed as himself. I didn't recognize the other competitors. Their faces appeared on the big screens and Venus was all too eager to wave and blow kisses. Solaris acted as if there were no audience watching him at all. He remained bored and emotionless, but the crowd loved him anyway.

"What'd I tell you?" Michael murmured in my ear, making me jump a little. "Fucking *Hunger Games* shit, right there, love."

CHAPTER 55

NEST OF SNAKES

NYX

My heart wouldn't stop pounding. Soon it would pave a hole through my ribs.

Jedidiah sat next to me, dressed as Death, keeping his hand in mine. He was my pillar, my strength. I didn't deserve him but without him, I would have crumbled to dust long ago.

It wasn't love, this thing happening between me and the High Lord's son. Perhaps it could have been. But that ship had sailed.

I meant what I said last night. He was right. I was afraid of him, the night we met. I remembered it all so vividly. We'd been making eyes at each other all night. He was so tall and handsome and powerful. He turned heads when he entered the room. All the girls flocked to him, touched him, and wanted to talk to him. The crowd parted for him as he made his way over to me. He had everyone's attention, and yet, he only had eyes for me.

Immediately, I knew. We could have been something. The potential between us was undeniable, even before we ever spoke a word to each other. We could have been a power couple. As he strode toward me that night under the bright lights of the club, our potential future flashed before my eyes. We could have had it all.

It terrified me. I'd never let a boy close enough to hurt me before.

One look at Jedidiah Stone and I knew he would crash through all the walls I'd spent my entire life building up. So when he held out his hand and asked me to dance, when the electricity coursed between us and my stomach flipped upside down, I did the only thing I knew how to do.

I'd hurt him. Humiliated him. I made sure that when he thought of my face and my name, they were tainted with resentment and fury.

I made him my adversary. I liked it like that. I looked forward to seeing him every time we went out. I searched for him in every crowd. And when our eyes locked, I found that safe, familiar disdain and disgust I was used to finding in the eyes of those I cared for. The way my mother always looked at me. It was safer that way, to be the object of his ire.

Despite all my efforts to keep him as my opposition, after everything, it was Jedidiah at my side now. Not Emilia, not Natalia or Faye or the goddamn Luminary. It was Jedidiah, his hand in mine. Because now, we had a purpose.

This wasn't about love. This was about war. This was about survival.

He caught me staring at him. He looked fucking magnificent with his skull-painted face. He'd let me do it, too. Sat there so patiently as I'd drawn his beautiful features into a realistic looking skull, turning him into the dead man he already felt like he was. My beautiful ghost.

My vision was fluid like I was on drugs. Unfortunately, I was sober as a judge, though the idea of being under the influence of a dissociative started to sound appealing.

Soon, the Battle of Elements would take place. The most powerful Celestials from our Society worldwide would face off down on the field. To entertain not only those of us watching from the crowd but those watching from behind the Veil.

When the musical performance finished, the High Lord took center stage once more and gave another haughty speech. A speech I didn't hear—my mind was too far away. Reliving memories of the way he'd tortured me. Electrocuted me. Chained me. Locked me in the dark, in the cold.

I glanced at Jedidiah, and he seemed to be reliving his own hell. His father, our noble High Lord, stabbed him and shoved him off a mountain to his death.

I squeezed his hand in mine. A wordless promise. *He will get what's coming to him.*

Aries used his staff to cast a protection circle in the middle of the field, much like the elemental ring back in the Sphere, to ensure no magic could escape into the crowd.

"Let the thirty-third Hallows Eve Battle of Elements commence!" our High Lord declared.

Two Celestials came out then. Their faces were all over the big screens. A male and a female, both lovely in their own way. Air and earth. Aries introduced them as Atticus and Farah, powerful Embodied Celestials from overseas.

The audience cheered for them. My blood was running cold.

Intense war drums began to play as the lights dimmed and the two competitors got into a fighting stance in the center of the protection circle.

Aries returned to his VIP box, right next to the field, the best seats in the house. Our reigning Luminary, Delphyne, was in there with him. Brit Dawn from Celestial Post sat with them, and Aro from Veneficus, along with a few others I didn't recognize. I hadn't seen any other Priestesses from Luna tonight. I wondered if they had even bothered to come.

I hadn't seen my mother, either. Surprised she wasn't down there sitting next to Aries.

It felt like I was watching the events play out from outside of my body. Nothing felt real. It didn't feel real that soon I would be down in that ring, fighting for my life against Solaris Adder. How would it even happen? I was supposed to be in prison. My identity was disguised, and no one had seen through my glamour, except maybe Emilia.

The night tolled on.

The battles played out, one after the other. Earth collided with wind and made a mess. Fire met water and became hissing, vengeful steam. Celestials fought each other, tooth and nail, with magic and combat. The audience went wild as spirits clashed.

Venus St. Claire entered the ring. She'd changed from her Hallows Eve costume and now rocked her signature red fighting leathers. The audience cheered for a solid two minutes, just for her. She faced off with Maverick, the basketball star. It was definitely the most impressive segment of the night so far. Which was ironic, seeing as how they were in the 'lesser league', being only Emerged rather than Embodied. What did that say? That the newer generation was more powerful than the older ones? A curious thought, indeed.

Venus's crystals challenged with Maverick's electric air made for a bright, loud, extravagant fiasco. Their Hollywood natures really came through—they knew how to put on a good show. Knew how to give the people what they wanted. Maverick would jump and propel himself twenty feet up in the air to hit Venus with lightning from above. She would swing around on vines and shoot crystal bullets at him, and he looked pretty when he bled. Their battle was more like a dance. A colorful, calculated, dangerous dance.

Venus won. And she looked damn good doing it. How annoying.

While the audience was going crazy for her, I noticed my friends rising from their seats below. Natalia led Emilia, Faye, Destiny, and Michael down the stairs—they were leaving. Where the hell were they going?

Jedidiah let go of my hand and rose to his feet.

Panic spiked my blood instantly.

"Where are you going?" I demanded breathily. I stood up with him, my heart pumping erratically in my chest.

Jedidiah, my person, my strength, dressed as Death incarnate, leaned down to put his lips to my ear. "I have to go. Trust me, Nyx. Trust us. We have a plan."

"You're leaving me." The realization made me weak and dizzy. *Please don't leave. Please don't leave me. I need you.*

He gripped my shoulders, those stormy eyes locking with mine. Even with his face painted as a skeleton, he was bewitching. "Never. Never, Nyx. I'm not leaving you, but I can't help you from here. Solaris is about to take center stage. It's almost time. Please, just trust us." He pressed his lips to my forehead. "You got this, baby."

He left me with that, turning away and descending the stairs, leaving me alone in the stands.

Trust us.

I wanted to. With every fiber of my being, I wanted to trust them. I did.

But it was fate I didn't trust.

Aries didn't leave his box when he spoke this time. He accelerated his voice with magic as he introduced the next competitors.

"Now is the moment we've all been waiting for!" our High Lord announced. "Next in the ring is the Celestial that's taken the Society by storm. A powerful, mysterious young man with magic from the Old World. Our Society hasn't had a shadow summoner in over a thousand years. Introducing, for his first public debut, the Darkbringer Solaris Adder!"

My heart fell out of my body before he even emerged in his whirl of shadows. Dead center of the protection circle.

The crowd lost it.

Solaris didn't react. He didn't wave or smile. He stood down on the black grass, his face a mask of stone. He wore his signature black jacket with ornate silver buttons. My heart thudded horribly as his silver eyes swept over the coliseum. His ethereal face bombarded me from every angle, being shown on all the big screens. I didn't need to look at the faces around me to know he was easily entrancing everyone with his supernatural magnetism.

He was everywhere—larger than life.

It felt like someone shoved a white-hot iron down my throat as I realized he was looking for someone in the audience. Looking for me.

"I must admit, it was difficult to find a worthy opponent for the Darkbringer," Aries went on. "After much consideration, we decided the only fair competition would be an Embodied fire bearer. Luna Academy's finest!"

My blood turned to ice. Who—?

An explosion of flames on the black grass made the audience startle and gasp. Priestess Bridget emerged from the fire. The flames dwindled around her, fizzling out at her feet.

My hand flew to my mouth. No.

"The lovely, Exalted Priestess of Fire, from Luna Academy—Bridget Hayden!" Aries bellowed.

The audience released an oooh which evolved into cheers and whistles.

She must have been in one of those chariots from before, but I hadn't noticed her. I'd been too focused on Solaris and Venus. She wore her fighting leathers, her red hair tied back in a sleek, high ponytail. Her face was etched with indignation and determination. She didn't acknowledge the crowd. She stared only at Solaris Adder, who regarded her back curiously.

No. This was bad—really fucking bad.

Bridget was powerful, yes. But Solaris was Solaris.

A foreboding, dense feeling manifested in my stomach.

"Let the finale begin!" Aries shouted, and the war drums began to play.

Bridget lowered into a fighting stance. Solaris remained poised, spine straight, arms folded behind his back.

What happened next was a blur. A blur of horrific images straight out of a nightmare.

Bridget summoned fire over her hands and shot it at Solaris in a furious torrent that would send anyone else running. Solaris didn't move a muscle. A shield of shadows manifested out of thin air, ricocheting the flames back to the sender. Bridget dodged the boomeranging fire, grunted, and tried again.

Solaris didn't even have to lift a finger to ward off her attacks.

The crowd was dead silent.

Bridget attempted a few more times to hit Solaris, unsuccessfully.

With a flat, unimpressed look—almost an eye roll, as if this were so beneath him—he unfolded his hands from behind his back and splayed them outward, summoning his wicked power.

Shadows rose from the ground at Bridget's feet.

She went to summon flames to combat the ascending darkness when suddenly her eyes clouded over with black. All the big screens displayed her face to the audience, revealing the way the shadows were harassing her from within.

The crowd gasped in dismay.

Bridget's jaw went slack, her face crumpling with horror. Her eyes had morphed into pits of endless black, a scream tearing out of her throat as she collapsed to her knees.

What was happening?

My heart thrashed a mile a minute as I watched, trying to understand what in the seven hells was going on. Solaris stood apathetically, watching the Priestess on her knees. He didn't appear to be doing anything.

Every second that passed seemed to unleash more devastation for Bridget. She screamed and cried as if the film of shadows over her eyes was showing her things we couldn't see.

"No!" she screamed, her hands flying up to cradle her head. "No! Not you! I'm sorry! Please, NO!"

The crowd murmured with confusion, none of us quite grasping what we were seeing.

Shadows smoldered around Bridget, who was in another world. A world of terror and tragedy. She fell to the ground, writhing and calling out, begging for mercy, begging for it to stop.

Priestess Bridget was one of the most powerful fire bearers in the entire Celestial Society, and yet, she stood no chance against him. Her fire magic was nothing compared to what he brought to the table.

The revelation of that permeated the coliseum.

The audience wasn't cheering or reacting. Everyone had fallen eerily quiet, unsure of what was happening. Even the drums had stopped. This wasn't the fun, colorful, exciting show from before. This was cold and harsh. Dark.

Not a performative fight, but a psychic assault.

At that moment, it hit me. What he was doing. He told me before, the power of shadows "was deeper and far more personal" than I could imagine. *To be haunted by your own ghosts is the most merciless of fates, for the demons that belong to us, are the ones that will eat us alive.*

He had unleashed her own shadow upon her.

She yowled and writhed on the ground, reliving her deepest horrors and traumas. What might one see if the darkest corners of their internal world were suddenly brought into the light?

Solaris flicked his wrist, sending snakes of shadows after Bridget, to finish the job. She remained utterly defenseless on the ground, screaming as the tethers of darkness slithered over her body, entering her eyes, her mouth, and her nose.

He kept looking around—looking for me.

My heart dropped like a stone to the bottom of the ocean.

If I didn't stop this, if I didn't show myself, he would kill her. This was his way of summoning me.

I rose to my feet instinctively and descended the stairs, pushing through even though my limbs felt like fucking jelly.

Solaris continued to consume Bridget with his sentient darkness.

"Stop!" I cried. I pressed my fingers to my throat, enchanting my voice to be louder. "STOP! I'm here! Stop!"

My voice thundered through the coliseum, causing a confused stir of murmurs and whispers.

"Solaris!" I shrieked, trudging down the stairs, nearly tripping over my own feet. "I'm here! STOP!"

He heard me. He stopped. He withdrew his shadows and released the Priestess from his wicked power.

The floating eyeballs found me, showing my face on the hovering screens as I made my way down to the field. Nobody recognized me for who I truly was, though. No one saw past the reptilian eyes, blood-red hair, and razor-sharp cheekbones.

I almost yanked off my Medusa headpiece and tossed it to the side. But as my fingers touched the cold metal of the serpent headpiece, something told me to stop. *Keep it on*, a phantom thought urged.

Not one single soul tried to stop me as I reached the bottom of the arena and hopped over the border, landing on the black grass outside the electric protection circle.

Solaris watched me through bright eyes, teeming with emotions I didn't care to read.

"Let me in," I demanded, standing outside the forcefield.

Bridget's frazzled gaze met mine. No one made a single sound. Not even the elites in the VIP box. Aries watched through wordless contemplation. Nobody seemed to be breathing.

"Firefly, is that you?" Solaris mused playfully.

"You know it is. Let me in the circle. Face me. One on one."

Solaris grinned, and for a moment, he did nothing. I could feel the audience on the edge of their seats. My heart was out of control, thrashing so violently I thought it was going to hurl itself out of my throat.

After he let the suspension fester, he raised one of his silver-ringed hands and banished the protection circle Aries had cast. The High Lord blanched at that, at how effortless it was for Solaris to override his magic. In the same moment that I moved closer to him, Solaris flicked his wrist and sent Bridget flying across the field. The audience gasped, but Solaris paid them no mind. As soon as I was close enough, he cast the protection circle once more, trapping me in here alone with him.

This was it. The reality of that tried to penetrate my awareness, but something about all this just felt like a distant dream.

Jedidiah had been right before—all anyone cared about was a good show. No one did a single thing to stop any of this from happening.

I happened to steal a glance at the Luminary of Luna Academy, sitting next to the High Lord. I didn't know that woman at all. She'd always been hard to read but I never knew how much she really kept hidden until now. Her pale face was set in stone, no emotions betraying her. Though, when we locked eyes, I saw a deep, ancient knowing in them. She looked as though she were watching something she'd seen before. Or something she had been expecting to happen. I couldn't let myself ponder what that meant.

I took my place in the protection circle, face-to-face with Solaris Adder.

The crowd didn't know how to react.

As I gazed upon my own personal hell incarnate, everything else faded away. Faded into nothing. Every moment in the last couple of months had been leading up to this. Fate was a heavy weight on my shoulders, threatening to bring me down, and never let me up again.

The stars overhead blinked down upon us, wedging bets on which one would walk away victorious.

"You made it," Solaris said, a strange edge to his tone. He eyed the golden nest of snakes on my head. I wondered why it almost appeared to pain him.

"No thanks to you," I retorted icily. The protection circle amplified our voices so the whole coliseum could hear us.

A loaded pause. "I did come for you, you know."

My heart flipped. I swallowed hard, letting his words roll off. "Well, you were too late."

"I guess I was," he whispered.

A beat of heavy silence passed.

"You fucked up, you know that? You could have had me at your side, Solaris." The words just tumbled out, taking both of us by surprise. "You could have made me understand. It didn't have to be this way. We could have become allies—organically. All of this was unnecessary. I just wanted you to know that before we start. I want you to know how badly you fucked up. And no matter how this ends tonight, you'll never have me the way you truly want me."

His jaw muscles flexed, evidence of the way my words affected him. I caught a glimpse of the regret hiding behind those metallic eyes.

I waved a hand and dismantled my glamour, revealing my true self.

The coliseum erupted with startled gasps and murmurs. Some of them even booed me. Me, the criminal, the thief. Me, the girl who dabbled in black magic. Me, the girl who should have been rotting away in prison.

Me, the girl who used to be on top, the one they all couldn't wait to see fall.

My chest burned, my palms sizzling, longing to unleash fire.

I glanced over at Aries, basking in the horror that exuded off his features as he realized it was me. I gave him a steady look, letting him see the truth on my face. *I'm coming for you.*

But then I turned back to Solaris as white fire ignited over my hands, licking up my arms and fanning around me like a banner. *But, you first.*

CHAPTER 56

ORIGINAL TONGUE

EMILIA

"Somebody better start explaining what the fuck all of this is right now before I lose my goddamn mind." Jedidiah snarled with impatience as he took in the scene.

I couldn't blame him.

He had his hood down now, and his face was painted as a skull. Nyx had obviously done it for him, since it was clearly *American Horror Story* inspired. It was a little startling how much the whole Death look suited him.

Natalia had led us through a secret passageway that led to a bunch of hallways and rooms below the coliseum. Meaning, we were directly underneath the field. The vibes were beyond creepy, and it didn't get any better when we reached the room she had set up.

The room was empty, save for all the magical paraphernalia. It was a strange, abandoned place—it might have been some kind of office before, but no one had been down here in a long time. The floor was pale tile, the walls dreary blue, and there was a whiteboard on the wall. A complex language I didn't recognize. It wasn't even Latin. It felt like an ancient, forgotten tongue. Reading it gave me chills, even though I knew not what it said.

And then there was all the shit Natalia had set up. Clearly, she'd been here yesterday or something, getting everything ready.

In the center of the room on the floor, was a giant, oval-shaped mirror. Around it was a circle of thick salt peppered with white candles. Outside of the salt circle, sat a pile of leather grimoires, a cluster of potion vials, some black crystals, and a jar of crushed herbs.

Natalia's brown eyes swept over each of us. Destiny looked like she wanted to bolt. Faye was eerily calm, and Michael hadn't said a word. Jedidiah continued to fume, glaring at Natalia, awaiting an explanation.

She sucked in a long breath. Standing next to the magic circle on the floor, dressed as a classic witch, it felt like we had traveled backward in time. She reached into her dress and pulled out two peculiar silver objects. Two metal rings with sharp-toothed edges, big enough to fit on a man's wrist.

"Michael and I Dreamwalked together a few nights ago, just the two of us." She held up the two rings. She showed us how they opened and closed, like clamps. "That's where I got these. Michael brought them back from the Dream Realm. I've never told any of you much about my family because we are estranged. I don't see them or talk to them. But my father is a collector—he has a bunch of magical objects, most of them quite insidious. Michael and I traveled into my father's dreams and stole these. They are magic-blocking cuffs.

"Originally, the plan was to find Solaris's weakness or the source of his shadows and cut him off. Unfortunately, I think his own emotions are the source of his shadows, so I had to figure something else out. My dad will be furious when he realizes these cuffs have been stolen. And we should all fear the wrath of Artemis Ambrose if he finds out it was us. These things are lethal. Worse than the iron chains the High Council used on Nyx."

She gestured to the whiteboard. "Anyways, this is a script," she said. "A script for a dream, written in the Original Tongue. Faye helped me translate this, using some books that had been passed down in her family. This language is forbidden today. It is intended for only gods and goddesses and has the power of instant manifestation and must be used extremely carefully."

The five of us shared quick glances.

"This mirror will ensure Michael's dream is a direct reflection of where we are now. The script and the mirror will allow him to dream of this exact place—the coliseum, and all the people in it. It will be a perfect mirror of this reality. With the Veil being so thin, it will essentially be the merging of two worlds. The waking, and the dreaming.

"Three of us will drink the elixir and join Michael in the Dream Realm. The other two will take this herbal mixture that ensures you stay out of the dream and remain anchored here in the physical world as guards. Those of us who cross over into the Dream Realm will go back up to the field and intercept the battle. You guys will distract Solaris with magic so I can get close enough and put these on his wrists. He will lose access to his magic and Nyx will win. And it will be pretty fucking ironic and poetic, too. Considering what he did to her."

My heart loudly thrashed all over my body. Behind my eyes, in my chest, in my stomach. I looked to the others, to see how they felt.

This all meant we didn't trust Nyx to win on her own.

If she knew...

Jedidiah's stormy eyes narrowed. He looked intimidating, dressed as the Grim Reaper, holding the scythe at his side suggestively. "Are you serious? What is this shit, a Leonardo DiCaprio movie?" He shook his head, disgusted. "This cannot be your master fucking plan."

"It will work!" Natalia insisted. "Look, I've done my research. The Goddess made Michael for this purpose. He has the power to bring objects out of the Dream Realm, and he can heal people in his dreams—his dream can be used to put these on Solaris. Once we do it in the dream, it will manifest into reality. We will be up there in the ring, helping Nyx, yet remaining unseen. Solaris won't know what's happening—he won't know how to fight back. We can help Nyx win this. This is how."

"It feels like playing God," Destiny muttered, fidgeting with her fingers.

Jedidiah scrubbed a hand over his face. "Bloody hell. Why don't we just Astral travel? Sounds a whole lot easier than this!"

"Because!" Natalia cried. "Solaris always has access to the Astral Realm. We aren't safe from him there. The Dream Realm, on the other hand, is out of his reach. He won't be able to sense or harm us."

"You sure about that?" Jedidiah snapped back.

"It will work," Faye murmured. "Who's going into the dream?"

"I am," I answered right away.

"I have to be there," Natalia said. "It should be me, Faye, and Emilia. Jedidiah and Destiny can stay out and keep watch."

Destiny's shoulders sagged with relief.

Jedidiah grimaced. "All you're going to use me for is watching over your bodies? Are you stupid? I'm the most powerful one here. I should go in."

"Two seconds ago, you didn't even believe in this plan." Natalia quipped.

"Using this kind of magic—it's dangerous," Faye said to him, gesturing toward the whiteboard. "Using this language will cause a shockwave of energy throughout the ether. It could be picked up by someone—they could sense us down here. You need to make sure no one gets to us. Your own father might catch wind of what we are doing. Only you can face him."

Michael watched everyone, saying nothing.

Jedidiah sighed, aggravated. "I am worth so much more than this."

"If you don't want to be here, then leave," I snapped at him.

He shot me a dark look.

"I'll stay out with Destiny if you don't want to be a part of this. Screw off and go watch from the sidelines out there if that suits you better." My heart slammed fiercely as I spoke, knowing he could explode at me. I was bluffing, too. Completely bluffing. I did not want to stay out and keep watch. I just wanted him to agree to this.

To my surprise, he stood down. "Fucking fine."

"Come on, Michael," Natalia cooed, reaching out to grab his hand. He took it, without question. My stomach knotted as the beautiful witch led him into the salt circle and directed him to lie down on the oval mirror.

My chest rose and fell. Michael, dressed up as an ominous version of Peter Pan, took his place on the mirror. This was too surreal. Michael, my crush from my mortal hometown, was the centerpiece of this entire plan. Without him, saving my sister wouldn't be possible. My stomach felt uneasy and warm.

Natalia offered him the vial with the liquid in it—the elixir to make him sleep. His brown eyes, behind that mask of shadows, flicked to me before he took a sip. Something unspoken coursed between us. I opened my mouth to say something, but no words formed on my tongue. A moment later, he sipped the tincture, and lay back, his eyes already fluttering shut.

"Come, all of you," Natalia insisted. We moved in closer. She handed me a dark crystal before she gave another to Faye.

Me, Faye, and Natalia lay down outside the salt circle, around Michael, holding the dark crystal over our chests.

Destiny and Jedidiah stood over us, watching wordlessly.

Natalia sipped the tincture next and then passed it to Faye, who passed it to me. It was bitter and unpleasant, but I choked it down.

The world started to slip away immediately.

"See you on the other side," Faye whispered.

CHAPTER 57
CLASH OF SPIRITS
NYX

All anything ever came down to was a moment.

Moments were all we had, really. That's what life was. Everything mundane would be forgotten, lost in the sea of passing time. But certain moments stuck out and lit up our timelines like a string of lights, whether they be glorious or horrific or heartbreaking—moments stayed with us. They forged us.

A moment could forever change you. A moment could shape you. And a moment could fucking ruin you.

I knew I was stepping into one of those moments now. We both were, him and I. Our fates bound; we were in this together, all eyes on us. So, what would it be? Change, shape, or ruin?

Perhaps all three.

Solaris Adder waited for me to make the first move. He stood like a stone statue, stoic and unwavering. His magic pulsed through the air around us, making the atmosphere dense and all-encompassing.

The floating eyeballs buzzed and bobbed over our heads, circling, and following us to make sure they captured every angle. No one wanted to miss a thing.

I did my best to block them out. Block it all out. The audience. The

High Lord and the Luminary. Mine and Solaris' faces all over the big screens. The nagging wonder of where the hell my sister and my friends went—ditching out right before shit hit the fan.

Just be here. Now.

Solaris made a vague gesture, barely a flick of his wrist. I winced, expecting to be hit with a subtle attack, but nothing came. He grinned impishly. I felt nothing. What in the seven hells did he just do?

He nodded slightly toward the VIP box. I followed where he pointed, my chest tightening when I found Aries Vanderbilt clutching his throat. His eyes were clouded over with black, his face contorting with the terrors of his own shadow.

The Luminary caught on to what happened. Her pale blue eyes met mine briefly before she put her hand on the High Lord's shoulder and portalled him out of here.

My jaw fell open.

No one noticed, though, since all the cameras were focused on me and Solaris.

But why would he...?

I inhaled a long breath through my nose. He was clearly trying to distract me. I wouldn't bite the juicy worm he dangled in front of me. I wouldn't lose focus. White fire flickered over the flesh of my hands and arms, longing to be wielded against the man who stood before me.

The man who stole my life from me. Who'd disarmed me, backed me into a corner, stripped me of everything I was, and made me nothing. The man who fluttered in and out of my life like a ghost. The man who sought to force his will upon me. The man who brought me to a dragon. A dragon who proved the glory of my lineage was not yet lost.

How could Solaris be the root of both my darkest and greatest moments?

"I would kill to know what you are thinking, Firefly," he said, his voice barely more than a whisper.

"I'm thinking fuck this," I snarled back. We stood down here on this black field, circling each other like alley cats. Neither of us had made a move. The crowd held their breath. "You wanted this, Solaris. You condemned us to this fate. So get on with it."

"I came for you, down in those dungeons. But you were already gone. You were with him, weren't you? Somehow, he managed to find you first. The Groundshaker."

His words had my brows coming together in befuddlement. How could he possibly bring up Jedidiah right now? I snapped a cold laugh, shaking my head. I searched between his metallic eyes, trying to sniff out his motivations. I expected to find envy or at least disdain in him, but instead, he appeared...curious. Curious in a way that made it seem like he admired me. But that made no sense so clearly, I just wasn't reading him right.

"Like calls to like," Solaris went on, his voice casual yet sharp. "You may find solace in him now, Firefly. But it will never compare to the primordial dance of light and dark. You will always be drawn back to me. You might as well accept that."

A horrendous heat rose up the back of my neck, spilling across my cheeks. Everyone in this coliseum was listening to the bullshit he was spewing. The white fire writhing over my flesh spiked with my fury. I stepped forward, my lips tearing back over my teeth with a snarl.

Solaris's eyes brightened. "That's it," he coaxed. "Unleash yourself. Show them what a glorious little weapon of mass destruction you are."

My chest rose and fell. Every fiber of my being wanted to do just that. Desperately. My magic begged to be released tenfold. Each second of holding myself back made me feel heavier, hotter, nearly blinded by my own power boiling over. I ground my teeth together and held my fire, despite all my baser instincts urging me to do the opposite.

"*You* unleash yourself, Solaris. Show them what you are."

He grinned. "Oh, they will know soon enough. They think I have forgotten what I am. Like you have."

I saw red. My body vibrated, fire writhing up my throat. Smoke escaped my nostrils as I exhaled, and he chuckled under his breath, as if he were winning.

"You've said that before," I ground out. "That I've forgotten what I am. What does that mean?"

"You know I don't give out answers for free," he murmured, grinning.

Solaris stepped closer to me. I fought to stand my ground and not retreat.

"You said I fucked up by choosing to do what I did to you," Solaris's voice wrapped around me like a passive-aggressive caress. "But I didn't. You needed it, Nyx."

The world went dark as he pulled us both into the shadows.

I couldn't help but gasp when the coliseum and everyone in it vanished. No lights, no cameras, no big show. Just the two of us, facing off in the darkness.

He stepped closer to me, and this time, I stepped back. My breath puffed out before me, and my arms were flushed with chills.

He laughed darkly, shaking his head at me as if I were a child that needed a good scolding. "I saved your goddamn life, Nyx Morningstar. You may hate me now, but that will fade. You can't stand there and act like this experience hasn't changed you. Sharpened you into the weapon you were born to be. You should be thanking me. I forged you."

I sucked in a sharp breath, the burning in my chest nearly causing me to combust. "You—!"

He cut me off. "And don't think I don't know what funny little stories you've made up in your mind. You think I've done what I've done to you because I *fear* your power." He tossed his head back and laughed. Laughed at me. "Quite the contrary, Firefly. I want nothing more than to see you rise to the glory of your full potential. But I couldn't have you discovering what that means—not until the timing was right."

"*Stop*," I insisted, desperate to keep my voice even. "Enough of this."

"There is something bigger at play here. I *had* to do this, Firefly. One day, you'll understand."

"Solaris," I breathed. "I don't care to hear any more of your psychobabble. I don't give a fuck why you did what you did. Take us back."

Of course, he didn't relent. "Even if I told you the full truth, you'd refuse to see it. But soon the hall of mirrors will close in and outrunning the truth will no longer be an option. For anyone. You and I are meant to conquer, side by side. The personifications of light and dark. Cosmic opposites brought together.

"You think you know who the enemy is, but I promise you, the *real* powers that be are much darker—much more conniving and deceptive than you can imagine. The ones who split the world in two, the ones who keep humanity asleep, the ones who pit Celestials against each other as competition and tell you social climbing is what's important while they corrupt this realm and weave it with their artificial web..."

I was shaking my head vigorously, an instinctive reaction. In truth, every single one of his words hit me like a bullet. But now was just not the time for this conversation. He was trying to throw me off—and it was nearly working.

"Stop," I growled, my jaw clenched. "Don't do this. Send us back. We have a battle to finish."

"We have a *war* to finish, Firefly. Shake your head and deny it all you want. In your bones, you know my words are true. This is your fate."

"You know *nothing* of my fate, Solaris. All you have done is force your will upon me. That is not *fate*. That is tyranny."

His eyes darkened. "You really think I have forced my *will* upon you?"

Something about his tone and the look on his face had my stomach in knots.

He splayed his arms slightly and shadows began to whirl around me, caressing my skin, tentacles of dark smoke. My heart slammed, that heady magnetic feeling pulling at me from the inside. His magic enveloped me, his eyes locked with mine. The sensation was sinfully euphoric, and I found myself moving closer to him, one traitorous step at a time, until the space between us was nonexistent.

"I could have forced my will upon you long ago," he purred. "So much could have been avoided if I had done so."

He tipped my chin up with his fingers. Electricity swam through my veins, my mind whirling with adrenaline. I didn't understand what was happening. Why I couldn't move or look away or remember my own fucking name.

"But even better than that, why not force your *own* will upon you?" he whispered, watching my face, his eyes dropping to my parted lips as I panted. "Shadows cannot create, nor can they lie. Shadows only provide a dark reflection to the truths we refuse to acknowledge. You feel that tug inside of you? That temptation? It may be the shadows luring you in, but they only call upon what they find already within you."

I *did* feel it. His power penetrated my being, rooting around in the depths of my soul, digging up desires I never knew I had.

My breathing came out hard, my chest rising and falling. I couldn't look away from him, from those entrancing silver eyes. He reached out and brushed his thumb along my cheek, cupping my face lightly in his cold hand. A shiver tumbled down my spine. His closeness was addicting, and I couldn't quite remember why I'd been so furious before.

He leaned down, ever so slightly. "Show me what's truly inside you. Show me what you've been keeping hidden. What shames you the most."

My hands flew to the back of his neck, my fingers knotting in his dark hair. He gasped a little, the pulse in his throat visible under his pale skin. I couldn't think, couldn't breathe. The only thing that existed was him and his shadows coiling inside me, roaring through my blood.

I yanked his face down to mine, my gaze dropping to his lips before I slammed mine into them.

Somewhere off in the farthest corners of the universe, stars exploded, and angels wept.

He groaned into my mouth as I forced his lips apart with my tongue. My insides turned to a storm of ice and fire, exultant and disorientating. His hands gripped my waist, pulling me into him, our bodies welding together. I could feel his heart rocketing behind his jacket. He tasted like citrus, his lips smooth and cold against mine.

I moaned into him, gripping him hard, wanting more. *More, more, more.*

The world tilted off its axis, the kiss consuming me in ways I'd never thought possible.

And then the light flooded back in.

He willed the world to rise around us once again, the roar of the crowd and the spotlights above harassing my senses.

It took a moment for me to register.

We were standing in the middle of the field. In front of the entire Celestial Society. *Lip-locked.*

I jerked away from him, my lips tingling, eyes bulging out of my skull.

Horror clawed up the backs of my legs and ascended my spine, lighting my cheeks on fire. I stared at him in disbelief, his mouth shiny with my salvia. He looked just as shocked as me, breathing hard, a small smile slowly tugging at the edges of his mouth.

The mouth I had just been kissing.

All restraint I'd been holding onto died.

A boom of arcane power—*my* power—shook the coliseum. I surrendered to my baser instincts, morphing into a ravenous elemental force. White-gold fire erupted out of me and rushed at Solaris in a torrent of blinding light.

And I screamed. I screamed, I screamed, I screamed. From deep in my belly. Furious, disgusted, *humiliated*.

I would fucking *kill him* for that. I decided right then and there, this battle was to the death.

I think he saw that truth in my eyes.

He splayed his hands and unleashed his dark power.

A storm of shadows assailed the fire that came for him hungrily.

Our power clashed between us, two rivers of light and dark that hissed and smoked and thundered upon contact. Our elements came to life like ravenous beasts of dual natures, opposite forces out for blood.

It was indescribable, the feeling that rushed me as the full magnitude of his magic challenged mine. My veins became sizzling maps of electric charge, lighting up my skin. My hair blew around my face like I had stepped out into a windstorm. Every single cell in my body came to life, in full force. I'd never felt anything like it before. My fire propelled against his shadows, and I screamed as I willed them to override his darkness. *I must win. I must. Fuck this motherfucker.*

A wall of firelight and shadow built up between us, two otherworldly powers that matched each other's force uncannily.

Cosmic opposites brought together.

I gritted my teeth and summoned every molecule of vigor I had into this moment. A cry howled out of my throat, my white fire coursing even faster out of my hands. I *needed* to beat him. I couldn't spend my life enslaved to allegiance with him. I couldn't. I couldn't.

It was the first time I'd ever seen Solaris work up a sweat. No one had ever been able to stand against him—until me.

He countered me, but it didn't look easy. His shadows rushed out of him without relenting, his teeth clenched together, his brows furrowed and determined.

It was a fair fight. Infuriatingly fair. Neither of us could push past the other, not enough to be considered a victory. My fire was hot and bright enough to snuff out his shadows, but his shadows were more abundant and constant. No matter how much darkness I cast out, it kept coming at me endlessly, rushing out of him like a hemorrhage of black ink.

The spirits of light and dark continued to clash, hissing and smoking, building a wall of fathomless magic between us. Our powers attempted to devour each other. Light eating dark, dark eating light. They fought like viscous living creatures, jaws of fire and shadow snapping at one another in a battle to the death.

I screamed and howled, my fury outranking his. But despite my ferocity, his shadows held their own.

The impossible sight of white flames joining forces with swirling darkness made my head spin. A cosmic phenomenon. I'd never seen anything like it, nor imagined such a thing could exist. I shut my eyes to block out the dazzling truth, shrieking as I forced myself to push harder.

My eyes shot open to see my fire obeying my will, burning hotter and brighter, breaking the barrier of his shadows—*yes*!

He realized what was happening and his face changed.

His *eyes*. They morphed from bright silver to pits of fucking black. Demonic, soulless. Darkness embodied.

His true form revealed.

I knew he was about to unleash even more devastation, so I decided to pull a rabbit out of my hat. I'd never tried to use earth magic before— it had manifested naturally as a ground shake when I was enraged, but I'd never summoned it on purpose. If Jedidiah was right—if we really did Power Share—I had a trick up my sleeve.

I withdrew my flames and twirled away, making the audience gasp. Enough smoke blocked Solaris's sight of me, but I only had a couple seconds of freedom. I searched inside myself for a power that wasn't flaming hot. *Come to me*, I beckoned.

When nothing happened, disappointment and fear welled up my throat like bile.

Jedidiah could summon flame, but I couldn't summon earth.

I growled in frustration, curling my fingers inward as my heart rocketed against my ribs. The smoke was clearing, and I needed to do something. I begged that new, foreign power inside of me to manifest itself. Somehow!

The ground began to tremble, and I nearly whooped in excitement. *Yes!* Golden vines burst from the ground at my telepathic command. I watched in disbelief as they began slithering toward Solaris, who stood there in mute shock as the black smoke cleared from around him. His eyes had gone back to normal. As if they'd ever been *normal*.

It was at that moment that I realized I hadn't conjured vines. No, those were not *vines* slithering toward Solaris Adder.

They were snakes.

Living, golden snakes, hissing fiercely as they charged my enemy in defense of me. At least a dozen of them manifested from the earth, each one massive and exotic and entirely threatening. Solaris watched them come for him, and I couldn't understand why his face looked like that. Like this was the most devastating thing he'd ever seen. Like he was ready to drop to his knees and yield.

Instead of fighting back, he just watched, watched as my army of serpents assailed him.

At the last second, he snapped out of his weird trance and splayed his arms. Snakes of shadows met my snakes of living gold. The creatures attacked and consumed each other, the shadows turning my snakes to dust. My heart was pounding as I watched something I couldn't explain. This was not the magic I had intended to call upon!

Soon, the snakes were no more.

For a moment, neither of us made a move. Solaris stared at me with wild, feral eyes. His chest heaved. The audience was dead silent.

"How did you do that?" he demanded, his voice rasped and fractured.

I put on a cocky, aloof mask. "Wouldn't you like to know?"

He snarled something fierce, and I knew I was in for it now. But when he conjured his attack against me, I was ready. My flames hissed against his darkness, and we fell back into the same power struggle as before.

A river of shadow collided with a stream of flaming light, and neither one overcame the other.

CHAPTER 58

CHAOS MAGIC

EMILIA

I t worked. Natalia's plan—worked.

We became lucid, our spirits standing over our unconscious bodies on the floor. The ethereal blue filter enchanted the world, letting me know we were truly in the Dream Realm.

A startling truth hit me then. Michael wasn't here.

"It's fine," Natalia insisted. "He'll be somewhere. It's his dream. We have to go."

Faye and Natalia were still in their Hallows Eve costumes, so I assumed I was too. I followed the girls out into the strange underground hallway, letting Natalia lead the way back up to the field.

Time moved differently inside this dream. It was as if I blinked, and we were back out in the main arena. In the light, surrounded by outlandish people. Shit—had everyone looked this unsettling before? Everywhere I turned I saw morphing, disfigured faces. Terrible makeup and elongated jaws and teeth. Fear pumped through my blood at how wrong everyone looked. Demonic.

I spun around, confused. I couldn't even remember how we got here. How were we in the audience right now?

"Focus," Natalia's stern voice urged, drawing my attention at once. "It's easy to get lost in the dream. Stay focused, girls! You hear me?

Don't look at the people. They won't look like themselves. We're in a mirrored dream—but reflections can get muddied. Stay focused on why we're here—to help Nyx. Got it?"

Faye and I shared a quick glance and nodded.

We followed Natalia down toward the dark field. It looked the same as before, only now the air was tainted with a heavy blue.

Then I spotted my sister.

She stood amid chaos magic. A stream of furious white fire blazed out of her, clashing loudly with a river of darkness. Solaris stood opposite of her, his starving black power raging out of him.

The sight of them...

They weren't just wielders of light and dark—they *were* light and dark. Nyx's obsidian eyes had transformed into orbs of beaming gold, as if she had the sun trapped inside her skull. Solaris's eyes were pits of black, deep and endless, the windows into his wretched soul.

I blinked. What I was seeing didn't seem real.

The two powers merged in a way that made my dream body seize. Something was happening—

"Come on!" Natalia cried, hopping over the border, and running across the black field.

Faye and I hurled ourselves after her.

"Don't get too close, you two!" Natalia instructed. "Use your magic to intercept him!"

Faye splayed her hands and urged a staggering gust of wind to blow out of her and attack Solaris's shadows, pushing them away from my sister's fire.

I should have been doing something—using my magic to help my sister. But I was frozen in mute wonder as I watched what was happening between Nyx and Solaris's magic. Where her firelight clashed with his shadows, something was...forming. Together, the two polarized elements danced to create something new. Tiny fragments of light and dark clung together, orbiting and merging into what looked like an iridescent pool or window or...mirror. A mirror of darkness and star fire.

What in the...?

"Emilia!" Faye's voice yanked me back into the moment. "Do something!"

She cast howling wind at Solaris, intercepting his shadows and making him growl with confusion and fury.

Both Nyx and Solaris appeared extremely perplexed, but neither one backed down. Despite Faye's efforts, Solaris held his ground, his power bursting freely from him with little resistance.

For some reason, Nyx retreated. She withdrew her magic, allowing Solaris's shadows to knock her down—hard.

I watched Natalia decide it was now or never. She grunted before lunging herself at Solaris, those ominous silver cuffs in her hands. She got close enough and clamped one over his right wrist. He winced—he felt it. Instinctively, he jerked his arm in a swift motion, as if to knock something away. Just as she looped the second cuff around his wrist, his shadowy fist collided with her head, and it actually *hit* her. She went stumbling backward, miffed.

But it worked, what she did. The shadows snuffed out.

CHAPTER 59
COSMIC WONDER

NYX

Something was happening to Solaris.

His shadows battled with an invisible resistance that pushed them away from my flames.

My heart thundered as my eyes swept around, searching for the cause of this interference. No one should have been able to infiltrate this fight. We were enclosed in a protection circle that not only kept our magic in but kept other magic out. So, what the fuck was happening to him?

His lips tore back into a snarl, his face reddening with effort and angst. He refused to back down, but I watched his strength wane.

Something was wrong.

Not just because of Solaris—but because of what was happening with our magic as it clashed.

The wall of shadows and fire was forming into something else completely. Darkness latched onto fire and merged into an unexplainable cosmic wonder...

It looked...like a rippling pool of golden, fiery stars and velvet darkness. I'd never seen anything like it, never heard of anything like it, and that damn well terrified me.

Panic ascended my spine like a frightened serpent, and I reacted impulsively.

I retreated.

With a grunt, I withdrew my flames. A stupid, rash decision, not one I thought about before I did it. This time, I wasn't quick enough to lunge away from Solaris's power—it hit me right in the chest, hard and consuming. I went down, the wind knocking out of me, shadows corrupting my vision as my back hit the field. I stared up at the stars through the filter of black lace that clouded my vision. My mouth opened and closed like a fish out of water.

A handful of heartbeats went by.

My senses fought to gain control of themselves.

Solaris appeared over me; his silver eyes full of something that made it even harder to breathe than it already was. His shoulders rose and fell with his ragged breaths. His hair was a mess, his expression unhinged. He held up his arms, showing me the strange cuffs around his wrists. They were so tight around his skin, and *shit*, they had teeth, digging into his flesh, drawing blood. "Seems you have help on the other side, Firefly."

What the fuck?

I didn't know what that meant. I didn't know what was happening.

I blinked up at him, trying to rid my vision of black spots.

And then the strangest thing happened... A peculiar, ominous tune began to play. Loud enough it echoed off the coliseum walls. The melody felt wrong, grating down my senses like nails on a chalkboard. It reminded me of the tune that used to play in the little ballerina music box I had when I was a kid. An inverted, broken version of an old children's song.

People started screaming... What was going on? I tried to sit up, to look around, but I was weak. Solaris's shadows writhed inside me, corrupting my energy, my senses, and my body. I wanted to know why the coliseum was erupting with screams of horror. Chaos ensued, and I had no clue why. I stared up at the stars, wondering why they looked like a face.

CHAPTER 60
IN THE STARS
EMILIA

My sister was down on the ground. I went running over to her, my dream body flooding with panic and adrenaline.

Time moved impossibly, here in the Dream Realm. Fast and slow at the same time. It was different from being inside the memory, where events were fixed. This blue dream world was the opposite of fixed. This was chaos. I could hardly stay focused enough to process what was going on around me.

I stared down at my sister as she blinked up at the stars. She couldn't see me, even though I was right there. Solaris stood over her, glaring down at the shiny new cuffs around his wrists.

But beyond all of that, a chilling melody possessed the air, a strange horror tune that made every fiber of my soul tremble with the awareness of a threat.

The music was followed by an explosion of horrified screams.

"Something's happening!" Natalia cried.

I tore my attention from my sister on the ground, scanning the audience. At first, I didn't understand what was happening. People were screaming and running—running from what?

"Vampires!" Faye screamed. "It's vampires!"

"What?" I breathed, still confused. The dreamy blue filter over the

489

world made it hard to comprehend the atrocities taking place up in the stands.

I squinted, my heart sinking as I realized Faye was right. Vampires with bright red eyes and sharp, pointed fangs were stalking the Celestials who were desperately trying to escape. Tackling them to the ground and—

Oh, my Goddess.

Vampires—there were so many of them. I noticed them earlier when we first arrived. I thought they were just Hallows Eve costumes.

"Why isn't anyone fighting back? Why aren't they using their magic?" I asked desperately, chest rising and falling.

"It's the music!" Natalia cried. "The distorted tune—it's a magic blocking frequency! They can't fight back!"

The three of us shared a loaded look.

Faye raised her hand, summoning a whirl of wind over her flesh. Her magic here in the Dream Realm still worked. "But we can."

A mutual understanding bloomed between us.

"Are you okay, Natalia?" I asked, anxiety threaded in my tone. "Solaris, he hit you!"

"I'm fine," she insisted. Natalia held out her hands and two wooden spears—or stakes, rather—manifested in her grip. She wasted no time before she beelined it for the stands, tossing the stakes with extreme precision, taking out two vampires right away.

The Coliseum was flooded with them, the entire place turning into a bloodbath. Everywhere I looked, I saw a Celestial getting their throat ripped out by a demon with glowing red eyes. Fear possessed me on every level, rendering me useless.

Where in the seven realms is Michael?

My dream heart hammered, the sapphire world spinning around me. I was not built for this. For Dreamwalking, for fighting my sister's battles, for taking on a horde of rogue vampires. Cement formed inside me, hardening me. I could hear my mother's voice in my ear, telling me how useless I was. She was right.

I couldn't move. I was fossilized in place, watching as Faye and Natalia ran up into the stands, into battle. Fierce, powerful women who didn't back down in the face of evil. I made no move to join them.

Tears burned a path down my cheeks, shame coating me like hot wax. Celestials and vampires alike stopped their discord in the stands just to point and laugh at me. Laughing in a way that was horrible and demonic. Somewhere in the back of my mind I knew this wasn't real, they weren't really laughing at me. My own fears had found me, here in the dream. But it didn't make it any less terrible. It didn't make my pathetic weakness any less true.

I tilted my head back to look up at the stars. To ask them why they made me this way. What I found up there in the cosmos, though, was something that rocked me to my core.

A face in the sky—a face made of stars.

I inhaled a sharp breath as I gazed upon the phenomenon in the dark velvet abyss. The stars clustered together in perfect formation to make a human face. Eyes, a nose, lips—those lips, shining with starlight.

Michael. He was *in the stars*.

My tears became that of wonder and awe.

His eyes were shut, forever peaceful.

A soft, wistful sound escaped me.

My hand flew to my chest, my sobs coming to a stop. Michael. He was in the stars.

A newfound inspiration burst out of a tiny seed inside my being. I brought my focus back down to the moment, my face settling into a mask of determination.

I stood on the field, taking it all in.

No one was laughing anymore.

To my left, Solaris Adder was helping my sister to her feet. In front of me, Faye and Natalia whizzed around the stands, taking out vampires left and right. With magic and combat. They were powerful, yes, but they were outnumbered. Two against hundreds.

The red-eyed devils had the upper hand, a hefty Celestial body count building up in the stands. Some Celestials were fighting back— but the odds were stacked against them. They'd been drinking enchanted spirits and taking psychedelics, and now they had no magic.

I knew what I had to do.

CHAPTER 61
AS OLD AS TIME
JEDIDIAH

"I'm going up there," I told the little bald chick—fuck, what was her name? Hope? Faith? I couldn't remember and it didn't matter. Something was happening up on the field. The screaming was audible from all the way down here. Not to mention my Spidey-senses were buzzing off the charts.

Her brown eyes were wide and panicked. "We have to stay and watch over them!" She gestured to the four of them sleeping people on the floor.

"You're a fireling, right? You can protect them. I need to go see what's happening."

"But—"

"Listen—I'll cast a glamour over the door. No one will be able to find you. You'll be fine, alright? I'm leaving."

The girl was still protesting as I darted out of the room, turning back only to summon my power to put an illusion over the door. When nothing but a plain wall remained, I turned and shot out of there as fast as I could.

I emerged back up to the surface and my ears were bombarded with the shrill cries of battle. I gripped my scythe, which was a hell of a lot more than just a costume prop. It was made of solid metal, heavy and sharp enough to slay a fucking dragon.

My heart rocketed behind my ribs, threatening to pave a path out of my flesh as I ran towards the opening of the arena.

I made it back into the light, and that was when I heard it.

When it *possessed* me.

A musical tune, creepy and inverted, a horror-movie version of a child's song.

The melody did something to me. I felt it, tangibly. It snuffed out my magic like a candle in the wind.

"What the fuck?" I muttered, stepping out into the stands.

Solaris and Nyx stood together in the field, but they weren't fighting. They were staring out into the audience.

People were attacking each other. Killing each other. Blood—there was so much blood. But why would they be—

"Hello, handsome," a high-pitched voice to my left spoke. I turned to see a tiny woman with raven hair, a child's face, and eyes redder than the devil's dick. She cocked her head to the side as she regarded me. "You look lovely as Death. Our brother was right about you, after all. Look at you—so valiant. Instead of fleeing, you run straight into battle to defend your people. A fearless warrior. Though I always did believe it was a thin line between valiance and foolishness."

I stared down at her, a shiver running down my spine. I knew right away. She was a vampire.

I looked back to the carnage happening throughout the coliseum and suddenly it all made way more sense.

A vampire attack.

"You're cute when you're miffed," the vampire mused. "You know who else was soooo cute? Your ginger friends. Oh lord, they were delectable. I crossed paths with them in the foyer of that fancy hotel above your little boy scout camp and I couldn't contain myself. I just haaaaad to taste them."

My heart was a concrete block thrashing behind my ribs. The sky seemed to fall as the revelations of her words settled over me.

This horrible little creature murdered the twins. And for some reason, she wanted me to know.

Shock immobilized me, and all I could do was gape at her.

She seemed pleased. "I'd love to taste you too, but I admit, I get pretty hot n' heavy when I feed, and I'm not into incest. So I guess someone else can have you." She flashed me an unsettling smile with her fanged, blood-stained teeth.

My body reacted for me while my brain sputtered out like an old, rusted engine. I swung the scythe at her with an instinctive lunge. Not my best work. She laughed maniacally while she ducked and dodged the blow. With rapid speed, she jumped right over me, landing a couple levels above.

"Don't let me distract you!" she giggled. "Don't you want to go down and save your little girlfriend? One girl, caught between two brothers. Isn't *that* a story as old as time!"

I growled like an animal and shot toward her, but in a blur of motion, she darted away and landed behind me, making me whirl.

"I'll see you again soon, handsome," she promised. "Tell our daddy I say hi."

She disappeared like a phantom.

What the fuck?

Nothing she said had time to process because the second she darted away, another vampire came flying at me.

All I saw was a wet mouth full of jagged teeth and two red pits to hell as I swung the scythe just in time, swiping the head clean off. It rolled down the steps, red eyes bulged and frozen in terror forever. I didn't waste a second. I released a growl of pure rage, taking off with the fervent instinct to defend myself and my people.

Everywhere I looked, there was a Celestial with a parasite latched to their throat.

Everyone's Hallows Eve glamours were glitching. No one had wings or horns or halos, not like before. Now they looked indecipherable from mortals, being devoured by a dark power far greater than them.

I used the scythe to disembowel a female vampire who had a Celestial woman in her grasp.

I repeated this several times over, making my way through the blood-soaked stands.

But what I really needed to do was get to the source of the haunting music that was rendering my people defenceless.

CHAPTER 62

SUMMONER

NYX

I backed away from Solaris, shaking my head, my entire body vibrating with dread so potent, my vision spun. "*You* did this. You. This was your plan all along!" A sob broke out of me as I gestured to the stands where chaos and devastation took place.

Hundreds of vampires had been hiding in plain fucking sight and they were out for blood.

And blood did flow.

There wasn't a damn thing I could do about it either because I was trapped down in this stupid protection circle with Solaris Adder.

"No," Solaris insisted, his tone firm, his eyes wide and teeming with obviously fake emotions. "I didn't. I swear it, Firefly. I didn't plan this."

"LIAR!" I screamed, throwing my hands out as I shot a ball of fire at him.

He dodged it but he didn't strike back at me.

I released a wanton cry and shot flames at him again. And again. He weaved out of the way each time, his silver eyes full of something that made me even more murderous and distraught than I already was. How *dare* he try and appear mournful over this.

"Dismantle the protection circle!" I demanded with a ragged sob. "We have to help them!"

"Your magic still works in here!" Solaris countered.

"What good does that do!" My eyes scoured around us, taking in the massacre.

I noticed the strangest thing. A Celestial woman hurled herself onto the black field, running for her life away from a snarling vampire. The vampire closed in, and my heart seized—but right before he was about to get her, he jolted as if he'd been *impaled*. A stain of blood manifested over his chest, pooling through his shirt. His red eyes popped open with shock before he went down to his knees. His skin began to decay— turning gray and hardening like stone before he dispersed into a pile of gross, fleshy ash.

I'd read once before—that was what happened to vampires after they'd been staked.

I must have been losing my damn mind because it literally looked like an invisible person killed him with an invisible stake.

"Firefly!" Solaris's voice had my attention right away. "We can draw them in here," he said, his voice rushed and urgent. "You can summon them down to us, and when they're close enough, we'll dismantle the protection circle. And then you can finish them off with your fire."

My chest heaved as I glared up into those shiny, metallic eyes. "Why would I go along with any of *your* plans?"

"Because it's the only way."

"Fuck you, Solaris! You tricked me! This entire time, you've been distracting me. You wanted war and now you've started it. LOOK at what you've done!"

"I didn't! I didn't, Firefly. This was *not* my plan. I swear it. Tonight was supposed to be about me and you. I signed a goddamn Celestial Oath! Why would I blow it!"

"Because you are PSYCHOTIC! Now let me out of here! I have to help them!"

"It was Ra'ah!" Solaris exclaimed, his voice rough with ragged emotion that sounded a whole lot like betrayal. "My sister did this. If it were me, I would be dead! I would be breaking our Oath!"

Undeniable truth rang through his words.

I stumbled back, my chest heaving.

"That may be true," I growled, bile rushing up my throat, making it

497

nearly impossible to speak. "But you helped her. I heard part of that conversation you two had in the penthouse when you thought I was asleep." *I heard it and I've been denying it to myself until now.*

Horror bled over his features, his chest rising and falling. "Then you would KNOW I told her NO."

I shook my head. "You must have changed your mind!! *Look* at what you've done," I told him, and after a moment of resistance, he listened to me.

My lips tore back over my teeth and instead of going to fire like I always did, I chose a more traditional form of violence. I tore the Medusa headpiece off. I wound back my arm and cracked Solaris square in the fucking face with it while he was distracted by the carnage. The sound of breaking bones gave me a rush of adrenaline. Blood pissed from his nose and lips as he roared, and he went down.

I would make it my life's eternal mission to see this man bleed daily for all the horrors he caused.

He made no attempt to counter me with magic. His nose was bent and broken, and his cheek probably shattered too. Yet he did *nothing* to fight back. It infuriated me even more. I tossed the nest of golden snakes aside, stalking him like a lioness after her prey as he shuffled away from me on the ground.

"Go ahead," Solaris rasped. "Do your worst."

A low growl rumbled from the back of my throat as the white fire crackled to life over my hands.

This was it.

I could end him right now.

My chest heaved with my heavy, uneven breaths. The world around me was bloody chaos, and yet, I only had eyes for the man before me. He looked so pretty, down on the ground, broken and bleeding. At my mercy.

I held my hand out, fingers splayed. "You don't deserve my fire," I growled as I lifted him into the air with telekinesis.

He hung there, suspended in mid-air, ten feet off the ground. Just staring at me. Not even attempting to break free.

"FIGHT BACK!" I bellowed. "Don't you dare fucking give up now!"

"I cannot," he admitted, causing my face to crumple into a grimace.

I gritted my teeth together and stepped forward, eyeing my prey. A fly caught in a spider's web. He was truly helpless.

"Fine," I muttered, curling my fingers inward. *Snap*. He hissed as his arm bent at an unholy angle, falling limp at his side. "I. Am going to. Break. Every. Single. One of your bones." *Snap*. "Then. I will tear out your soul. And feed it to THEM!" I gestured to the stands, fire crackling over my fingers.

A ringing shriek to my left had my neck snapping in that direction. It wasn't a Celestial who screamed—it was a vampire. A hideous, demonic sound. My eyes landed on the subject, and what I saw next made no sense.

The vampire cried out to the heartless sky as something impossible happened to him. My jaw went slack as I watched. Hard blue ice manifested from the bottom of his feet, rising all the way up to the tip of his head. Freezing him in time, his face stuck as a mask of pure terror. He stayed like this for only seconds before the ice combusted, shattering the remnants of the vampire into oblivion.

Ice.

Emilia!

Where was she? Panic took hold of my limbs as I searched for my sister, horrified that she was here right now. How did her magic still work? If anything happened to her...

But I didn't see her. Anywhere. I didn't see any of my friends. All I saw were colorful Celestials scrambling for the exits. Some of them were fighting back, but the odds were not in their favor. Without magic, they were hardly stronger than mortals.

A whimper escaped me, the feeling of helplessness choking me.

Then it happened again—a vampire was taken out by an invisible stake. Beside him, another was thrown across the arena by a vengeful gust of wind.

It's them. Wind, earth, and ice. Faye. Natalia. Emilia. It had to be.

They'd left right before Solaris and I took to the field. What the hell were they up to?! Some Astral shit—

"Nyx!" Solaris called my true name, awakening something primordial inside me.

I'd gotten distracted and my telekinetic hold on him must have faltered. He gripped me by the top of my arm with his good hand, turning me to look into his fathomless eyes. His face was stained with blood and ash, his expression urgent. "We must summon the vampires to us. And then you are going to light them up. Do you understand?"

I hesitated for a beat.

The Coliseum was alive with the sounds of terror and death.

"No," I growled. "Just tell me how to dismantle the protection circle and I will go help them myself!"

"Shadows can lure them down here, away from everyone." His face was solemn, his words ringing true.

What other choice did I have? Every second I wasted, every moment I spent focusing on my hatred for Solaris, I allowed the vampires free reign.

"How do we do it?" I asked, hating it. Hating that despite everything I was looking to him for guidance.

He stared down at me for a moment, a silent battle taking place behind his eyes. Then he slid a silver ring off one of his fingers, off the hand that hung limply at his side because I had broken his arm in two different places. He held up the ring, the one with the oval black stone. He offered it to me. "This ring is infused with my magic. Put it on. Then you can summon them. Shadows have the power to penetrate inside them, find their desires and lure them down to us with them."

"Like you did to me," I hissed, my eyes burning. "Does your wicked power have no end?"

"My wicked power is divine. We have no time to waste!"

"Why do I have to do it? Summon them yourself!"

"These cuffs cut me off from my magic," Solaris explained bitterly. My eyes widened. "It doesn't matter now. You must put on this ring and summon them. And you must use your will to dismantle the protection circle. You can do it, Firefly. You can do anything."

I didn't have much of a choice. My people were dying.

I had no time to ponder any of this. I definitely did not have time to ponder the fact that Solaris couldn't access his magic right now. Karma's timing was insane.

I did as he said and slid the ring onto my biggest finger. It didn't fit, but I still felt the raw power hit me straight in the solar plexus. I made a strangled sound as I adjusted to the heady dark magic that now amplified my own.

Oh, my Goddess.

The shadows felt euphoric.

"Splay your arms, focus intently, and say this charm: *Vocare sanguinem pastores.*" Solaris guided me.

"What?!" I hissed. "I can't just—!"

"You MUST! Bloody hell, I told you your school was a farce. You are so unfamiliar with spell work that it makes me sick."

I shot him a dirty look. "Are you seriously insulting me right now?"

"Repeat after me: *Vocare sanguinem pastores.*"

I splayed my arms, my eyes squeezed shut.

Somehow, I managed to chant the spell. It came out as if it already existed within me. My voice bellowed with authority.

I became the master of puppets, making all red eyes turn to me. They stopped whatever they were doing, stopped feeding off my people long enough to hear my dark siren song.

"*Vocare sanguinem pastores!*"

Over fifty blood-soaked vampires gravitated down to the field. Coming at us from every angle.

Each breath I drew was tainted with the stench of death. How many had fallen tonight? The stands were littered with bodies.

I couldn't handle it.

It wasn't supposed to be this way. *This* was never meant to happen. I knew the road ahead was going to be cursed but I had a clear picture of what that curse would look like. I had it all figured out, who my enemies were, who needed to be vanquished. Solaris, Aries, his anonymous council, the Luminary. *They* were the problem. An army of vampires led by Solaris's sister was never part of the goddamn deal!

Rage unlike anything I'd ever known ignited in the core of my soul. I was familiar with rage, yes. But this thing awakening inside of me now was a monster I'd never met before. A beast that had been sleeping in the depths of me for so fucking long, just waiting for the right day to emerge. It yawned and stretched inside me before it slithered its way into the light, peeking out through my eyes at its approaching enemies.

The inverted music box tunes finally stopped. I hardly noticed.

The vampires were right outside the protection circle now, stalking toward us like a horde of zombies.

With Solaris's magic amplifying mine, all it took was a single thought from me, and the protection circle went up in smoke.

An ear-splitting alarm rang through the coliseum, shaking the very earth under our feet. It took me a moment to realize the alarm was me. My battle cry.

I splayed my arms and arched my back as the energy inside of me burst free at last.

The vampires howled in agony, and it was music to my ears as they fell prey to my Celestial fire. Raging white flames exploded from me in a shockwave and claimed the entire field, burning away the grass, burning away the fucking filth. The magnitude of my magic was incomprehensible. Not of this world.

Everywhere my eyes touched caught fire.

I felt as if I were the conduit for a much higher power.

Perhaps I was. Perhaps the fire exploding out of me was the wrath of the Goddess herself. The wrath of all those who came before me, like the Luminary suggested that night. My ancestors roared in my blood, fuelling me. Their fury was mine. All this rage and vengeance that had been pent up and suppressed for millennia, finally set free. Through *me*.

My wrath did not just manifest as fire, but as an earthquake too. Protesting groans sounded from the Earth as it trembled and cracked. Fissures spread like a map of veins from under my feet, traveling across the burning ground.

At that moment, I wasn't a woman. I was a *dragon*.

Furious and powerful and enormous. I scorched the earth and turned my enemies into piles of fucking ash. It was *glorious*.

I shook the world, the stadium collapsing in on itself. Pure adrenaline coursed through my veins and made me feel larger than life. My fire had no limits—it licked its way up the stands, claiming everything.

The Celestials running and screaming were now running from me. From *my* wrath.

This was my true form. I was not made to be civilized. I was made for chaos.

The Goddess created me this way, so I could bring this wicked world to its knees. Prophetic, in a way. I stood right over the spot in the field where I had buried the dragonstone. This was my plan all along. I could feel him, stirring below me...

Bury it in the earth and release it with fire.

I glanced over to share the moment with Solaris, but he wasn't there. My brows lowered and I looked around, but I didn't see him anywhere. Not until I looked down.

He was a pile of ash at my feet. Nothing left but a few smouldering embers devouring the remains of his black leather boots.

It was like a sword through the heart. I fell to my knees. The scream that tore out of me was a ragged, ungodly sound.

CHAPTER 63
IN-BETWEEN
EMILIA

I shot upright with a howling gasp, my hand flying to my throat. My spirit projected back into my physical body with an actual crash.

The room spun into view, but nothing stayed still or solid. My pulse thundered under every inch of my flesh.

The last thing I'd seen in the Dream Realm was my sister quite literally exploding. With the colossal white fire that had a mind of its own.

It wasn't natural, that magic. There was no way that was all Nyx.

There had to be something higher at play here. Aries said it himself. The Clash of Spirits was an event for the world's unseen.

I had the feeling that our friends weren't the only ones assisting Nyx from the ethereal realms.

Suddenly a blood-spattered skeleton face was all up in my space. Jedidiah. "Come on!" he was saying. Over and over. "You guys need to wake up. The place is burning down. We have to get out here!"

The next thing I knew, I was on my feet. I didn't know how it happened but there I was, swaying like a dead tree in the wind. Panicked voices blared around me. I couldn't make out any of their words. My vision wouldn't stay still. My body and my spirit were estranged from each other, not wanting to click back together.

I smelt smoke and burning plastic.

Faye was up. Destiny held the door open, screaming at me to come on. My feet wouldn't move.

Natalia was still unconscious. Jedidiah held her limp body in his arms as he urged us to get out of here. Why wasn't Natalia waking up?

Something warm touched my shoulders and spun me in a different direction. Michael. He was right there—safe. Alive. His sharp, copper crown matched the lighter shades in his deep eyes. His mask of shadows had vanished, leaving his face clear and true.

Michael's face. It had been in the stars.

My lips parted and some strangled sound escaped my throat. I hurled my arms around him, unable to verbally express the waves of emotion drowning me right now.

He spoke softly into my hair. I didn't catch what he said. I was trapped in some in-between realm, unable to solidify here. He scooped me into his arms like a baby, and then we were moving—running. Making a break for it. Attempting to escape my sister's wrath.

We made it out. Somehow.

I kept thinking I was still inside the dream. Time moved all wrong, all choppy and spaced out. Blackness kept trying to consume me. Every time I thought I was grasping the reins of consciousness; I lost control again. Michael was there, though, right next to me. Each time I saw his face, it was painted with a little more worry.

I don't think I'm okay.

CHAPTER 64

FIREBORN

JEDIDIAH

P lumes of thick, dark smoke billowed mercilessly into the sky, painting the night black.

The white flames of judgment devoured the Memorial Coliseum. Everyone who had escaped stood outside, watching. The grand front archway eventually imploded, the Olympic rings crumbling to dust.

Nyx was still in there.

For some reason, that didn't worry me. Knowing her, she'd walk out of the fire unscathed. I just hoped Solaris Adder didn't make it out alive.

It was a shit show. There was no way this could be hidden from the mortal realm. Their fire trucks and ambulances were already here.

CSA's were here too. Celestial Special Agents. Sort of like the supernatural version of the FBI and CIA, only these motherfuckers were armed with chaos magic and telepathy. They wore all-black leather suits and dark glasses, walking around and questioning everyone.

Nyx's little sister kept passing out. Her mortal boyfriend held her on the ground, trying to keep her awake. Before, she'd been covered head to toe in ice, but now she was just damp and shivering, her lips blue from her own coldness. That girl would probably never be the same after this.

506

Natalia hadn't woken up from the dream yet. I knew that kind of magic was fucking sketchy. Faye kept trying to wake her, to no avail. I had a bad feeling about it. But so much was going on, I found it hard to focus on the well-being of some girl. In fact, it seemed ridiculous for them to be here. I gave them my portal globe and they left back to the safety of Luna Academy. I promised I'd bring Nyx back as soon as she came out.

CSA's attempted to Compel the mortal first responders to leave. It wasn't going very smoothly. I scoffed to myself, hoping tonight was the night our existence was finally outed to the world. About fucking time.

After a while, water elementals huddled together and summoned rain.

Storm clouds flooded in from every direction, lightning crashing over the flames just as the heavens released a torrential downpour.

The rain pelted down but the fire remained unscathed, white flames roaring defiantly without relenting. As I took in the storm, the destruction... I couldn't help but think... We needed this.

DESPITE THE RAIN, THE FIRE BURNED FOR HOURS.

The bright flames were made of magic. They'd long devoured the fuel it would take to keep a fire going, but they burned for eons without the need for any.

It was dawn by the time the flames extinguished. A violent dawn, the sky streaked with black and crimson as the sun ascended in the East. Everyone was still here, watching. Even the mortals, with their fire trucks and news crews. I wondered how the CSA would spin this one. Perhaps no magical evidence would be left behind. But the undying, white-gold fire had spoken for itself.

My father didn't even bother to show up.

Fucking. Coward.

Speaking of my father—what did that little vampire bitch mean when she said 'our daddy'? She literally tried implying that my father was her father. She implied we shared a brother. That was impossible. I was Aries's only son. I'd grown up an only child.

My mother would have told me if I had some long-lost psychotic siblings. When my mom left, I'd understood why. She begged me to go with her—escape all this bullshit and live a quiet, humble life. I loved her, and I hated this city, but some unexplainable instinct inside me made me stay. And as fucked as everything was right now, I didn't regret it. I had work to do, mountains to move, and empires to see fall.

There was *no way* that vampire was related to me. She was just a mind game-playing succubus bitch. She'd murdered my friends and wanted to fuck with me even more. Shit! I should have gutted her. I'd been too shocked to do a thing—I just stood there and let her talk her shit. That would haunt me for the rest of my days. I prayed that by some twisted grace of the gods she survived tonight, just so I could murder her myself.

Fuck all of this. I needed to go find Nyx. She hadn't come out yet. It had been hours. The worry officially set in.

I stalked away from the main cluster of people gathered outside of the fallen coliseum. The stone walls were crumbled and smoldering, some pieces remaining more intact than others. When I was sure I was far enough around the bend and out of sight, I started looking for a way inside. Now that I possessed fire magic, I should have been okay to head into the smoke and the cinders. The smell was a bit much, though.

"Jedidiah!"

I turned to find Emilia Morningstar scurrying over to me. The girl was pale and damp, her lips still blue. Her dark hair was a mess and her silver dress was ripped and wet. She approached me alone, a vacant yet determined look in her eye. I glanced behind her thoroughly to be sure no one saw her follow me here.

"Where are you going?" she asked me. She handed me my portal globe and I took it, eyes roving over her. She'd been gone for hours yet hadn't cleaned herself up.

"Where do you think?" I muttered, gesturing toward the mess of smoking stones. It seemed like I wasn't going to find a clear path into the destroyed coliseum, but that didn't mean I couldn't make one.

"I'm coming with you," Emilia insisted.

"At your own risk," I replied, finding no point in arguing. I splayed my hands, my fingers curling inward as I called upon my earth magic. I willed the fallen stones to pave a path for us, and I didn't have to look behind me to know the girl followed me.

"Natalia still hasn't woken up," she said as we moved forward, her voice low with fear. "It's been hours."

I held my arm over my nose, coughing at the potent scent of burning carnage. "I told you guys that was a stupid plan."

She didn't say anything back.

The Memorial Coliseum was now a gaping, smoking canyon. As if a meteor had crashed into the earth. The ground had completely sunken in, and the stands all burnt away to nothing but ash and rubble. Good thing we got out when we did. If we'd been under the field a moment longer, we would be dead.

Down in the center of the pit that used to be the field, I saw something pale with dark enormous wings.

"What the fuck?" I murmured aloud, my heart hammering. Emilia stood next to me, staring down at the same ominous thing. We shared a loaded glance before either of us made a move. Her ocean-blue eyes were different from what I remembered. That day I toyed with her in the Elemental Sphere, she'd been so soft. Naive and innocent. That shy, girlish shine she used to have in her eyes was gone. She was hard now.

I used earth magic to pave a safe path down into the pit.

My brain wouldn't grasp what my eyes were seeing.

The world moved in slow motion, black smoke rising from the crisp ground. Emilia and I made it to the bottom, but we didn't dare to approach the impossible winged creature that crouched there in the ashes.

Enormous feathered wings fanned out behind him, the shade of dark, hardened blood. A deep threatening red, just a whisper away from being black. Solaris's naked skin shone with a pale glow under the light of the moody dawn. His mahogany hair blew around his face as his metallic eyes peered down at the girl in his arms. He crouched over her, murmuring to her, trying to get her to wake up. His wings beat the air urgently, stirring up dust and smoke.

Nyx's eyes were shut, her skin and hair painted black with ash.

A thin, serpentine creature wrapped itself around her leg, its tail long and pointed, leathery wings still slick with newness. Its scales shone like real gold reflecting the sun. The creature made a juvenile sound, which was both bird-like and reptilian. Smoke seeped out of its nose and mouth as it crawled up Nyx's naked body.

A *dragon.*

My throat dried. My heart failed to beat. The whole fucking world stopped. Emilia stood frozen in my peripheral vision as we bore witness.

Solaris scooped Nyx up like a baby, the golden dragon curled and tucked safely on her chest, its tail wound around her arm. He rose to his feet, those massive, dark crimson wings fanning out fully behind him, shining bright red where the light touched them. He stared at us silently, holding the unconscious Nyx in his arms. That was when I noticed he had Natalia's silver cuffs on his wrists. They bit mercilessly into his flesh, trickles of blood dripping to the blackened ground. His eyes were swimming with unshed tears, but other than that, his face betrayed nothing.

They were mythic.

Solaris's knees bent slightly, and then with a heavy beat of his wings, he propelled into the sky with startling speed. They vanished into the clouds, leaving a streak of fire and shadow in their wake.

ACKNOWLEDGMENTS

First of all, thank you so much for reading! No matter how you felt about it. Thank you.

Second, I finally *did it*. I finally published a book. Can you believe it? Not that I really had a choice—Nyx Morningstar would simply not let her story turn into another one of my forgotten drafts rotting away in Word.

The story you just read has existed in my mind for years. I tried once a few years ago to bring it to life and failed miserably. Last year, in 2022, I came back to it and restarted. This time, it *flew* out of me. This world, these characters, they are so alive. And this first book? We barely scratched the surface of the tale that is yet to unfold.

Thank you to my dear friend and editor Serena Gee, for being my first reader and my first fan. You believed in this story as much as I did and you helped me forge it into the flaming sword it was always meant to be. Without all of your hype and input, I literally would not be sitting here writing these acknowledgements. Can you imagine how bad Nyx would haunt me if I flopped this? I'm eternally grateful for all the life you breathed into this story.

Thank you to my amazing daughter Ophelia for letting me write this book. Days and days of Mommy on her computer, scowling at a screen, typing vigorously, you never gave me a hard time. You are the light of my life and I hope one day you read this book and know the only reason it exists is because you allowed it. My little boss! I love you.

A huge thank you to my love, Caden, for supporting me and believing in me and for allowing me the space and privacy to bring this book to life. You are my rock. I couldn't have done this without your support. I promise one day you can read it. Maybe.

Thank you to my lovely friends Angel and Shawna for being some of my first readers and loving this story! Your encouragement fuelled me!

Thank you to my mom for raising me in a way that never allowed my imagination to die. Our life may have not been perfect but you never let my fire go out. I burn because of your love. I hope this book didn't freak you out too much!!

And once again, thank you to YOU, the reader.

This is just the beginning.

XO, Fibi.